# THE ROMERO STRAIN

## THE DEAD, THE DAMNED, AND THE DARKNESS

## TS ALAN

*ISBN:* 978-1-7328136-9-4 *(softcover)*

*ISBN:* 978-1-7351711-0-4 *(mobi)*

*ISBN:* 978-1-7351711-1-1 *(epub)*

*First printed 11/10/2017*

*Second Edition published by TS Alan 01/16/2021*

*Edited by* Kevin Fern

*Cover art by* John Becaro

*Cover design by* TS Alan

# CONTENTS

*In Memoriam*
*Herbert Smith*
*(1953 – 2012)*

*Special thanks to*
*Paul A. Wiese*
*and Kevin Fern*

"That which is abnormal to nature is a monster..."

— Dean Koontz, "Frankenstein: City of Night"

# PROLOGUE

## AFTERMATH

FOR PARAMEDIC J.D. NICHOLS AND HIS DOG MAX, APRIL 8TH STARTED out as any other day with an early morning walk along the streets of the Lower East Side. Nevertheless, that morning was not to be an uneventful beginning to another day.

Unbeknownst to the residents of New York City, a highly virulent pathogen based on a rare human receptor gene and owl DNA had escaped the night before from a Department of Defense Biosafety Level-4 complex located under the lowest level of Grand Central Terminal. By morning, the virus had spread over the city infecting many of its sleeping inhabitants. Within a few weeks, most of the world's population had become infected and turned into the living dead or mutated humans.

Coming to the aid of a girl named Marisol, J.D. quickly realized her pursuer was no mere crazed person. Fleeing to a nearby power facility for help, they soon found themselves being chased into the service tunnels and through the city's underground by an undead horde. Along their subterranean flight, they gathered other survivors, and attempted to make it to Grand Central Terminal, where J.D. believed help would be found. However, their hopes quickly ended when J.D.

was bitten and they discovered Grand Central had been overrun with the undead.

Knowing he had limited time to help his fellow survivors, J.D. struggled to find a safe haven for his companions. In their search they stumbled upon an enigmatic scientist named Richard France, who had become disoriented in the labyrinth of service tunnels underneath the terminal. With some coercion from J.D., France divulged he had fled a secret government bio lab known as the Grand Central Complex (GCC).

When the true nature and scope of the Trixoxen virus was revealed, J.D. learned that genes linked to his Irish ethnicity would either save him from becoming one of the undead or more likely cause him to mutate into what Doctor France called a transmute, one of the very creatures that forced the doctor from his lab.

With no food, little water, and no place to go, the group made a risky decision to access the complex using the unwilling aid of the doctor. Driven to save his companions before he mutated, J.D. made a bold move and entered the complex alone. What he discovered inside made him question everything France had revealed, and his discovery was enough to put his mutation into remission.

When France finally divulged what truly happened in the underground complex, the group was relieved to hear that the living dead would eventually perish, and they would be able to return to the surface, if they could co-exist with a new breed of humanoid—transmutes—that would inhabit the world above.

As the last of the living dead began to perish and the group's resources were nearly depleted, the survivors made the decision to seek another sanctuary. Finding a new refuge at the 69th Regiment Armory, on Lexington Avenue between 25th and 26th Streets, the group hoped to begin again, but the human race proved itself to be the greatest monstrosity of them all.

# PART I

---

# THE DEAD

"Our dead are never dead to us, until we have forgotten them."
– George Eliot

# 1

## THE FIGHTING IRISH

THE COMMANDER'S OFFICE WAS A ROOM LINED WITH 69TH INFANTRY relics dating back to the Civil War. It was also a room stained with blood. The corpse of Colonel Walter Travis sat slumped in a chair. He had shot himself in the head, but as J.D. Nichols rolled the colonel away from his desk, he had no idea why.

J.D. looked down at the desk. Next to a half full bottle of Irish whiskey and a dirty glass etched with the unit's insignia were two printed papers that had been neatly placed side by side. The one to the left was dated 08 April 2014, and was a two-page document. The other dated 09 April 2014, wasn't even a full page. J.D. picked them up and began to read. They were operational reports on the letterhead of the HHC Rear, 1/69th Infantry (M), 3rd BDE, 42nd ID. Besides both reports being detailed and detached they contained information about the timing of the military's response to the outbreak. On the morning of the outbreak the U.S. Army Medical Command (MEDCOM) had declared a FPCON Delta for Grand Central Terminal at 8:00 a.m., at which time the 69th had been put on alert but not yet called to the armory for active duty. J.D. was well aware of why MEDCOM had been the ones to declare the force protection condition instead of the City of New York. By announcing they had received highly credible intelligence that a bioterrorism attack on Grand Central Terminal was imminent, the military could proclaim it their jurisdiction, and seal off the area and send in their Special Ops Rangers without raising suspicion to the true nature of their mission. The revelation of this fact neither surprised nor shed any new light upon what J.D. already knew. The military's mission to contain and cleanse the true threat that was below Grand Central in a secret government bio lab had failed. Their experimental virus had gotten out and spread across parts of Manhattan hours before their containment undertaking had even started. Realizing it was too late, MEDCOM then attempted to find an antiretroviral to stop its spread but they couldn't. A zombie apocalypse ensued and humanity lost. As J.D. read through the papers, he discovered why Colonel Travis might have committed suicide. However, there was no entry in the operational report that stated it was the reason for his fatal self-inflicted gunshot wound.

As he reached for a small diary-like notation book, his companion Max let out a sigh of boredom. J.D. looked to his German shepherd and said, "I know you'd rather be searching the building, but this is important. All right?" Max made no comment but instead laid on the floor, putting his head upon outstretched front legs, and then closed his eyes.

J.D. sat on the edge of the desk and paged through the hard cover journal. It was Walter Travis' personal account of the events at the Lexington Avenue armory during the first days of the viral outbreak.

*April 8, 2014 - This morning at 1000 hours, Companies A and C were called to active duty in regard to a potential biohazard threat. The threat turned out to be an infectious disease of unknown origin. Once again, the men under my command have been called upon to manage re-supply for food, drinking water, and health and comfort items to our troops on the east side of the city, along with the armory being purposed as a secondary MEDCOM—designated FOB MEDCOM Bravo —because of our hospital facilities. Seven of my men, including my friend First Lieutenant James Alexander—who I spoke with at 1300 hours and had stated was on 23rd Street and 10th Avenue—have not reported for duty. I have been unable to contact any of them as of late this afternoon.*

*The first incident of the infected attacking without warning was a shock to us. We had heard rumors and radio reports early on that the dead were coming back to life and eating the living, but we felt that was mass hysteria. None of us realized how true it was until our own sick started dying and coming back to life. With a heavy heart I issued an order to shoot those who succumb to the infection, this after several troops who were classified as deceased by medical staff abruptly came back to life and attacked them. We discovered the only way to stop them was by bullets to their heads.*

---

*It is 1700 hours as I begin this update. Medical, food, and water supplies started arriving by 1330 hours and continued for about two hours. Weapons and ammunition arrived last. A few unusual items arrived with these including several flamethrowers. By mid-afternoon the 642nd Engineer Support Company had completed its mission objective of erecting razor wired perimeter fencing and perimeter lighting.*

*Shortly thereafter encounters with the infected dead became more frequent until it culminated with a group overrunning the afternoon watch assigned to outer perimeter defenses. The entire squad was killed.*

*I have been to war and have heard the screams and cries of the injured and dying. But what I have experienced today, of my men, my colleagues, my friends, being ripped apart in such a savage manner was horrifying, and frightens me more than any battlefield I ever fought on.*

*After reporting the loss of my men to command, they ordered me to abandon further watches outside the fence and gave orders only to shoot to kill if I felt the security of the base was a risk. By 1630 hours those rules of engagement were upgraded giving us authorization to open fire under the widest possible circumstances, permitting unrestricted shoot to kill in order to protect the integrity of the armory.*

*I ordered the placement of gunners on the roof to aid in eliminating any further threat to our welfare. However as soon as we kill the infected dead that approach the fence, others quickly take their places. There is now a continual flow of what my soldiers are calling zombies. Their corpses are now stacking up along the fence line. I do not know if these "zombies" are truly the living dead or not, but if they continue to grow in number, I fear bullets will not be able to stop them from breaching the fence.*

*A side note: James and the other six men who did not report to duty are unreachable. God protect them.*

---

*It is evening, around 1900 hours as I write this. Many of my men have contracted the virus. Several men close to me, whom I have served with for many years, have already perished. I fear it will not be long for me either. I believe I am infected. If our NBC protection gear had arrived earlier instead of arriving with the 548th CSB perhaps most of my men would not have become infected. We are placing our dead in the facility's basement, though as of now I believe no one shall ever find these heroic men and give them a proper burial.*

---

*It is nearly 2300 hours as I write this journal entry. Complete quarantine of the five boroughs was initiated earlier this afternoon, but I fear it has come too late. MEDCOM HQ has informed me that many of the city's PODs, and the Park Avenue Armory, have been lost. Our position has also been compromised for a second time. At approximately 1840 hours the infected dead began attempts at breaching the security fencing. I addition to live fire, I gave orders to use flamethrowers to hold back the horde. Shortly afterward the commander of the 3-2 Stryker Brigade Combat Team, which is supporting our security efforts along our perimeter fencing, informed me that they have now gone through half of their ammunition supply. Shortly after 1900 hours it was evident these measures were in vain. I ordered the perimeter lighting to be disconnected and rigged to the fencing in hopes this would dissuade further attempts at entering the compound. However, this did not deter the infected dead; the electrified fence seemed to enrage the hordes that are determined to enter. Moments after electrifying the fencing they were able to rip the entrance gates down and enter the inner perimeter. Nothing seems to stop their determination at destroying us. By the time my men had begun to secure the first set of heavy wooden entrance doors, the infected dead had set upon them. I was forced to sacrifice two of my men by locking them out in order to secure the inner doors before the infected dead could gain entry. My men pleaded with me to save them but there was nothing I could do but stand in the hallway and listen to their screams while being devoured. Their cries were unsettling and still disturb me.*

*Efforts by MEDCOM HQ to develop an antiretroviral to combat the disease have not happened and time is running out to save the city. The depth of this epidemic is catastrophic. The infected dead are killing and eating the living. Soon there will be no one to save or a reason for a cure.*

*Command first informed me that withdrawal of military personnel would commence at 0600 hours tomorrow if a cure was not found by then. Shortly thereafter command changed that order and informed me that no new intakes were being allowed into Madison Square Garden and that the base was being sealed off due to the overwhelming number of the "undead" they have been encountering. The situation was becoming dire and all positions in New York would have to be abandoned. Withdrawal of MRIID and CDC personnel would begin at 0200 hours and that personnel under my command were to report to the main command base. When they heard that the undead had overrun our outer defenses and it would be impossible for us to rendezvous, they agreed to an airlift by helo from the roof. I was given orders to make sure only those who were uninfected were ready for transport. I was ordered to shoot all personnel who were infected to ensure no problems with the exfil.*

*I cannot and will not with good conscience order my soldiers to kill one another unless they have succumbed to the virus. The fate of the remaining ill shall be in the hands of God, not in the hands of man. I will, however, ensure the safe withdrawal of all remaining uninfected. I have sent Staff Sergeant Becker and a fireteam up to the third floor to seal the hospital wing and eliminate any threat before sending my remaining uninfected to the roof, and instructing them that they have authorization to secure the roof with any means necessary in order to guarantee their safe evacuation. Several of my soldiers who have contracted the disease are not showing characteristic symptoms. The virus seems to be affecting them differently. Before Doctor Harlonson became ill, he told me he believed it was a mutation. Corporal Reilly and Private Harrington are experiencing changes in their skin color and texture, which is beginning to become leathery and grey in tone. There is also significant change happening in their eyes and, after losing their ears, they have grown smaller ones with slightly larger canals. They are also showing signs of severe agitation and light sensitivity. They have been isolated in a room to themselves under armed guard, sedated, and secured to their beds.*

*Though all vehicle, train and plane transportation in and out of the five boroughs had been restricted early on in order to contain the viral spread, it appears this quarantine has indeed come too late. News reports from around the world indicate major outbreaks in many countries throughout Eastern Europe and South America as well as the United Kingdom, Ireland, France and Canada. The CDC has classified it as a Category 5 Pandemic for the United States, projecting that the virus without interventions will lead to an extinction level event.*

*A great deal of the city's electrical grid has failed. We are equipped with three backup generators to run our electrical needs. However we are limited to the amount of diesel we have stored in the basement. There is a refuel truck outside, but even if we could get to it*

*I don't think it will matter. There may be no one living here in a few hours that will need its use.*

------

*April 9, 2014 - It is now 0245 hours and this will be my last journal entry. More and more of the undead have gathered outside. It seems like the entire city has succumbed to the plague. I have heard unusual noises coming from somewhere inside the building. It sounded like the calls of owls. Shortly ago there had been attempts by my men who are now the undead to break into my office. But for the last fifteen minutes I have heard no one beating on my door.*

*Staff Sergeant Becker had called earlier for reinforcements but I could not send any. Though I have not heard from him since, or know if he was successful in his mission, I have no choice but to order the last of my non-infected soldiers to the roof for exfil. HQ has informed me that ASOC will send a helicopter to transport them to Stewart ANGB for final withdrawal. I pray that my soldiers make it safely out of the city.*

*I tried several times throughout the day and evening to get a hold of my wife and children, to hear their voices, to know they are alive, but I know they are dead or worse. All is lost and this virus drains me of my energy and my mind. Before I become too incapacitated, I will follow Command's orders. I will kill myself. It is better I die than to become one of the unholy abominations that now roam this metropolis.*

*Faugh an Beallach!*

J.D. closed the journal and picked up the reports and tucked them under his shirt. He now knew the circumstance behind the colonel's suicide. J.D. would not show his discovery to his friends. They had all endured enough horror and trauma in their fight for survival. J.D. would spare them the disturbing facts of the fall of the 69th Infantry Regiment, for in the end all the soldiers had died as heroes, even the commander.

As he looked down at Max he smiled. It had been a long and arduous four-month journey of survival. His group had survived a zombie uprising and found sanctuary inside the GCC, only to have to abandon it and seek shelter above in a post viral world. It was a world in which the living dead had perished but two mutated human species had risen. They had lost one of their members against the most aggressive of the two species that had claimed post-apocalypse urban New York. The ones they called half-mutes. Indeed, it had been a difficult path to survival, but along the way his group had bonded and had become as close as family, and his dog Max had made it through with him. He smiled as he saw his furry friend napping and wondered how many other humans and animals may have survived.

## 2

## RYAN'S HOPE

*APRIL 8, DAY 1.*

Ryan had left his Bronx apartment early that morning, shortly before 9:00 a.m. He walked six blocks and boarded the Seventh Avenue Express 2 without ever having turned on the news, as he usually did when he awoke. He arrived at his agent's office around 10:00 a.m., never noticing the commotion in the streets as he walked from the Times Square Subway Station west along 42$^{nd}$ Street, up 8$^{th}$ Avenue to 44$^{th}$, and then west to his destination between 9$^{th}$ and 10$^{th}$ Avenues.

It was the after excitement of the meeting with his agent and signing the contract for a lead role in a children's movie, and the fact that he had his iPod ear buds firmly planted in his ears, that had made him oblivious to everything around him, which was unusual for him since he was always a consummate and observant New Yorker. The meeting barely took a half hour and when he left the office of Bret Adams Ltd, he headed directly to the Galaxy Diner on the corner of 46$^{th}$ Street and 9$^{th}$ Avenue to meet a few friends he hadn't seen in a while for a late breakfast.

Ryan and company always liked to sit directly opposite the counter seating, which was three-quarters of the way to the back of the restaurant on the 46th Street side of the building and in between the two sets of folding window doors, and today was no exception.

He passed under the familiar black and white awning that hung below the large black sign emblazoned with white letters spelling out "Galaxy Diner," and accompanied by artwork of the planet Saturn. Upon entering he was greeted by the hostess, a very petite, early twenties Latina woman with her dark hair pulled back into a ponytail.

She smiled and nodded at him in acknowledgement as he approached her, and then let him pass. She had recognized him from the numerous times he and his friends had patronized the establishment. Ryan had made an impression upon her with his good looks, strong physique, and glinting smile. She had flirted with him from time to time, hoping he would notice she was interested, but he had dismissed it as her just being friendly, even after Jeff had told him that the hot looking hostess had a thing for him. This was probably the reason he dismissed her intentions. If Jeff said she was interested, then she definitely wasn't, because Jeff was a known practical joker.

Ryan returned the smile and gave her a "Good morning" as he walked toward the back of the restaurant to his way to his awaiting friends.

The diner was the choice for struggling actors with limited financial means, or for anyone, for that matter, on a budget. Although the food never lit the culinary world on fire with its carte du jour menu, it was gastronomically exemplary when it came to diner food, especially for Ryan, with its vegetarian omelets.

It wasn't until he sat down with his friends that he heard the news; it seemed it was the talk of the establishment.

"Terrorists my ass," he heard someone exclaim from the booth behind him as he attempted to order a "Farmer's Omelet," a multitudinous concoction of three eggs with fresh spinach, tomato, onion, mushrooms and cheese and served with potatoes and toast, whole wheat for him.

"It's that Goddamn avian flu I tell you."

"Avian flu," someone countered. "What do you know about avian flu? Does avian flu make you go crazy and attack someone, or the dead come back to life?"

"*Bullshit!*" the unseen man in the booth behind Ryan countered. "The dead coming back to life. That's just not possible. It's mass hysteria, I tell ya, that's all."

Finally, after the group had ordered he asked his friends what all the talk was about.

"Wow!" Ryan commented, keeping his voice low so the patrons in the talkative booth behind him wouldn't hear. "Rather the animated conversation behind us. Terrorists and avian flu?"

Tracie asked him, "Haven't you heard the news? Grand Central was shutdown a few hours ago because of a possible terrorist threat, and there's a pronounced outbreak of influenza that is apparently affecting a large portion of the city."

"More like *infecting* the public," Jeff said, attempting a pun.

"That was bad," Ryan replied to Jeff's attempt at humor. "But what's all this about people attacking one another?"

"Oh, that. The news reported a few incidents of assault early this morning by people who were acting irrationally, that's all. It happened on the east side," Tracie assured him.

"I guess I should have watched the news this morning," Ryan remarked.

"I heard," Don spoke up, "that the dead were coming back to life and eating people."

"That's just stupid," Jeff said, shaking his head.

"No, I swear. That's what I heard."

Jeff asked, "Oh yeah? And where did you hear that?"

"1010 WINS."

"You're making that up. 1010 WINS would never report such trash," Jeff adamantly rebuked.

"No," Don refuted. "I swear! I heard it this morning, right before I walked out the door."

Jeff commented, "That's about as real as that UFO video the Syfy Channel broadcast back in 2000. Turned out to be an actress who was hired to do this promo."

"I don't see how that applies here," Don told Jeff.

Jeff contested any possibility of the unexplained being possible. "UFOs, zombies, vampires, Frankenstein. That's all Hollywood. If the news reports something outrageous then it's gotta be some kind of hoax."

"You mean like *War of the Worlds* on Halloween night," Ryan added.

"What about the Devil… or God?" Tracie asked him.

Jeff responded, "What about them?"

Tracie clarified. "Are you putting them into that category, too?"

"Of course not," he replied, with a slight tone of offense to Tracie's question.

Don responded, "So what you're saying is that God and the Devil are real but vampires and UFOs don't exist?"

"Absolutely!" Jeff declared.

Tracie interjected. "Well that's a bit narrow-minded don't you think?"

"How's that?" Jeff asked her.

"Well. You presume by your belief that God and the Devil exist, but you've never seen either of them, have you?"

"No, but—"

Traci didn't allow his counterpoint; she wasn't done with hers. She shook her finger at him, letting him know there was more to come. "Well, since you cannot prove that God or the Devil exists, then how can you dismiss the existence of UFOs or vampires? There are more reports of UFO sightings every year than divine manifestations."

"Yeah, *but*—" He stopped, trying to think of a comeback, a valid point Tracie would buy.

Tracie prodded, "Yeah, but." She paused ever so briefly before going in for the kill. "See, that's so typical of you, Jeff. If you can't explain it or it doesn't fit neatly into your world, you dismiss it. You suffer from the clash between faith and reason. The inability to believe the unbelievable."

"That's not all he suffers from," Don taunted, as he tossed a French fry at him.

Abruptly the volume of the 42" High-Definition television in the back dining area rose—the young Latina hostess having turned it up—the voice belonged to Pat Kiernan of NY1.

"Due to a bioterrorism threat at Grand Central Terminal, the New York City Office of Emergency Management in conjunction with the United States Army Medical Research Institute of Infectious Diseases has issued a statement declaring that as of 2:00 pm Marshall Law will go into effect for all five boroughs. In accordance with this enactment, all train and subway service in and out of the City of New York will be suspended. All bridges and tunnels along with the FDR Drive and the Westside Highway will be closed with exception to authorized personnel. In addition, if you live or work within a five-block radius of Grand Central Terminal, you are required to remain where you are until further notice and instructed to turn off any air intake systems, to close all windows and doors, and to seal them if possible.

All personnel from the Office of Emergency Management, Department of Environmental Protection, Department of Health and Mental Hygiene, law enforcement, fire department, emergency medicine physicians, and technicians should report to their place of employment immediately, Furthermore, all conEdison power station and Verizon telecommunications engineers and technicians are urged to report to work immediately. Anyone not requested to report to work should stay at home. If you are at your place of employment, stay there until further instructed. Stay inside. Do not attempt to go out. If you are caught out after 2:00 pm today, and are not authorized, you will be arrested.

Once again, due to a bioterrorism threat against Grand Central Terminal, the New York City Office of Emergency Management in conjunction with the United States Army Medical Research Institute of Infectious Diseases has issued a statement declaring..."

"Marshall Law just for a threat? *Seriously?*" Ryan commented.

"Told you," Don said to Jeff.

"Well, I didn't hear anything about the dead coming back to life," Jeff told him.

"Well," Tracie announced. "Something is going on. I think it's time for us to leave. That's only a few hours before they suspend the subway. I don't want to get stuck here."

Tracie motioned for the waitress to bring her the check. When the checks had been delivered and distributed, Don and Jeff went to the cashier booth at the front entrance to pay their tab. Tracie waited for Ryan to finish the last bites of his omelet. Ryan hated eating in a hurry. He loved to savor his meal and socialize with friends while eating. Gulping food down was never a pleasant experience for him.

Tracie knew his habits, likes and dislikes. They had been friends for a long time, and for a time roommates, until Tracie moved to Hollywood when she was cast in a crime drama. She was staying with Ryan, in the same apartment she once had shared with him, while she visited. They were very close and enjoyed spending as much time together as possible. They were nearly as close as brother and sister. Though neither was currently involved, there was never a thought of being anything more than friends.

As she sat with him watching him fork the last bite of his omelet, a mushroom falling out of the folded layer and down onto his plate, they couldn't see or hear the commotion on 9th Avenue.

It was a mild, sunny day with wisps of thin clouds streaked across a bright blue sky and a barely perceptible cool breeze. The past few days had been warmer than usual for this time of the season, and the Galaxy Diner had decided to take advantage of the sun's glorious early warmth by opening its small sidewalk patio for those patrons who were eager to sit outdoors and enjoy the beauty of the day.

There had been only three patrons seated at the front in the enclosed sidewalk dining area. There was a couple, in their early twenties, holding hands across the table as they ate pancakes and waffles, each sharing with the other their syrup-soaked breakfast. There was also a single patron, a gentleman in suit and tie, reading the *New York Times*, and sipping on his third cup of black coffee. The couple stood and began to point across to the other side of the street. They stared for a moment, turned to look at one another as they briefly exchanged a few words, and then turned their attentions back to whatever had caught their interest across the avenue.

The curious act caught Jeff's eye as he was about to exit, causing him to stop, and then make his way over to the open, large folding window doors that separated him from the outdoor dining area to view the couple's animated exchange.

"Hey, Don," he called to his friend, who was paying his bill. "There's something going on across the street."

Don turned to him after handing the cashier the check and money, and, in a creepy voice, he tried to imitate the zombies from the video game *Resident Evil 4* that he and Jeff often played together. "*Matano!*"

"Oh, fuck off. I'm serious."

"C'mon let's go," Don told him, as he collected his change from the cashier, and then made his way out the exit. But Jeff wasn't listening. He remained engrossed in the commotion across 9th Avenue, trying to determine what the young couple had been pointing to. Don walked out and stood in front of the barrier of the sidewalk café and motioned to Jeff to join him. Jeff's face filled with a look of fright. He frantically motioned to his friend, and yelled to him to turn the other way. As Don did, he was struck.

Hit full-force like a quarterback blindsided by a linebacker in a blitz play, Don crashed over the thigh-high metal barrier. Thrown face forward onto the young couple's table, the force of the impact sent him crashing to the ground. His head struck the concrete step-up to the folding doors. Don was dead before the creature began to rip away at the soft flesh of his throat.

Jeff let out a loud and panicked, "Holy shit!"

Startled and afraid he turned to run, but found himself blocked by patrons who had come to the folding windows when Jeff had begun to yell his warning to his now dead buddy.

A face of sickened flesh, drenched in the blood of his mutilated friend, looked up at him, and then instantly bounded through the opening. Stumbling, unable to make a rapid retreat, and blocked by the gawking patrons, Jeff crashed backward with the ravenous creature upon him. Another wild-eyed, sickly drawn face of a man abruptly breached the archway and savagely snatched a retreating, panic-stricken patron.

---

Ryan and Tracie could hear Jeff's shouting, as he called out to Don to turn around. It was not unusual for Jeff to be noisy and boisterous, but it was highly unusual, although not totally out of place, for him to be making a spectacle of himself in public. Jeff, after all, was loud and raucous by nature, loved to irritate his friends whenever possible, and had a need to be the center of attention. Except his call to Don seemed to have had an urgency and intent of warning, not one of rowdiness.

When the crash came, followed by the terrified, panicked cries of patrons in the front part of the restaurant, Tracie and Ryan had just stood up from their table and were about to head to the cashier. The commotion and fleeing guests quickly brought their attention to an event that was not Jeff's doing.

At first, they thought a deranged homeless man had thrown something through the open partition and had now entered the restaurant to menace its patrons. That was what the scenario seemed to indicate by the presence of the man coming toward them clad in a filthy trench coat, dirtied and torn jeans, and sneakers with the toe of the shoe missing on the left foot. Within seconds they both realized the seriousness of the situation. The man grabbed the Latina hostess and tossed her to the ground and began to gnaw at the woman's face. Ryan stepped forward to help, but as he did, he saw another charge. This time it was a wild-eyed, sick-faced female, who definitely did not have the appearance of a homeless person.

Ryan quickly turned to Tracie and grabbed her hand. There was only one escape, and that was to the back of the restaurant. As he turned to pull her, she was suddenly yanked from his grip. Tracie stood in the grasp of the attacker, her arms flailing, her body shaking, and the thing's face buried in her neck.

Stunned, Ryan momentarily froze while he watched his best friend being eaten alive. All he could think of doing was to tackle the both of them, hopefully hard enough that Tracie would land solidly enough atop of her assailant for it to let go so he could pull her free.

His tackle worked, but Tracie's body had gone limp. As he desperately pulled her away, spurts of blood pumped from Tracie's torn and chewed neck. The tumbled female rose. However, she wasn't interested in Tracie's lifeless body. The bloodthirsty female now had her angry sights set on eatus interruptus—Ryan Duncan.

The sick, flesh-crazed woman stepped forward, and as she did a busboy leapt down on top of her from the top of the diner's counter, swift, fluid and as dramatic as a professional wrestler coming off the high rope down upon an unaware opponent. Smashing her to the ground the busboy plunged a large bladed cutting knife deep into the women's chest. Ryan attempted to go back to Tracie's aid, but as he did the female creature got the upper hand on the busboy. Ryan realized he was helpless to save his best friend. He turned and ran.

There was only one place these things had not invaded and that was the very back of the restaurant near the kitchen entry. Although there was no back door, an escape through one of the folding windows was possible. As he searched the wooden and glass panels that made up the southern wall of the diner for the lock bolts to unlatch them, out of the corner of his eye he glimpsed the female creature. Crimson-stained like a scream queen in an over the top splatter horror film, and with a knife protruding from her chest, she came at him. Ryan took flight into the kitchen to find a weapon.

A cook confronted Ryan on his intrusion but was interrupted when the blood drenched female bounded through the kitchen doors. When the female bit into the cook, the man let out a wail. The rest of the kitchen staff panicked and fled into the dining area not bothering to help their fellow employee.

Ryan saw the open basement door. There was no other choice. He bolted through the doorway , quickly slamming and locking it behind him, and then fled down the stairway to the large underground storage room that nearly ran the length of the restaurant.

The tympanic sound of angered pounding resonated down from the stairwell door filling the subterranean storage room and his head. For a moment the room spun around him, adrenaline pumping through his body making his heart pound and his breath short. The sound was relentless. He placed his hands over his ears, trying to drown out the frantic drone of thudding fists against metal.

He moved through the basement, his hands remaining firmly against his ears, searching the well-lit cinder block tomb for anything he could use to defend himself. Mops, tables, chairs, a walk-in cooler, and cans of food, but where were the knives?

The quiet before the storm, the silence in between cannon barrages —as quickly as the thunderous kettledrum door had begun to turn out its demonic symphony it fell silent.

He had once received the book *The Zombie Survival Guide: Complete Protection from the Living Dead* as a birthday gift from a house manager during his run in the musical *Altar Boyz*. It was a humorous look at how to survive a zombie uprising. Though Ryan had found it amusing, it was just a work of fiction, not a true survival guide. Nevertheless, now two thoughts, two references from the book, filled his head: There are no places that are safe, just places that are safer, and the zombie may be gone, but the threat still remains. He found the knives and took stock of the available provisions. In a locker belonging to one of the staff he found an iPod. He perused the music artists: ABBA and a whole lot of Mexican metal bands. ABBA. He couldn't believe it. He had auditioned on three separate occasions to be an ensemble performer for the Broadway jukebox musical *Mamma Mia!* based on the songs of ABBA. Three auditions and no gig, he still harbored a slight resentment over it. Given the choice of being eaten by zombies or forced to listen to ABBA music... Well, he was glad he had his own iPod with him.

On day two he felt ill, like he was coming down with the flu. Ryan was certain it wasn't avian influenza and that he had contracted the zombie virus. Within 12 hours he felt as if he was knocking on death's door. Then he passed out. He had no idea how long he had been unconscious, but when he awoke the lights to the basement were off and his illness had passed.

Ryan had contracted the viral pathogen. Unbeknownst to him his partial Irish ethnicity was his saving grace. He had inherited a single copy of the mutated receptor gene CCR5-D32 from his mother, which allowed his immune system to eradicate the infection. If he had two copies of the gene, he would not have become ill. Ryan had no idea why he hadn't turned into a zombie but he was glad he was still one of the living.

After several weeks of hiding, Ryan had no choice but to re-emerge from his basement sanctuary. Though his food and beverage stocks were satisfactory and with rationing they could last a month more, it was the foul odor of his feces, and that his candle stock was nearly depleted, which drove him above ground.

The living dead were everywhere and he knew he was not going to be able take on the throngs that roamed the streets and survive if he attempted to find a new hideout or tried to make it home. He would have to survive where he was for the time being. However, he knew he could not live in the basement for much longer without becoming ill from the decaying fecal matter or going stir crazy in the darkness, so he cautiously reinforced the kitchen entry with a makeshift barricade as best he could until an opportunity would present itself for him to leave.

After spending three months at the diner, Ryan noticed the living dead appeared to be slower and rottener then when the outbreak began. The living dead seemed to be dying. Another week or so, Ryan believed, he could leave and make his way home.

A couple of days later a group of men armed with knives and clubs came scavenging. Luckily for Ryan the group had no ill will toward him. The five men were led by a priest, and shockingly the group was from St. Clement's Episcopal Church, located less than 300 feet west from the diner on 46th Street. Father John apologized for the intrusion and explained they had come searching for food to help feed some neighborhood parishioners and their families, who had taken refuge in the church when the plague broke out. Ryan would not and could not allow children to go hungry. He gave Father John everything he had and in kind Father John invited him into his flock, and that is where

Ryan would remain for many weeks until the day he was captured by marauders while out scavenging.

———————

Everyone at St. Clement's had several jobs; Ryan's was scavenger and childcare. It was easy for him to watch over the children; he was an actor and singer so his talents were much appreciated by the youngsters. As a scavenger he felt inept; he really didn't know how to defend himself, and though there were no longer zombies roaming the city, one of their scavenger teams had reported they witnessed a hostile band of survivors. They had seen the marauder group execute two people for the supplies they had been carrying.

Ryan dreaded supply-scrounging detail but it was a necessity. He had been feeling ill for two days before it had been his turn to go out with the three-man team. He was in pain and had red splotchy sores on his lower back and below his ribs, as well as a few small patches on his arms and lower part of his neck near his collarbone. The ones on his lower back and side had begun to blister. There was no skipping his turn. Everyone needed to pull his or her weight if they all wished to survive, so out he went.

Ryan's team had been out for four hours and had collected enough supplies to fill the SUV they were using. No one of his group heard the approaching men but as they exited the small shop they were scavenging, an assembly of heavily armed men confronted them.

Ryan and his companions were on their knees with their hands atop their heads. A scar-faced man with a pistol in his hand was looming over them.

"What makes you three assholes think you could come into the boss's territory and steal from him?" the scar-faced man asked.

One of Ryan's companions fearfully whimpered, "We're sorry, we didn't know."

"You didn't know?! *You didn't know?* Well, let me enlighten you, *asshole*. Everything and *everyone* on the Westside, from the Bronx to the Battery belongs to Stone. He's the Goddamn King of New York.

And those are his supplies you're stealing and putting into his SUV. So, one of you three assholes is going to have to pay for this attempted thievery. The scar-faced man cocked his pistol and put it to the back of the whimpering man's head. "Is it going to be you?" Ryan's sniveling comrade began to uncontrollably sob as the scar-faced man moved down the line. "How about you?" he asked Ryan's next companion. "Or maybe you?" he then asked, pressing the pistol barrel against the back of Ryan's skull.

The other members of the scar-faced man's group didn't say a word as the marauder leader continued. "Damn. I just can't decide," he announced. "I know, how about our newbie decides?" Scarface turned to the only man that wasn't carrying a weapon. "Wiese. I think it's time you stepped up. Here's your opportunity to earn your place in our group, become one of the chosen few, the inner circle." However, Wiese didn't answer. "What the fuck, are you deaf, Wiese? Get your ass over here and take this pistol," he said with irritation. Two marauders brought Wiese forward. Scarface put the pistol in his hand. "Now pick one of these assholes and shoot him in the head," he ordered. Except Wiese couldn't. He stood in front of the three kneeling men trembling. The scar-faced man grabbed Wiese's pistol hand and placed the gun against the whimpering man's head. He put his finger over Wiese's trigger finger and said, "All you got to do is squeeze, like this." Scarface squeezed Wiese's finger and forced him to pull the trigger. The pistol clicked. The whimpering man wet himself.

"Wiese, you *asshole!*" Scarface admonished. "You really are useless," he continued as he snatched the pistol away. "You forgot to load the chamber." Scarface pulled back the slide and without saying another word shot the urine soaked sobbing man in the forehead. Brain matter sprayed out the back of the man's skull. "Now that's how you fuckin' kill somebody!" he joyously announced, being thrilled over his act. However, Scarface wasn't done with his terror tactics. "You?" he addressed a long, scraggly blonde-haired man, placing the pistol to his head, "What's your name, asshole?"

The scraggly haired man softly replied, "Billy."

"*Billy.*" he repeated, and then sarcastically asked, "Is that it or are you having trouble remembering two of them?"

"Miller. Billy Miller."

"Well, Miller, Billy Miller, it's your lucky fuckin' day. You get to take a ride." Scarface gestured to his men. Three of them stepped forward, seized Miller, restrained his hands behind his back, and then put a hood over his head. Scarface moved to Ryan. "Okay, asshole. What's your name?" Ryan looked up and that's when Scarface saw the soars on his neck. "Holy fuckin' Jesus!" he blurted out. "This asshole is got those fuckin' mutant blisters. Can't take his sorry ass back to Stone, so we should have some fun, instead. You two," Scarface said, pointing to two of his men, and then directed, "And you, Wiese... Take this infected motherfucker to that place with the fuckin' cube. That last place we saw those fuckin' crazy mutants. Tie his ass up, slice him up a bit, and leave him for food. And don't fuckin' come back until you wash up and change your clothes. Don't want any of that mutant shit coming back with you. Got it?" he asked the three.

"Got it," one of them replied, and then the hood went over Ryan's head.

## 3

# LOCK, STOCK AND BARREL

*DUTY ABOVE HONOR AND FAMILY ABOVE DUTY.*

That is what Lieutenant James Alexander's father, who had also been a soldier, had taught him. The highest duty of any man was to the safety and well being of one's family, and if that interfered with one's duty to one's country then so be it. Family, Country, and then God. And that is why he did not report directly to the 69th Infantry Regiment as ordered. Instead, James went to the Hearst Tower, home to *Elle* and *Vogue* magazines, to see if his wife Ann-Marie was safe.

Ann-Marie had been with the publishing firm for seven years as an editor. James had met her when she enrolled in one of his evening yoga classes he taught. They took an instant liking to one another and began to secretly date, though all of Ann-Marie's as well as James' friends knew they were dating. So when the couple announced their engagement three years later, they were astonished that no one was surprised at the announcement. To everyone else, the secret rendezvous, vacations together, and the large amount of time these two "friends" spent together was so obvious.

James was a good-looking man with a muscular physique and a strong face, and many of his students often told him he reminded them of a young Billy Blanks. James was quieter than Ann-Marie, who liked to go regularly to the pub for a couple of pints and listen to Irish Folk music. James, however, liked to spend his time away from noisy crowds and preferred restaurants over bars. There was never a compromise between them. In each of them they had found a mate who allowed each other the freedom to do what they wanted when they wanted, but still they found time for one another. James joined his wife once a week at the pub, and Ann-Marie met him for dinner once a week at James' favorite Indian restaurant. They were by everyone's accounts the most perfect couple they had ever known, and the only surprise in the relationship to their friends was why it had taken them three years to decide to get married.

The urgency of James getting to West 57$^{th}$ Street was upper-most on his mind, for when his wife had left for work in the morning, she was feeling a bit weak and tired. She wasn't sure if she was coming down with the flu or if it was caused by being seven months pregnant, but she decided, since she was only a little sick, to go to work.

James was unable to reach her on her work telephone or on her cell phone, so after numerous attempts to contact her he decided to go directly to her office. By now panic had spread throughout the city and upon arrival he had found that the building was in the midst of a security lockdown, the large rolling steel cage doors lowering to hermetically seal the building. Being an Army National Guard Officer and being familiar with building security, they let him in with barely a moment to spare. That, and the fact that he told security if they refused him entry, he would blow the door open—an idle threat since he carried no grenades and the doors were blast resistant.

Ann-Marie was indeed ill; she and many others had been infected. He had planned on taking his wife to the armory, where hopefully the doctors could help her, but the outside world had become unsafe; the dead were killing the living, and the building had now been sealed. So he and those employees who still remained prepared themselves for an uncertain and possibly lengthy wait. It was only a matter of hours before those who were infected began to succumb to the virus, only to return from the dead minutes later. The first had been a surprise when springing back to life, attacking and biting several other employees who had come to the aid of the creature's first victim. It was evident that the rumors and apparently outlandish news reports were correct— the dead were coming back to life to consume the flesh of the living. James without hesitation terminated the living dead thing with a shot to the head. He had seen enough zombie movies to know what needed to be done. However, there were several hundred employees who had stayed inside as instructed by the Office of Emergency Management and CDC, and most were showing advanced signs of the disease, including his wife. Ann-Marie, though, did not become one of the living dead. She changed. She turned into a frightening and monstrous grey creature.

James did not understand what was happening to his beloved, but when she had fully changed he was unable to kill her, not only because he was deeply in love with her, but also because of the baby inside her womb. Ann-Marie had fled, escaping toward the outer part of the floor, leaving James with slash marks across his chest.

The wounds, though deep, were not immediately life threatening. He knew they would need medical attention, but the firm's wellness center was situated on the 14th floor and by now the certified nurse practitioner along with the certified medical assistant were most likely zombies.

There were nine of them remaining on the 23rd floor. The pantry, one on every floor, had enough food staples for a few days, but would not sustain them much longer than that even with rationing. The elevator would have been the quickest way down, but provided no visual of the level until the elevator doors opened. Too much of a risk not knowing how many infected were roaming around. So, James opted for the stairs; at least the exit doors provided a small window so they wouldn't be blindly entering a floor.

They had been lucky. There had been no undead lurking in the stairways, but the 14th floor was a different story; the undead were everywhere. There were no more bullets, only spears fashioned from broom and mop handles found in the janitor's supply room. James had told the others they should stay and if successful he would return with food, but he knew the odds were against him. He had only one volunteer who went with him, and when they saw the number of the undead prowling about, they knew to enter would be futile, so they returned to the 23rd floor disheartened.

James was a soldier and was not going to allow the living dead to stop him from his mission. He devised a plan and with the help of his one and only comrade, they hoped to diminish the number of the undead by luring them into an elevator and sending them down to the lobby. It was a dangerous but ingenious plan and, in all practicality, feasible, provided the undead remained single-minded in their desire to go after the living. Jonas McGann would be the bait since he was the lighter of the two, and James was the stronger. However, he alone, even with his strength, diminished as it was from his wounds, would not be able to lift Jonas quickly enough to safety. It would require a second person.

There were only three other men, all executives. To James they were useless, pathetic "suits," who refused to lend a hand, didn't want to get involved, for that would require them to actually do physical work, to soil their hands. It was a woman, a small Lilith of a young lady who volunteered. She would not be strong enough to help pull up Jonas, so she volunteered to be the bait.

Though the plan was simple it had its inherent risks. Liz Hudson would be suspended from the elevator's ceiling, utilizing the emergency trap door to make a hasty exit, which solely relied on James' and Jonas' ability to extract her quickly. The elevator doors would open to the 14th floor, Liz would make noise to get their attention and then be quickly pulled up to safety, with the doors closing, trapping as many undead as possible. The elevator would descend to lobby level to allow the trapped to exit. If the plan was successful all the living dead would exit, the doors would once again close and Liz would be lowered down in order to press the appropriate button to return to the 14th floor, where they would repeat the process. If they refused to exit or were just too brain dead to leave, they would be forced to climb up to the 23rd floor utilizing the interior elevator shaft ladder, and then would continue with their evacuation using another car to lure in a second group. As a precaution Liz was given one of the sharpened broom handles as a defensive weapon and if necessary, to use it to stop the doors from automatically closing if the undead did not immediately run into the car.

On the first attempt only three of the undead made it onto the elevator and exited at lobby level. The second attempt was much more fruitful with nine that made it into the car, but as Liz was making her escape, jabbing at the ravenous creatures with the improvised weapon to ward off their attack, two of them grabbed hold of the spear and tore it from her hands. These undead were highly agitated and did not want to exit when they reached lobby level. Instead they stayed in the car jumping up toward the open hatchway in an attempt to fill their need to feed.

Upward the there of them went climbing the narrow ladder back to the 23$^{rd}$ floor, and then crawling over to the next car that was waiting for them. Down into the car they lowered her, upside down with their makeshift harness made from telephone cords and computer cables. The buttons had been pushed, the car descended, they prepared themselves, but the undead were ready, waiting by the elevator doors. They charged before the doors had fully opened. Liz plunged the replacement spear at the horde as it surged at her. It pierced the lead attacker through its left eye, running through its head and lodging in the back of its skull. But there were too many and James and Jonas were not quick enough. The undead latched onto her long blonde hair that had partially fallen out of the back of her blouse, having been tied back and tucked under a bra strap. Liz screamed in agony. Her hair was being ripped out in large chunks. The elevator descended as they finally got her through the hatchway. The blood flowed from the large area where the flesh and hair had been torn away. The wound was a dark mass, but the blood that ran down her face and soaked into her white blouse was rich and red. She looked like Carrie the night of the prom.

It was imperative to get to the 14$^{th}$ floor. Liz needed immediate medical attention. Though her head wound was severe it was not life threatening, not yet, not unless it became infected. The journey up the shaft was long and arduous, and the pain for her excruciating, far more than she could take. She fell in and out of consciousness, which made the trip up more difficult and hazardous.

James had all the contingencies covered he thought, but he hadn't considered an injury. So as he pried open the elevator door he knew that it would be up to him to try and get the medical supplies that were now urgently needed.

To risk his life foolishly was neither noble nor heroic. A new plan was needed and it was needed now. James needed a real weapon, not a stick. As he paced the floor back and forth talking to himself, Jonas overheard him muttering about needing bullets or another pistol.

He commented, "Too bad my brother isn't working today; he'd have a gun."

"What did you say?" James asked. "Why would your brother be carrying?"

"Because he's an assistant chief of building security. That's how I got this job."

"He carries a weapon. Are you sure? I've never seen any guard here carrying a hand gun."

"That's because floor security isn't allowed weapons, but those in the command center are."

Without knowing it Jonas had come up with a possible resolution. If his brother carried a weapon, then perhaps there was another security officer who had been on duty in the command center who also had a weapon.

Anyone could access the command center floor; it was on the first basement level that was shared with the mailroom department. As the elevator opened both Jonas and James stood poised with spears at the ready, but there were no undead waiting.

They stepped into the corridor. The sign on the wall in front of them pointed left for the direction of the mailroom and right to the command center. Sensors allowed for lights to be turned off when there was sufficient daylight or an office was vacant. The doorway that led to mail room operations was dark, but the opposite full height glass entry wall revealed a well-lit corridor beyond its archway.

A chilling, sinking feeling shivered through them. Either someone was still alive or there were undead moving about behind the closed doors. They cautiously walked the short distance of the corridor toward the main reception area of the command center. As the long reception counter came into view, they could see no one stationed behind it. Making their approach, just feet ahead, they could see the tell-tale signs that there had been a struggle. Bullet holes riddled the wall across from the counter and some kind of blood splatter coated the floor, the color of which was not consistent with human pooling. James concluded it was from the undead. As they rounded the right of the counter, on the floor, chewed beyond recognition, was a man dressed in what was left of a grey suit. His pistol was feet from him in the midst of a large pool of the man's coagulated blood. James had no choice but to retrieve the weapon, but to his dismay the ammunition in the clip had been expended.

To each side of the counter was a door. To the left, the sign on the door stated. 'Offices.' The one on the right read, 'Locker Room.' Above each door was a security camera and to the right of each was an access card reader. James tried the door handle to the offices, but it was secured. He removed the dead guard's identification/access card. He swiped the card through the reader and the door release clicked. They chose to access the security offices first. This to him was the logical choice to find weapons and/or ammunition. It was where Jonas' brother, Jason, had his office.

As the door swung inward, out charged a frantic creature. It lunged at James and impaled itself directly onto the sharpened broom handle he had outstretched. The creature kept its momentum and the wooden fashioned spear drove through it, the tip of James' weapon protruding through its back. The creature was relentless and it furiously thrust James backward, almost knocking him off balance. The creature crept closer, impaling himself further down the shaft of the spear. Jonas raised his lance up and thrust it under the monster's chin, driving it upward into its skull, but the thrust was not hard enough to penetrate into its brain. The ravenous undead creature grabbed frantically at them, trying to drive itself completely down the spear in order to get a hold of James. They both drove the creature back, pushing down the corridor of the offices and slamming it into the adjacent wall.

The end of James' lance punctured the interior wall and abruptly stopped. The creature grabbed onto his arm, dug its nails into him, and pulled itself closer. Only inches away from being able to sink its teeth into James the creature grew even more frantic. With one final upward thrust Jonas put all his weight behind his weapon and drove the creature's head to the wall, ramming the broom handle into its brain and through the skull. The tip of the now dulled weapon imbedded slightly into the partition. The zombie went limp, its body now held up by the imbedded broom handles supported by the shaken two. They both released their weapons. The creature fell forward, its torso sliding along the last few inches of the shaft that had been impaled through its midsection, and flopped to the floor.

Jason's office was locked and the key card James had taken from the reception guard did not allow access to any security director's office. The secured doors were too difficult to penetrate without some type of tactical entry tool, such as a ram or hammer, and there was no time to go searching.

The creature that had attacked them had been a well-built, black male in his early to late 50s—Jonas having guessed, based on having been introduced to him by his brother when he first started his employment with Hearst Publishing. James rolled over the corpse to search for a weapon. His name had been Herbert Lee Smith, according to the picture identification he wore around his neck, and he too, like Jason, was an assistant head of the security for Hearst Tower. Under the man's buttoned suit jacket was a shoulder holster. Herb was carrying a Glock 19 with a magazine capacity of 15 rounds not including one in the chamber.

Like James' U.S. Army issued Berretta M9 pistol, the Glock also used 9x19mm Parabellum cartridges and both weapons had a reversible magazine release button that could be positioned for either right- or left-handed shooters, which was preferable since James was left-handed. But 16 cartridges would not be enough. He hoped Mr. Smith kept additional ammunition in his office.

James relieved Herb of his keys and security badge, and went to his office. Inside the bottom right desk drawer of the assistant security director's large oak desk—rank having its perk of real wood—was a small, rugged, grey-colored, survivor dry box. James probably could have just knocked open the small lock, but instead he used Herb's keys. The box's contents revealed two loaded clips of ammunition and two 20 round boxes of Speer GoldDot ammunition. Though one box was partially empty, James was sure there was enough ammunition to adequately eliminate the undead of the 14th floor.

# 4

# FOR A NEW LIFE BOUND

*OCTOBER 14, DAY 189.*

J.D. Nichol's team parked the Stryker facing the Franklin D. Roosevelt Drive underpass at South Street, between the yellow New York Water Taxi ticket booth and the pea soup green colored South Street Seaport Museum Visitors Center. There was more than enough room for a large helicopter to land.

J.D. watched and waited, gazing not at the sky but back across South Street, past the Heartland Brewery, beyond the Fulton Market building, up the plaza toward the Titanic Memorial Lighthouse at Pearl Street. He was watching to see if anything was coming, but the night was motionless.

Dawn was approaching, but for the moment he had time to do one final gesture of friendship for the man who was going to keep Marisol safe and protected, and that was to give him a birthday present.

He closed the upper hatch and lowered himself back into the truck. J.D. picked up a camouflage backpack from the cabin floor, turned to David and spoke, "Happy birthday, DD," and then handed him the bundle.

"*Birthday?*" he asked taking the pack.

J.D. was astonished. "*What?* You forget what today is? It's October 14^th."

"Shit. Didn't even think about what day it was. How did you know?"

"It was Julie. We were planning a surprise party for ya, but I guess you won't be getting any cake this year 'cause it's back at the armory. Chocolate I think."

"Double chocolate fudge," Kermit corrected. "And that would be an incorrect assumption. I packed some cake in my duffle bag. You've spoiled Julie's surprise."

"I just suck, don't I?" J.D. announced. "It would have been nice if someone would have said something," he snapped with slight irritation, glaring at Kermit.

Julie consoled him. "It's okay, J.D. I didn't know about the cake either."

When light finally broke, J.D. threw out a smoke flare to indicate their position. It was only a few minutes before the distinct sound of a helicopter broke the silence of the dawn. Sam pointed out it was an HH-60 Pave Hawk. J.D. was actually going to miss Sam's rambling lectures and excessive information. The helicopter landed, its side facing them with its manned machine gun protruding out the cabin window. It wasn't as foreboding as the helo he remembered with the large caliber machine gun mounted in the cabin door like from the film *Apocalypse Now*, but was still surrealistic as its blades echoed, cutting through the silence of the derelict sea port.

Everyone knew what was expected of everyone. Their departure had been thought out carefully. The men would immediately take up defensive positions protecting the women while they got aboard the helicopter. Then they would follow, first Sam, followed by Kermit, then finally David.

J.D.'s pleasantries with the helicopter crew were brief. When the payload had been handed off to the crew sergeant, he signaled to his team. They deployed as discussed. Marisol came first with Max on his leash, then Julie leading Otter on his leash. Their rescue was suddenly interrupted. Half-mutes were coming. The sound of the helicopter had attracted them.

"I got unknowns coming in, unknowns coming in!" the gunner sergeant called out. J.D. saw the gun move and the half-mutes running toward his friends from the plaza. They had only moments before they would reach the pier.

He helped Julie get Otter aboard.

"Half-mutes," J.D. said aloud, shouting over the propeller noise, which now began to spin up. "If you shoot, you'll only attract more. My team can handle them," he told the sergeant. "Just get ready to go."

He quickly moved away from the chopper toward the Stryker. Kermit and Sam were already running toward him, while David covered their retreat. He met David half way. The half-mutes were nearly upon the two of them. J.D. pushed aside his carbine and unsheathed his bolo machetes.

J.D. quoted him the character Kane's line from the film *Highlander: The Final Dimension*, about seeing him in hell.

David's pause was brief; he correctly responded with Connor MacLeod's line about being the judge of that. J.D. was going to miss their interchange of challenging one another to movie quotes. He hadn't known another person who was as good as David and it was rare that J.D. could best him.

J.D. couldn't stop them all. A few ran past. He heard the whirling blades of the chopper grow louder, and then the roar of its machine gun. He didn't have time to look behind; he had just hoped David had made it. He thought he heard Marisol's cries as the helo lifted off. Then something struck him. His leg collapsed under him. He went down. He had been shot from behind. He saw half-mutes falling in front of him, but saw more coming. He knew he was too far from the safety of the Stryker. He struggled to stand. His thigh flared in penetrating pain. He tried to work through it, but he knew he wasn't going to be able to stand very long. He could feel the blood flowing out of both holes the bullet had made when it passed through him.

The rattle of the machine gun stopped; the helicopter moved away. He had been left behind even if he had wanted to go. There was no escape for him now. More half-mutes came running toward him. He tried to escape to the water, but it was as far in distance as was the truck. He would have to make his stand where he stood. He twirled his blades ready for the onslaught.

J.D. looked up to the sky. The helo had gone, but he gave one last challenge to David. He spoke the same final words as the Nexus-6 replicant Roy Batty uttered right before his death in *Blade Runner*, except left out the part about dying. J.D. didn't expect David to shout back a response. The helicopter his friends had departed in was heading to rendezvous with a transport plane that would take them to England, where a coalition of British and American forces had established a refugee community. The antiretroviral they were carrying back with them would help that population's survival. Unfortunately, J.D. could not go. He did not want to be a lab rat because of his mutations caused by the virus. Besides, someone had to protect Ryan and Doctor France, who were totally inept at survival. He wasn't sure who he'd miss the most, his human friends or his canine buddy.

J.D. took a battle stance as the half-mutes drew down upon him, and then shouted, "Okay, David," his voice resonating throughout the South Street Seaport. "This one's for you!"

When the first one came at him, he was able to decapitate it. Then there were two more, followed by a third. He dispatched them, too. Then there were six more furious creatures charging. He killed three before the rest struck him down. His blades fell with him, releasing from his hands. More of the half-mutes joined in, clawing at him, biting him, trying to rip him apart.

Then came a feeling, something he had never felt before, so primal, so evil, so overwhelming. It was a need to survive, but more. It was a need to kill those who threatened him. He felt his mutation surge. A loud, ear-piercing screech came from deep within him and burst forth. The creatures that were trying to slaughter him suddenly released him and covered their ears. The deafening sound that J.D. made rang out filling the city's silence. It was an unnatural, frightening screech.

In that moment, the moment the creatures released him, he pulled his MPK5 around and fired it into the creatures before him. As his father had told him many times, 'If you don't have a backup, you don't have a plan.' Those that had stopped in their tracks as they ran to join in the frenzy now began their rush toward him once again. J.D. quickly rose. He felt no pain; he felt nothing, except the need to kill. He moved toward them and let out another deafening cry. He raised his weapon up again and was going to fire when he heard a familiar reply. It was the call of Luci. She too was a transmute, but more genetically altered than he was. The calls from the rear sent the half-mutes into a panic; they feared the loud piercing sounds. J.D. unleashed a barrage of gunfire at them as most began to flee, but his weapon quickly went empty. There were less than a dozen remaining and showed no sign of desiring to retreat. Two bold creatures appeared to be hungry for his flesh. They continued their advance. J.D. unshouldered his weapon and threw it to the ground. He ripped the gloves from his hands and exposed his short but razor-like talons. He ran toward them to meet them head on, to show them he was not intimidated, and to show them he was the apex predator. One suddenly changed its mind and fled, but the others held their ground. Suddenly Luci appeared, seizing one, and knocking it to the ground. A frenzied brawl commenced. Screeching from Luci and guttural noises from the half-mute filled the air.

J.D. struck the others head on. There was no martial arts training in his attack; he was in instinctive animal mode. He swiped and tore at them with his talons. A severed finger from one of his enemies fell before him. Most turned in fear and took flight seeing the carnage this strange smelling and fearsome half-human was doing to their kind. J.D. slashed his talons across a female half-mute's chest, ripping deeply into her flesh. As the creature fell, J.D. jumped atop of it and began ripping out its throat, pulling a necklace from it as he did. The blood gushed upward splattering onto his face and sunglasses, saturating his clothing. A shrill cry came from the half-mute with the missing finger that was still with a few others. J.D. raised his bloodied hands into the air and screeched angrily at them, letting them know they had been warned. They quickly retreated. With his face still flush with the fury he felt, he stood up and walked several feet toward the Stryker. Intense pain suddenly seized him. He collapsed, unconscious.

# 5

# CALL OF THE WILD

J.D.'s CALLS FROM THE SEAPORT ECHOED THROUGHOUT THE CITY, traveling all the way to the West Side and as far north as Central Park. What little noise there had been from the creatures that now inhabited the city had abruptly fallen silent on his first cry. Birds had scattered, rodents had fled, and even the light breeze that whispered through the Seaport seemed to have gone silent. Nonetheless there was one creature that heard the cry and was compelled to reply. There was one creature that knew the distinct tonal acoustics of his screech, one who had heard it before, and that was Luci. She had been the mysterious shadow that David had reported trailing them on their trip to the rendezvous point, and it was she who had come to his aid. Except there were others that emerged, not at first when the first call rang out, but after the conflict was over and the Seaport was again calm, with only a few gulls and a breeze making noise.

There were only a few who came to investigate but even the few could be a threat. They were inquisitive, but also an aggressive species. These grayish-blue colored creatures with hide-like flesh were just one of the mutations that the plague had spawned. These were not the infected reanimated, but as Doctor France once told him, "These are the infected altered."

Richard France had been the scientist who had accidentally created these creatures while experimenting on humans with an aggressive virus called Trixoxen. This had been the virus responsible for turning the world's population into the walking dead, the plague that had destroyed the world, and the disease that had even mutated J.D. The virus J.D. had named the Romero Strain.

The small parliament of human/owl hybrids was bold in their approach. Their large, solid black eyes, which now lay under brow ridges that had receded to become flush with the cheekbone bones to form a facial disc, studied him. There had been another distinct change to the facial structure. The temporal bones were now channeled and led from the facial discs to large holes in the skull where ears had once been. The female, however, was spared total loss of the ear; a small vestige of what had once been still remained.

The group inched closer, their sharp, jagged teeth revealed, razor-like talons upon elongated fingers extended and ready. Luci cried out to them, giving them warning not to approach. Nevertheless they were curious and wanted to see, to see the one that gave out these cries of warning. Luci screeched at them to stay back, but these were males and had a more aggressive mindset. One was bold, far more than the others. He came closer, and Luci reacted aggressively. She rose quickly and lashed out at him, striking him across his chest with her outstretched talons. Her swipe ripped at his chest, enough to abrade his flesh but not enough to penetrate below its tough exterior. However, Luci's physical act had been enough for him to realize that the female was serious in protecting this creature and the warning she had given was enough to make him retreat; the others willingly followed.

She went back to J.D. again and sat down, placing his head in her lap and rocking back and forth as she cooed and stroked his face. He was unresponsive at first, but slowly awoke to discover her above him.

"Luci," he whispered, with a slight smile. "You're always saving me."

Her robust, pungent odor stung his nostrils.

"Luci needs a shower. Luci stinks," he said to her, in short sentences with simple words.

She smiled back. He knew she understood. Though speech was beyond her capability she could still comprehend the meaning of words, the tone of a voice. J.D. had been right all along; the doctor knew little about the creatures he helped create. Doctor France had not fully studied nor tested the transmutes. He had made assumptions—though he emphatically declared that his statements in regard to the transmutes' intelligence levels, retained memories of being human, and aggression levels were based on the facts of his research—based solely upon preliminary studies. In fact, he had barely enough time to spit before the first transmute had been whisked away by the DoD after he had reported the phenomenon to his superiors. Doctor France's continued experiments had spawned three others, a female and two males.

Luci was to be the only of the three who was to be transported to Fort Wyvern in California, when the men in unmarked black uniforms came for the second time. But, their agenda was far more than just securing a mate to the original male; they had also come to shut down the research facility.

However, Luci had unknowingly escaped her fate when the two males of her species went berserk in an attempt to save their own lives, helping to destroy the research labs and killing most everyone in the facility. She, however, had survived the soldiers' attempts to kill her. Injured and weak, she managed to crawl to a darkened area of the facility to rest and heal. Then this strange creature came. It smelled of both human and her own kind. This strange smelling male saved her, fixed her wounds and mated with her. From that day forth she was bonded to him. She was his mate for life.

She had stayed close to the facility even after J.D. forced her to leave. She followed him to the armory and saved him from the transmutes that had made it their home. She stayed close to him as much as possible, letting him see her from time to time under the cover of darkness, but never too close as to be seen by the others.

Luci had sensed something that morning was different. The humans who now inhabited the former home of her kind never came out before dawn, not since they took up residence. It was odd for her to see them rustling about in their machine, so she was curious. When they had departed through the gates that separated her from her mate she stealthily followed. She was drawing near, but staying out of visual contact with them when she heard the loud whirl in the sky. She hid, out of instinctual necessity. Except she was intrigued by the noise. Somewhere in her mind she had heard it before, and something told her not to be afraid. She watched as this whirling machine came down from the sky and landed on the pier. She tried to remember where she had heard the noise and seen the machine before, but it would not come back to her. She grew sorrowful. There was something missing in her, she knew, but couldn't remember what it was. Then she saw them, the others.

She was afraid of them as all transmutes were. The others were dangerous. They killed her kind and sometimes fed on their insides. But the others were mostly day creatures. They hid away at night and were seldom seen, unless you made noise. Noise attracted them; noise made them angry. These that ran toward the whirling machine were angry and hungry. There were too many of them; she could not help her mate. Though her body wanted to go, her instincts forced her to stay hidden.

Then the frightening repeating noises of the "guns" came. It was a word she knew and a sound she was familiar with. The guns that made the pain. The guns they used to hunt her. The guns that killed her kind. The guns the bad humans used at the armory. The noise that filled the air brought back the memories she couldn't understand; disjointed fragments of her past. The pictures inside her mind of wearing spotty brown clothes and a gun. The memories of her shooting a gun. It was all so confusing and frightening. She curled up shaking, waiting for the noise to stop, waiting for the bad things inside her head to go away.

Then the cry of her mate came, so loud and resonating, so powerful and compelling. She had to answer him, she had to go to him. Now he lay in her lap. He was like she once was, limp and weak and unable to defend himself. He was bloodied from the gun, like she had been. She stroked him as he spoke so gently to her.

J.D. had dressed his wound, applying a pressure bandage to

suppress the blood flow. He had been lucky the bullet that passed through his leg missed the artery.

"Luci. We go. To the truck," he pointed. "To the truck. We go. We go now."

J.D. needed to reach the truck. The Stryker could give them an impenetrable sanctuary from the half-mutes if they decided to return. Inside the truck was also where he needed to be in order to get back to the armory. He wasn't sure if he was going to be able to drive with his damaged leg trying to apply pressure to the vehicle's gas pedal, but he had to try, for he knew there was no way he was going to walk or crawl all the way back without being attacked, if he could even accomplish the act of walking.

"Up, Luci. Up," he instructed her.

She supported his weight as he tried to hobble to the Stryker ICV with her assistance. Luci abruptly stopped.

"Luci. We go. We go to the truck."

Luci shook her head no. He was astonished. He had never seen a response like this before. She was telling him no like a human. Suddenly Luci scooped him up into her arms and carried him to the open doorway of the Stryker. He was amazed at her strength and ability. He had forgotten about transmute strength, and though she was a female she was unbelievably strong for her frame.

He retracted the gate behind them and with her help he hobbled to the communications station. He radioed to base; he hoped that Ryan or the doctor would hear. He knew that Ryan was expecting him, but now he wasn't calling base to let Ryan know he was going to be late; he was radioing to let them know he was in distress. Except his calls went unanswered, so he was left to help himself. He crawled into the driver's position; the truck had been left running as he instructed Sam to leave it.

"Luci sit. We go. Okay?"

Luci sat down; J.D. released the brake and stepped on the gas. The vehicle lunged forward then stopped. A loud cry of pain came from J.D. His leg wasn't going to allow him to depress the gas pedal. He tried again this time using the other foot. The truck began to move once again, but then he put the brake on. It wasn't going to happen. He was in too much pain and discomfort to try the awkward left over right foot to push the pedal. It was time for an alternate plan, and that was pain medication. If he could inject a small amount of morphine into himself the throbbing pain should diminish enough to be able to use his right foot.

He injected himself. The pain should have gone away in a few minutes, but it hadn't. He thought it must have been the transmute in him, so he prepared another syringe, this one stronger. This time the pain went away, but it was too much medication. He felt himself drifting away.

"Oh, shit. Night, night time," he told her as he felt himself losing consciousness.

## 6

# THE SUPERIOR MAN

DOCTOR FRANCE SUSPECTED SOMETHING HAD GONE WRONG WHEN "THE colonel" did not immediately return from seeing the others off and it concerned him. Not because he was directly worried about J.D. Nichols' welfare but that of his own. France knew he was between a rock and a hard place. Going to England with the others was not an option. There would be too many questions on how he knew so much about the plague and how he developed an antiretroviral. However, he also knew he was totally unprepared to survive on his own. Though he was a brilliant scientist and Mensa member as he had pointed out to his former fellow survivors, he was acutely aware that some other faculty than his intelligence was necessary for survival. His superior intellect did not include that ability. He would need to rely on a guardian, and that protector was Mr. Nichols. Nevertheless, he certainly wasn't going to go on a manhunt; it was simply too dangerous. He needed to get someone else and his options were limited.

Doctor France knocked on the locked door but there was no response. He knocked again, and then addressed the occupant behind the door, keeping his voice low. "Mr. Wiese, are you still there?"

Paul responded, "Is that an attempt at humor?"

"No, Mr. Wiese. I leave that for others."

"So who the hell are you and what do you want?" Paul asked.

"Simply," the doctor replied, "your freedom."

"Well then open the damn door and let me out," Paul retorted.

"I am afraid it is not as simple as that. To begin, I do not have the key."

"Brilliant. And who the hell are you?"

"Doctor France, your only ally. I have come with a proposition. One that will certainly be of interest to you."

"How about you stop flapping your gums and get to the point."

"Fair enough. Mr. Nichols has not returned from his outing and I fear he may have run into some difficulty."

"Who the hell is Nichols?" Paul asked.

"That would be the leader of this facility. You know him as the colonel."

"You mean the asshole who calls me Piss Pants?" Paul scoffed sardonically, "No loss there."

"I can understand your reason of dislike. He does come off as a bit brutish at times. However, Mr. Nichols is… How should I say this so you clearly grasp the full breadth of your situation? Mr. Nichols is a man who is not afraid to get his hands dirty when it comes to dealing with hostilities that would compromise the safety of those within these walls. And he has more than effectively proven his abilities at hostility resolution on several occasions. He is also the kind of man that you will want as an ally rather than an enemy."

"Why should I give a damn? If he doesn't return then all the better for it."

"You do not quite comprehend yet, so allow me to elaborate. Mr. Nichols does not trust you. He believes you to be a spy. Therefore, if he does not trust you then Mr. Duncan will not either, especially since your companions tried to kill him. For those reasons I am sure that Mr. Duncan will be inclined to execute you as a precautionary measure. On the off chance that Mr. Nichols returns under his own volition, what do you think will happen to you then? He is convinced you are an infiltrator. With a few well-placed words I am sure I can convince him of that. Now do you comprehend?"

"Yeah, I get it. I'm in a lose/lose situation. But you're not telling me everything, are you? If you're asking me for help, then that means you must be desperate. And that makes me ask myself, why? Simple answer is you don't have anyone else to help, do you? So it would appear I have the upper hand in negotiating terms of whatever proposition you have," Paul said.

"Let me assure you, Mr. Wiese," France began to succinctly explain. "We may be a smidgeon under-staffed but you are locked behind a door with no chance of getting out unless you come to my terms. Now on the off chance that you decline my proposition, Mr. Nichols does not return and Mr. Duncan does not shoot you, the probability of this facility falling into the hands of your former associates is highly probable. Now if Mr. Nichols is correct about you, and you are a spy, you have nothing to worry about. However, if he is incorrect as I suspect, what do you think your former associates will reason when they discover you locked up? Being the educated man that I am, I would presume you were attempting to seek comfort and aid from the enemy. However, that is just me."

Paul knew everything Doctor France had stated was correct, and if there was the chance of freedom and not being executed as a spy, then it was his only option for survival. "So, what are you proposing?" Paul asked.

"I am certain that Mr. Duncan is as concerned as I am over Mr. Nichols' late return. Having observed his budding relationship with Mr. Nichols, I can conclude that there is a bond of developing friendship, undoubtedly enough to motivate Mr. Duncan in going to Pier 17 to find out if something indeed went wrong. If you were to agree to accompany him on this endeavor it would certainly be in your favor, not only in the eyes of Mr. Duncan but also in Mr. Nichols'. And when it comes time for the decision on your fate, I will give full recommendation that you be granted asylum, as you had previously requested, being that you selflessly risked your life for the betterment of all."

"And how do you propose I accompany your Mr. Duncan, if I'm locked in this broom closet?"

"Your release will be forthwith; of this I am sure. However, be advised Mr. Wiese, although Mr. Duncan is a man of better virtue, he is also a man you do not wish to trifle with. He will not hesitate to kill you if given the slightest provocation or doubt in your intention on aiding him in his effort at retrieving Mr. Nichols. Do we have an understanding?"

"Not quite. There's one non-negotiable codicil."

# 7

# DOWN A RABBIT HOLE

THE ROOM WAS SMALL AND THE LIGHTING POOR, THOUGH ADEQUATE. Paul Wiese sat on the floor with his back up against a file cabinet waiting for a promised release by the armory's doctor, who had visited earlier with a proposition. Paul had come to the armory to seek their help, but had been considered hostile and sequestered to a cell to await judgment. He knew the story he had to tell, the story that must be told not only for his own saving grace but for the children. For it was the children, all children, that needed to be saved. Except he had not been allowed to tell what needed to be said, of the horrors the children were enduring under Edward Stone and his enforcer Richard Barlow, the one who pretended to be a former corrections officer. He had seen and heard things that frightened him to his core, and he knew if he spoke up against either of them that both would not hesitate to take great pleasure in torturing him to death. So he had followed his orders, biding his time to make an escape and to find someone—military, police, anyone—to rescue the children.

But now here he sat. He did not know how long it had been since Doctor France's visit and he did not know how much longer it would be, if at all, before the doctor's promise would be fulfilled—one hour, three hours? Now with nothing to keep his mind occupied he tried to remember happier times. He thought of his childhood, but all in all those were not fond memories. His father had died when he was very young and his mother, who did the best to raise him after the loss of her husband, had the years taken away from her far faster than normal. She too died way too young, from multiple sclerosis, at age 58.

His youth was not marred with all bad memories. There had been one great happiness in his teen years that had lasted into his early twenties, his band. At the age of sixteen, by sheer act of being in the right place at the right time he was hired as lead singer for the start-up pop band called Twilight. He had been at a friend's house most of the afternoon and by evening the light mid-winter's snow had turned into a full storm. By the time the evening came, the snowfall had grown heavy and the visibility had turned from reduced to beyond poor. The winds were stiff and frigid, blowing snow drifts into the street and making it difficult for vehicles to travel.

This was the night his friend John was holding auditions in his basement for a lead singer. Though the musicians were able to make it before the weather turned foul, it now looked like the singing auditions were going to have to be rescheduled. That is when Paul announced he could do it. His friend was surprised at his sudden and brazen announcement. Paul had never once mentioned being interested in joining a band nor did he ever once tell anyone he could sing. The truth was he never had an interest in being in a band until that moment, and though he had never sang before anyone previously, he knew he could do it. They were all surprised at his vocal talent and how many songs he knew, and he was hired that night.

There was a reason he had suddenly decided he wanted to become a singer. It was partly ego to be able to be up in front of people and performing, and then there were the girls. He hadn't had much luck with girls; in fact, he had no luck with girls, but he knew this would change once he was out front performing.

He had been right. Within a few short weeks of playing live gigs, the word got around about this fantastic new Top 40s band and the skinny, attractive, lead singer with the sexy, swooning voice. For the next seven years he would perform and never have a problem with

getting a girl. Nonetheless, by the age of 24 he found himself in a delicate situation. After a show in Cleveland, he had taken a very attractive, thin but buxom brunette back to his hotel room. After several
hours of unabated, intense sex she suddenly told him, 'By the way I'm
fifteen.' Whereupon she got up, showered, dressed and then left. He
realized then that he was getting older but the girls in his audience
were still remaining young, a little too young. He realized then he
didn't want to be fifty and touring the lounge lizard circuit and
sleeping with underage women. Then there was the security issue.
Would people even want to come out and see him when he was fifty?

A lot of his high school friends had gone to college, gotten well-
paying jobs, and were now raising families. One such friend had
become a teacher and told Paul about the job security it brought him. It
was what he was looking for and needed, a job that would pay well
with benefits and a retirement package. He had kept the band together
while attending the State University College at Buffalo and even kept
performing with it the first two years he had begun to part time teach.
It all came to an end when his mother died when he was 29.

The house in Williamsville was now his along with receiving a
large life insurance benefit. Now that his mother had passed there was
no reason for him to stay in the Buffalo region. He had stayed only
because in the last five years his mother had grown increasingly ill and
he was the sole care provider for her. There was nothing to keep him
and he wished to try and live where he had always wanted, New York
City.

He now had the resources to make his desire a reality, to live in
New York City. He had fallen in love with the city the first time he had
performed at a small club in the West Village, the now defunct Village
Gate. He would keep the house and rent it out, just in case, to fall back
on if needed, but would relocate to Manhattan and try finding a job
there as a teacher. It hadn't taken him long to find an apartment; he had
used a finding service and though he felt the fee was a bit high, they
had found him a comfortable one bedroom in Greenwich Village. The
following month he moved in and it wasn't very long before he was
substitute teaching for the City of New York. Within three years he had

gone to full time. By year five he sold his house in Williamsville, took the money, and invested it in a roomy, two-bedroom townhouse in Greenwich Village. The following year he met his future wife, Karen, who had come to his school to substitute for a colleague of his. He asked her out on their first meeting; two years later they were married.

He had been expecting his first child when the plague came. Karen had been three months pregnant. He couldn't understand why he survived being ill and she didn't. She died in his arms, then abruptly rose from the dead and attacked him. He had been forced to bludgeon her to death with a hammer in order to survive. For two days he sat next to her corpse and cried until the foul stench of her decaying body brought him out of his daze.

He had survived by sheer will. He owned the top floor of the six floor building in which he resided. He was able to make it to the basement to find a few minor building supplies and an axe in a maintenance room. He boarded up his windows as best he could, and then proceeded to his neighbor's apartment to scavenge for food and other supplies. He hoped there were other survivors in his building, but knew it was unlikely. One floor at a time he used the axe to gain entry and two out of three times he used the axe on his zombie neighbors. The supplies he had gathered were not enough. His long-term survival depended on more food items, so he was forced to go to the roof and climb over to the next building. He did this with the buildings to each side of his, and though his encounters were few with the living dead, he had decided it was best he didn't tempt fate; what he had gathered would have to be enough until he ran out. He did his best at barricading the roof access door and the building entry doors. He then proceeded to barricade himself inside his townhouse and wait until the noise of the outside world dissipated.

He ate and drank as little as possible to conserve supplies. He only used his candles and flashlights when necessary and tried at all costs to stay away from the windows. It had been over three months now and he had not heard any attempts to break into the building by the front doors, the roof access, or his own doorway. Although he had heard little, with exception of some high-pitched screeching that resembled that of owls, he was unsure what would lie in wait for him. As food was now running short, he would be forced to leave the safety of his home and go out and seek supplies.

Gunshots, there were gunshots. Had the military finally come to kill the walking dead, or was it survivors he wondered? But if they were survivors were they killing other survivors or the dead? Crashes from below! Someone was coming. They were breaking into the building, ripping apart his protection, making their way up one floor at a time, not stopping because they could see he had broken into the floors below. They were coming straight up for him pounding at his door, not asking if anyone was alive, just smashing his door down.

There were five of them, five armed men pointing their guns at him. He dropped his axe and surrendered; there was nothing he could do. They put a hood over his head and took him, smashing him in the skull and knocking him out.

There were others in the room when he awoke, all of them men. He had found out that women and children had been taken too, but no one had seen them since. There was a small man, a dwarf. He had been stripped of most of his clothes. His upper body was adorned with many tattoos. He had been beaten and was near death. He was unable to speak. The others told him that the man had demanded to know where they had taken his daughter. When he had done so one of the captors told him 'the little bitch was entertaining his boss.' They then took the dwarf away and after an hour he was returned beaten beyond recognition and with his tongue cut out. The man who had taken the dwarf was named Renquist, or at least that was the name on his prison guard uniform he had been wearing, but no one knew for certain.

One by one each man was taken. Some returned battered and beaten, some did not. Paul was taken too, for what he found out was what his captors called indoctrination and reconditioning. It was nothing more than mental and physical abuse to beat the fight out of you and attain absolute obedience through intimidation and cruelty. He had learned quickly to succumb to their wishes. He discovered that those who had not returned to the basement were those who now followed this madman. Those who returned to the basement usually were the ones that would perish there. Every other day they would come and remove the dead and dying, only to bring more 'fresh meat' as replacements for indoctrination. They had taken the dwarf, the one the others called Tattoo, the following day to the 'meat pit.'

He had decided it was better to do what his captors told him and made him do than to be beaten and tortured to death. One beating had been enough for him; he acquiesced to their authority. In doing so he hoped to find an opportunity to escape. At first he only thought about escaping and getting as far away from the city as possible, but the more he kept hearing about the captive children and young women the more angry he grew. He had overheard comments, disturbing comments— whispered words about the upper echelon and their sick and perverse acts of sexual cruelty, violence, and pedophilia—so disturbing that it made him vomit. What if his child had lived? he asked himself. What unimaginable atrocities could have befallen his child? He knew he had an obligation to escape and, if possible, find help for the children. His resolve was hardened when he was assigned to 'dead meat duty.' Someone had to dispose of those deemed unfit to serve in Stone's New World Order, and it was Paul's turn as part of his conditioning. However, it wasn't the few dead from the basement that bothered him, disgusting as it was to move a bloated, fetid corpse, it was the disposal of the abused and murdered children. Though Paul never saw the bodies first hand, he knew that the bed sheet wrapped bundles by their size and weight were not those of adults. He was going to escape and find a way to free the remaining children, whether it was with help or by himself. He would see Stone and his men dead for what they were doing.

J.D. had inadvertently given Paul the opportunity he had been looking and hoping for, a way to escape Stone's clutches. The one that called himself Colonel Plissken—he knew that was not his real name —had interceded at Astor Place and prevented his overseers from ruth-lessly and brutally murdering Ryan Duncan. He knew what his chiefs were going to do was immoral but was afraid that if he attempted to intervene, he too would be killed. It was wrong but he needed to stay alive if he hoped to save the children. J.D. had spared Paul's group, giving them warning to stay out of his territory. When J.D. told them to run, Paul was the first to flee and headed west toward Broadway. Paul needed to lose his companions if he wished his freedom. He saw an opportunity to make his escape and ran down the steps of one of the north uptown entrances to the N and R trains and into the darkness. Paul had hoped to make it to the tracks and hide in the tunnel, but he had not realized that he had run to a place with no escape. It hadn't occurred to him that the entry gate at the bottom of the stairs might have been shut and secured, but lucky it was ajar. In Paul's hurried attempt to get inside, he had not seen the obstacles before him. As he pushed through, he tripped over the remains of an MTA worker. He stumbled, tripped over another body, and then fell face forward to the ground in the middle of the station. He scrambled quickly to get to his feet, only to find he had fallen in the midst of a myriad of corpses. He heard Stone's men following in his footsteps down the entrance stairs. There was no time to make his way through the turnstiles, onto the platform, and down into the tunnels, and even if there had been, it appeared that access was gated off. In an effort to avoid capture, or worse, Paul quickly crawled toward the southeast stairs to make an escape, only to find it was secured. With nowhere to go, the only idea he had was to start screaming, to scream the way he had heard so many others scream during the first day when the living dead began their takeover of the city.

The clamor of fast-paced footsteps down the stairs immediately halted. Paul heard whispered voices near the bottom of the stairs, and then retreating footfalls. Paul sat hunched by the southeast exit a few feet away from the secured gate. The light that came through the large, black iron bars was just enough to give him comfort, but the style of the gate resembled those used in prisons. He felt like a prisoner waiting in the darkness. He waited to make sure his pursuers had truly left, and that it was safe to make his escape.

With his freedom he could now make a plan at rescuing those Stone and his men held captive. However, who would help him? He knew of only one survivor group the one led by "Plissken." It would be a risk to approach them considering the warning he had received about staying out of their territory. Nonetheless, he knew they had a moral compass. If he sought out another survivor group it was possible, they could be as equally evil as Stone's group. If he could get this man to listen to his story, then perhaps there was a chance his survivor group would help. Nevertheless, that decision would have to wait. What he needed to do next was find shelter and food before dark before the night creatures emerged.

As he sat on the floor of the locked storage room biding his time, his thoughts shifted to the state of the armory. When he had been placed in custody after approaching, there had been two armed men with the colonel. There had been an intimidating, well-built older black man and a short, thinner man the colonel had addressed as Sam. He recognized the two as part of the team that had rescued Ryan. Except where were they now and the others that had been with him those two weeks ago at Astor Place? Had they truly abandoned the colonel and their armory stronghold? Who then was left to help to defeat Stone's formidable survivor group?

"Shit," Paul stated with an uncomfortable tone. He *really* needed to piss.

# 8

## A CRY IN THE WILDERNESS

J.D. WAS OVERDUE. HE SHOULD HAVE BEEN BACK TWO HOURS AGO. Ryan was worried. There was something wrong and he knew it. The strange cries that echoed throughout the streets were a sound that had a familiar tone, but never so loud or frightening. It was the reverberation of a transmute, but it had been so piercing that it had sounded as if every transmute in the metropolis had simultaneously called out in some eerie death shriek.

He went to the communications room and tried to radio J.D., but he was not familiar with the equipment, and his attempt did not elicit a response. J.D. had been right; he wasn't prepared to survive on his own. He needed the support of others, as he had when he first banded together with other survivors at St. Clement's Church.

Doctor France entered the radio room, and told Ryan, "I heard you attempting to contact Mr. Nichols. Are you aware you were using the public address system?"

"Do you know how to operate this equipment? The colonel is overdue, and there was this screech. Did you hear it?" Ryan asked, slightly panicked.

"As did the whole city one would surmise."

"It was the colonel, I know it. He needs help. I have to go to the rendezvous point."

"Do not be so impetuous, Mr. Duncan," France told him, and then warned. "A solo outing is ill-advised. The bad element is certainly keeping this facility under surveillance. You would make a very easy target."

"Then we should both go. Strength in numbers, less likely to be attacked."

"You and I both know that my strength is in my intellect, not in physical prowess. I am far from the best candidate for this quest. Besides, leaving this facility unsecured will be the quickest way to lose our refuge."

"You're the only one left," Ryan reminded the doctor.

"You are forgetting Mr. Wiese. I am sure he would be more than willing to aid you."

"The man tried to kill me," he reminded the doctor. "And J.D. doesn't trust him."

"You are being a tad over dramatic. Besides Mr. Nichols is overly suspicious and irrational at times due to the chemical and physical changes within the frontal lobe of his brain that occurred during his transformation. His trust issue I feel in this case is unwarranted. Mr. Wiese came here not only to seek asylum, but also for our assistance in an important matter. A matter that may also relate to the people that went missing from your former survivor group."

"And how do you know this?" Ryan asked with suspicion.

"I had a brief chat with the man during my examination of him, before Mr. Nichols struck him in the larynx and dragged him off. I think if you asked Mr. Wiese for his assistance, he will be most agreeable."

---

Paul had come to terms with Doctor France, and the doctor had given his word that he would speak with Ryan as well as J.D. in regard to Paul's codicil in their agreement. Paul had already been incarcerated many hours before Richard France came knocking, enough so that he needed to urinate badly, but he refused to wet himself or urinate in a corner of the room. J.D. called Paul Piss Pants for a reason that was meant as humiliation. Paul had urinated himself at Astor Place when he thought J.D. was going to kill him. Paul refused to be the butt end of someone's amusement again, especially from J.D., who had without regard callously punched him in the throat and nearly crushed his windpipe right before being locked up. Now as he felt the pain and urgency to relieve his bladder, he hoped that France would be true to his word, so he could get out and use a bathroom proper, instead of the floor.

Ryan had been a kind and gentle soul before Stone's group found him and two co-survivors scavenging for food for their small band. But the humiliation, the degradation, the anguish, and the trauma that he had suffered by their hands had caused him to harden. He was no longer going to be a victim. He stood in the archway with a pistol in his hand, and though he was a pacifist at heart and the majority of his experience with a firearm had been with a BB rifle when he was younger, it didn't mean he was unwilling to use the weapon or incapable of shooting someone at close range if it was in defense of his own life.

He was plain in his words as he explained the situation, attempting not to give away any vital information that could be used as intel if Paul Wiese was really a spy as J.D. suspected.

"You've heard my request," he told Paul. "Will you help me or do you prefer to stay locked up until the colonel returns?"

"You mean *if* he returns"

"I give you my word, if you help me, I'll listen to your story, and if I believe you are true and sincere, I'll help you in whatever way I can, as I know the doctor will."

"Let's just cut the crap and pretense. You're not military. And this colonel of yours, he's not military either. You're only asking me for help because you have no other option. Whatever the reason, everyone has chosen to leave, which makes them smarter than you and whoever else was stupid enough to stay behind, because the group that forced me to join them is definitely the same group that attacked this place. I know this because I heard talk when I was with them. And they want this place.

As for the one you call Renquist, he's not the boss—that's Stone. He's one sick fucker with no moral compass who will not hesitate to fuck you in the ass and slit your throat at the same time just for his own amusement and gratification. There's nothing more I'd like to see than that depraved son-of-a-bitch emasculated and eviscerated for the things he's done and continues to do. And if this colonel of yours is some kind of badass who can end him, then hell yeah, I'm in."

# GUARDIAN OF THE FALLEN

CORPSES OF HALF-MUTES GREETED THE TWO AS THEY PULLED THEIR vehicle onto the creaking wooden slats of the pier and in front of the apparently abandoned Stryker. The waterfront felt ominous. Ryan had been here several times. He remembered the large crowds that gathered during the summer tourist season, filling the restaurants, visiting the many ships, watching the street performers, and patronizing the shops. The atmosphere then was festive, almost carnival-like, but for Ryan it felt like a time that was so long ago, a fading memory of the time before the plague that silenced his beloved city.

It was fall now, the season waning and the winter months looming, which only added to the silent and eerie feel on the aging, unattended pier. A light cool breeze blew through the promenade, and seemed to cry for those days of man, the days of joyous noise and revelry. Though Paul had never been to the Seaport, he felt it too, a chilly tingle running through him as he and Ryan cautiously made their way from their ICV to the back of the other. The truck was still running, but the rear deployment gate was secured. They knocked hard on the rear gate, but there was no answer. Ryan thought it was possible that J.D. could be inside, injured, unable to respond, so he told Paul to climb up and see if a gun port hatch was unlocked. Ryan stood guard as Paul made his way up over the slat armor to the gunner's turret. A loud cry came from Paul as he quickly jumped down from the vehicle.

"*Holy shit! Holy Shit! Holy Shit!*" he repeated frantically. "There's —there's one of those... creature things in there, and it's got your colonel. I should have taken my chances and stayed at the armory. He's done for."

Ryan needed to know for himself. He couldn't just leave the man who was instrumental in his rescue behind unless he was positive, he was dead. Ryan peered cautiously through the hatch, with weapon at the ready, and was shocked at what he was witnessing. He had expected, by Paul's reaction, to see the transmute feeding on J.D.'s corpse. What he discovered, what he couldn't believe he was witnessing, was a female creature cradling J.D. in her arms, like she was comforting him, protecting him.

He was astonished at the tenderness and attention it was giving J.D. The creature looked up at him, but made no threatening motion, gave no warning to stay back. It was like she knew that Ryan had come to help.

Ryan withdrew his weapon, smiled and said, "Hello." He was about to introduce himself when Paul called up, nearly demanding to know why he hadn't killed the thing. Ryan stood up and told him to shut up, that it appeared the creature wasn't hostile and that J.D. may still be alive. Paul just muttered. Ryan turned his attention back to the female creature.

"Where was I?" he addressed her. "Yes. My name... My name is Ryan. *Ry-an.* I'm a friend. *Friend.* Do you understand? J.D. is friend."

Luci made a light noise in response to 'J.D.'

"*J.D.* Yes, J.D."

Luci made more noise.

"Yes, J.D. is friend. Like me... I need to see my friend. I need to see J.D. Okay? I need to come in, look at him," Ryan told her as he gestured to the inside of the truck.

Ryan knew he was about to take a big risk. These creatures were known for unprovoked attacks, but this one seemed different, almost human. Nevertheless, he was also acutely aware that they were smart and it could just be a ploy. He could see no way of getting her out of the vehicle, and to try and shoot her could potentially cause J.D.'s death in the process, provided he was still living. So, Ryan had no choice but to go through the hatch to J.D.'s aid and hoped he wouldn't be seized the moment he dropped his legs through the opening.

Paul warned him not to go, that he would end up like his commander, but Ryan refused to heed his words. He slipped down into the vehicle as Paul was still talking away. There was a small platform about four feet into the vehicle. Ryan placed his feet on the metal stand and ducked down into the ICV. Luci had now backed away from J.D. and was hunched in the rear corner near the back exit, making light clacking sounds. Ryan spoke softly and gently to her, explaining what he was going to do. Ryan checked his pulse; it was weak but noticeable. J.D.'s shirt was soaked in blood and there was a large amount of blood spatter on his face, but it didn't appear to be his. Ryan looked at the leg bandage, and though it was blood soaked, the blood flow appeared to have ceased. To the best of Ryan's limited ability he surmised that he was just unconscious. After trying for several minutes to explain to the female creature what had to be done, he still had no idea if she understood the urgency for him to take J.D. back to armory. Instead Ryan crawled into the driver's seat, radioed Paul it was time to go, and then proceeded to drive away.

It was noon when they finally arrived back at the armory. Ryan tried to coax Luci from the truck while Paul went to get the doctor and a stretcher, but Luci refused to leave his side. Paul warned the doctor of what they brought back, but the doctor refused to believe Paul's fantastic tale. After all, he was more familiar with the transmutes than they were, and he knew that these creatures were incapable of such human emotions. When France set eyes upon her he knew that J.D. had been right, when J.D. had told him that he and Luci would be reunited at some future time.

"Oh, my God!" France exclaimed. "Luci."

Luci's reaction was less than cordial, it was menacing. She clacked and screeched, warning the doctor not to come near.

"You know her?" Ryan asked the doctor.

"Yes," he responded hesitantly. "She was a... patient of mine, long ago."

"Well you seemed to have made a great impression, doc. For all our sakes you better get back to the hospital. Paul and I will bring him up."

Luci followed them into the armory, trailing slowly and cautiously behind, keeping a close eye on her injured mate. Paul was concerned and a bit frightened at the prospect of having this creature 'stalking' them into the armory. Ryan assured him that if this Luci wanted to have done them harm, she already had plenty of opportunities to do so. Ryan's optimism did little to relieve Paul's anxiety.

It was evident that Doctor France was not going to be allowed to examine J.D. and he gave them a stern order that it was in the best interest of everyone that the creature be put down. Doctor France put up such an argument in necessitating the act that Ryan questioned him on his motive, and when the doctor refused to explain himself, Ryan told him in no uncertain terms that Luci was not going to be harmed in any manner. It was apparent to him that she and J.D. had some sort of mutual bond, and when asked about this, the doctor again refused to elaborate with the exception to stating that they had a history.

It was Ryan who gave J.D. the exam after the doctor explained what needed to be done and what needed to be recorded. It was also Ryan who eventually cleaned J.D.'s wound and changed his bandaging while the doctor was forced to stay on the other side of the room because Luci refused to leave J.D.'s side. As Ryan carefully wiped away the dried, crusted blood from his leg, Luci began to tap soundly on his back and make light noises. When he turned around Luci was gesturing up and down her body with a closed hand.

Ryan thought he understood her hand gesture. "Yes, Luci. I'm cleaning. I'm cleaning his wound."

Ryan turned back to attend to J.D.'s leg, but Luci still wanted his attention. She tapped on Ryan again, and when he turned around again she again made the same motions. Ryan did not know what she wanted.

"I don't understand. I don't know what you mean."

Luci raised her arms in the air and held out her long fingers. She fluttered them in the air as she lowered and raised her arms several times. She then stopped and looked at Ryan.

"I'm sorry, Luci. I... I don't know."

Luci abruptly ripped off her shirt and stood in front of Ryan naked, revealing not only her breasts but also her pregnancy. Ryan looked down at her stomach, but Luci wanted his attention. She tapped him again, and then picked up the small bowl of bloodied water Ryan had been using to wipe away J.D.'s dried blood, and then poured it over her head. She then again made the arm motions. He now understood. Luci wanted to be clean, too. She wanted a shower.

"*Shower?* You want a shower?"

Luci lightly pawed at Ryan's shirt. It was a yes, she wanted a shower.

"Then take that infernal beast to the showers, Mr. Duncan," France demanded. "It will give me opportunity to thoroughly and properly assess Mr. Nichols' wound.

Ryan gestured for Luci to follow and she did.

# 10

## THE LIEUTENANT OF INWOOD

OCTOBER 18, DAY 193.

J.D.'s leg had nearly healed when he heard Paul's voice over the intercom announcing someone had driven up to the 26th Street gate, and was calling out to be let in. J.D. was perplexed to the circumstances on how "Piss Pants" had gained his freedom and why he was in the comm room. However, it would have to wait. The timbre in Paul's voice told him that the man was genuinely concerned over the arrival at the gate. J.D. quickly dressed and armed himself, and was too much in a hurry to greet Luci properly as he bolted from the door into the hallway where she sat on the floor patiently waiting for him. J.D. paused long enough to tell Luci to go inside his room and stay, and then hurried away down the stairs and out of sight. It would be many hours before J.D.'s return.

The man was dressed in an Army uniform and was holding a pistol.

J.D. and Ryan greeted the man with raised weapons and an order to lay down his firearm and kick it away. The commander then ordered the man to put his hands on top of his head, and place his back against the fencing and to tell anyone else in the vehicle to step out. Although the man assured him he was alone.

"State your business," J.D. ordered.

"I've come to see Colonel Travis."

"What for?" Ryan asked.

"I'm Lieutenant James Alexander of the 69th Infantry Regiment. He's my commanding officer."

"First Lieutenant James Alexander, Alpha Company?" J.D. inquired.

"Yes," he confirmed, and then asked, "May I stand and present myself?"

"Granted," J.D. confirmed, "but slowly. And keep your hands on top of your head." When the soldier had turned around, J.D. asked, "Where the hell have you been soldier? Colonel Travis listed you as FTR, presumed dead."

"I can explain," he began, and then realized that the two men before him were not soldiers. J.D.'s mismatched uniform and age, and Ryan's incorrect shoulder sleeve insignia alarmed James. "Wait, you're not a Colonel. And he's not of the 69th! What the hell is going on? Where's Colonel Travis?"

"The Colonel is dead, along with everyone else. If you had been here you'd know that."

"That still doesn't explain who you are?"

"We can discuss that in my office, Lieutenant."

Not having much of a choice with two guns aimed at him, James surrendered.

"You are to go with my lieutenant to see Doctor France for a physical, after which you will report directly to my office for a debriefing. And you better have a damn good reason why you just suddenly showed up. Is that understood, Lieutenant?"

"Affirmative," James halfheartedly confirmed.

"Lieutenant Duncan, unlock the gate please," J.D. instructed.

"Yes, sir," Ryan replied quickly and respectfully, as if he were a real warfighter.

After picking up the man's pistol, J.D. re-secured the gate, all along

keeping a watchful eye on the Humvee. His keen vision saw no movement in the vehicle or in his visual plane of the surrounding area, not
even a half-mute. He radioed to Paul it was clear and that they were
returning.

J.D. was suspicious, especially at a soldier who had been listed as
presumed dead showing up six months after the fact. Even if this man
was truly Lieutenant Alexander, it didn't mean he was not cooperating
with others to gain access to the armory for their own reason.

---

J.D. knew much about the fall of the armory and how the brave men of
Companies A and C had perished in their fight for survival. After all he
found Colonel Walter A. Travis' journal and operational reports. So, he
knew that Lieutenant James Alexander along with six other soldiers
never reported to the armory. However, J.D. also knew the lieutenant
had been nearby. So why hadn't he reported, why after all this time did
he finally decided to make an appearance, and where had he been for
all those months? That is what J.D. intended to find out.

---

"First Lieutenant James Alexander, 1st Battalion, 69th Infantry Regiment, A Company, DoD Identification Number 193726886," he
repeated for the third time to the suspicious "officer" who sat behind
Commander Travis' desk.

J.D. replied, "You want to repeat that a fourth time or would you
rather sit down and discuss your miraculous appearance after six
months?"

"No disrespect, *Colonel*, but I don't believe you're military. And
I'm not obligated to tell you anything."

"You doubt I am the commander of this base?"

"You may be commander but you're sure the hell no colonel."

"And I say this MPK-5 I have pointing at your crotch from under the desk out ranks you. So, at ease soldier and take that seat in front of you."

Begrudgingly he complied.

J.D. tossed a small diary in front of the seated man, and then said, "You, Lieutenant, according to Commander Travis' daily operational report dated 8 April, were reported in route to base at 1300 hours. However, you failed to report for duty, and now six months later here you are. That journal in front of you belonged to your late commander. It's his personal account of what happened here. Open it. Open it to the first tab and read the passage to me."

"What?" James responded, pretending not to understand J.D.'s instructions.

"I want you to read the first marked passage to me aloud. Now pick up the book and read!"

James opened the book to the first tabbed section and read the passage aloud as instructed.

*"April 8, 2014 - This morning at 1000 hours, Companies A and C were called to active duty in regard to a potential biohazard threat. The threat turned out to be an infectious disease of unknown origin. Once again, the men under my command have been called upon to manage re-supply for food, drinking water, and health and comfort items to our troops on the eastside of the city, along with the armory being purposed as a secondary MEDCOM—designated FOB MEDCOM Bravo—because of our hospital facilities. Seven of my men, including my friend First Lieutenant James Alexander—who I spoke with at 1300 hours and had stated was on 23rd Street and 10th Avenue—have not reported for duty. I have been unable to contact any of them as of late this afternoon."*

The lieutenant didn't seem to be fazed by the mention of his failure to report.

"Now read the next part where it's marked," J.D. ordered.

Again, James read aloud.

*"I have been to war and have heard the screams and cries of the injured and dying. But what I have experienced today, of my men, my colleagues, my friends, being ripped apart in such a savage manner was horrifying, and frightens me more than any battlefield I ever fought on...*

*...There is now a continual flow of what my soldiers are calling zombies. Their corpses are now stacking up along the fence line. I do not know if these "zombies" are truly the living dead or not, but if they continue to grow in number, I fear bullets will not be able to stop them from breaching the fence.*

*A side note: James and the other six men who did not report to duty are unreachable. God protect them."*

Lieutenant James Alexander was clearly shaken by the second passage he was forced to read.

"Now you want to talk about obligation?" J.D. asked. "You had an obligation to report to duty, an obligation to fight alongside your fellow soldiers, an obligation to your friend Colonel Travis, but you let your team down, your commander down and now they're all dead. Your desertion offends me—no it sickens me. You're right; I'm not a colonel. But I am the leader of this base and I have an obligation to protect those within these walls. It is my responsibility to determine if you are friend or foe, and my decision alone on whether you get to live, join us, or walk out of here with food in your belly and a weapon in your hand. So, you either tell me what I need to know now or I'll find some dark hole to lock you in until you're ready to cooperate."

James could not afford to be locked up. He had come to the armory to see if any of his 69th Infantry Regiment compatriots were still alive, explain his absence to Colonel Travis, and appeal to his sense of fairness and understanding as both a commanding officer and as a friend in hopes of securing aid and assistance. This was not about his welfare but that of others. The lieutenant knew it was in the best interest of those others to cooperate, and perhaps in doing so he could still complete his mission with the assistance of the man who now controlled the armory.

"Very well," James agreed.

J.D opened a thick file folder that lay in front of him.

"It states in your file that your MOS was Transportation Officer. It also says you were awarded a Medal of Valor in 2007 for going above and beyond the call of duty and were also given a service commendation in 2011 from Colonel Travis for outstanding duty. Furthermore, I see you are a certified kick box instructor. But none of this tells me why a soldier with such an exemplary service record failed to report to duty." It was perplexing to J.D. why a model officer with such noted courage and dedication to duty would betray everything he stood for. "You abandoned your regiment and your country in a time of catastrophic need. Why?"

"It's not what you think. I'm not a coward. I had to take up a defensive position in the Hearst Publishing building."

"And why there?" J.D. asked, knowing something was off with his answer.

"Sir?"

"Why that particular building, Lieutenant? Did you randomly pick it or was there reason you ended up there?"

"I was protecting some civilians."

"So you're stating that you decided, for no apparent reason, to go back up town, randomly pick a building to take up a defensive position so you could help a bunch of book editors instead of reporting directly to base as ordered? Is that what you're telling me?!"

"More or less," James replied.

"More or less. Interesting phrase more or less. It always seems to be used by those who are underplaying or exaggerating facts. So, which is it? Because according to the colonel, he spoke with you at approximately 1300 hours and he stated you were on 23$^{rd}$ Street and 10$^{th}$ Avenue and expected you shortly, but you never arrived and were unresponsive to his calls. That sounds like cowardice to me, unless you have another explanation for why you failed to report and chose to save a random bunch of strangers."

James did have a legitimate reason for never making it to the armory. He knew that Colonel Travis would have understood, and though he knew that what he had done was a court martial offense, he was pretty sure the colonel would have been sympathetic and only charged him with being absent without leave not desertion. However, he knew nothing about the man wearing the sunglasses and wasn't sure if he would be sympathetic to his reason.

"If I am candid with you," James Alexander began, "would you answer one question truthfully for me?"

"Do you one better, I'll answer yours first."

"If I had been a civilian and came to this base would you have offered me comfort and aid?" James asked.

J.D. was surprised at the question; it wasn't what he had been expecting.

"That's not a question I can answer with a simple yes or no. Not all are welcome. There are those that would take this base by force or subterfuge in order to control and deprive those in need of food, shelter, and medical attention. There are those who have tried, and I'm sure will try again. Those are the ones that we fight against, the ones that wish others harm, and that is why you sit before me. I need to know if you are one of those who wish their fellow man ill will or do you stand with what is moral and right. With that said, if you are a survivor and need help, that is why we are still here, and that is why we shine the beacon nightly."

James was satisfied with how J.D. had answered his question, and conveyed his story to the self-proclaimed leader of the armory in hopes the man would agree to help him. A half-hour later he and J.D. left the armory to save the Hearst Tower survivor group.

# 11

# THE GREENHOUSE

*October 20, Day 195.*

The nine survivors were weak, hungry and frail but alive. Their situation could have been worse. They could have been dead if it had not been for James' military training, ingenuity, and his great determination to stay alive. James' group was on their way to full recoveries with the help of Doctor France. Liz, too, had survived and was told that though there would be some permanent hair loss and scarring to her scalp, it could have been fatal if it hadn't been for Lieutenant Alexander's first aid skills.

With the survivors secure at the armory, J.D. and James returned to Hearst Tower two days later. It was James' desire to find his wife and see what happened to her, and to see if she had birthed the child she had been carrying. Though J.D. had caught scent of her several times, after several hours of searching they could not locate her. J.D. knew Ann-Marie was being elusive for a reason. He believed it was the scent of human from James.

As he and James started their departure, J.D. had an uneasy sensation that something was watching them. Rotating his head around, he scanned the interior, but could not find the source of his anxiety. James was too engrossed in his thoughts to notice J.D.'s 180-degree head rotation. As the two walked down the motionless escalator back to the lobby, J.D. realized what was causing his unease; he was being observed by a transmute. Though he couldn't smell James' wife, he was certain she was near. J.D. kept moving. It was best not to let James know Ann-Marie was watching them, especially since the creature had not made its presence known.

However, Ann-Marie and the child were ever present in James' mind. James stopped at the bottom of the steps. "Colonel," he addressed J.D. "I can't leave. Not without knowing. With your permission, I'd—"

"Negative, Lieutenant," J.D. interrupted, knowing full well what James was going to request.

"Colonel, please? I'm sure I can find her on my own. I just need more time."

"Lieutenant, you're not going to find her," J.D. told him. "She doesn't want you to."

"You can't know that, sir."

"I do," J.D. said, and then revealed, "I caught their scent several times, but she is evading us, hiding, afraid."

"*Their* scent?" James questioned, like he needed confirmation that he had heard J.D. correctly. "Then I need to find them, more than ever."

"Lieutenant, she's not afraid of me, she's afraid of you. You reek of human," J.D. told him like it was a bad thing. "I prefer not to have a dead lieutenant or a dead mother and child on my hands, and one of those outcomes is what will happen if you go hunting them down. She won't react well to your presence, especially if you corner her."

"With all due respect, I don't believe that will happen. Luci isn't afraid of you. And you made a child together. I don't even know if my child is a boy or girl."

J.D. had told James about Luci and her pregnancy, but he hadn't discussed it with him in great detail. Now he was going to have to clarify the uniqueness of his own situation so James could better understand. "Okay, James, rank aside," J.D. began. "Yes, Luci and I are going to have a child together. But you're not me. You're not part transmute. Being part transmute is the reason why I am more of a curiosity than a threat to them. Besides Luci..." J.D. paused momentarily knowing to fully explain the difference between the two transmutes sexes, and how Luci even differed from the few other female transmutes he had encountered, was a long conversation better suited for another time. "Let's just say Luci isn't like any other transmutes I've confronted. Luci is unique.

If you find Ann-Marie and your child, and if you manage not to get yourself attacked in the process, then what? You think it's going to be a happy reunion, and you're going to bring them back to the armory and live happily ever after? Think again. She's no longer human, James. She may have a fleeting recollection of you, but the memories of that life together are gone, and I can't allow you to endanger the armory by bringing her back—and before you tell me I did so with Luci, let me remind you of this: There's a reason why she remains away upstairs with me, and that's because she is aggressive toward most humans. As for my unborn child, not even Doctor France has any clue to whether she'll have the capacity to socialize with humans."

"But, J.D., I just can't forget them. I have a child. I want my child to be a part of my life."

"Then are you willing to kill Ann-Marie in order for you to be with your child? Because there's no way in hell she's going to let you take the baby from her."

James was silent.

"I didn't think so," J.D. confirmed, acknowledging James' silence as a sign he would be unable to kill his wife. Even if James had it in him, J.D. would never allow it. The child needed its transmute mother if it were going to survive, not a human father rearing it.

However, J.D. knew that James was not going to easily forget his wife or the baby he had never seen. His love for them would not allow it, and J.D. was certain James would eventually attempt to make contact, a reunion that would more than likely end in tragedy. J.D. had a resolution to the dilemma. It was a solution he hoped would give

James some resolution and comfort, and that was to act as guardian over them.

"I can only offer you this," J.D. began to explain. "I can act as their guardian. I can watch over them, bring them food, and if I see either is ill, as a paramedic, I will treat them using the best of my medical ability. I will tell you about my visits with them, and if it is at all possible, I will teach your child English, and perhaps one day you'll be able to talk to him or her as a father to a son or daughter." J.D. extended his hand and said, "I give you my word and my hand on it. Do you accept?"

James knew that everything J.D. had told him was true, and that the possibility of a family life or being a part of raising his infant was not presently viable. There was no other alternative but to accept J.D.'s offer, so he did, accepting J.D.'s hand and pledge.

"Good then," J.D. confirmed. "Now Lieutenant we get back to business."

# 12

## MOMMY'S LITTLE MONSTER

WHILE J.D. LOCKED HIMSELF AWAY FOR THEE DAYS AFTER BEING SHOT, Luci spent her time patiently sitting on the floor outside of J.D.'s room waiting for his acknowledgement. Ryan had brought her a clean shirt to wear, spread out a blanket, given her an extra one to cover herself, and even a pillow. He had never been sure if Luci actually had lain down, for every time he passed by, or had brought her a meal—though she never ate anything—she had been sitting clutching her bent knees with her head tilted slightly, carefully watching him. Ryan had even gone so far as to explain how to get to the bathroom. It appeared to Ryan that Luci was pinning for J.D. He was certain there was sadness in her face, like an aching of the heart perhaps, though Doctor France insisted she was incapable of such feelings.

J.D. knew Luci was outside his door. Ryan had told him so while helping to change his bandages. However, Ryan's revelation to her "condition" was a bit overwhelming to J.D. It was true he had repeated unprotected sex with her after he saved her life, but it never crossed his mind that he could impregnate her, nor had Doctor France brought up that possibility during their conversation about his intercourse with her, while they were still at the GCC.

J.D. tried to clear his mind of all that had transpired in the past 24 hours through meditation, but to his discontent he could not. He feared if he were unable to find his center and balance his chi, he would not be able to mend his soul, but moreover to purge the dark, disturbing urges he felt at the pier that continued to haunt him.

---

Luci was in the shower when he finally returned, after successfully rescuing James' group. She immediately came to the archway of the bathroom, forgetting to turn off the water. Her enlarged and rounded belly exposed, she stood peering at him sniffing the air, taking in J.D.'s scent. She screeched at him with piercing intensity. J.D. called back to her. She charged him, her wet nakedness striking him down. She tore at his clothes, ripping his shirt open, only to reveal his Dragonskin body armor. Luci pounded on his chest in frustration and discontent to the second layer he was wearing. He pushed her off, and then pinned her to the floor. Her scent was strong. Her body exuded a far more intoxicating smell than he remembered. He knelt before her spread legs, her vagina moist with anticipation. J.D. pulled off his shirt and body armor and tossed it to the floor. He frantically tried to unbuckle and unbutton his BDU pants, but his nails were getting in the way. Luci grew impatient. He stood up to de-pants himself, forgetting that he was still wearing boots. When his pants reached his ankles, he realized what he had forgotten, but it was too late. Luci had waited long enough. She stood swiftly and charged again, pushing him backward, off his feet, and down onto the bed. She was slightly irritated; he still had on his underwear. She ripped it from him.

Underwear was strange to her. Clothes were strange to her. Luci didn't need clothes. Her grey hide-like skin protected her for the most part, but there was an area remaining that still was her human skin, and though the skin's pigmentation had changed slightly to a light grey, it was still soft and supple. That portion of her body began directly underneath the larynx running down the front of her shoulders, around her full breasts, down the edge of the rib cage, into the pubic area and partially into the crease of her inner thighs, essentially covering her chest, abdomen and groin.

The sight of her voluptuous breasts with their enlarged nipples, and her swollen belly made him tremble with an urgency to penetrate her. He had been erect the moment she had pushed him to the floor, and Luci had waited too long to feel him inside. She mounted him and violently drove herself up and down on his engorged cock. He tried to sit up in order to push her off. He wanted to be the dominant one. He wanted to mount her. Except she refused his advances, and pushed him back down. When he tried again she forced him back, this time digging her talons into the front of his shoulders, letting him know that she was not going to have any of his male domination. It had been his own fault; she had learned quickly from him. It had been J.D. who had reacquainted her with sexual pleasure and the female orgasm.

The return of his Luci had helped to relieve his anguish and satisfy the physical side of his sexual needs. With Luci, though, it was not love. Nonetheless, the sex between them was still vigorous and rough, interspersed with moments of true tenderness, an intimacy that the doctor insisted Luci was incapable of due to neurological changes in both size and function of the overall frontal and temporal lobes of all transmute brains. However, France was not as intimately acquainted as J.D. was with Luci's sexual proclivities and emotions.

The sex was frequent. The sex was intensely gratifying. Then Caitlin was born, and the sex ended.

---

The birth of his daughter brought happiness and joy back into his life. She was physically less like a transmute than her mother but still retained a transmute appearance. She was also very much like her mother in human characteristics. She was born with eyes as blue as a gas flame, and as beautiful and brilliant as a benitoite gemstone. Her hair color, too, was red like Luci's, though more lustrous. She was her mother's daughter, with little, if any, resemblance to her father. Nonetheless, there was no doubt the child was his.

Ryan had helped with the birth, since Luci would not allow the doctor near her. It was for the best as she had every reason to want to kill the doctor. France had been the one to oversee the experiments on her. He was the one who had changed her from human to transmute, though that had not been the intention, but rather a phenomenon. Ryan became the child's godfather and secondary protector, and Caitlin would eventually call Ryan 'Elty Ryan', her own personal acronym for *Lieutenant* Ryan Duncan.

Luci had given birth quickly and effortlessly. Though she had carried her child for nearly seven months, their daughter had been born full-term. She was born early in the morning of October 31$^{st}$. This to him this was a sign of fortune for she had been born on the ancient Celtic festival day known as Samhain, or what most called Halloween, which is sometimes regarded as the Celtic New Year. The ancient Gaels believed that on October 31, the boundary between the living and the deceased dissolves, and the dead become dangerous for the living by causing problems such as sickness or damaging crops. In a way, she was a child of dissolved boundaries. She was neither trans-mute nor human, and yet she was more human than her mother and more transmute than her father. To J.D. she was the perfect mixture of both.

She was not weak like a human child. Caitlin weighed nearly nine pounds at birth, and had grown at an exceptional rate in just a few short weeks due to her inherited Spotted Owl DNA. France had told him that birds of prey were the fastest growing vertebrates and if her growth rate was anything like an owl, it was possible that in 8-9 weeks she could be walking. Although, France had given him the why to the rapid growth, he could not tell him how it would affect her life span. It deeply concerned J.D., but much like his own condition, there was nothing that could be done.

Caitlin was also born muscular. A lean, hard frame much like her father's. Her facial features were less pronounced than Luci's. Her teeth were less jagged. She had ears, unlike her mother who had just nubs, though Caitlin's had not fully formed. Caitlin also had human flesh, pink and supple in the same area where Luci's was light grey, and light bluish grey where Luci's skin was hide-like and darker. Caitlin's fingers were like her father's, not elongated. Eventually, when her talons would grow out, they would be slightly shorter in length, but still as lethal as J.D.'s. Like her mother and father, she had the ability to rotate her head 180 degrees, though she did inherit her mother's mildly elongated neck. She would grow equal in strength to both her parents, though her stealth and agility would be attributed to Luci, her cunning and intellect would be derived from her father. She also had the ability to quickly heal from injuries. As for the sexual aspect of her female gender, time would only tell if she was as sexually driven as her parents were. This, however, was far from J.D.'s mind as he gently held his newborn in his arms, ogling over the perfect child he and Luci had conceived. Well, almost.

Caitlin was a screecher—her voice, strident and shrill, echoed throughout the armory night and day. It was not just painful for himself and Luci, but to all of the people of the armory. After a week of Ryan fielding civilian complaints and bringing them to his attention on a daily basis, J.D. knew something needed to be done not only for the populace, but also for his own sanity. He decided that a private setting would be conducive for everyone. He thought about relocating his daughter and his mate to his old home—his pre-doomsday domain— his apartment on 13$^{th}$ Street. However, too many renovations needed to be done to make his residence livable again. Besides, Caitlin's incessant screeching would only attract half-mutes and perhaps Stone and his men, or others, and his apartment building was not easily defendable. There was only one viable solution—the unused top floor of the armory, where doors could be closed and Caitlin's noises could be muffled.

Sex was still absent in J.D.'s and Luci's relationship even after several weeks of Caitlin's birth. At first, he had thought it was postpartum depression, and so he did not try to force himself upon her. After a month, he could no longer take not indulging in sexual pleasure. When he tried to initiate sex, his advances were abruptly halted by an angry and violent response. Luci was not interested in any mating.

What J.D. had not realized was that the gene therapy injections he was giving her were not only affecting her physically but also altering her brain chemistry as some of her damaged human DNA began to be repaired. It was taking its toll on her physically as well as mentally. She no longer had a sex drive nor the energy to do much more than to breast-feed Caitlin. The virus she had been infected with had been developed using recombinant owl DNA. In Doctor France's human trials at the GCC, Luci had been one of the test subjects. Richard France quickly discovered the disease, which was meant to kill its host, had a different effect on some of those who had a mutated CCR5-D32 gene in their DNA makeup. Instead of death, it altered DNA on a cellular level, causing a metamorphosis into what the doctor would name a transmute. It did not alter nearly as much human DNA in females as it did with male subjects; an anomaly France was unable to figure out.

When J.D. had finally confronted the doctor about his own mutation, shortly after retaking the GCC, he discovered that he was beyond help and his mutation was permanent. In their adversarial conversation the doctor did reveal that it might have been possible to repair some of the mutation if he had had a pre-mutated DNA strain from him. J.D. had realized that though he could not be helped, it was possible Luci could be. Doctor France would have certainly taken samples from Luci prior to infecting her with the virus, and when hard pressed the doctor revealed he had.

Thirty days into the treatments Luci had begun to change, subtly, but J.D. had not noticed. It was the sixth week of therapy when the change suddenly struck him. He had been away from her for several days, concentrating on armory business, confident that Luci was able to take care of their child without any supervision. He had returned in the evening to find her sitting on the wooden floor of the bedroom in front of the full-length mirror crying, their daughter who she clutched to her bosom also crying.

He spoke to her trying to console her with a soothing voice, knowing she could not respond with human speech. Shockingly she did. She pointed to the mirror, and with a facial expression of repulsion and a tone of great lament she spoke, "Look. Ugly. Luci ugly."

Having previously only the ability to communicate with hand gestures and screech type vocalizations, J.D. was awestruck by the return of her human language. After initially being dumb struck, he reassured her, "No, Luci You're beautiful."

"No!" she insisted. "Ugly. Look," she told him holding up her hands.

"No, Luci. You look," he told her, holding up his taloned fingers. "Luci and J.D. the same. Caitlin the same." He raised his daughter's little fingers.

"Doctor hurt me. Doctor make me ugly. I no want to be ugly. I want die… Go. Go. No look at me."

He knew her anguish had been his fault. He had been selfish in his desire to return her to a more human state. He would discontinue the gene therapy.

She pushed him away. She was inconsolable. He could not calm her aching heart nor stop her tears with his words. The more Luci sobbed, the more Caitlin wailed. He sat on the edge of the bed for a moment, and then realized what might placate both his daughter and his mate.

He went to another room where he had stored some of his personal affects to retrieve the one thing that might calm them both; it was his Yamaha Arranger Workstation.

He had not played his keyboard or any keyboard for an extremely long time nor had he sung since that day in the truck when he and David traveled down Second Avenue on their way to McSorley's Ale House.

He had many favorite artists and knew how to play many songs from various music genres. There was one artist who he knew Luci cherished the most. Elton John had been a name that had attracted J.D.'s attention to a questionnaire he had read in the medical records that Doctor France had kept in regard to his test subject. In Luci's box, along with a few personal items, had been a file that contained a sheet of paper with various personal questions. In the document, Luci had stated that her music choice was mainly of the pop rock kind, mainly British artists, with one standing out significantly. Accented with asterisks on both sides of the name, was the words Elton John. This was Luci's favorite music artist, and it was with this single musician he hoped to calm her by singing the few Elton John songs he knew.

Running through several ballads, which elicited no response from her, J.D. then played "Blue Eyes." Though she did not stop her sobbing, it appeared Luci recognized the song. When he had finished, he smoothly transitioned to "Lucy In The Sky With Diamonds," hoping that hearing her name would calm her. It did.

She came to him with their child and put her hand on his. He stopped playing.

Realizing his terrible mistake, he turned to her and cupped his hand to her cheek, begging her forgiveness. "I'm sorry, Luci. I was selfish. I wanted you to be human again. To give you back your memories. To make you the way you once were. But that was wrong. I did it for me, not for you. And now all I have brought you is anguish."

She saw his remorse and understood the regret he conveyed. "I understand. You try to help. Make Luci b-better. Like at the... lab— laber... laba." Her words were stammered as she fought to find the correct pronunciation. But her mouth failed her. "The underground place. You save me. No harm. Make me better... But you send me away...I – I understood... I watch J.D. always. I find you and... help you, too. Now we together." She held up their child. "We make Cai – Cai... Caitlin. We f-family."

"Yes, Luci. We're family."

For the moment, Luci was now calm and content, but Caitlin still was dissatisfied. Luci placed her in the crib that was near the bed and returned to her mate. She pulled at him, beckoning him to the bed. She wanted him and it was the first time he had truly been invited in a romantic way. He accommodated her, and for the first time their love-making had been tender as well as passionate and not just aggressive and robust.

After several hours of loving one another Luci had fallen asleep. Caitlin, however, refused to follow her mother's lead. Though she no longer cried, she fussed, greatly. He moved his keyboard closer to her and watched his fidgety, noisy, non-compliant daughter as he tried to think what music might possibly soothe a picky transmute infant.

She had not appreciated Elton John as her mother did, so he needed to find something to her liking. After attempting Joe Jackson's "Love Got Lost," she was still an unhappy girl. She didn't seem to care for his rendition of "Phantom's Theme" by Paul Williams, and though he thought she got some amusement out of "Song For Whoever" by the Beautiful South, she still refused to fall asleep. Though more suited for accordion than piano, he played and sang the Shane MacGowan song, "Skipping Rhymes," which was based on the traditional children's song "This Old Man." However, it was apparent she was not fond of his favorite Irish singer. A spittle lip vibration came from her in protest.

"*What?*" J.D. declared, with astonishment to her disapproving verbal gesture. "Did you just give me a raspberry? Or did you give Shane Patrick Lysaght MacGowan a raspberry. Ya wee disagreeable child," he responded in a fake Irish accent. "How could you?"

He picked her up, cradled her in his arms, and gently danced around the room with her, singing "Good Night" by the Beatles.

"You, young lady," he playfully scolded. "You should be my biggest fan, not my biggest critic. Shall we try again?"

She stared up at her father and gave him an amused look.

"I will take that as a yes," he said to her, and then returned her to the crib.

He pondered what would put her to sleep. Something, perhaps, he thought, without lyrics, a tune that would be light and floaty. He knew just the piano piece, "Clair de Lune" from *Suite Bergamasque* by Claude Debussy. Caitlin fell asleep before he had played the last notes.

It had been a long time since he had played or sang, and now that his daughter had drifted off under the hypnotic spell of Debussy, he decided to play for himself.

Though J.D. had tried to keep his singing and playing low, as not to awaken Luci, he had unknowingly done so. Luci had watched and listened from her bed, the interaction between her mate and daughter. Finally, when Caitlin drifted off under the hypnotic spell of Debussy, and as he began to play Chopin's "Nocturne Op.9 No.2," she went to him. She looked at her sleeping daughter and smiled.

There was one other piano ballad that he knew Luci would take pleasure in, a song not by Elton John, but by Elvis Costello. It was from a film starring one of her favorite actors, Hugh Grant. The song was "She," from the film *Notting Hill.*

He began to play it, but before he reached the bridge of the song, only having completed half the verse that led into it, Luci coaxed him from his piano bench, and gently spoke three simple words, "Love. More. Now."

———

Love. More. Now.

There was happiness in his life again.

However, happiness is fleeting, like the setting of the sun.

# 13

## WEI JI

There was the long, piercing honking of a Humvee horn. They had
come like they had before, a strike force, but this time they had brought
more vehicles, military Humvees, more weapons and more men. If
they chose to lay siege to the armory this would not be a haphazard
attempt like what had happened previously. J.D. and his friends had
thwarted the attack without injury or loss of life to their group. The
men inside the armory were not his old tried and true, battle-experi-
enced comrades. He and James were the only ones who had any battlefield experience, so he knew that he would have to put on a strong
front to convince these men that any attempt to seize the armory would
be futile. He had known that one day, sooner rather than later, those
who had tried previously to forcibly take control of the armory would
return and try to accomplish what they had so miserably failed at the
first time. Paul had warned him Stone was coming.

The mid-November air was mild as J.D. approached the men who
had gathered in front of the north gate at 26th Street. The wind blew

lightly from the south to the north and it reminded him of those windy spring days on Second Avenue and 12<sup>th</sup> Street when he used to sip his vanilla hazelnut flavored coffee on the wooden slat bench in front of the Open Pantry, but spring was months away. However, J.D. had over dressed for the weather and it was apparent by the looks on the faces of the men behind the fence that they had taken notice of his outfit. There had been a reason J.D. was wearing a vest, gloves, a black military cap, and sunglasses along with his full military uniform. The vest was body armor for protection, but the other accessories were to hide his advantages.

"I'm looking for the one called Plissken. Lieutenant Robert Plissken," declared a tall man with a noticeable bald area on the crown of his head, as he emerged from the center of the group, and then sized up J.D.

J.D. responded to the man's inquiry. "That joke never seems to get old. It's colonel. Colonel Nichols. And what can I do you out of?"

"You're a funny man, *Colonel*. It's not what you can do for me it's what I'm going to do for you. Why don't you let me in so we can talk?" The man slightly raised the bottom hem of his shirt and spun around while simultaneously assuring J.D. of his intent. "As you can see I'm unarmed."

"Why don't you state your business before you decrease the property values?" J.D. snapped at the man.

"All right," he said with irritation, as he straightened his shirt. "I'm going to let you and your little toy army just walk away. Just walk away from the armory and everyone gets to live."

J.D. stared at the man's dirtied navy-blue colored shirt that was clearly too large for him. He was dressed in a uniform shirt from the New York City Department of Corrections. Above his left breast pocket, stitched to his uniform, was a name patch that read, 'A. Renquist', but J.D. knew this man was not who he was pretending to be.

"Just walk away and everyone gets to live." J.D. sarcastically repeated. "I'll tell you what. You just have Stone bring us the women and children and you got a deal. If not, tell him I'll be coming to get them."

"I don't know whom you're talking about," he feigned.

"I know you're not Stone. You're just one of his ass-lickin' dogs. So, go deliver the message."

The man grew angry at J.D.'s insult.

"I could shoot you right here."

"You could, but you won't."

"Ye—yeah we could just sh—shoot you."

"What are *you?*" J.D. asked the nervous, skinny man who stood next to Renquist. "The ugly inbred comic relief? I'd watch where you're pointing that gun, twitchy, or you might find yourself dead."

"Hey, who you, you ca—calling twitchy?" the red-haired man stammered in his reply.

"He's quick, too, isn't he?" J.D. snidely added.

"You're pretty bold for a man who came out without back up," Renquist said.

J.D. replied defiantly, "And you're pretty stupid if you think there's no one watching my back. We're done here."

J.D. turned and walked away from them. He wasn't afraid that they'd shoot him in the back, for he was being watched over, and J.D. was certain that the person who had sent Renquist did not want J.D. dead at that moment. Within several moments of returning to the armory, the horn of the Humvee echoed a second time throughout Lexington Avenue. He was being summoned again.

There was only one man at the gate this time, and it was Stone.

He was a man of medium size and height with golden blonde hair and crystal blue eyes. He did not appear menacing, but neither had serial killer Jeffrey Dahmer. When he spoke his voice was lyrical and sweet, and upon his blemish-free, baby-smooth skin a charismatic smile lit his face as he recited:

> *"Humpty Dumpty sat on a wall.*
> *Humpty Dumpty had a great fall.*

*All the colonel's horses and all the colonel's men*
*Couldn't put Humpty together again!"*

The nursery rhyme confirmed what J.D. had suspected all along. It had been Stone who scrawled the cryptic *Babes in the Wood* message on the wall at St. Clement's Episcopal Church.

J.D. snidely fired back,

" *'A wise old owl sat in an oak. The more he heard, the*
*less he spoke. The less he spoke, the more he heard.*
*Why aren't you like that wise old bird?'*

Now get to the point!" J.D. said with irritation.

Of all the nursery rhymes that had been recited to him in his childhood, he could only remember three in their entirety.

"I overestimated you, Colonel. I thought you a man of intelligence. Why do you not accept my offer? Your army has left you. The world is but an echo of the past. Whom are you fighting for?"

J.D. tried to be clever. He tried to come up with a movie quote for a response. He had once been a master of movie quote trivia. But most of the snappy lines seem to elude him and those he barely remembered seemed to be a fuzzy mixture of quotes from an amalgamation of films.

"I fight for reasons you would not understand. I have an obligation to protect the innocent. We stand between those who need our protection and those who would do them harm."

"Indeed… then why have you come to meet me if it is not to accept my offer?"

"I came to see your face, so that I alone may find you on the battlefield. And it would be wise for you to take note of mine, Stone. For the next time you see it, it will be the last thing you see on this Earth."

"We could just wait you out or take the armory by force."

"You've got a real hard-on for this place, don't you? You tried taking it before. How'd that work out for you? Before I lose it, I will burn it to the ground."

"You would destroy it?"

"Every stone, every brick. And every soldier you kill will take ten of your men before they perish. I swear to your God that this armory will be the end of you."

"Your armory is filled with civilians. If my men die so will they."

"I will not yield this armory and I will not stop until I have all those you've imprisoned. Those are *my* terms!"

"What is this armory worth, that you would sacrifice so much to keep it from me?"

"Nothing," J.D. spoke as he backed away. "And everything," he told him as he turned toward the armory.

Edward Stone walked away disappointed but with an even greater determination at defeating his adversary. "I will kill him, and piss on his dead corpse. This I swear," he muttered to the dark-haired, balding man, as he returned to his men.

J.D. Nichols knew that the hostages would not be released. He knew it was up to him and his men to rescue them. As the last truck departed and headed up Lexington out of view, J.D. turned back toward the granite sanctuary and walked toward the entrance. As he did he gestured up to the roof. A dwarf stood up, slung a rifle over his shoulder, and waved back.

J.D. had barely made it up the first set of granite steps when a shot, emanating from the roof, rang out—echoing throughout the compound. It was Peter Dunne—a recent survivor addition—who had fired, sending a fence scaling insurgent to the ground. However, it was not Stone's men who were on the offensive, it was half-mutes.

There were four more, and they were angry, aggressive, and hungry. A half-mute was more voracious than an undead and more aggressive than any transmute. This new creature had evolved from a mutation of the original virus.

Half-mute and transmute sightings had diminished since the onset of the changing season, and the sight of the four climbing the fence not only alarmed him in regard to their continued presence, but in their agility. What also alarmed him—and ran a shiver up his spine—was that when Peter had killed the first fence climber the others let out a cry of anger and anguish for their fallen companion. He had known these creatures to be furious and rapid in their attack, nearly in a blind rage, but he had never known them to show any sign of intelligence.

The half-mutes had been drawn to the armory by the sound of honking horns. They had not come as quickly to the noise as in the past, or in as large of a drove, but they had come, and they were now deadlier than they had ever been.

J.D. waved up to Peter and shouted to cease fire, and as he did the next of the group made it to the top of the fence, over the crown of barbed wire, and into the compound. Fast and furious it came; eyes filled with rage and hatred intent on laying clawed hands and jagged teeth into J.D.'s flesh.

Sidestepping, J.D. sliced his bolo machetes across the torso of the first partially naked creature as it lunged, inflicting two deep gaping wounds into its chest. Abruptly the sounds of machine gun fire came from behind him. The bullet riddled creatures dropped from the fence.

J.D. rotated his head around to see Lieutenants Duncan and Alexander charging out of the building. "Cease fire! Cease fire!" J.D. yelled. They did, but James had not stopped solely because he had been ordered to. The sight of his commander's head spun around like Regan from the *Exorcist* shocked him. Ryan saw James' anxiety and commented, "Great party trick, huh?" He hoped it would lighten James' unease, but it didn't.

J.D. quickly rotated his head toward the north just in time to see another two leap halfway up the gate. Moving forward, machetes at the ready, J.D. was prepared to greet the threat, but neither naked male creature made an attempt to scale any further up the barrier. As they gripped the fencing they looked around at their dead comrades, and then looked up at the approaching, sword wielding human. J.D.'s attention was drawn to the missing last finger on one of the creature's left hand. He vaguely recalled tearing a finger off one of them at the Pier 17 melee, but he doubted it could be the same half-mute. As J.D. got within feet of it, the four fingered half-mute seemingly shrieked a cry of bitter resentment and frustration, as it gave J.D. a cold glare and outstretched index finger aimed directly at him. It then fled with its companion.

The encounter had been odd. It was like the creature was giving him warning. J.D. knew that the razor wire was not enough to deter these creatures. A better deterrent needed to be placed atop the perimeter fencing.

# 14

## STONE COLD

J.D. KNEW LITTLE ABOUT THE MAN WHO CAME TO THE GATE AND demanded that they abandon the armory. What he did know had come from what Peter Dunne had written down in regard to his harrowing story of his brief captivity, and the story Paul had told them of his time under the rule of Stone and the one called Renquist, whose true name was Richard Barlow. Of Stone he knew even less, only that Barlow and Stone had been in prison together. What J.D. didn't know, what none of them knew and what they would never discover was Stone's past atrocities and the brutality he was capable of.

Edward Coleman Stone was born at Children's Hospital in Buffalo, New York and grew up in the Buffalo suburb of Tonawanda. A local family named Slayzek adopted him at age five, as his mother could not afford to look after her son. As a child, Edward resented his illegitimacy.

In 1996, at the age of eleven, he entered Tonawanda Middle School. Throughout the next three years he was recognized as a very bright pupil by his teachers, one who was sure to make a memorable mark in the world. They had no idea how right they would be. After starting at Tonawanda Senior High, he became idle and easily distracted, did not apply himself and began to behave badly. At school, he was inept at sports, but demonstrated a talent for music and learned to play the violin and cello. It was during this time that he developed a fascination with Nazi Germany, Nazi idealism, Nazi symbolism and the exploits of Doctor Josef Mengele.

In his junior year, Edward made his first court appearance and was given five years' probation for breaking and entry and grand larceny. A few months later, he was also given probation on a charge of vandalism for defacing a cemetery, having spray-painted a large Swastika on the side of a mausoleum. In June, two months before his 17th birthday, Edward left school with no GED to his name and found work as a porter for the summer at a Buffalo waterfront restaurant. The money he earned he used to purchase books. He had now developed an interest in the writings of the Marquis de Sade and Friedrich Nietzsche, with special interest in Nietzsche's theories of *Übermensch* and *The Will to Power*. He became increasingly interested in a philosophy that advocated cruelty and torture, and the idea that superior creatures had the right to control—and destroy, if necessary—weaker ones. Stone avidly collected books about torture and sadomasochism along with other paraphernalia related to domination and servitude.

At the end of the summer, he left the porter's job and became a janitor for the Amherst Audubon Center, a recreational ice hockey, roller hockey, and sports training/fitness complex. He also began drinking heavily and smoking marijuana. His employment at the sports facility was short-lived, being fired for drinking on the job and verbally abusing fellow employees. Having no income to support his habits and vices, the young man resorted once again to thievery. At age 18, he was sentenced to two years in the Wyoming Correctional Facility, a medium security prison located adjacent to the maximum-security prison known as the Attica Correctional Facility.

While incarcerated, Edward, hoping to avoid any further manual labor jobs and desiring to appear respectable, studied accounting. Upon his release, he returned to the home of his adopted parents and tried to find a suitable position; however, due to his criminal record he was unable to secure an accounting job and was once again forced to do manual labor to support his growing illicit fantasies and fixations.

What made him finally act upon his illicit fantasies of rape, torture and murder was not clear; however, for the next ten years he would claim 24 victims in four cities. In Buffalo he became known as the *Ellicott Creek Killer*, having dumped his tortured and mutilated victims along the banks of Ellicott Creek between the Town of Tonawanda and the Village of Williamsville; even going so far as to dump his last victim, a 15-year-old girl, in the murky waters that surrounded Williamsville's Island Park, which lay directly behind the village's administration building.

In Rochester, he was dubbed the *Salmon Creek Killer* and claimed five victims before moving to Albany to take another seven lives and become the *Lakeside Park Killer*, having disposed of his victim's corpses along the shores of Buckingham Lake, Rensselaer Lake, Tivoli Lake, and Washington Park Lake.

In the late winter of 2013, he arrived in New York City and killed his first victim in March of 2014. She was 14 years old, and stuffed deep into her throat he had left a nursery rhyme. Over the next 7 months he would destroy three more lives, all young girls under the age of twelve, before being caught by criminal profilers from the FBI's New York office.

That evening in March of 2014, in less than two hours of custody, Stone confessed to being the *Nursery Rhyme Killer*. However, Stone's confessions were just the beginning of his ruthless, brutal admissions. He made the interrogators ill. The more Edward talked about hurting woman and children, the more he seemed to enjoy himself, as if his outpourings were an opportunity to relive the experiences. When the police and FBI searched his home they found a torture rack, countless items of sadomasochistic paraphernalia, articles about the crimes—all the way back to his first victim—and the most disturbing evidence was discovered in a small plastic container under his bed. Inside the green box, Stone kept hundreds of photos of his victims, including heart-wrenching pictures of the children he bound, brutalized and sodom-ized. He also kept a chilling diary recounting the terrifying ordeals of his victims and the sexual pleasure he received from acting out his sadistic desires. He received the most pleasure from those victims who fought back, keeping them alive for days or weeks while repeatedly sodomizing, raping and beating them until they were completely emotionally and physically demoralized. The journal also contained meticulous entries of planned sadistic torture fantasies for future victims.

When the plague broke out he was at Rikers Island awaiting trial. He had been in the dining hall when the chaos from within began. Riots broke out, the prison attempted to go into lockdown, but the inmates and the living dead outnumbered the correctional officers. Most had fled the dining area, but a small group remained and barricaded themselves in, using tables and chairs to block all entrances. Stone, Barlow, and Matthew Downey—the skinny red-haired man J.D. referred to as Stutters—were the only survivors of the 17 men that had taken refuge together. One by one the inmates of the group had grown ill then died, only to return moments later as one of the living dead. One by one the group killed their fellow inmates, using chairs to split apart their skulls and bash out their brains until there were only three remaining. Toward the end they didn't even wait until their fellow inmates died, they began to kill each other as soon as anyone showed signs of the infection.

When the living dead had ceased to be and it was safe for them to leave the confines of their refuge they did so, taking with them uniforms of corrections officers and their weapons. They found the west side of Manhattan their destination, in particular, West 15th Street, a building, which held special meaning for Stone. It had been the residence of his idol Albert Fish.

# 15

# SUPPORTING THE SWORD

*NOVEMBER 15, DAY 221.*

J.D. and his original team never had an opportunity to get to the Javits Center; they had been rescued before they even had a chance to recon the facility. It had been many weeks since they had left, and after Stone's visit he realized his new team was going to need heavier fire power if they were to defend themselves against any further attacks, especially now, since they had refugees to look after.

He had taken James with him to do reconnaissance of the facility before he decided to take a full team to recover whatever they could from the fallen sustainment headquarters. James had been the logical choice; he was actually a soldier with combat experience.

J.D. mumbled as he drove, repeating the rhyme that Stone had recited over and over again.

From a book of nursery rhymes that J.D. Nichols' grandmother often read to him when he was a child, Humpty Dumpty was as an egg that had fallen off the wall he had been sitting on, shattering its shell with no one able to put him back together. He also knew that in the

18th-Century "Humpty Dumpty" was a reduplicative slang for a short and clumsy person.

The meaning behind the demented limerick could have meant that if he was clumsy and made a mistake, Stone would be ready to take advantage of it. Except to interpret the rhyme in its literal form was to dismiss Stone as just an unstable sexual predator, and to disregard the fact most serial killers, though they do poorly in school, are very intelligent with IQs in the "bright normal" range. Nichols knew there had to be a deeper meaning to the nursery rhyme. However, the answer eluded him.

"Sir, what exactly is your obsession with Humpty Dumpty? You've been repeating that rhyme for days."

It had actually been over a week.

"Stone," he replied, candidly. "Stone… 'Humpty Dumpty sat on a wall. Humpty Dumpty had a great fall,' " the colonel spoke recited, in a clear but irritated tone. " 'All the colonel's horses and all the colonel's men. Couldn't put Humpty together again!' It's got to mean more than its literal translation."

"Humpty Dumpty was a cannon, Colonel."

"Cannon? What the hell would Stone be yammering on about a cannon for?"

"I don't think it was the cannon he was talking about. See, in 1648, during the English Civil War, there was a cannon mounted on top of Saint Mary's at the Wall Church in Colchester defending the city against a siege. Colchester was a Royalist stronghold. The enemy, the Roundheads—or Parliamentarians as they were sometimes called— were the ones laying siege to the city, and they were loyal to Cromwell and against King Charles. The Roundheads destroyed the church tower, blowing the top of it off, sending "Humpty" tumbling to the ground. The King's men tried to repair the cannon, but failed. This having been one of a number of setbacks, the Royalists were forced to lay down their weapons, open the gates of Colchester and surrender. The attack had lasted 11 weeks. That nursery rhyme of yours, that's only the last verse." He paused briefly, scratching an index finger to a cheek, as if trying to recall something. "I think the rest was:

*'In Sixteen Hundred and Forty-Eight*
*When England suffered the pains of state*
*The Roundheads lay siege to Colchester town*
*Where the king's men still fought for the crown.' "*

James paused as J.D. quickly slowed their vehicle. The road ahead required J.D. to drive around several overturned cars that partly obstructed the roadway. James continued:

" *'There One-Eyed Thompson stood on the wall*
*A gunner of deadliest aim of all*
*From St. Mary's Tower his cannon he fired*
*Humpty Dumpty was its name*
*Humpty Dumpty sat on a wall... '*and so on.

I would think if Stone is as intelligent as you seem to believe, he's going to attack the armory, again. And the next time I don't think he'll just bring Humvees and rifles."

"So, his men are the Roundheads, we're the Royalists, and the armory is St. Mary's... And I'm guessing I'm not One-Eyed Thompson, I'm Humpty Dumpty."

"Yes, sir—No disrespect, Colonel."

"None taken... You remind me of someone I once knew. You study literature, too?"

"Sort of, sir. My wife... my wife and I are Irish, sir..."

James had hesitated when he first said 'my wife is.' For one blink of the eye he almost was going to correct himself and say, 'was.' However, Ann-Marie was not dead, just gone from him but not totally lost. J.D. had kept his word and had even brought back a few digital photos after each visit, so he could see how quickly Michael Adam Alexander was growing.

"She was born and raised in Athenry, County Galway. She lived there most of her life. Speaks Gaeilge, too... I never truly had an interest in that part of my ancestry before I met Ann-Marie. I wanted to know as much as I could about our culture and the history of her country. I became so fascinated with the Irish-English conflict that I decided to know more about the history of England, too."

"Well, that makes you smarter than me, Lieutenant. I'm Irish, mostly, but know damn little about Irish history. I drink at McSorely's Olde Ale House and sing Shane MacGowan songs. That's my Irish."

The only part of J.D.'s Irish roots that he knew much about came from his mother's side of the family, which were mainly stories about his relative Peter O'Donnell. So when he told James that he was Irish by lineage and had no heritage—jokingly referencing Shane McGowan and McSorely's as an ethnic baseline—he had not been truthful. However not knowing his complete ancestry made him feel like an empty bottle of Bushmills whiskey, Irish on the outside and unfilled on the inside.

Though J.D. had not been as proficient in the history and culture of Ireland as James, he knew a great deal about Irish-American history, especially when it came to the City of New York.

J.D. pulled their vehicle into a lot of freight trucks on the corner of West 35$^{th}$ Street and 10$^{th}$ Avenue, parking the Humvee out of sight as a precaution. They would only need to travel by foot one long city block to reach the Javits Center.

After careful surveillance of the massive glass and steel structure that spanned four city blocks, something struck J.D. as peculiar. Amongst the abandoned military bunkers, torn down perimeter fencing and endless decayed bodies, it appeared that the dead had been pushed aside to make a pathway into the building at the south set of 34$^{th}$ Street entrances.

He tapped James on the shoulder, and then pointed to the area he wanted him to view and said, "Take a look over there? See where the bodies appear to have been moved on the sidewalk, in front of the center doors on the far section? Looks like someone cleared a path."

James pointed his binoculars at the place J.D. had pointed to. J.D. stood up, removed his sunglasses, and spoke again. "Actually, I'm sure of it. Those bodies have been moved."

James tipped his ACU Digital Camouflage fatigue cap back. "How do you see that from—" James began to question as he looked at J.D., and then realized his question was pointless. "Oh, yeah."

"I'll lead," J.D. said. "I have the eyes." He pointed south along the sidewalk to indicate the direction they were to head. He placed his sunglasses back on and proceeded.

When they were directly across from the doors where the corpses had been disturbed, they crossed over the toppled perimeter fencing and entered into what had been a security buffer zone. As they did so, J.D. noticed two distinct depression marks that appeared to come and go from the south. The two lines were multiple tire depressions, which had left clear tread patterns on the aged remains of the dead. J.D. gestured to the imprints, and James nodded in acknowledgement. They stopped in front of the pathway that led to the doors, pausing briefly while J.D. peered into the abandoned building.

The two cautiously approached the glass doors, using the pathway someone had made. At the archway, they paused once again to allow J.D. to scan the interior one more time before making a decision to enter or not. The broken glass of the doors lay shattered mainly upon the interior concourse.

J.D. knew the multi-leveled Javits Center fairly well. He had been here several times with his friend Phil, when they attended the annual Cycle World International Motorcycle Show, which was held each January. Phil owned Whiskers; it was the store where J.D. bought Max's food. Phil was an avid motorcyclist, and had taken J.D. out many times on the back of his Harley Davidson. Phil had even offered to teach J.D. how to ride, though J.D. never took him up on the proposition.

The immediate interior of the exhibition floor was as he remembered, with the exception that it appeared that someone had turned the building upside down, and then downside right again, with the entire contents of the building now strewn everywhere, much like a snow globe after you shake it and the snow has landed haphazardly.

He had a feeling that something was amiss, but couldn't see anything overtly wrong. What he did see, as they walked under the archway and into the building, was a giant room before them filled with pallets of what appeared to be fuel drums. As they cautiously made their way deeper into the complex, they came to the wide archway that allowed admission into the exhibition hall known as 3E.

The exterior glass windows allowed just enough light into the massive room to see their way around. The two had stopped short of entering into what looked like the vehicle maintenance bay. There was a Stryker, an Engineer Squad Vehicle (ESV) variant with a plow attachment, three Humvees, a Light Medium Tactical Vehicle (LMTV), a MTV, and several fuel tankers along the southern wall. Several of the vehicles looked as if they had been disassembled, perhaps in the midst of servicing when the chaos ensued. Running perpendicular to the vehicles were vehicle parts, tires of all sizes, and munitions for the various vehicle weaponry. Directly in front of where they stood, they could clearly see drums marked, 'FLAMMABLE / Diesel Fuel;' the scent and taste of which hung heavy in the air, but there was no indication of any of the steel drums having been toppled over. Everything inside this large hall appeared to be well organized, which struck J.D. as odd.

They moved on, proceeding to the next room. This one was smaller and narrow. It appeared to be a dispensing area for uniforms and accessories, including boots and body armor, according to the signage in front of the entrance.

There were many pallets—most of which had been knocked over—of food items, toilet paper, and medical supplies. Most of what J.D. surveyed had been eaten away by rodents; a lot of the spilt boxes appeared to have had their sealed tops ripped open, as if someone had been foraging through the various containers. It appeared that someone had been here, possibly several times.

Beyond this room was the 3A hall, only accessible if they walked through the room before them or utilized the stairs that led to it from Level 2. This is where the weapons and ammunition were most likely to be. But there were only two of them, too few to be wandering in by themselves without backup, he thought. There was the possibility of booby traps, transmutes, or worse, half-mutes waiting for them. It was better to stay in the open area until they had a full team to penetrate into that region to find out exactly what 3A contained. This was just a recon mission, and J.D. had seen enough to know that they needed to come back and salvage whatever was still viable, especially vehicles, vehicle parts, and much needed fuel.

# 16

# FOB MEDCOM

THERE WAS ONE OTHER LOCATION J.D. WANTED TO VISIT BEFORE HE and James returned to the armory to plan their salvage strategy, and that was to check out Madison Square Garden/Penn Station—known as FOB MEDCOM HQ.

As they drove down 33$^{rd}$ Street toward their new destination, J.D. abruptly halted the vehicle in the roadway, put the gearshift into park, and looked at James.

"I figured it out," he told his lieutenant. "There're no bodies!"

"Bodies, sir? No bodies, where?"

"At the Javits Center. There're no bodies at the Javits Center."

"Begging the colonel's pardon, but we were walking over bodies everywhere."

"No, James. Just civilians. We were walking over dead zombies stacked up outside the building. But there were no soldiers, anywhere. Doesn't that strike you as odd? Not one body of a soldier, not one discarded weapon."

"How can that be?"

"And did you notice the heavy smell of diesel, but the entire bay seemed to be in order. Not one diesel drum toppled? So, you tell me, Lieutenant, who would remove all the dead bodies from inside the building and separate the soldiers from the corpses of the other undead?"

The question he posed to James was a question he was sure he had an answer to.

"The military?" James answered, puzzled. "But if they came back for the fallen, why would they tidy up?"

"Exactly, Lieutenant. They wouldn't. Nor would anyone else, which leads me to think that perhaps a few soldiers may still be using it. After all, you survived. And that vehicle bay is way too tidy."

"That could explain things," James commented. "You going to turn around and have another look, sir?"

"No, not now. Want to check out MEDCOM HQ. See what's left over there."

The forward base headquarters was where main logistics and operations had been conducted. J.D. had known this from reading operational reports that he discovered at the armory in the former base commander's office.

The carnage he and James surveyed from atop their vehicle was overwhelming, far greater than the state of the armory had once been in and surpassed that of the Javits.

It had been chaos here. Almost every defense had been overrun and torn down. Vehicles had been upended, fencing torn and twisted from their metal posts, bodies—soldiers and civilians alike—carpeted the immediate area, strewn out like the contents of a woman's handbag dumped upon a bed, the owner having frantically searched for a misplaced item.

The wreckage of a destroyed Black Hawk helicopter, which had plummeted from its rooftop perch, lay mangled near the loading dock. It appeared the helo had spun around like a top causing the rotor blades to fragment with such fury that a sizable segment had embedded in the cab of a nearby Medium Tactical Vehicle.

The reek of death still clung in the air, Mother Nature needing more time to erase the fetidness of so many decaying corpses. James and J.D. stood in silence atop the Humvee as they looked out, absorbing the decimation, each reflecting upon their own mortality.

"There but for the grace of God go I," James whispered.

Although, J.D. did not believe in any one supreme being over another, he too knew he had been blessed. "Amen." Then abruptly he turned to James and whispered, "Eleven o'clock. Movement. Behind the truck... Cover me."

J.D. jumped down from the vehicle. He had seen something. No, he had seen someone. Someone was moving about, hiding amongst the shadows of the loading dock bay, watching them, and using the back end of a supply truck as cover. He was sure of this.

His keen eyesight had not misled him. It had not just been a play of light gleaming off metal, reflecting into darkness and dancing like flickering candlelight upon a shadowy wall. The movement was real, not an illusion, and the closer he drew toward the back of the truck, the more his adrenalin began to surge through him, elevating his senses and making him more aware of his transmute side. It was a human. He could smell it.

Stealthily he made his approach toward the loading dock, winding his way around debris and bodies. J.D. could see clearly now into the low light area of the open bay. There was someone at the back of the truck, and it looked female. She was watchfully studying him.

"You behind the truck. Step out and away from the vehicle, and identify yourself."

There was no response.

J.D. called out again. "I can clearly see your position. Step out and identify yourself. We're not here to hurt you," he assured her, in a calm but authoritarian tone. "We're here to help."

Again, there was no response.

He knew she was still there, and though he had lied to whoever was hiding about clearly being able to see her, he could see the shadows her movement cast under the vehicle.

"Please, Miss," he addressed the unknown figure, hoping that a correct gender statement would persuade the person that indeed he could see her clearly. "Make it easy on the both of us, comply to my request. Don't make me have to come and get you."

An answer came. It was in the form of a sudden burst of machine gun fire.

"Goddamn it," he yelled in her direction. "Why you shooting at me?"

Another burst of gunfire came in the direction of the overturned Humvee J.D. was using as cover. The projectiles pinged against the vehicle's metal skin.

James let out a burst from his weapon, peppering the corner of the vehicle from where the gunfire originated. J.D. radioed to James and told him to keep laying down cover fire; he was going after the shooter.

Lieutenant Alexander did as requested. Small bursts of gunfire pulsed from James' weapon until the Colonel Nichols had successfully made his way to the truck. Machine gun raised, he came around the end of end of the truck prepared to let loose a barrage. Except the MTV M1085 Long Wheel Base (LWB) truck hid no enemy, just a standard operation container that held boxes of Army Meals Ready-to-Eat (MREs).

Into the shadowy bay he went, believing it to be the way the assailant had fled. However, as J.D. crossed the threshold of the loading dock and stepped into the building, an abrupt sound of rapid gunfire came from behind. It was James. Something was wrong. James was not shooting toward the dock; he was shooting in another direction. J.D. knew it could only be one thing. Since he did not hear return fire from an enemy, he knew it could only be half-mutes.

James had never seen an enraged half-mute extremely close up, nor had he done close-quarters battle with any. Now, much to his dismay, he was confronted by a group of them. They were completely different from the living dead he had killed and what his wife had transformed into. Although half-mutes slightly resembled transmutes, it was like comparing a soursop to a durian; both were a thorny fruit but the durian was far the more ugly and formidable with its spikey pokers. The face of a half-mute was dotted in red splotches with traces of grey mixed into its yellowish pigmented skin like it had jaundiced. Although the eye sockets were sunken and the eyes were as large as a transmute's, the eyes also bulged. The eyes were nearly clear, too, but there was moderate constriction in the pupils caused by miosis. Doctor France had determined by autopsy that this was brought upon by lesions on the brain stem. This meant that their visual acuity in the dark was drastically diminished and would prevent them from stalking the metropolis at night. There was also a ridge running from the start of the brow ridge that extended down and around the cheekbone. The delineation was more distorted yet distinct in detail than a transmute's facial characteristics. They were also mildly irradiated, having been exposed to fallout of nuclear radiation that had drifted in from the Indian Point Power Station in White Plains, New York, just 24 miles north of the city. Although this had no direct correlation with their mutated features, it could have been the cause of their brain lesions.

Nevertheless, none of the information he had learned about these creatures presently mattered. To the lieutenant, they were just ugly and dangerous and were trying to kill him, and the only bit of intelligence that was useful was that these once-humans were almost as easy to kill as any human could be.

By the time J.D. had made it back to the truck, James had eliminated four of his would-be attackers, the others fleeing when they saw J.D. rushing toward them. J.D. and James kept careful watch for nearly five minutes expecting another attack but none came. For the moment, silence was their ally, which gave J.D. a chance to check the corpses of the half-mutes. As J.D. stood above the first dead half-mute a piercing shriek echoed off the buildings. The cry was shrill and angry. J.D. and James stood back-to-back, poised and ready to take on another enemy attack, but as they looked around trying to determine the enemy's location no attack came. J.D. wanted to dismiss the call as coming from a different half-mute but he knew differently. The cry had been as distinct as his own. It had come from the four fingered half-mute. When the danger was over, and they we sure the threat had fled, J.D. turned his thoughts back to the girl.

The shadowy figure that had escaped into the dark depths of Madison Square Garden was definitely human female. Transmutes and half-mutes don't shoot machine guns, and the only zombie J.D. had ever known to use such a weapon was Bub from the film *Day of the Dead*—and all the real living dead that had ravaged the city were now decaying like the metropolis itself.

J.D. had never been inside the backside of The Garden. It was vast. With his LED flashlight illuminating his way he walked the dark back corridors, where music artists like The Who, Led Zeppelin, Iron Maiden, AC/DC and numerous other rock and sport legends had once walked on their way from the dressing rooms to the stage.

He realized that his pursuit of the unknown person might be as fruitless as Robert Neville's search for Matthias, the leader of a band of psychotic albinos called "The Family," in the early-70s film, *The Omega Man*. Heston's Neville, searched endlessly for his enemy only to have his enemy in the end hunt him down, spear him in the guts, and finally die a slow death in a decorative water fountain. His recollection of this never triggered a parallel between his unyielding hunt for Stone and Heston's relentless pursuit of Anthony Zerbe's character Matthias.

It was a waste of time he thought to himself. She could be anywhere in the building or not in there at all. The distraction of getting shot at had masked his assailant's escape. J.D. returned to the truck load-in area. He stood on the dock. There had been only one other route of escape that she could have taken, and that was the pedestrian walk that lay between Madison Square Garden and Penn Station, which linked 31$^{st}$ Street to 33$^{rd}$ for foot traffic. Whether the elusive girl had fled into Penn Station or to 31$^{st}$ Street, J.D. realized a continued search for her would be futile.

# 17

# BIGTREE AND LOTT

*NOVEMBER 17, DAY 223.*

It had been two days since James and J.D. had explored the once busy convention center making their preliminary survey. The Javits Center proved to be a location that could not only supply food, weapons, and clothing, but also needed fuel for the armory's generators and vehicles.

The early morning was crisp and chilly, but not too cold for a late November's day as they exited their vehicles parked at the large roll-up gate of the building's rear load-in door for hall 3E.

J.D. had not brought many men with him, since there were few that he felt were capable to accompany him, and of those who had volunteered for "military" service, only a few had qualified on a weapon. Of those soldiers, he left four behind to help keep the armory secure. He had also left James behind, not wanting to, but had felt it safer since he could deal with the pressure of an attack if Stone or another hostile group decided to take advantage of the decrease in armory forces. Instead, he brought Second Lieutenant Ryan Duncan and new recruits Privates Peter Shumacher and Douglas Tyler. Schumaker was a former dentist who had volunteered for service in hopes of aiding J.D. in rescuing one child in particular, his son, while Tyler had been a Sandhog—one of New York's legendary urban miners. Douglas Tyler had been working on the Second Avenue subway line when the plague came to pass. He was also a jazz drummer by night and J.D. had taken a liking to the thirty-something year old early on, mainly because he was a fellow musician who had some great stories to tell—both of his time as a Sandhog and as a drummer.

Amongst the civilians there was Paul Wiese, a baker, a storeowner, and a welder/fabricator named Finlay Mackay. The baker, like Private Tyler, had been brought because he was physically strong and had experience driving larger vehicles. The storeowner was also physically capable and could help load the trucks. Finlay the welder was the one person he knew could most benefit the mission. He was the one that could breech the load-in door with minimal noise and effort, without the use of an explosive device.

They had chosen to enter the facility by the load-in entries in the rear of the building for two reasons, the first of which was that J.D. did not wish to alert anyone to their presence by parking vehicles and disembarking personnel out in the open. Secondly, there maybe someone hiding inside who may have laid booby traps. Walking across a large room in extremely low light was not a risk J.D. would allow anyone but himself to take.

Torching through the large, heavy steel roll down gate used for vehicles took less than fifteen minutes. They chose the gate instead of the adjacent metal exterior door because Finlay Mackay told J.D. it was a duo-form door, meaning it was constructed of multiple layers of steel, and would take longer to remove than cutting through the gate.

After pulling the cutaway section from the gate, J.D. was the first to cross the threshold. He immediately stopped as he stepped into the immense structure of the 3E exhibit hall. The Stryker Engineer Squad Vehicle (ESV), which had had its weapon system pointing toward the front of the building two days prior, was now pointed directly at him.

He did not react to the 50-caliber remote weapon station that allows the gunner to fire from inside the vehicle, but calmly looked around for a moment, making a cursory glance at the rear end of the ESV, and then stepped back to the opposite side of the makeshift entry to his men.

Though the rear hydraulic gangway was retracted, he did notice that the access door on its left had no lock on its exterior handle. When Corporal Sam Drukker from his original team had acquired the first Stryker from its sentry position outside Grand Central Terminal, he had imparted some useful information in his rambling dissertation about the vehicle.

When the access door at the rear of the vehicle is not padlocked, it either means the door is unsecured or that its occupants had locked it from the inside. Since there was no lock on the exterior handle and the main gun was pointing to the bay door, the odds favored that the vehicle was occupied.

J.D. did not believe it was mere coincidence that the heavy caliber gun just happened to be pointing in their direction. Even if someone had come and gone inside the ESV, what would be the point of redirecting the weapon system toward the rear of the building when the front entryway was the optimal place for uninhibited access into the hall? He knew that the Stryker was occupied, but the question was, by whom? The Army? Stone's men? Other survivors?

It was most probable it was someone who knew the intricacies of the vehicle and how to maintain it. It had now been eight months since the city had fallen, eight months since any vehicle other than those used by his team, and those of Stone, had sputtered pollution into the air. Not only would someone need mechanical knowledge, but also operational knowledge of its electronics. It was, in all likelihood, the military.

There was no use in trying to commandeer any supplies with the possibility of being killed, and to openly challenge the Stryker's occupants would be fatal. Out gunned, out positioned, and possibly outmanned, there was only one solution he could think of, present himself and his three full garbed soldiers as a true military unit in hopes the ruse would last long enough to flush out whoever had taken up strategic position inside the Stryker.

After a brief rundown of the situation and his tactical plan of approach, he ordered the civilians to back the vehicles away from the large door. J.D. took point and led his team in, appearing as military as possible. Each took position as they had been instructed. The "colonel" approached the rear of the ESV, and with his rifle butt he rapped on the entry door.

"You in the vehicle. This is Colonel J.D. Nichols, United States Army, 5th Special Forces Group. You are occupying military property. Make your presence known, immediately!"

No reply. He tried a different tactic.

J.D. remembered what his old survivor friend Corporal Drukker had said to him about the Stryker units, and hoped he remembered correctly.

"Attention! 3$^{rd}$ Brigade, 2$^{nd}$ Infantry Division," J.D. bellowed. "Make your presence known. Arrowheads, you are ordered to report."

J.D. awaited a response, and after a moment, when none had been given, he was about to reach for the handle of the access door, when it popped ajar with a creak, and then slowly opened. Cautiously a tall, thin corporal stepped out followed by an average height specialist, both with weapons raised. Their uniforms bore the insignia of the 3-2 Stryker Brigade Combat Team, also known as the Arrowhead Brigade, out of Fort Lewis, Tacoma, Washington. He was glad that he had actually listened to Corporal Drukker's over indulgent informational sessions, and even more so that he correctly remembered what Sam had imparted to him. However, J.D. could not be certain that these men were actually soldiers, just because they were dressed in uniforms.

"Stand down," J.D. ordered, "and relinquish your weapons." The two soldiers refused to comply, even though they were out gunned. "I gave you an order."

"Not until we're sure you are who you say you are," the tall corporal stated.

"Did you not hear the Colonel's direct order, soldier? You will stand down. And you will do it now!" Ryan barked out. "Or you will be terminated with extreme prejudice. Is that clear?!"

Ryan's father had been a career army officer, and Ryan had been a "military brat." Having been exposed to the military way of life, Ryan knew that respect was of the utmost importance not only in the military but in home life. He also knew that the only way their ruse was going to work was if these men truly believed they were military, so he acted accordingly.

The two soldiers realized they had possibly made a strategic error. They had compromised their fortified position by coming out of the Stryker without ascertaining that the men before them were actually military. Being out gunned they also realized the outcome of engaging in a firefight would not be advantageous. The two acquiesced, surrendering their weapons, and hoping the soldiers before them were actually military.

Ryan immediately relieved them of the rifles, ordering, "Hands behind your head. Step forward, and on your knees."

"Is there anyone else in the vehicle?" J.D. asked them.

The two men looked oddly at him. They had seen his bare hands. Then they looked at each other, both realizing they had made a horrible mistake.

"Soldier, the colonel asked you a question," Ryan addressed the corporal. "Is there anyone else in the vehicle?"

"No, sir," the man replied in a slightly confused tone.

J.D. signaled to Ryan to check the truck, as Privates Schumacher and Tyler stepped forward, machine guns still poised ready to engage the pair if necessary.

"Clear," Ryan called out, as he emerged from the Stryker.

J.D. ordered his men to lower their weapons and take up surveillance positions. Returning to his captives, his next order was addressed to the both of them, though his words were directed to the black-haired corporal. "Stand and identify yourselves, soldiers."

The corporal replied with a blank stare and no verbal confirmation to his identity.

Ryan immediately backed his commander again. "Are you deaf, son? The colonel told you to identify yourself! Is that understood?"

"Sir, Corporal John Lott," the soldier finally responded, in an indifferent tone, as he began to rise from the concrete floor.

The other soldier followed his partner's lead.

"Is that how you address a superior officer, Corporal?" Ryan continued, barking at the soldier with an authoritarian voice. "Insubordination is unacceptable, soldier. You will address the commander properly. Is that understood?"

The two snapped to attention and put hand to forehead in saluting position, the corporal returning with a, "Sir. Yes, sir."

"Colonel Nichols gave you an order, son. Now identify, friend or foe?"

"But, sir—"

Ryan had a suspicion they were about to question not only his colonel's mutation but also his age. Ryan's father had retired from the United States Army as a Lieutenant Colonel. The average age of the typical military rank of Lieutenant Colonel is 45 years old. J.D. Nichols was 28.

"No buts, soldier. This is not a democracy. This is the United States Army. You will identify immediately. Or you will be considered hostile and taken into custody. Have I made myself clear?!" he shouted at them, like a drill sergeant giving orders to new recruits on the first day of training.

The soldier held his salute as he reported, even though he suspected that they were not actual military.

"Sir, Corporal John Lott, 296th BSB, 3-2 SBCT, Bravo Company, Fort Lewis, Washington. DoD ID number 7807036741."

Ryan and J.D. were satisfied that they were true enlisted men; the corporal delivered his DoD ID and not a serial number, which was no longer used. But as an extra precaution, J.D. gave the corporal one other question.

"MOS, soldier?" he inquired.

"Combat Wheeled Vehicle Repairer Level Two, *sir!*"

J.D. saluted the man, and the soldier completed his hand salute.

"Excellent," J.D. replied, then put his attention to the accompanying soldier. The enlisted warfighter was different, different than any survivor. "Okay, soldier, report. Name, Rank, MOS."

"Sir, Bigtree, Gordon. Specialist. 296th Brigade Support Battalion,

3rd Brigade, 2nd Infantry Division, Company B, Fort Lewis, Washington. MOS: Special Electronic Devices Repairer, Level One."

"Very good, soldier." J.D. saluted him, and the specialist returned by releasing his salute.

"And what is your nationality, Specialist?"

"Nationality, sir? That would be Cayuga, sir."

The colonel replied, "You're Native American."

"Yes, sir," Bigtree confirmed, not certain what his ethnicity had to do with the present situation.

"Any Irish, English or other European ancestry in your blood, son?" J.D. inquired.

"Not that I am aware of, sir. Just Cayuga—Begging the colonel's pardon, is it important?"

"Well, Specialist Bigtree. Let's just say that you have screwed up Doctor France's Odds Ratio model."

Bigtree looked at him with puzzlement, not understanding to whom or what he was referring to.

"Now, gentleman... My name is Colonel J.D. Nichols. I am commander of the 69th Regiment Armory, formerly known as FOB MEDCOM Bravo. I'm sure you have many questions, including how I hold the rank of colonel at my apparent young age, and what has happened to my hands. All these questions will be answered at a debriefing. As of this moment this convention center is under my jurisdiction and its contents now the property of the 69th Regiment Armory. As for the both of you, consider yourself members of the 69th until further notice. Disregarding a direct order from a superior will get you restrained and/or shot. Do I make myself clear, gentlemen?"

"Yes, sir," they both replied, simultaneously.

"Good... Lieutenant Duncan."

"Yes, sir."

"Bring the civilians in, we're burning daylight."

# 18

## CHAIN OF COMMAND

"So, LET ME UNDERSTAND THIS, GENTLEMEN," J.D. SAID, VERIFYING what he had just been told. "You spent all these months living inside the Stryker and it never occurred to you to leave? Why not?"

"We could have taken off with the Stryker after the shit hit the fan," Lott said, "but besides that being desertion, where the hell would we have gone? Bigtree and I did our best to defend the supply depot but, in the end, there were too many of those zombie son-of-bitches. After everything settled, we buried what was left of our dead and were hoping to return to Fort Lewis, but we couldn't raise them on SATCOM, or anyone military for that matter. So, we just stayed, not sure where to go.

Then, about a month ago, the ASC was infiltrated by insurgents. First came a recon team, and then a few days later at two squads of men. They pilfered food, weapons, fuel, and most of the Humvees. The next time they came back we were prepared. We set some booby traps. Took out four of them. That was a week ago, sirs. We thought that they had returned when we saw the torch cutting through the door."

"Why didn't you just destroy the base and go home?" James asked. "I would think you'd want to see if your family was still alive."

"I have no family, sir, only the Army."

"And what about you?" J.D. asked, directing his question to Bigtree. "What about your family?"

"My mother died when I was young, sir. My only brother was stationed in Iraq with the 2$^{nd}$ Squadron, 3$^{rd}$ Cav. My father... My father, sir. I buried him. He was our CSM. He died kickin' zombie ass, sir."

"I'm sorry to hear that, soldier."

Bigtree asked, "What now, sirs?"

"Yes. What now? First let me tell you a story," J.D. replied. "And hopefully it will answer some of your questions."

J.D. explained his backstory and how he became the base's commander along with the current situation of the armory to the two potential recruits. Bigtree and Lott still could not understand why Lieutenant Alexander, an officer of the United States Armed Forces, would follow the orders of a civilian let alone how he could allow a civilian to command a military installation. That was treason.

It was apparent to both J.D. and James that further clarification to the military state of the country was required.

J.D. took off his sunglasses and set them on his desk. Though he had told them about his physical changes, the black color of his irises was an oddity that drew their attention.

"Let me make this clear," J.D. told them with a louder voice than normal, trying to snap them out of their fixation on his eyes. "The United States of America as you knew it no longer exists. Uncle Sam is dead. The DoD is dead. There is no more Army. There are no more Marines, Air Force, or Navy. The only surviving U.S. forces are in England as part of a coalition force. And gentlemen, you missed your opportunity for that evac two months ago. They're not coming back. You're stuck here like the rest of us. Since the military no longer exists and there is no more president to obey, or country to protect, there is no one to hold you to your oath of enlistment.

You could join us. I could use soldiers with your skills. I'm in need of not only combat trained men, but men of your MOS... Or go your own way. We'll give you each a Humvee, weapons, ammunition and rations. I won't think any less of either of you."

The colonel sat up in his chair, straightening himself, and then informed them, "But be advised," he said with outstretched index finger. "If you decide to stay, you'll be under my command. And the authority of this command is not to be taken lightly. We may not be the U.S. Army, but we still maintain this armory as a military installation. Anyone who has been given a rank has earned it, and the respect that goes with it... My XOs are Lieutenants James Alexander and Ryan Duncan. As a soldier of the 69th Regiment you would report to Lieutenant Alexander for duty assignments. We can offer you food, shelter, healthcare and a lot of hard work and long hours. But as soldiers you should already be used to that. You've heard from James and me. You know what we're up against and what we want to accomplish. So, gentlemen, time for you to decide. Are you in or out?"

Lott responded. "With all due respect, I'd like to think about it."

J.D. was quick and firm with his response of no. "You decide now. When you walk out of this office you're either a member of this team or escorted to a Humvee."

"May I ask a question of the lieutenant, then?" Lott asked.

J.D. gestured to the soldier giving him permission.

"Lieutenant. Why is it you stay here under the command of a civilian?"

James responded, sincerely, to his question. "I came to this armory seeking help for the group of civilians I was with. Colonel Nichols didn't have to help, but he did. He took our entire group in, gave us food, shelter and medical assistance. No, he's not a soldier, but what he's doing here, the lives he's saving, the cause he's fighting for, that's why I joined. For me it was the right thing to do. It was the only thing. There are people who need our help and this regiment is making a difference. I am a soldier. And I am still a guardian of freedom."

"You trust him that much, sir?"

"I do," he confirmed to Lott. "He has earned my respect and trust. And he is a fine commanding officer."

"Then consider me in, sirs," Corporal Lott said, as he took a saluting stance.

"Welcome aboard, Corporal Lott," Colonel Nichols congratulated him with a salute "You are hereby promoted to sergeant." J.D. turned his attention to Bigtree. "Well, soldier. What say you?"

Specialist Bigtree stood up and took an at attention stance. He snapped his fingers to his head in a saluting manner.

"I too am a guardian of freedom, but I must respectfully decline. If any of my people are still alive, I'd like to help them out. So, I choose to leave."

"Very well," J.D. responded. "The lieutenant here can make the arrangements. Best of luck to you soldier."

The total of *real* military personnel was now at two.

# 19

# MARAUDERS

It was the seventh trip to the Javits Center in four days. Each trip J.D. had taken the same team with him, the same men who had accompanied him on the first salvage mission. But in addition to those seven he had also included John Lott who knew how to operate a Stryker.

The Stryker ESV that Lott and Bigtree had made their home remained operational ready; the two soldiers had seen to that. Though the ESV was a great addition and was useful with its large plow in clearing debris and vehicles out of the way and widening the route back to the armory, it wasn't needed for subsequent salvage trips because it did not have the cargo capacity, and because J.D. said, '…It smells like ass.' He refused to let anyone use it until it was fully sanitized. Lott and Bigtree had for many months, ate, slept, and defecated in the close quarters of the Stryker's infantry compartment. Instead the salvage team used the Stryker ICV that was already at the armory.

Most of the trips to the U.S. Army sustainment headquarters had consisted of removing as much salvageable food and sundry items that still remained intact. Rodents had made meals of a great amount of the MREs and toilet paper, but spared much of the military clothing and footwear. This was their second time in which they concentrated on removing weapons, but mainly munitions, which were comprised primarily of ammunition for individual and crew served weapons—the heaviest armaments being hand grenades, standard 40mm rounds for the single-shot grenade launcher attachment for the M-4 and M-16 machine gun, and cartridges for the Stryker weapons system.

A great portion of the hand grenades and grenade launcher rounds, had been buried under a roof collapse. J.D. was surprised the force of the collapsed ceiling hadn't detonated an explosion of epic proportion. With the damaged ammunition boxes partially buried, and having been exposed to rain pouring in from the large roof opening, J.D. was forced to forego recovery of most of the munitions cache. However, Sergeant Lott assured him that it was unlikely the water deluged boxes of munitions suffered any compromise. Nonetheless, J.D. felt that it was prudent not to disturb the debris that covered the live ammo.

Having filled two LMTVs with as much munitions as could be salvaged, along with the remaining clothing, the four-vehicle convoy departed using 34th Street as their main thoroughfare across town. Sergeant Lott drove the lead vehicle, a Stryker ICV. Paul Wiese was at the weapons station and Private Peter Schumacher was assigned to communications. Following the Stryker were the two cargo trucks, followed by a Humvee. Behind the wheel of the Humvee was Lieutenant Duncan. Seated next to him was Private Doug Tyler. J.D. stood in the gunner's turret of the Humvee, facing the rear of the vehicle. He moved his head back and forth, utilizing his transmute ability, watching the rear as well as the rest of their flanks.

As the Humvee neared the intersection of 10th Avenue, J.D. noticed something odd, something out-of-place—it was two City of New York Department of Sanitation collection trucks. Both were on the east side of the avenue, fifty feet from each corner. This was wrong. These trucks had not been there on previous trips. He looked at the cab of the truck at the northeast corner. He clearly saw someone behind the wheel.

*"Ambush!"* J.D. screamed over their communications system. "Ambush. Move! *Move!* "Don't let them cut us off. Punch it, Ryan. Punch it!"

---

As the Stryker approached the intersection of Dyer Avenue, a sanitation truck quickly sped across the street and crashed into it, forcing the armored personnel carrier to careen sideways up onto the sidewalk.

---

It was too late. J.D. heard the crash ahead of him and then the sanitation trucks behind closed off the street. He rotated himself around and repositioned the machine gun as he called to Ryan to get out from behind the LMTVs. Ryan moved right. Ahead the Humvee crew saw the sanitation truck that had plowed into the Stryker. Another white garbage truck moved into the intersection. Someone was trying to box them in.

---

Suddenly the Stryker lurched and slid sideways with a thunderous crash. John Lott was at the wheel but had not seen the threat vehicle approaching. His command helmet struck the instrumentation as the Stryker abruptly stopped. Disoriented, it took him a moment to comprehend what had happened. Something hefty had hit the vehicle, but John had not felt an explosion, which meant it that it must been a large non-explosive object moving at a high rate of velocity to have caused such an impact as to have forced the 22+ ton, slat armored Stryker sideways.

---

Ryan stepped onto the gas. J.D. pulled back on the bolt latch release of the M2 Browning machine gun and released a barrage of .50 caliber projectiles at the city vehicle. He knew what was ahead was not a military operation. The army would have simply blockaded the roadway with military vehicles and shown their superior strength. No, this was someone else. Perhaps Stone. Perhaps other survivors. Whoever they were they were not military, and they had hostile intentions. These were marauders.

––––––

The light utility vehicle at the lead position slammed on its brakes and skidded to a halt less than fifty feet from the intersection as the large white truck before them completed its blockade. The LMTV that followed did the same and almost rear-ended the first. Abruptly as the sanitation truck had appeared, it quickly reversed position. As the rig backed away it revealed four military Humvees obstructing the team's escape.

––––––

Speeding to the intersection J.D. could see that the men with their weapons raised were not military personnel. He squeezed the trigger on his crew weapon again, this time aiming at the Humvees, and, again, 550 rounds per minute burst from the Browning's barrel. Except without the firepower of the Stryker, J.D. was out gunned. The enemy returned fire. Two of the four Humvees before him were armed with the same caliber machine gun as his, and J.D.'s 4-wheel drive vehicle was not an up-armored variant, and therefore did not have a ballistic windshield. When the enemy fired from all of their four positions, they targeted the charging Humvee. A multitude of ballistic hits ripped through the Humvee's grill and into the engine compartment. With a fierce explosion, the hood of the Humvee blew up into the air in a twisted mess, partially blocking Ryan's view. Then abruptly the front tires blew out. As Ryan tried desperately to control the vehicle, a hail of bullets ripped through the windshield striking him. The Humvee jolted, flipped on its side, and then skidded along the street toward the enemy.

---

"*Ambush!*" Jonas McGann heard his commander cry over the armory communications system. He immediately paged Lieutenant Alexander, trying to keep the panic from filling his urgent call.

James had been in the armory's basement, in the "dojo," sparring with Peter Dunne. Still dressed in his workout attire he quickly headed to the second floor.

"It's the colonel, sir," Jonas responded. "I heard the commander say, 'ambush.' Then it sounded like gunfire and an explosion. Then the comm went dead... I can't raise anyone, sir. What should we do?"

"Call all base personnel to arms. Take up defensive positions. And keep trying to raise the colonel."

"But if they're under attack—"

"Private," James interrupted, "it could be a ploy. We defend this base and the civilians. Is that understood?"

"Yes, sir."

"Then deploy the men. Immediately."

---

Sergeant John Lott made his way to the troop compartment to check on Paul Wiese and Peter Schumacher. As he stepped out of the driver's area he heard the sudden eruption of gunfire and then an explosion. He knew that they were under armed attack. He saw that his men were down; both Paul and Peter were on the floor. John knew he must get to the weapons control system. As quickly as he could he brought it online and turned the weapons platform toward the enemy.

---

The Humvee slid to a stop less than thirty feet from the intersection.

J.D.'s head spun with a multitude of flashing prickles of light. Everything was out of focus. He heard shouting, but he couldn't comprehend if it was friend or foe. Roughly, without warning, he found himself being dragged from the turret he was haphazardly hanging out of. A great roar filled the afternoon air. He was abruptly released.

---

John grabbed the joystick of the fire control computer, turned it left and aligned the targeting sight on the monitor, and then depressed the firing mechanism of the Stryker's MK19 grenade launcher. Each enemy vehicle exploded in rapid succession, sending the opposition fleeing.

---

The base personnel had deployed, each taking up a strategic position on the armory's roof. James pulled the Stryker ESV across the entry to the armory, and then took a seat behind the communications console. Peter Dunne sat behind the weapons station and watched for any sign of the enemy through the targeting monitor. They waited.

---

Bruised, battered, and still shaken from the Humvee trauma, J.D. thought he heard the sound of the Stryker starting, but he wasn't sure. What he was sure of was the sound of pained cries from inside the destroyed Humvee that now had gone from a smoldering front end to an inferno. J.D.'s instinct as a paramedic kicked in. He felt a rush of adrenaline and a burst of whatever it was that fueled his transmute side, and everything became clear.

Whoever had tried to pull him so briskly from the open hatch had fled. A brief glance of the Stryker told him that John was alive and on the move. Bursts of fire erupted from the Stryker and crashed to the street, laying down a thick cover of smoke. It was the ICV's M6 smoke grenade launcher.

Doug Tyler was dead. His face had been ripped apart. The tall, thin private had been killed instantly. His body now lay atop of Ryan. Ryan struggled to get himself free of the weight of the dead man and out of the Humvee. J.D. pulled Doug's corpse out of the vehicle, and then grabbed onto Ryan, pulling him by the collar of his Improved Outer Tactical Vest (IOTV). Dragging him several feet into the street away from the vehicle, the Humvee's gas tank abruptly erupted. J.D. immediately fell across Ryan to protect him.

Ryan's face and forehead were bloodied. Glass fragments from the windshield had peppered him. Most of the facial wounds were superficial, and none had penetrated his eyes; his tactical sunglasses had protected him. However, there was a wound to his left arm that was severe.

Luckily, most of the bullets that had passed through the upheaved hood and windshield had missed Ryan. Those that did hit him were fragments, which mainly struck the front trauma plate of his IOTV stopping penetration. Ryan had truly been fortunate. If the shots the battered his vest had not shattered, Ryan would have been fatally wounded. Though his IOTV was able to withstand a direct impact from a 7.62mm bullet, it was incapable of stopping .50 caliber.

The penetrating wound to Ryan's left arm was just past the vest's enhanced side ballistic insert. The bullet fragment had lodged into his deltoid. It was not an immediately life-threatening wound, but the jagged slug was imbedded deep into the muscle causing severe pain and blood loss.

The exchange of gunfire had not stopped after the four enemy Humvees had been destroyed. The enemy had continued to blindly shoot through the smoke screen. John Lott had freed the Stryker from the garbage truck and backed the ICV up near their overturned burning truck, simultaneously lowering the Stryker's rear deployment door. The Stryker's heavy caliber machine gun let loose on the advancing rear guard, taking out three of the enemy before the marauders ceased their advance.

Paul Wiese and Peter Schumacker came to J.D.'s aid, shouldering the semi-conscious Ryan into the Stryker. J.D. waved and radioed his LMTV driver teams to fall in behind the lead vehicle. It was time to make their escape. From the dissipating smoke came more rapid bursts of gunfire, but it didn't appear to be directed at them. J.D. realized why. The distinctive shrill cry of Four Fingers the half-mute came from just beyond the smoke.

J.D. radioed his team and gave orders to move out. As he turned to jump onto the retracting door of the Stryker, a half-mute charged through the dissipating smoke and struck him down.

Tumbling, the two landed in front of the oncoming trucks that had fallen in line behind the ICV. There was no time for the first driver to stop. A loud thud and crunch came from under the carriage of the LMTV.

The Stryker slammed into the burning enemy Humvees, smashing them out of the way. Peter called to John to tell him that their commander was down. The Stryker kept moving forward, picking up speed. The rear deployment door closed. John had his orders—move out and do not stop for any reason.

The second truck driver saw the mutilated corpse of the half-mute and his commander scrambling to his feet. J.D. had barely cleared the front of the first truck. There was no way he could have survived trying to let the tactical wheeled vehicle pass over him. Though the vehicle's ground clearance was 22 inches with a full payload, the clearance at the under axel was scarcely over 14 inches, and J.D. had a backpack on.

Almost as soon as the driver had stopped another half-mute leapt on the driver's side. The flesh-hungry ogresque creature tried frantically to grasp onto the closed driver's door window, but kept failing, which only enraged it more.

J.D. was on the passenger side of the vehicle. He grabbed the door handle only to find it locked. He yelled to Finlay MacKay to move out, as he climbed up in between the cab and cargo bed—using the spare tire that was secured to the back of the cabin for an anchor—and pulled himself over the rail and onto the supply boxes.

The half-mute had not given up. As the truck began to move, it again leapt up, this time grabbing onto the handrail of the vehicle's cabin. The creature quickly moved to the rear of the cabin and crawled around the extended air intake tube. J.D. was on the radio, ordering Finlay to pull ahead of the other cargo truck and alongside the Stryker, letting John know he was going to jump onto the top of the ICV and access the gunner's hatch.

J.D. saw the thing frantically trying to climb over the boxes and into the bed. *It was Four Fingers!* There was no point to try and do battle with it on a moving truck by using his blades. J.D. reached for his pistol but as he did Four Fingers fearlessly charged. He never got the pistol from its holster. Instead, J.D.'s fast twitch reflexes of his transmute side and his martial arts instinct simultaneously kicked in. He used the creature's momentum to heave it off the back of the truck. J.D. was certain that would put an end to the creature that apparently had been stalking him. J.D. was wrong. Four Fingers tumbled for a moment then stood up. Four Fingers let out a cry directed at J.D. It was as loud and shrill as previous encounters, but this time it was much angrier. For a moment Four Fingers stood in the street glaring and pointing an index finger at J.D., as the truck drove further away. Then Four Fingers limped away. J.D. was certain this wasn't going to be the last time he would see the mutant.

---

J.D. knew it wasn't a wise choice to leap from one vehicle to another while doing 45 mph. He always wanted to be a stuntman, but even stuntmen used precautions. His precaution was to have the vehicles slow to 20 mph. He threw his backpack over first to lighten himself. He nearly overshot his toss.

The Stryker moved left to avoid a car, the LMTV swerved left, just missing the vehicle as he heard John shout, "Obstacle, move left," over the comm system. J.D. lost his balance and fell back onto some crates. Recovering, he leapt from the truck. It was ungraceful. He landed on his stomach, rolled, and struck his head on the slat armor. His helmet absorbed the impact. He radioed his men he had made it. The vehicles sped onward, back to the armory.

---

Inside the vehicle, J.D. quickly released Ryan's vest using its hidden release lanyard, which was designed to allow medical personnel easier access to the casualty and remove the components. J.D. cut away Ryan's left sleeve with a pair of trauma sheers and exposed the wound.

He placed a compression bandage on Ryan's deltoid and told Peter to keep pressure on it. Ryan looked up at his commander. J.D. wished he had some Yunnan Baiyo herb or Celox to act as a hemostatic agent to stem the flow of blood, but he didn't.

"I'm going to die, aren't I?" he asked J.D., believing the wound was life threatening.

"Die? That would be an inconvenience to me, Lieutenant," J.D. told him, as he prepared a syringe of morphine and then injected it into a vein.

Ryan spoke, fearfully, "I don't want to die."

"Good. You won't. But if it makes you feel better, Ryan, how about I order you not to?"

Ryan smiled. "Yes, sir."

Ryan drifted off. The morphine had taken effect.

---

The skirmish had been brief, perhaps no more than four or five minutes, but the results of the firefight had been devastating, far more than just the physical loss of life. J.D. had been careless, and he knew it. Doug Tyler's death, Ryan's injury, and the emotional devastation that would carry over to everyone in the armory had been a result of his under planning. James tried to console him,; trying to convince him he was not at fault, that they simply did not have enough men to keep the armory safe and to assign to needed away missions. Nevertheless, this did not ease his guilt.

He once had a brief conversation with Kermit in regard to his idea of how to flush the transmute flock out of the armory. Kermit had warned him, "There's no room for bravado or carelessness."

J.D. had responded with, "Every plan has an inherent degree of risk, but risk is the price you pay for opportunity." It had been his plan so he entered the building alone. Getting the transmute flock from the building had worked but bravado almost got him killed.

Nonetheless, J.D. had not taken the risk alone at the Javits. Poor planning, carelessness, and a bit of bravado had been his downfall, and the price of opportunity had been too high.

Lott and Bigtree had told him about the scavengers, but in his arrogance and over confidence he hadn't planned for that probability. He should have had more men. His men should have been better trained. Most were civilians, not soldiers. Soldiers went to basic training for ten weeks. His men barely had four weeks of minimal training.

The High Mobility Multipurpose Wheeled Vehicle (HMMWV or Humvee) he had used was inadequate in battle. He had used one that had belonged to the 69th Regiment, one that had been abandoned at the armory. These were just standard Humvees, not a variant, no "Up-Armor" kits installed.

What had happened could never happen again. Immediate changes needed to be implemented and he knew it. It would start with abandoning the use of Humvees that were not properly equipped for battle, a more intense and longer training period before allowing men into the field, having more men trained on the Stryker systems, and mainly taking any potential threat, no matter how insignificant, as a real danger.

---

The operating room had been prepped by Doctor France, who had been informed that Ryan had been wounded and needed immediate surgery. France was not informed of the extent of the injury, so he assumed the worse and prepared for most battle trauma scenarios, equipping the operating room with an overabundance of all things needed for major surgery. France was relieved to see the injury Ryan sustained was not massive, though by the damage to the deltoid he knew Ryan would have to keep his arm immobile for an extended period, followed by a regimented program of physical therapy.

J.D. had conducted the extraction of the bullet from Ryan's arm. However, he had to have Doctor France close the incision he had made that allowed enough room to insert a surgical probe, Kelly forceps, and retractor into Ryan's flesh to retrieve the fragment. Doctor France also had to remove the glass fragments from Ryan's face and forehead. Even if J.D. had clipped his talons, he still would not have had the manual dexterity to properly tie sutures or remove tiny bits of glass.

Continuously throughout the procedure, J.D. kept rubbing at his left biceps. It wasn't until after Ryan's surgery that he discovered that Four Fingers had given him two deep scratches. The lacerations had an itchy and burning sensation to them, and they were still bleeding. France was concerned. He knew half-mutes had some residual radiation to them as well as some very bad bacteria under their sharp nails, which he had discovered while doing an autopsy some months back. France gave him several medications, and told him to take them until he said otherwise. When J.D. asked about any side effects or bad interactions they might have with the medications he was still taking for the leg wound, the doctor dismissed his concerns with an offensive tone. J.D. didn't take France's remarks as anything more than being his usual dickish self, and never thought about it again.

When all was done, J.D. changed his clothes and departed the armory. He needed to retrieve Douglas' body.

# 20

# A LITTLE NIGHT MUSIC

THE NIGHT SKY SANG WITH THE SOUND OF BURSTING MUNITIONS, lighting up the city with a pyrotechnic extravaganza that was reminiscent of a Macy's Fourth of July celebration. Flames danced, licked, and grasped at the stars. It was a glorious blaze, a symphony of sight and sound. It made J.D. grin with perverse pleasure watching the pyrotechnic display.

He was alone, standing on the roof of a nearby building looking west toward the Jacob K. Javits Convention Center. Though he was a safe distance away, he was still close enough to feel the fire's heat upon his face, which suffocated the chill from the brisk night air around him.

After the ambush, J.D. knew that trips to the convention center were too dangerous until they were better prepared, but by then he knew whoever had attacked them would have finished clearing out what they had left behind. J.D. was not going to allow this to happen. Never leave anything your enemy could use, especially if it could be used against you. If J.D. and his men couldn't have what remained, then neither could anyone else.

The entire sky grew brighter with its dancing flames and fireworks as the north end of the Javits became engulfed. There hadn't been this much nightglow since the world went dark. Anyone who was still alive in the city would see the orange glow and hear the exploding ordnance. He hoped one particular group of men would take notice, those who had attacked their convoy. He waited patiently, watching the roadways for headlights. His fortitude soon paid off.

Three vehicles came from the north, down 11$^{th}$ Avenue, slowing and then stopping in the intersection at West 37$^{th}$ Street. The exploding munitions were preventing them from advancing. They paused and then retreated. Turning east toward 10$^{th}$ Avenue the column of vehicles disappeared. A moment later they emerged heading west on 36$^{th}$ Street, heading toward J.D.'s position.

The three Humvees passed his building and stopped just before 11$^{th}$ Avenue, facing the main entrance to the convention center. J.D. patiently waited for the occupants to make their exit. He watched them, studied them. He saw their faces clearly. His night vision was superior. He did not see the stuttering man, the one that pretended to be Stone, nor the real Stone, and he was certain that this group were what remained of the marauders who had attacked his team on 34$^{th}$ Street.

What he was about to do he could not do to Stone's gang. He needed Stone alive, alive to tell him where the abductees were being held. The men below, the men on the street, the men who had shot the truck out from under him, the ones who had injured Ryan—those who had killed Douglas Tyler—those men… those men would die tonight.

J.D. raised the Milkor M32 multi-grenade launcher that still contained five rounds of 40mm air-consuming thermobaric shots and pointed it toward his enemy.

It had been against his morality to take another's life, but that was before it became a kill or be killed world. Although the thought of killing another human had once sickened him, the thought of Douglas Tyler's shattered face and partially burnt body sickened him even more. He knew this action would change his life forever. His detective father had told him that when he shot and killed his first perp, it had been the most traumatic experience in his life, one that remained with him forever. Except, J.D.'s planned action was more than self-defense. It was an ambush motivated out of a need for revenge.

There was no going back. He was about to cross the line. His eyes were on his enemy, who were heading toward the building entry. *No one fucks with my family,* the voice in his head said. He put his finger to the trigger and sighted in on the lead vehicle.

He hesitated.

How easy it would be to kill with the single pull of a trigger, he thought. A man needs no courage to hide in the darkness and kill his enemy from afar. If he could not face his enemy in battle then how could he lead others into combat?

He pulled the trigger.

The thermobaric shot over and passed the vehicles at 262 feet per second and rocketed into the Javits Center. The large glass frontage exploded, raining down fragments of glass like a fierce hailstorm. The percussive blast hurled his enemies from the entryway back onto the pavement.

He who fights with guns and knives is a *coward*, he told himself. He must face his enemy with his hands and feet and nothing but! Let that be the measure of his true strength and courage.

Stunned and confused only four of the nearly dozen men began to rise. A man furthest from the blast zone stumbled back toward the vehicles. He grabbed a two-way radio from the driver's side seat and began to call. That is when he saw J.D. approaching. The man grabbed his pistol and pointed it at him, giving warning. "Don't move!" Nonetheless, J.D. knew he needed to be a few more feet closer in order to disarm the man before any of his friends arrived. J.D. attempted to engage the man in conversation to distract him as he cautiously advanced.

"I heard the explosions. I came to see if anyone was hurt," J.D. told him.

"I said don't move. I'll shoot!" the man informed him.

J.D. was exactly where he wanted to be—point blank range. He stopped.

"Raise your hands!" the agitated man instructed.

The man holding the gun expected J.D. to comply and did not expect to be disarmed. J.D. quickly raised his left hand and grabbed the pistol by the slide and redirected it down as he twisted. Before the man had any clue as to what was happening, J.D. had firm control of the weapon when his right hand came up and punched the man three times in the jaw. J.D.'s right hand then went down underneath the sideways pistol and grabbed the back of the hammer, and then rotated the weapon 180 degrees, breaking the man's trigger finger. It snapped like a dry twig, and as it did the dazed man cried out painfully. J.D. rotated the pistol back to release the man's broken digit from the trigger guard and pulled the weapon free. The man collapsed to the ground unconscious.

The others did not immediately see J.D. coming, and by the time they realized that they were under attack he had disarmed and incapacitated them. He had made a decision that taking prisoners could be profitable in extracting information about this group's strength and location, instead of leaving corpses strewn about. He then moved to the enemy that had not risen, those closest to the Javits entry. Four of the six that lay closest to building's entry had not survived the blast, but he didn't need more than a few prisoners anyway. The remaining two were severely injured but still alive. He pulled them back from the blazing building toward the street to examine them.

One by the truck, three that stood, and six on the ground made ten. But there had been eleven he had counted from the top of the building. The other had fled or... J.D. heard the footfalls closing in. "Don't move!" an angry voice shouted at him from behind. "Don't fucking move, you stupid son-of-a-bitch."

The man was nearly behind him when J.D. was given the order to stand up. He did what was commanded, but as he did he stepped back. The man rammed the tip of the automatic rifle into J.D.'s spine. It was exactly what J.D. wanted, to know how close the weapon was to his person.

"I said—" the man began, but his words fell short as J.D. rotated his head around, giving the man a ghastly shock, and giving J.D. the opening to rotate his body to the outside. The weapon discharged as he did. As J.D. put one arm under the rifle and grabbed the stock taking control of it, he pulled the weapon forward and rotated it, slamming the barrel into the side of the man's face. J.D. had the rifle in hand as the man collapsed to his knees. J.D. released the magazine and tossed it aside, and then threw the M-16 rifle even further away.

"Hands on your head," J.D. ordered aggressively, as he unsheathed one of his machetes as a threat. The man complied. "I recognized you. I saw you in the garbage truck. What is your name?!" J.D. demanded to know.

"Who are you? *What* are you?" the man asked, his voice trembling as he gazed into the blackness of J.D.'s irises and then peered at the claw like fingers.

" 'I am the flail of god. Had you not created great sins, god would not have sent a punishment like me upon you,' " J.D. told him, quoting Genghis Kahn. "Do you understand? Now what is your name?"

"What does it matter? Just finish it," the defeated man groggily responded.

J.D. commanded, "I want to know the name of the man who helped kill a friend of mine and nearly killed another. Tell me this and maybe I'll kill you quickly, instead of cutting you from groin to gullet," J.D. told him, pressing the blade against his throat.

"It's Michael. Now get it over with."

J.D. wasn't through with him. He needed to know what had incited the man's group into ambushing his. "Why did you assault us on 34<sup>th</sup> Street? What did we do to your people to provoke that attack?"

"Hostages. We needed some of you as hostages."

"*Hostages?!*" J.D. questioned the man's nonsensical comment. "Hostages, *why?*"

"Our children. Our women. We wanted them back. If we had some of your people, we thought we could trade them back for those you took from us."

J.D. was shocked at the revelation. "Now who's the stupid son-of-a-bitch? You killed my friend for nothing. We're not those people."

J.D. wanted to kill the man for what his group had done, but he knew he couldn't. There had been enough tragedy caused by Stone and he would not be the source of anymore suffering for this group.

"The killing stops. Do you hear me? Too many people are dead over this mistake. We're not the people who took your children. We've suffered the same. But I know who he is. We can move forward as enemy or forward as ally. But it ends tonight."

The Javits Center creaked loudly behind them as the steel of the structure began to give way.

"You know who he is?" Michael asked with surprise.

"Yes. And I'll never stop hunting for him."

The building began to heave, as the intensity of the flames grew hotter and higher. The darkness that was night melted into near day, as the fire glowed brightly lighting the sky.

"Then perhaps my enemy's enemy could be our friend. But that is not up to me. I'm not in charge," the still glassy eyed Michael told him.

J.D. heard a cry. For a moment, he thought it was Four Fingers, but the timbre in the creature's shriek was different. He looked to the distance and saw them—*half-mutes!* The noises and the brilliance of the Javits engulfed in flame had roused them from their hiding places. J.D. had not thought of this. Half-mutes were day creatures and their constricted vision made them blind at night. However, with his pyrotechnic destruction of the convention hall, J.D. had inadvertently transformed night into day.

"Get down," J.D. instructed. "Get on your belly and don't move. They're coming," he warned.

Michael was muddled, as he saw J.D. pull out his other blade. At first he thought he was about to be decapitated, but then realized that the man in front of him had a dire look of concern on his face. Michael understood something bad was coming. He did as J.D. ordered.

J.D. walked toward the oncoming creatures. He let out a loud screech in warning. A few halted in their advance taking heed of J.D.'s notice, and then fled, but eight others stood their ground. Another cry came again, and then the pack charged forward, razor fingers extended and at the ready to slash and tear the flesh from J.D.'s bones for a meal.

Michael Panton lay on his stomach trembling while he witnessed the carnage. He had never seen any person move so swiftly or kill with such fury and ferociousness, as did the man with the machetes. As the man finished slaughtering the day stalkers—as he knew them by—

cleaving the last one's head cleanly from its body with one swing, he cried out with a piercing screech almost like an owl. Somewhere in the distant darkness came return screeches, all with owl like sound but none with such an intensity of timbre of voice as the one before him. It had sounded unworldly. Michael knew the man who had just slaughtered almost a dozen day stalkers was also definitely not human. He also realized that whatever this fellow had become was exactly the ally his group needed to help hunt down the group that had killed many of his fellow survivors, and abducted their women and children.

# 21

# ENEMY MINE

THE ANCIENT PROVERB "THE ENEMY OF MY ENEMY IS MY FRIEND" IS widely attributed to the Arabs, but it is actually much older. It originated in the 4th century B.C. in India. Kautilya—the "Indian Machiavelli"—wrote about the idea in the Sanskrit military book, the *Arthashastra*. It was a book that J.D. had read. However, J.D. had also read the *Art of War* by Sun Tzu, and knew very well that an enemy could be unpredictable and treacherous. He was not going to fall into a trap.

Under the cover of darkness, hours before sunrise and the appointed time, J.D. Nichols and Peter Dunne set off for the rendezvous location that had been mediated by Michael Panton and Paul Wiese to discuss a collaboration between the two survivor groups in hunting down Stone and his men. However, just because Michael Panton seemed sincere and willing to cooperate in said combined effort, didn't mean that the chief of his group would mutually agree. After all, Michael did tell J.D. that it was not up to him but the group's leader, and to trust that the meeting was in good faith would be foolish, especially since J.D. had killed some of their company. With the possibility of the meeting being a ruse to lure J.D. into the open, he had fully prepared strategies for the meeting place as well as for the armory if it came under attack in his absence.

The meeting had been set for 8:00 a.m. at a neutral location, Bryant Park on the upper terrace of the Sixth Avenue side of the New York Public Library. Although the park was tree lined, it was late in the year and the leaves had fallen from them allowing a better view of the park and surrounding areas. There was only one vantage point for an ambush—unless you were a highly trained sniper that could hit a target from an extremely long distance—and that was the library that would be shadowing the negotiation.

J.D. had guided Peter through the building's dark interior to the optimal viewpoint of where he believed his enemy would strike if they were looking to assassinate him. They did not discover any of Panton's group waiting, but it did not mean that they wouldn't take up position at the window. It was shortly before 3:00 a.m. J.D. and Peter waited silently. James had orders to pick J.D. up on Fifth Avenue in front of the library a few minutes before the meeting. An hour before sunrise, J.D. heard the shuffling footsteps of several people. He and Peter moved out of sight as two beams of light bobbed in the darkness on approach. J.D. would wait before making his move, he wanted to make sure the two men got settled and reported to their leader that they were in position.

---

As agreed, J.D. had brought only three other men with him, all fully garbed in battle dress uniform not only as an intimidation tactic but also as a show of unity. They had also brought with them the remaining two wounded men that J.D. had taken back to the armory for medical attention after the melee at the Javits Center. The third injured person from the group—one who had only suffered minor injuries—had returned with Michael as a show of good faith to prove that J.D.'s group meant them no ill will. This token J.D. hoped would be a catalyst for a meeting, and it had.

Arriving in two Humvees at the designated location, J.D., Paul and

James escorted the two recuperating guests back to their group. However, the meeting was not to be cordial.

After Michael Panton introduced his group's leader, Kane Dinger, and the men accompanying them, Paul in turn did the same. Their leader asked J.D. to join him on the terrace, gesturing to a chair that J.D. knew would have been the perfect position for the two gunmen to have the best shot. J.D. declined the man's offer, and before the leader could say anything, J.D. addressed him.

"Everything that has transpired between our two groups happened because of a misunderstanding," J.D. reminded Kane. "Good people on both sides have died because of this. We came in good faith hoping to move forward in a mutual relationship at working together to rescue those who have been taken from us, and to punish those who are responsible. But you have not. You would have me sit to assassinate me."

The seeming charismatic leader responded from atop the terrace, "Is this how you start off a negotiation, with accusations?" Kane smiled slightly but pleasantly, giving no sign of treachery. "We are as eager as you to find those who were stolen from us, so why would we want to kill you when it would be mutually beneficial for us to work together?"

"Then the two men with the rifles in the library above are not your men?" J.D. asked.

Michael asked Kane, "What is he talking about?" However, Kane did not reply, but kept his focus on J.D.

"The only men I have are those before you," he assured J.D., the leader's voice reflecting nothing but genuine sincerity. However, J.D. knew differently.

"Then perhaps," J.D. responded, "we should ask them?" J.D. then called into his all ready active headset, "Lieutenant, bring the two captives forward."

A moment later Ryan Duncan, a pistol in one hand and his other in a sling, brought two restrained men with pillowcases over their heads to the bottom of the terrace steps, and made them kneel.

J.D. removed the men's hoods to reveal two frightened men with

Gorilla tape across their mouths. Both men looked to the man at the top of the stairs with bewildered expressions, one struggling to call out.

With a shocked look Michael commented, "Jesus, Kane. What have you done?"

J.D. heard Michael's remark and realized he was unaware of their leader's plot.

Kane pulled his sidearm free and pointed it at J.D. The others followed suit by aiming their rifles at J.D.'s men. Paul, James and Ryan returned the threat with their weapons at the ready. Michael stood flabbergasted not knowing what to do.

"I have the high ground, Colonel. Now tell your men to drop their weapons and back the hell up. We just want you," he told J.D., and then cocked the hammer of his pistol as a threat.

"Kane, are you insane? These men can help us," Michael burst out.

"Mind your place," Kane notified Michael, "or suffer the consequences." The man turned his attention back to J.D. "*Now*, Colonel!"

J.D. smiled knowingly as he raised his hands as four of Kane's men cautiously made their way down the short terrace stairway. He looked up at Kane and said, "Kill the shepherd and the sheep will scatter."

A shot rang out from the window above. Blood and brain matter splattered, spraying into the morning air. The bullet ripped through Kane Dinger's skull, and then struck one of his men through the back who had been directly in the bullet's path. The three remaining men attempted to strike back, only one managing to get a shot off before J.D.'s men gunned them down, leaving Michael and the two restrained men alive.

J.D. and his men slowly backed away from the corpse strewn staircase, momentarily keeping their weapons aimed at Michael before turning and running.

Michael was dumbfounded at all that had transpired and overwhelmed to be alive. He watched as J.D. and his men fled to their trucks parked on 40th Street. He didn't move to the bound men until the colonel's vehicles sped away. Then it struck him to why they had departed so hastily when they had the upper hand. *Day Stalkers!*

It had only been two days since the Bryant Park confrontation when Michael Panton brought his group of fourteen to the armory gates for an unconditional surrender. His fellow survivors were mostly made up of women and teenagers. Of the adults, there were only four men remaining, including Michael. The two who had planned on ambushing J.D. from the library window were not amongst them. Michael revealed that they had been expelled from the group after being beaten nearly to death, the collective retaliation for the two attempting to take control of their group.

However, J.D. had only allowed the group inside the perimeter fence under guard, until he could be certain of Michael's intention. He had also placed his sharpshooter on the armory's roof just in case of any trouble, like he had done at the library. Doctor France protested greatly against the commander's decision to leave the ragged group exposed outside to the elements as well as possible attack from Stone, when it was clear to him that their deteriorated condition posed no threat to the armory. J.D. was firm in his decision; there were just too many refugees all at once to allow them into the inner sanctum, and it was a risk he was not willing to take. He ordered the doctor to conduct his medical exams outside and to see to their feeding.

For over three hours J.D. and James repeatedly questioned Michael about his group, their deceased leader, where they originated from, and how many of his people were kidnapped. Michael explained that he had only been with the group four months, having arrived with his niece who had been one of the five kidnap victims a month after their arrival. Kane Dinger had ruled the group with authoritarian ways in dealing with threats to his community from inside and out, and only accepted lone survivors or small families. However, Michael told them, after Stone's group attacked them and stole their children, Kane became increasingly deranged because of the loss, and was consumed with finding the men who had taken them. J.D. realized that Dinger was as equally maniacal and power hungry as Stone, and could not hold their deranged leader's wrongs against them, especially since none of Kane's goons were still a part of the group. J.D. allowed them into the fold. Michael volunteered to be a soldier in the war against Stone.

## 22

# NORRIE-MILLS

J.D. knew that he and his men would not be able to make it back to the city before dark. It had taken them double the time to get to Mechanicville then it would have if the chaos of world's end hadn't made the journey longer, slower and more treacherous. They had used Route 87 for the most part to get to their destination, avoiding all but the outskirts of Albany by utilizing Route 787. Avoiding major cities was a must. They were one vehicle and four men. Avoidance with anything that could hamper or halt them in their journey was necessary. They had explored Mechanicville for several hours, and J.D. had been right; it was a choice location to relocate. The hydroelectric plant could provide for all their non-fossil fuel needs.

On their journey and in their exploration of Mechanicville, they had not come across any survivors nor had they encountered any half-mutes. J.D. hadn't truly expected to come across any humans, but he had anticipated confronting a few half-mutes lurking around the town.

J.D. stood in front of the large roaring and crackling fire he had built, watching the orange flames leaping up like demons' tongues licking at the dusk. The heat and beauty of the fire soothed his chilled bones, but not his mind. Like New York City, Mechanicville was also occupied with rotting zombie corpses. However, decaying zombies were not what was troubling him. What he had discovered on his solo search into a few buildings that piqued his interest, were the remains of several carcasses of eaten transmutes. The disturbing find was disconcerting and he knew that only a non-human predator was capable of taking down a transmute, and that was a half-mute. Though it had been distressing, he told no one of the discovery, not even Ryan. However, he did tell Ryan to keep the team on high alert because he had an uneasy feeling that half-mutes were about. The discovery of the mutilated and dined upon corpses of his half kin was concerning for another reason also. If they were going after a stronger prey as food, then they were becoming more aggressive, more desperate, as well as cunning. J.D. knew it could potentially be a threat for the survival of the transmutes as well as his own people.

As the Stryker had made its way slowly through the park and into the tent camping area, they had spotted at least a dozen deer grazing. When he and his pre-apocalypse friends visited here before, they would always slow their vehicle and watch the deer that would gather at the break of the woods, just a few yards from the road's edge. This evening there had been more than he had ever seen before, and it brought about opportunity. A deer could provide not only nourishment for many; it would also raise the morale of the armory's inhabitants.

J.D. was not a large game hunter and therefore had no experience or knowledge of field dressing a kill, and neither did any of his men. Instead, he used his knowledge of anatomy, as he gently cut into the deer from belly to sternum as careful as possible as not to puncture the bladder or cut into the intestines. After discarding the parts that were inedible into the park garbage can that still stood at the edge of the road near the cabin's driveway, they hung the beast up in a tree, securing it high enough that no animal could get to it.

Ryan sat directly behind J.D. on the bench of the decaying, weather-stained picnic table, eating a strip of well-cooked venison. Although, J.D. thought the deer was a bit gamey, it didn't diminish the enjoyment he got from eating his portion medium rare. His desire for his barely cooked meat was by taste preference and not because of a transmute craving for raw meat. Though there were rumors that his night outings alone were to satisfy his transmute need to feed upon live animals, this was false. The few rats and other small game animals that he had captured were strictly for James' wife and child.

While Sergeant John Lott continued to cut more wood for the fire, Jonas McGann stood amongst the oak and hazelnut trees and rotting flora on the rise that helped obscure the cabin from the road. The stalwart young man, Lieutenant Alexander's protégé, looked down the paved roadway toward the base of the incline—which had now begun to vanish into the fading light of the day—watching vigilantly for any intruders that would come up the hill. J.D. had doubted that anyone, or anything, would be in such a remote area with the chill of autumn taking its grip. Nevertheless, after his gruesome discovery in Mechanicville, he could not rule out the possibility, so he had assigned guard shifts just in case. J.D. was a firm believer in that you could never be too careful or too prepared, especially after the 34th Street ambush debacle.

Jonas took his duty seriously. This was his first away mission. He had never gone out on any patrol, but had been assigned inside the armory to the communications center, as well as other menial duties. James knew he was capable of any task to which he was assigned; after all, it was he who helped James at the Hearst Tower when others refused. And it was Jonas who helped to save James' life in the basement as they went against the enraged zombie that had once been an assistant director of building security. Now that the lieutenant was sure of Jonas' combat skills it had been time to let his apprentice prove himself. James had recommended Jonas for the mission, and Jonas knew if he failed, he would not only fail in the colonel's eyes, but more importantly he would disappoint his mentor and the man who helped him to survive. Failure was not going to happen, not on his watch.

J.D. had chosen to make camp at cabin five, not only because of its tactical advantage—being a cabin atop the summit that was obscured behind a tree line rise—but also because it was a cabin he knew well.

This was the cabin that he, Shiyab, and two other St. Vincent's EMTs had shared while spending off-duty time together camping for the past four consecutive years. This was Norrie-Mills State Park in the town of Staatsburg, just north of Poughkeepsie. It was their place of peace, a place where he and his friends came once a year for a week. It was a place where they did not have to worry about the demands or their jobs or think about the horrors that sometimes accompanied them. Here they could unwind, relax and rest their souls.

Cabin five usually had an obscured view of the Hudson River, due to the heavy surrounding tree foliage. However, there was one exception and that was an opening between two young oak trees that formed an inverted V that allowed a direct view of the wide river while seated at the picnic table. From the table, J.D. used to sit gazing out onto the serene murky water, occasionally seeing a sailboat, or a tugboat pushing a barge, heading north against the current. Silently, J.D. stood reflecting as he gazed out to the flowing water. His favorite thing had been building a roaring campfire in the park-provided steel pit, sitting back in his New York Giants lounge chair while drinking a beer, or a glass of Jack and Coke—depending on his mood for the evening—and listening to echoes of clattering train wheels and the long resonant sounds of the locomotive's horn as it passed by the park to and from the Poughkeepsie, NY station. The group never came during the peak camping season; they always choose to go camping after the second week of September. It was much quieter, and three out of the four years they had stayed in the park, they had been the only cabin dwellers. Though the quiet and surrounding beauty of the park was still pleasant, the thoughts of the sights and sounds of the past were not. He missed the tugs on the water and the sounds of distant trains.

The lock on the door that separated the small, enclosed porch to the cabin's interior broke easily under the weight of J.D.'s right boot. He stood just inside the entranceway, reflecting for a moment, as he slowly scanned the unlit interior. The cabin had a musty smell, but it didn't matter; familiarity was comforting, and opening all the windows to air out the small space would diminish the odor. The cabin remained as he had remembered, though usage and time had worn and weathered her a bit more than he recalled. It was, for all intents and purposes, the same as it had been the previous fall, right down to the same furniture.

All for the moment was right, in a world that had gone so wrong. He hoped that for a few hours there would be peace for himself and his companions. J.D. half smiled as he washed the deer blood from his hands under the chilly water of the kitchen sink. The well-fed water pipe still worked. Like those in Manhattan these too still functioned due to the sloped angle from its source that gives the park's feeder pipes natural pressure. After shaking his hands to dry them, he closed the door as he departed and returned to his men and the warmth of the fire.

Tonight, there was a clear sky and bright half-moon. Its reflection shimmered and danced upon the glossy finish of the Hudson River current. As he gazed out, between the two trees that afforded him his panoramic view, he expelled a sullen breath, aching to see the lights from receding tugboats painting serpentine ribbons of oily colors on the inky black water. But there was only the glimmering of the night sky lapping at the watercourse, a pale substitute for the night-lights he loved to watch.

At 1:00 a.m. John and Ryan had retired to the luxuriousness of the cabin—not having to sleep in the confinement of the Stryker—while Jonas had withdrawn into the safety of the vehicle. J.D. stood guard. The diminished fire crackled behind him as he leaned up against a young maple tree in the brush staring down the road. The rotting foliage under his feet filled his nostrils with a scent that was pleasant and reminiscent of previous stays. He could distinctly smell the fragrance of decaying hickory husks from one of the numerous genus of trees that were a part of the surrounding forestation. In the distance came a series of loud cries. It sounded like the baying of wolves, but J.D. knew there had not been wolves in these parts for a great many years.

The night abruptly drew still with a deathly, ominous silence. The faint rustling and stirring sounds of the creatures of the night stopped. There was nothing, not a leave rustling, not a twig breaking, just silence. A few pops came from behind, but he knew it had only been the burning wood releasing moisture. Then he heard it—faint, light, swift. He looked down to the lowland and glimpsed moving specters at the foot of the hill. Fiendish shadows paced and intertwined, moving back and forth across the road with heads hung low to the ground. He could see what they were. The group stopped, then turned and ran fiercely up the incline. It was dogs, a pack of nine, and he could sense they were hungry and dangerous.

He knew what had drawn them. It was the scent of deer carcass that hung from the tree. J.D. stepped out of his hiding place and into the center of the roadway to greet the oncoming carnivorous horde. He had not shouldered a carbine this night; instead he was armed with his bolos and kept a Glock holstered on his leg. However, J.D. did not reach for either weapon as the pack drew near. He stood staring back at them, his arms extended from his sides, his fingers flexing and his breathing heavy. As the wanting dogs drew within striking distance, J.D.'s transmute voice rose up and bellowed forth in a piercing screech that sliced through the night.

He charged them. The Rottweiler pack leader leapt into the air. J.D. reached out and caught the animal in mid-flight, thrusting his talons into the leader's throat and then throwing the attacking canine to the ground. It was dead before it could yelp.

Another vicious predator leapt at him, but J.D.'s reaction was light-ning quick. He whipped his arm outward, slamming his forearm across the Shepherd's ribs, cracking them. It yelped loudly as it collapsed to the ground. The rest of the pack was now on him. They pulled him to the ground. J.D. pushed one dog high into the air off his chest, then turned, and with a raking handful of talons slashed deeply into another. The dog screamed in pain. The pack fled.

J.D. quickly jumped up unscathed, except for minor tears of his clothing, and pursued the fleeing pack through the woods and down an adjacent hill toward cabin number one. He was on the hunt.

---

The piercing, resonant cry abruptly woke the team. Ryan knew the call well. He had heard it before when J.D. had been in distress. J.D.'s screech that mid-October morning had pierced the city's silence and echoed through the streets from the tip of lower Manhattan to the armory and beyond. He ran from the cabin with weapon in hand with John quick at heel, the two meeting Jonas, who was emerging from the bowels of the Stryker.

J.D. was not at his post. They called out to him, but there was no response, just the distant howling of perhaps coyotes on the move. Ryan moved the team forward out of the thicket. Emerging and stepping only several feet onto the gravel of the roadway, his feet suddenly met a large mass. The abrupt and unexpected meeting of foot and object nearly toppled him. Ryan tripped, stumbled forward several feet but regained his balance in time so as not to fall. The melee had only lasted seconds, but the carnage of it lay about. As Jonas' flashlight swept over the moist ground it revealed two dead dogs—a Rottweiler with its throat ripped open and a German shepherd with compound rib fractures.

---

J.D. could hear the labored breathing of the animal he injured. His eyes were keen and quickly saw that the dog had taken refuge under a thicket of wild raspberry bushes. Its gaping wounds crimson wet, in shock, and in severe distress, the dog lay dying. The Golden Retriever had only made it less than a hundred yards from where the encounter had occurred before its injuries forced it to discontinue its flight. J.D. cautiously approached. The dog could barely raise its head as the victor stood above peering down at his near kill. The retriever whimpered slightly. The bloodied dog gave in, too badly injured and no longer able to defend itself. The canine knew its time was over.

---

J.D. had only been gone a few moments. A twig snapped and the three of them, still standing in the roadway, quickly turned with guns poised, trigger fingers at the ready, toward the sound. Flashlights bobbed and swept across the darkened woods, probing the sinister, primeval depths for the source, but they could see nothing but trees and brush.

From out of the darkness came a call, "Stand down," their colonel's voice reverberated, notifying them that it was he who was approaching. It took another few seconds for him to emerge from the darkness of the woods into the moonlight of the opening. In his arms he carried his limp prey.

"Go clear the cabin table and light the room. I have an injured dog that needs immediate attention," he instructed, with urgency in his tone.

His men didn't question him; without hesitation, they did what he had ordered. J.D. laid the dog down on the table. The canine's breath was shallow and heart rate weak. It needed immediate medical treatment.

There had been a standing order. No one, absolutely no one, kills transmutes or dogs unless it is in self-defense and only then must there be no alternative. J.D. had killed two in self-defense and injured another. However, he harbored no ill will against the animals that attacked him. They were hungry and they were doing what came natural to them, to hunt. Although the pack had fled and the danger was over, J.D. had chased the remainder of the group into the dense primordial wood not to finish off the attackers, but to save the one he had injured.

---

J.D. once again washed bloodied hands under the chilly tap water of the kitchen sink, this time drying them with a rag from the Stryker.

The commander examined the animal for outward signs of rabies. In the time of man, New York State had been one of eight states east of the Mississippi River to conduct oral rabies vaccination baiting programs for control of rabies in raccoon, fox, and coyote populations. But those times were gone, and if the dog had been bitten by any infected wildlife in the park, then it was highly probable that the dog was infected too. Though J.D. did not have a veterinarian background, he knew what signs to look for, having had his own dog. This dog appeared not to have any symptoms.

With the help Ryan, J.D. then stitched and dressed the dog's four slice wounds that it had suffered from the talon strike. He had also cut the imbedded collar from the dog's neck, excised the dead flesh and stitched it back together. The tag on the collar read, "Barkley."

The dog was no longer in pain for J.D. had injected him with a small amount of morphine to ease its suffering, and to relax the animal so it could be attended to. The procedure had taken nearly ninety minutes. J.D. sat impatiently at the table, fidgeting with his medical kit, waiting for the unconscious animal to awaken.

His patience ran out when the contents of his pack had been stored back into their proper places for the third time. Waiting by the animal's side just made him more anxious now that he had nothing to do, which only added to his irritated state. J.D. stood, looked down at the dog, stroked its head lightly with affection, and walked toward the cabin door. He stepped outside to the fire and stoked it, placing a few more pieces of wood on top of the hot coals. The new wood smoked and crackled, taking a few moments to flame up. He would have to be patient now. There was nothing else he could do to hasten the animal's recovery. Barkley probably needed several more hours before he would wake, and by then the dawn would begin to wipe the stars from the sky like letters from a chalkboard.

Ryan sat down next to his leader, his arm still in a sling and in minor pain from the jar he received tripping over the dead dog.

"How's the arm?" J.D. asked.

"It hurts."

"When we get back," he told Ryan, "I'm gonna do some acupuncture on that arm. I'll help, greatly."

Ryan reached into the utility pocket of his left pant leg. He brought with him something that he hoped would alleviate his commander's tension and take his mind off his rescue. "Here," he spoke, unscrewing a cap from a metal flask, and then handing it to J.D.

J.D. examined the container, and then sniffed its contents.

"Ahh," he said, "Old Number 7." He took a swig and then handed it back to Ryan. "There a reason you brought this? Pain reliever?"

"A good XO always sees to the needs of his commander," he replied.

"You know if we were in the *real* Army," J.D. responded, "I'm sure that carrying around alcohol would get you time in the brig."

"I think you mean *stockade*," Ryan gently corrected. "A brig is in the Navy."

"Okay, stockade."

"Well, *if* this was the old guard, then you'd be in the stockade, too, for impersonating an officer during a time of war."

"That's very military of you, *Lieutenant*. So, I guess then there's only one thing I can do about us drinking on duty?"

Ryan inquired, "And what's that, Colonel?"

"Have another drink and be glad we're the new guard." Though alcohol had no inebriating effect on J.D. due to his high metabolism, he still enjoyed the taste. He took a last swallow from the small flask, and then asked, "Anymore?"

## 23

## BARKLEY'S BIG ADVENTURE

BARKLEY WAS A GOLDEN RETRIEVER SOMEWHERE AROUND FIVE YEARS old and met many of the breed standards. Barkley's head appeared balanced and well chiseled with a powerful, wide and deep muzzle accented by a black nose. His eyes were a dark brown, set well apart with dark rims. His coat, though mildly matted on his chest and abdominal regions, was flat and its color a rich, lustrous gold of various shades.

His gait and movement had been powerful with good drive and long stride. This J.D. had noticed, as Barkley had been the one that had struck him down. Barkley in his former life had been someone's pet, or perhaps, even a show dog. Certainly, many of the breed standards were evident, and in all likelihood, Barkley was AKC registered. Nonetheless those days of being man's best friend were behind him. He was now a free animal with a new family.

This dog had not been the first J.D. had rescued since the aftermath of the plague. There had been one other, and that had been Otter. Otter was a four-year-old chocolate lab and had been owned by an acquaintance, Rick Bush. Rick, like J.D., had been a regular patron at McSorley's Ale House. Rick was the only other person—J.D. being the first —to be allowed to bring their dog into the establishment. There were health code laws in the City of New York that prohibited animals into businesses that served food, with the exception of service dogs. Max, in a broad sense of the definition, was a service dog. Max and J.D. had gone to search and rescue school and were volunteers with the New York City Urban Park Service Search and Rescue Team. Why Pepe, the manager, allowed Otter into the pub he never understood, and never asked.

The appearance of Rick's well-mannered canine at the entry of the alehouse was not only unexpected, but a bit of a shock. Otter had managed to escape his home and had not become a meal for transmutes or half-mutes. Though J.D. had never seen either species eating a house pet, it didn't mean it wasn't happening, for both were certainly not surviving on rodents alone. On top of that Otter had come to the familiar place while J.D. and his old companions had taken a few hours to get away from the armory. Otter must have smelled their scent and came searching, and J.D. was happy that he did.

The sleepy fingers of dawn slowly stretched out across the night sky filling the horizon with beams of glowing orange until the grey of night vanished into the coming of day. It was morning and with the pending new day it was time to complete the rest of their long journey home.

There wasn't much to stow into the Stryker ESV, and within a half hour's time they were prepared for departure. Barkley was semi-conscious as J.D. began his leave from the cabin, having had one last look at his patient. He dropped several small pieces of venison on the floor and made sure that the doors of the cabin were propped ajar so that his convalescing canine could leave the safety of its shelter when it was ready.

Barkley was not Max. Furthermore, J.D was not in the market for a pet, especially one who had reverted to a feral state. There was no room in his heart for any dog but his own. He was no Max he kept telling himself, and he was doing the right thing by leaving the wild canine behind.

The rear door of the Stryker began to retract.

Jonas called to his commander, "Colonel, sir?"

"Yes, Private."

"Sir—the dog," Jonas spoke in a half statement/half question.

"What about the dog?

"He's here, sir," Jonas answered his commander in a concerned tone. "He's feet from the door."

Barkley sat and then dropped the deer meat he had been carrying in his mouth. The rear ramp had barely retracted when the retriever made his presence known to all inside the truck.

Barkley lived up to his name. He was a very vocal animal. Nonetheless the ramp closed and the Stryker pulled away from the cabin leaving Barkley still sitting and barking.

The vehicle had not pulled more than a dozen yards down the cabin's drive when it abruptly halted and the rear door lowered.

Jonas called out, "Barkley, come. Come, Barkley."

However, the dog just cocked its head slightly to the side and looked at the private with an odd gaze. Barkley made no attempt to comply with the private's request; instead the canine began to bark franticly.

"Sir, the dog won't come," Jonas said, as he turned to the colonel.

J.D. shook his head with disappointment. "Private, if you can't even get a dog to follow orders, how will you ever mange to command a team?"

The colonel stood and went to the gangway. With a loud snap of his fingers and a commanding "Tsst," the dog was silenced. "Barkley," he said to the animal in a calm, assertive, in charge tone. "Come. Now."

The dog picked up its food and slowly and calmly made its way down the gravel drive, up the ramp of the Stryker and into the troop compartment. Barkley's big adventure was about to begin.

# 24

# HUNTER AND THE HUNTED

IT WAS MID-EVENING ON A LATE DECEMBER DAY. CHRISTMAS HAD nearly arrived, and there was no Santa.

They needed someone to play Santa.

J.D. refused to be Santa.

He couldn't be Santa. He knew this. His daughter would know it was him. All the children would know it was him. His owl eyes and talon fingers would give it away. No, he told himself. Santa may have been fat and jolly, but he wasn't a freak. Caitlin's first Christmas was going to be special. "Dawd" was not going to be Santa. Besides, he and Ryan were to be the entertainment. It was to be a day of music, merriment, ham dinner, and Santa Claus.

He would not order Peter to play an elf—that would be degrading —but he would order Paul to be Santa, and John and Michael to be Santa's helpers. That was one command decision he enjoyed. It was good to be king, and not Santa.

J.D. scanned the MRE food supply list.

01 - Chili with Beans

02 - Pork Rib

03 - Beef Ravioli…

… 22 - Chicken with Dumplings

23 - Chicken Pesto and Pasta

24 - Chicken with Salsa.

Twenty-four MRE menu items but no ham. It was bad enough that the government hadn't had number 18 - Turkey Breast w/Gravy & Potatoes on their MRE menu list since 2002, James informed J.D. prior to Thanksgiving, but now he found out that they did not have ham on their menu either. "What kind of Department of Defense would not have ham as a menu item?" J.D. thought. He flipped through the other food stocks list. Still no ham. He cursed silently to himself, shaking his head slightly with disappointment, and then handed the inventory list back to Paul.

They had canned tuna, corn, canned peas, canned potatoes, canned yams, and even canned gravy, though mostly of the beef and chicken variety. They even had supplies to make apple and cherry pies. But no ham! "Unacceptable," he told Paul for a second time. "Have Lieutenants Alexander and Duncan report to me immediately. We're less than 36 hours away from Christmas and we're lacking a proper feast."

"We have a lot of canned Spam, sir," Paul half commented/suggested.

"*Spam?!*" J.D. fired back with disdain and irritation. "Are you out of your mind, Wiese? This is a holiday! Damn if we're going to serve anything but a proper holiday meal. And why am I finding out about this now? Isn't this part of your administrative duties?" he asked him, nearly livid.

"Yes, sir. But with all due respect, I file a report for your review every week, sir," Paul informed his superior.

J.D. ignored Paul's reminder for he knew it was still probably sitting in the pile of unread reports on his desk. "Damn it, Wiese. Now we're going to have to rearrange duty assignments so I can take a team out tomorrow and find ham. This would never have happened if Kermit were here."

And that is why J.D. found himself and his team of eight at an Upper Eastside supermarket clearing the shelves of all the canned hams and some other items. It wasn't that there weren't closer grocery stores, but those had been cleared out and the food distribution warehouses he knew about were either in the Bronx or Astoria, which were too far. Furthermore, the stores in Lower to Mid-Westside Manhattan were in the area of Stone and his men, and J.D. and crew had no time for a hostile engagement over a ham dinner.

When finished, part of the team departed with the ESV, leaving James, John; and himself behind with the Humvee. There was one more stop J.D. wanted to make before heading back to base, and that was Penn Station.

He had not given much thought to the girl he had seen nearly a month ago. If she had any sense she would have vacated the area, and for the winter found herself a more suitable and hospitable place to dwell.

The temperature of the clean, crisp, biting late December air seemed colder than any other year he could remember. He was sure that it was the lack of heat being generated by the thousands of cars that used to fill the metropolis's atmosphere on a daily basis. The cleaner air was welcome, but the chill was not.

Standing at the front of the truck that he and James had discovered previously, he discussed with John the feasibility of resurrecting the 5-ton, 6-wheeled long cargo vehicle.

As they stood with the vehicle cabin propped up, revealing the engine, and discussing the possibility of jumpstarting the motor—providing the fuel had not been tainted with water condensation—J.D. abruptly caught movement out of the corner of his right eye. It was coming from the same area as the last time he had visited. It appeared to be the young woman from before. She fled quickly.

He hesitated in pursuit, not sure if there was enough daylight left to chase the phantom again, but then changed his mind, grabbed his 9mm submachine gun and was off. This time he did not move toward the loading dock area, but headed for an entryway under the colonnade that was above the same pedestrian path that he believed the mystery girl had used for her prior escape.

J.D. ran after her with more speed and agility than an Olympic hurdler. He was amazed with himself. Though he knew he had better reflexes because of his enhanced fast-twitch muscle fibers, he had not run with any intensity of act or determination of purpose since he had become trans-human. He jested to himself as he reached the entry that he was Velociraptor fast.

He knew the underground structure fairly well, enough to be able to navigate the subterranean corridors with relative familiarity. If one was to hide and survive for a long period of time and were trapped or chose to seek refuge in the darkness of the lower level of Penn Station, then one would want to seek shelter in a place were food would be abundant, and that would be the sanctuary of the food court promenade.

The automatic glass doors that led from the pedestrian walkway into the Pennsylvania Station complex had been shattered. Geometric fragments of glass covered the ground like crystalline hail, and crunched under his boots as he crossed the threshold of the outer world of light and into the darkness of the stairwell of the labyrinth.

He barely turned on the weapon's tactical light when he turned it off again. The flashlight could give away his position and he didn't need it at the moment; there was enough natural light for him to see adequately, providing he removed his sunglasses.

The path down the stairs to the main level corridor was clear, but as he neared the bottom a hail of automatic weapon fire greeted him.

"Buddha's balls!" J.D. cursed to himself, as he jumped over the right sloping handrail of the stairway enclosure to use as cover. The young woman *really* didn't want him to catch her. This just made him want to even more.

J.D. couldn't see her position, even using the weapon's scope. However, he was no longer on the receiving end of rapid fired bullets, so he cautiously made his advance, stepping over the remains of a soldier's corpse. As he moved from the stairwell into the wide passage-way, he observed the sealed archway to his right to what had been the entrance to the NJ Transit Ticket & Information windows, which led down into the pavilion for train access to NJ Transit Tracks 1–8. Oppo-site this was another entry, just a few feet ahead to his left. This entrance was to the lower level that would bring you down to the inter-secting corridor of the lower main concourse, the one that served as access for the Long Island Rail Road Waiting Room and for Tracks 13–21. This entry too had been sealed off, which meant the food court promenade was inaccessible from the direction in which the girl had fled.

As he stepped to the blocked entry, he kicked something. On the floor was a discarded MRE pack. The girl must have dropped it when she fled, but the displaced food seemed oddly out-of-place.

If the girl had fled straight ahead to the Seventh Avenue/West 32nd Street exit, the lost MRE should have been more toward the middle of the hall. From his vantage point J.D. could not see if the gates had been closed and secured at the exit's header, but he needed to confirm if she had escaped that way. As stepped from the barricade a noise from behind drew his attention. A lower panel that made up the wooden barrier had dislodged and fallen free. It was too much of a coincidence.

He peered through the hole. The passageway was unobstructed. He knew someone had cleared it, for to the left, where the three banks of escalators were located, the wells were filled with porter carts. Then he heard a clatter deep within the darkness. The adrenal began to pump in him again as he made his way down the dark stairwell. He wasn't chasing her so he could kill her; he was chasing her for the thrill of the hunt. The exhilaration of this pursuit was different from the hunter/prey searches he did for Stone's men. This quest was for fun and curiosity's sake. J.D. hadn't felt such a rush since he was pursuing Barkley through the thickets at Norrie-Mills.

At the bottom the exit had also been walled. However, it was loose. He didn't have to push on the board too hard for it to come out of its recess, but it did not fall clear. It seemed like something on the other side was blocking it. The board was clearly free of its framing. If it wouldn't fall forward, perhaps it could be pushed aside, J.D. hoped. He gripped the board's edge and pushed it left. The board slid away, revealing a mound of porter carts haphazardly lumped atop one another. The young woman must have hastily attempted to use them as a secondary deterrent and to keep the board propped in place.

The carts had not been stacked high and could be easily be crawled over. It would leave him momentarily vulnerable. He moved across them as covertly as he could. No attack came. J.D. had now entered the lowest concourse, which was the LIRR level of Penn Station.

He activated two Cyalume ChemLight sticks and tossed them ahead of him into the wide corridor. He had no choice but to use them as an aid to give him the visual acuity needed to effortlessly navigate. He listened and looked. The scent of must and stale air stung his nostrils. It was dank and damp from lack of ventilation on this level, unlike the one above, and signs of structural deterioration from water seepage were clearly evident by the debris that had fallen from the ceiling and was now scattered upon the floor.

There was no fetidness of decaying flesh. No signs the dead had overrun the lower level. There were no bodies, at all, like there had been on the upper level. Perhaps then, he thought, it was possible for someone to have taken refuge and survived the ravenous hordes of the living dead.

He looked down the hallway toward the intersecting corridor. Silence and darkness, with the exception of a few vermin, was all there seemed to be, and eerily reminded him of some ancient and lost under-ground city he had seen in a documentary on the History Channel. He tossed out a few more ChemLight sticks. Before he pushed on, he knew it prudent to call James and give him a situational report. J.D. told his lieutenant that he had found the woman's path of escape and if he could not locate her within twenty minutes he would head back.

J.D. cautiously made his way past the LIRR Waiting Room and the tracks it served to the intersecting corridor of the lower level concourse to where the LIRR ticket windows and food court were located. He tossed out ChemLight sticks to mark his path, and used the halogen flashlight on his machine gun to guide the way. He had wished he had brought his M4. It had a Trijicon optical sight that was superb for dark conditions. His rail-mounted light gave away his position.

Right. He felt the need to go right. The right was also the shortest part of the concourse corridor before him. To his immediate right was the long row of Long Island Rail Road ticketing windows, after which came Tracks Raw Bar & Grill. Bordering the restaurant—separated only by two archways to Track 17 and Track 19—was McDonalds, the last storefront on the southeast side, across from the entrance to the Broadway-7<sup>th</sup> Avenue subway line.

He kept close to the wall of ticketing casements as he made his way east to the entrance of Tracks Bar. The grill-type roll-down security gate to the tavern had been retracted and secured, and the inner wooden doors were closed. He peered through the grillwork searching the black depths of the interior. As the halogen light pierced the establishment's heart his instinct to go right paid off. In the far back past the long bar area, there were a large number of bar stools and other items stacked in the booths along the walls that formed a makeshift protective barrier. It appeared that someone had constructed this in an attempt to further obscure any interior view from the closed blinds of the south entrance windows and door. The rear doorway also had obstacles placed in front of it.

J.D. would not be able to gain access to the pub by way of the main entry. He had not brought bolt cutters with him. If there were another corridor that led to the back entrance of the pub, it was not via the way he had traveled. The entryway next to the pub led down to the platform of LIRR Track 17. This appeared to be the only way that might lead to the back entrance. After tossing a light stick through the archway—it bouncing on the bottom steps and rolling onto the platform below—he immediately noticed a portable outdoor lantern resting on the bottom step. He scanned the stairway's header with his flashlight. There, too, one step below him was another lantern.

After traveling nearly a hundred feet along the darkened platform and ascending the opposite stairs, he emerged in an adjoining passage and to the establishment's rear doorway. There was also a long pedestrian walkway that led away from where he emerged and ran in a westward direction. An inlaid decorative tile sign on the passageway wall read, 'Hilton Passageway.'

There was no reason not to breach the entry. He knew if he left it for another time there was the possibility that whoever had shot at him, would flee and seek safer shelter elsewhere. Besides he needed to know who this elusive person was. He just couldn't let it go.

He was about to strike the glass door near the lock mechanism with the stock of his machine gun to break the glass enough to reach in and unlock the door, but he stopped. If he did it would be loud and he would lose the element of surprise. He needed a rag or something to deaden the sound, but he had nothing. Then, on the off chance, he decided to see if the door was actually locked. It wasn't. Then J.D. got a suspicious feeling that the door was purposely left unlocked for a sinister reason. He knew the girl was a survivor and a fighter, and highly doubted she would accidently forget to lock it. He also knew that the doorway he stood before was the most vulnerable point of entry from an occupant's standpoint. It had to be a trap.

J.D. pulled the door back ever so slightly, just enough to give a narrow gap between it and the doorframe. He scanned the opening. He had been correct. He found an attached thin wire. The door was booby-trapped.

"Oh, you fool," he whispered. "But I will not fall victim to one of the classic blunders—the most famous of which is never get involved in a battle of wits with the Man in Black, but only slightly less well-known is this: Never go in against a trans-human when death is on the line," J.D. stated, bastardizing part of a well-known movie quote from the film *Princess Bride*. He fake laughed, "Ha, ha, ha," as he snipped the wire with his multitool.

Indeed, the elusive girl had been clever. The wired door had been jerry-rigged to a hidden M16 rifle. If he had fully opened the entry, J.D. would have been on the receiving end of a magazine full of 5.56mm caliber rounds.

The makeshift table and barstool barricade had been easily pushed aside. Carefully and methodically he made his way through the dining area toward the bar clearing every possible hiding area, including the bathrooms that were in an alcove to his left. Moving ahead, several feet from the recess was a unisex/handicapped bathroom. This, too, proved to be empty, but upon the long countertop with its deep basin there had been signs that someone had been using it. A woman's disposable razor, a can of shaving cream, and several bar towels sat to the left of the sink while two battery operated lanterns, one each on opposite sides of the countertop, sat under the large wall mirror.

Another recess on the left, much larger than the first and opposite the shellfish prep counter, lay between the final booth and the bar. Entering, he discovered an office, a storage room, and a large kitchen that ran behind the bar wall. The office had been converted into a living area, camping gear adorning the space. It was unoccupied as was the storage room.

He swept through the kitchen but found no one lurking under shelves or in any corner. There was only one other place within the immediate space where someone could hide, and that was the walk-in refrigerator unit. However, J.D. decided to leave it for last, opting to clear the rest of the establishment first.

He made his way along the serving side of the long wooden bar. At the end of the bar, there was an area on the patron side that had been obscured to him from the outside front doors. Cautiously approaching with gun at the ready, he came to the boot of the long L-shaped bar. He quickly popped his head and weapon over the bar counter, but there was no one cowering or waiting to blast him on the other side.

There was now only one place that the female in question could have taken refuge, and that was the cooler. He stood to its side near the handle side of the door. A slight smile suddenly came to his face. The last time he stood at a cooler he had discovered Army Master Sergeant Kermit Brown taking refuge inside, who would later become a team member and close friend.

He knew that anyone who has been in isolation for long periods of time could suffer detrimental effects, both mental and physical, and could become agitated very easily and be extremely violent. Though he knew the young woman had been pilfering MREs from the MTV, he had no idea if that was the extent of her trips to the outside world. J.D. had already been on the receiving end of her agitation twice, so he knew his approach needed be gentle, until it was time not to be gentle.

J.D. wrapped moderately on the door.

"Hello. This is Colonel J.D. Nichols... I am in charge of the 69th Regiment Armory on Lexington Avenue. You may have seen our light shining in the night sky. We may not be Motel 6," he jested, trying to lighten the situation by referencing a once well-known television commercial, "but we can offer you shelter, food, water, and a shower... However, since we're a bit pressed, I'll need an answer now, 'yes' or 'no'."

There was no answer. The gentle approach had failed. He knew he needed to be more direct. "Let me make this clear. Vacate the cooler immediately," J.D. said in a calm but assertive tone, "with your hands above your head where we can see them or we will make a forced entry."

He hoped the repeated use of "we" would encourage whoever that lay behind the steel barrier to rethink their position and surrender. He just hoped that whoever it was in the cooler didn't have superior firepower.

There was still no answer. It was possible that he had the wrong location, and this had been a futile attempt to get a corpse to surrender. Had someone made this makeshift bunker only to succumb to the plague or was the person behind the door still alive? "Nah," he told himself. She was inside and it was apparent she would need to be forced out.

J.D. looked at his watch. His twenty minutes were nearly up. It was time not to be gentle. He unhooked a M84 Stun Grenade from his vest and prepared to toss it into the cooler. This Noise and Flash Diversionary Device, as it was sometimes referred to, could produce a blinding flash of 6-8 million candelas and a deafening 180 decibels of sound pressure. A detonation of this device would incapacitate any potential threat inside for up to a minute.

J.D. pulled back the handle on the refrigerator unit. The latch refused to free. Someone had jammed the interior release handle, preventing the door from opening. There was no way he was going to unleash his machine gun upon the door handle, not with the possibility of ricocheting bullets. It would have to be blasted open. He reattached the M84 to his vest and paused to think.

He had no C4 explosive to render a small, directed charge, only a fragmentation grenade. A hand grenade was like using a sledgehammer to swat a fly, complete overkill. There would be collateral damage; the blast would be multi-directional. He had once called Corporal Drukker a nit in regard to foolishly wanting to use several hand grenades taped together to blow off the door of a heavily fortified U.S. Army command railroad car. Now he felt like the nit.

He reached into his backpack and pulled out some Gorilla tape, and then taped a M67 above the door handle. So blind in his ambition to find out who was behind the door, he did not even give warning to the occupant of the pending explosion.

J.D. squeezed the 14-ounce explosive device's handle to release the safety pin pull ring, and then released his grip activating the time delay fuse. He quickly ducked around the cooler. He hoped he was protected enough not to be in the way of a high velocity fragmentation. He may have been hard to kill, but his mutations did not make him indestructible.

The exploding grenade roared through the restaurant and its reverberating resonance carried throughout the underground hallways, and faintly rumbled to street level.

---

James and John suddenly stopped work on the truck. The light rumble concerned them, and they were sure it was most likely connected to their colonel's pursuit of the elusive girl.

James immediately radioed his commander, but there was no reply.

---

The door to the cooler was now ajar, but he was not about to fling the door open and go charging in, guns ablaze, like in some old John Wayne war film. He squatted next to the unit and cautiously pulled back on the exposed portion of the lip of the door, slowly opening it to try to peer inside without exposing himself. The noise of the mutilated metal door brought the answer he had been waiting for. A sudden eruption of gunfire pelted the inside of the thick door just above where the handle had been.

"Well, that's just rude and not very nice," J.D. scolded the occupant with the attitude.

A female voice immediately responded to J.D.'s condemnation. "I'm just givin' it back, *asshole!*"

He was surprised at the gunman's sudden need for verbal exchange. He countered, "Well, who shot at whom first? It was you!"

"I never shot at you. You're stupid as well as an asshole!"

"You have a filthy mouth! You should be ashamed."

J.D. always thought rude language from a woman was unbecoming and ignorant.

"You shot at me last month," he reminded her, hoping to reacquaint her with that lost memory, "by the overturned Humvee near the loading dock."

"That was you? Sorry I missed!" she yelled, and then rattled off another burst of gunfire.

---

James and John had already entered the main hallway of the upper concourse when they heard the distinct sound of distant automatic weapons fire. The hallway toward the east was gloomy but not dark, for the eastern portion that lay before them cast light from the stairwell ahead. But the day grew short and the corridor would soon be black. Time was of the essence if they were to locate where the gunfire had originated.

James once again radioed his commander. He awaited a response.

---

J.D. had decided to sit, leaning his back up against the doorframe of the refrigeration unit, when he started his repartee with the girl who had taken up a defensive position inside.

James' voice came faintly over the radio. J.D. had forgotten he had put in earplugs just prior to releasing the grenade. He took them out.

"Say again, Lieutenant."

"We heard explosions and gunfire," came a concerned voice. "We're on your Six. What's your situation? Over."

"Nothing to worry about, Lieutenant. I'm just negotiating. Think I'll have a resolution momentarily. Hold your position. Over."

"Affirmative. We'll hold. We're at the top of an open stairwell leading to a lower level. Over."

"Out," J.D. replied, and then turned his attention to the girl. "Okay. Last chance."

"What gives you the right?" she asked, and then squeezed off a few more rounds.

"As you wish," he told her, placing his earplugs back in.

He unclipped the "bang-flash" that he had reattached to his vest, pulled the door open a few inches more and tossed the grenade in.

Though the container muffled the sound of the explosion, it was loud even to his restricted hearing. He was sure that she, and anyone else that might be with her, was no longer a threat.

He pulled opened the door. Plumes of smoke wafted out, and the strong scent of burnt explosive powder drifted to him and stung his nostrils. In the back slumped on the floor he could see the one who had been evading him. He cautiously approached, rifle aimed, and kicked the weapon clear of the apparently unconscious girl's reach.

Securing the girl's hands and feet with plastic tie fasteners, he then picked her up and carried her from the restaurant over his shoulder. She was a survivor. She had faced the hordes of undead and lived. This was a girl who refused to give up her freedom and succumb to someone else's will. He admired her audacity. She was a fighter, and J.D. knew with training she would probably make a great warrior.

James and John were surprised at the bundle he carried over his shoulder as he emerged from the escalator onto the main concourse. With all the "negotiating" they heard they thought his adversary had been eliminated. The three of them made a cautionary exit, well aware that the explosions may have drawn more half-mutes, but day had become night and half-mutes did not roam the darkness.

After giving her a cursory exam—she appeared in good health, though a bit undernourished—J.D. laid her across the rear passenger seat, and then closed the door. He signaled to John they were departing. John revved the big diesel engine of the MTV truck in response. He had repaired it. The truck had only needed a battery jump from the Humvee. Today had been a good day. There was ham dinner for Christmas, resolution to the mysterious person, and a truck full of MREs. There really is a Santa after all, he thought, until Krampus in the back seat awoke. No bad deed goes unrewarded!

---

The ride back to the armory would not take very long and upon arrival J.D. would place her in the capable hands of Doctor Richard France, former government virologist and molecular biologist, and designer of the Trixoxen virus, who post apocalypse had become the armory's medical physician, and remained throughout a pompous ass.

J.D. had hoped to arrive home without any incident, but before he and James had completed half their trip, their prisoner awoke, whereupon she began kicking J.D.'s seat back, screaming expletives and demands of immediate release with noncompliance resulting in bodily harm to the reproductive organs.

He turned to her, pulled off his sunglasses to reveal his mutated eyes, and told her to shut up or he'd gag her.

A resounding, "Fuck you!" was given as a response, with no apparent fear or revulsion at the sight of her captor's black eyes.

J.D. was not going to get into a juvenile argument or exchanging expletives. He had given her an option, and she had refused it.

"Lieutenant, would you please pull over," he requested James.

J.D. pulled out a roll of camouflage cohesive wrap from his medic's bag. The Humvee came to a stop. The truck that John drove pulled up behind them.

J.D. opened the rear vehicle door. He grabbed her secured feet and abrasively pulled her out the door.

She resisted him and his efforts to wrap her mouth by trying to bite him, but they were futile and short lived. Having secured her mouth, he picked her up, swung her over his shoulder like a sack of Ready Mix, and went to the back of the truck. Opening the rear hatch, he secured her in the cargo bay behind the rear seat.

The rest of the trip back to the armory was much more pleasant.

---

J.D. was not kind when he dragged her from the back of the truck and carried her over his shoulder through the armory for all to see. She feared for her life and had been afraid that her capture was purely for his sexual gratification and amusement.

He had taken her alone to a large room and then roughly put her face up on an examination table.

With knife drawn he warned her plainly, "Do this my way and save yourself a lot of discomfort. Do it your way and I guarantee you will bring a world of hurt upon yourself. Understand?"

With anger in her eyes she venomously cursed him from under her gag, and then tried to kick him in the groin. J.D. knew why she was being belligerent and defensive. However, he was not that kind of man to do what she thought he was going to do to her.

J.D. put a firm, pinning hand to her chest, stuck the knifepoint under her chin, and asked, "Now do you understand?"

She had no choice but to capitulate. The freak with the weird irises was bigger and stronger than she, and he had already proven he would go to extremes to take what he wanted. She nodded she did, but promised herself she was going to shove that knife of his into his guts —*with a twist!*

J.D. rolled her to her side and cut the plastic tie from around her hands, which had been secured behind her back. He then sat her up and told her to raise her feet, and then cut them free.

"Where the hell is France?" he asked himself, as he looked around. He yelled out, "France...! *France!*" He turned his attentions back to his captive. "You can take the gag off. But no screaming and no trying to escape. Just sit there."

Again, he yelled out for Doctor France, but received no response.

"Now," he addressed her, and then was suddenly interrupted by his daughter running toward him from the opposite end of the large room.

She came to him and grabbed onto his legs. "Dawd. Dawd, Dawd... *Dawd!*"

"Cat," he responded firmly. "You know you're not supposed to be up here. This place is for sick people. Why aren't you with mom?"

"I am."

"I'm sorry, Cat. I don't see mom."

"Mawm get exam. She with Elty Ryan and Dokee Frans."

He knelt down to his daughter. "With Doctor France?" he asked with disbelief. "But mom doesn't like Dick. She wouldn't go see him. You must be mistaken?"

"Dawd," she cried, disappointment in her tone. "Caitlin no lie. I good cat."

"Of course, you are, Cat. But—"

Caitlin pointed at the girl. "Is she sick, Dawd?" she asked, interrupting her father's sentence.

"I don't know, Cat. Maybe. That's why we're here."

Caitlin tugged on her father's shirt and whispered in her ear.

"I don't know her name," he responded. "I don't know if she's a good cat or a bad cat."

Caitlin turned her attentions to the dirty-faced girl sitting on the examination table. She smiled at her and then curtsied.

"My name is Caitlin. My dawd call me Cat. What your name, pease?"

"Katherine," she told the curious child, returning the smile. "My dawd calls me Katie," she told the child, but not mockingly.

"Would you like be my friend?" Caitlin asked.

Before Katie could answer, J.D. spoke, "I don't think so, Cat. Katherine is only visiting."

"But dawd. You make her stay. She no go. Pease, dawd. Pease!"

"Why is it so important that she stays?"

"Cause. She no afraid. She no afraid of Caitlin. She smile at me... Beside. Tomorrow Chrismiss. Pease, dawd. Make her stay."

"Caitlin. Time for you to go get Doctor France for me. I'll talk to Katherine. Maybe she will stay."

She whispered in her father's ear for a moment than hugged him and ran back the way she had come.

"Cute kid. Don't see any resemblance though."

J.D. got up in front of her face. "Is that supposed to be humor?"

"That's not humor, that's observation. Your daughter is kind and gentle; you're just an asshole!"

"You brought it upon yourself. If you weren't such an obstinate, petulant child you wouldn't have found yourself gagged and tossed in the cargo hold."

She slapped him in his face. He raised his hand in response and she cowered.

"Consider that a warning," he sternly informed, as he lowered his arm and pointed his index finger at her. "Next time my hand will fly."

"Why did you bring me here? What is it you want from me?!"

"Nothing," a voice came from across the room. It was Doctor France. "Do not let the colonel bully you, miss," he told her as he approached. "The colonel may appear to be brutish, but do not let his rough exterior and lack of charm frighten you. He is too much the gentleman to strike a woman, even one that strikes him first. Is that not correct, Mister Nichols?"

J.D. did not respond to the character assessment, but instead said, "And where the hell have you been? Didn't you get the message I had a patient coming in?"

"Of course, I did. However, I was otherwise engaged with your wife, excuse me... *mate*. Besides since I was not notified that it was an emergency, I thought it best that Mister Duncan and I finish my examination of Luci first."

"Has something happened?"

"Need I remind you that because of your gene therapy meddling, Luci needs a weekly checkup and blood test due to her condition? Just routine. Everything is fine... Now, do you not have to be somewhere? Polishing your swords, browbeating your subordinates or searching for the children? I am fully capable of examining this patient without your supervision."

"Polishing my swords. You're real funny, *Dick*. I get the picture. Just watch this one, doc. She's a firecracker. If you have any problems, I'll be right outside the door."

J.D. began to walk toward the door, when Katherine called out to him.

"Hey, asshole, what did your daughter whisper to you before she left?"

J.D. turned around and gave her a big smile.

"Poo. You smell like poo."

Katherine smelled herself. The asshole had been right. She did smell, but not like poo.

# 25

# THE GIRL IN THE SHADOWS

KATHERINE O'HANLON, WAS A BALLET DANCER AND WAS 24 YEARS OF age. J.D. took an immediate liking to her, though their first few interactions had been extremely adversarial. Besides the fact that she was thin, tall and beautiful, with long silken auburn hair, she had become an apt pupil. This was what J.D. liked most about her, her ability to quickly comprehend and learn every martial arts technique he imparted to her.

Katie had come to New York City from Milwaukee, Wisconsin after graduating high school to continue her ballet studies at The School of American Ballet at Lincoln Center. The fluidity of the movement, the freedom of expression, the technique, variations, pointe, adagio, these were all things that were second nature to her and helped her to quickly learn Bruce Lee's Jeet Kune Do techniques.

Her ability and stamina amazed J.D. In those aspects she reminded him of Bonita, a young woman he once fell in love with in the Philippines when he was a teenager. Bonita had been a champion stick fighter and one that had not only bested him but also brought him into manhood. Katie's feistiness and stubbornness, though, reminded him of Marisol, and this is why he was not attracted to her. However, there was nothing romantic in their relationship. This was a bond between student and teacher and a relationship of commander and subordinate.

Though her parents helped to support her, she still needed a job. She chose an occupation she was familiar with, waitressing. It was a job she had done during the summers when she was attending high school. She was at Tracks Raw Bar & Grill when the plague broke out. She had graduated by then from waitress to bartender. Being her first bartending job, she was given the morning/afternoon shift.

By 2:00 p.m. the day of the viral outbreak Katie and her fellow employees had been evacuated, taken into Madison Square Garden for safety and to be monitored. The underground of Penn Station and the surrounding blocks were sealed, preventing intrusion into the safe zone. But hopes of survival quickly vanished. The city's power had failed; mass panic gripped the city while more and more people were becoming the living dead. Inside MSG, where the DoD had set up their headquarters, the situation had gone from under control to a Charlie Foxtrot by early evening, an Army acronym for cluster fuck. From the outside the undead had gathered by the thousands, only being held at bay by the resolute, valiant ranks of the 3-2 Stryker Brigade Combat Team. On the inside civilians and soldiers alike were succumbing to the virus. By 10:00 p.m. that evening the military knew that the city was lost and an evacuation of military personnel and the uninfected civilian refugees was needed. As a final solution, to ensure the disease would not spread, all troops and civilians that showed any sign of infection were to be immediately terminated. However, as the order of eradication commenced, chaos turned to mass panic. Both infected and non-infected ran to escape their execution. Then, abruptly, the guns of the ICVs fell silent, allowing the undead to breach the inner security fencing. FOB MEDCOM was now being overrun from inside and out. In the pandemonium and confusion Katie escaped, fleeing to the only safe place she knew, back to Tracks.

There were two entrances to Tracks Raw Bar & Grill. The main entrance was located on the LIRR level of Penn Station adjacent to the LIRR ticket windows. The other was on the same level but was adjacent to a less trafficked exit of the NYC Transit Broadway/7th Avenue

Line. She knew both entrances well, but thought if she could get to the back entrance, she could lose anyone that may follow her in the maze of passages.

Katie heard the rapid patterns of machine gun fire all around. Bullets spattered into a column next to her, shattering the tiling, fragments exploding into the air. A piece, catching her in the cheek as she ran past, initiated a small trickle of blood. She did not pause; she knew her life could end if she did. She ran east toward the 7th Avenue/West 32nd Street exit. She had intended to make her escape using the underground passages that would lead her to a set of stairs into the Hilton Passageway and to the rear entrance of the restaurant. But as she approached it was blocked with a wooden barricade. She barely paused as she searched the structure looking for any weakness, but there was none. She turned to another entrance that was across the hall and directly behind her, but it too was blocked. She quickly scanned the large entranceway. There was a board that appeared to be partially loosened at the bottom right corner of where the stairway had been located. This was the entrance to the lower level that brought you to the intersecting corridor of the lower main concourse, the one that held the LIRR Waiting Room for Tracks 13–21. She pulled the wood away easily from its frame and the concrete wall it had been nailed to. There wasn't much room, but she squeezed herself into the opening. The stairway had been filled with porter's carts. They had been haphazardly tossed down the stairs to fill the well. She struggled to pull herself in, and was almost clear when someone or something grabbed onto her foot. Its grip was tight and it began to pull her backward. She struggled to hold onto a cart, pulling herself forward. She wriggled her foot, trying to maneuver it so that whoever was pulling would pull the shoe free. Suddenly she felt her body lunge slightly forward. It worked. She quickly pulled her leg in. It was barely enough. She felt frantic hands grasping at her, lightly touching her foot. She wormed headfirst down the stairs between the carts beyond the reach of those who had tried to pull her out. She hadn't gone far when she realized that if she reached the bottom headfirst, she might not be able to free the boards that surely blocked her exit. But it was too late; she couldn't go back. There was only forward.

The well was dark and difficult to navigate. Though it had been only minutes it had felt longer as she weaved her way up, over, down, and around the obstacles before her. She no longer heard machine gun fire or the screams of the dying. She heard only an occasional noise at the top of the stairs, but nothing tried to come for her. It took her an hour of contortion-like manipulation to reach the bottom of the stairs. As she slipped through the last cart she slid into a hollow space. When the military had thrown the carts down the stairs they had not aligned properly to completely fill in the bottom. Though the space was tiny Katie had enough room to turn herself around. She was happy that she had chosen dancing as a profession. Her tall muscular build with her thin stature and agile flexibility had saved her life.

The boards had kicked away easier than she had anticipated. However, the prospect of crawling along the floor in the dark to her place of sanctuary frightened her. As the wood panel fell away a low luminescence lit the darkness. She crawled from the hole to find that the emergency lighting of the LIRR concourse was still operating.

She had not been able to roll down the security gate when the Army had escorted her and Theresa away. *Theresa!* In all the confusion and her flight for survival she had nearly forgotten about Theresa. She and her co-worker had been taken together into The Garden, but Theresa had become sick and the soldiers took her, even after pleading with the men to let them stay together. She knew her colleague was dead now. Only she was left, and she was determined to live.

The front doors were locked; she had been able to deadbolt them before she and Theresa had been hurried along, and she had taken the keys with her. She opened the wooden doors. Her familiar place was dark but comforting. She unlocked the large silver locks that hung on the side tracking and removed them. She rolled down the gate and locked herself inside.

The eerie light from the corridor filtered through the slats of the gating, casting a checkered pattern on the floor, lighting the entry way in a pale glow. She did not feel truly safe. There were things that needed to be done to help secure her immediate future. She headed toward the back of the restaurant.

When the news had broken about the pandemic that was sweeping across the city most of the employees fled for home. Katie and Theresa did the same. Except the subway system was in chaos. The platforms were packed with panicked riders, who were pushing, shoving, and fighting one another, all trying to get into overcrowded subway cars. Katie and Theresa had no choice but to return to Tracks. As Patrick the general manager departed, concerned over his family, he had given Katie the keys and told the two to lock themselves inside. The two women secured the rear entrance by locking the fully tempered heavy glass door and stacking bar stools and a stainless-steel table in front of it. They had also closed the blinds to the windows that allowed a view to the Hilton Passageway. Though they had rolled down the main entrance gate and locked it, they had not closed the inner doors. If rescue were to come they knew they needed to be visible; if they closed the doors there were only a few panes of glass to allow someone from the outside to look in. They had waited several hours before the Army came and took all the people who remained in the lower levels of Penn Station to safety.

Katie had no idea how long she would have to stay underground and hidden away. Do the living dead die? They did if they were the type of zombies that were from the film *28 Weeks Later*. What if they weren't that kind of zombies? What if they were the other kind that would only die if you shot them in the head?

She took stock of what provisions she had. She knew she had enough food for about three months. There were plenty of beverages, too. The water was still running, so she would be able to wash and use the bathroom. She surmised there was enough toilet paper to last for a couple of months. Nonetheless, she knew that all she needed was not within the comforting confines of the restaurant. There were a limited number of votive candles for illumination, and there were only two flashlights with apparently no spare batteries that she could find anywhere. This would be a problem. The thought of having to spend countless days, weeks, perhaps months in total isolation without the luxury of lighting would be unbearable. She also needed something to sleep on, a new pair of shoes—the pair of men's New Balance sneakers she had found in the manager's office were too big for her—and some Tampons. She knew where to find all of the items, and that was at Kmart.

Down the corridor to the left, past TGI Fridays, past the Haagen-Dazs ice cream shop, and past Dunkin Donuts was Kmart. However, when she arrived she found that the security gate had been drawn and secured with two large, heavy-duty locks, one on each side of the gate rail. She knew where the batteries were—they were to the right as you crossed through the entrance hall into the main area of the store—close to the checkout registers. They were far out of reach with no way to remove the locks, and she knew she wasn't going to prowl around the underground of Penn Station looking for a LIRR maintenance room in search of a pair of bolt cutters. She rattled the gate out of frustration, and then realized that might have been a mistake. The entrance she stood before was actually the basement level to the store. The main entrance was one level up and a street over on the south side of 34$^{th}$ Street; the underground floor was actually larger than its ground level. The noise she had made could attract whatever may be lurking in the upper parts of the store. She paused to listen, and watched for sights of anything prowling in the murky light. After a moment, she was mostly satisfied that she hadn't roused anything's attention. She went to the other gate to the left, which was at the smaller entranceway to the left of a large display window. She surveyed the gate. This one had no locks on the two side rails. She looked down at the floor. She stared momentarily in disbelief. The floor lock had not been secured. She knelt down, thinking her eyes had played a trick on her in the low illumination, but it was true, the high security padlock had not been secured into the wide, hardened solid steel body.

She cautiously raised the grill style gate up into its recess. Though the gate had been left unlocked there was still the matter of the sliding plate glass doors that barred her entrance. On the very top of the archway was a three-position switch that read: Open, Close and Off. The indicator knob was pointing to 'Open', but the doors were sealed.

She tried to open them by squeezing her fingers in between the lips of where the doors met and pulling them back, but there wasn't enough room to get a grip. She needed to be able to slip something into the crack and pry it open enough in order to pull them apart, and then it occurred to her—the large, heavy gauge kitchen knife she had brought. With some finagling the door opened. She slipped in and proceeded to the checkout area to acquire a shopping cart and to stockpile needed batteries. She grabbed a few snacks too, the usual "junk food" you always find near the checkout registers.

She pushed her cart down the main corridor heading north to the personal care section. After stocking up on soap, shampoo, and feminine hygiene products, she made her way toward the sporting goods area. Sporting goods was further into the low-lit recesses of the store and would bring her closer to the escalator that led to the main level. Though going to the bedding area upstairs to get a pillow and blankets would have been optimal, it was also the most dangerous thing she could do. If there weren't creatures roaming around upstairs already looking for a meal, the sight of her through all the glass windows that made up the building's exterior would certainly be an invitation for a dinner. It was dangerous enough doing what she was doing by entering into an unknown and potentially life-threatening situation, and she was not about to tempt fate by purposely putting her life at risk all for the sake of comfort. The sporting goods section was close enough to the tampons that she could quickly grab a sleeping bag or two and get out and back to the relative safety of the bar.

Luck, for the moment, was on her side. There were more batteries on the end cap of the aisle as well as flashlights and portable lanterns on display in the middle of the aisle opposite the sleeping bags. She loaded up, and then turned her cart to leave when she was abruptly confronted by what appeared to be a homeless man blocking the exit into the main corridor.

"Where you going with *my* stuff? It's mine, do you hear? It's mine. Put it back, bitch!"

The man was filthy and smelled of piss and foul body odor. He came at her. First grabbing the cart and pushing it back into Katie's hips, and then trying to push the cart out of the way to get at her. Katie raised the knife up that she held between her hand and the handle of the shopping cart. As the man reached out to grab her she swiped at him, partially severing several of his fingers. He let out a blood-curdling scream of agony. She didn't wait, she pulled the cart back enough that he was now directly in front of it, and then slammed it with all her strength head on into him, sending him crashing to the ground.

She ran as fast as she could, propelling the cart toward the exit. She could hear him cursing her with "cunt" and swearing he was going to find her and kill her. For her own safety and peace of mind she closed the security gate behind her and locked him in. She couldn't take a chance at him fulfilling his threat or the living dead being alerted to the commotion. It was safer this way. It was a matter of *her* survival.

# 26

# A HALF-MUTE NEVER FORGETS

*JANUARY 11, DAY 278.*

The return of his Luci had helped to relieve his anguish and satisfy his carnal trans-human needs, but the New Year had brought tragedy, and Luci had been savagely murdered. So this day he left the responsibilities of the armory and child care behind to seek respite from his stress and torment. Reflecting on the words of Buddha, "Do not dwell in the past, do not dream of the future, concentrate the mind on the present moment," he decided to teach martial arts to anyone who had a desire to learn. It was for this reason that he found himself traveling south, not by foot as he so usually did—and not under the cover of darkness —but in an "Up Armored" Humvee early in the morning with Barkley by his side.

Today was Barkley's first road trip since arrival to the armory. For a long time, J.D. kept the retriever locked in the basement before he felt comfortable taking him on walks outside the armory gates. J.D. didn't like to keep Barkley confined, although the basement was extremely large, but whereas his former canine Max—named for Max von Stephanitz the creator of the German Shepherd breed—was intelligent, affectionate and social, Barkley was particular about who he would allow near him. He was very well behaved and affectionate when it came to Katie and Caitlin, but ornery when it came to any male who tried to touch him, with the exception of J.D. This led J.D. to believe his previous owner had been a female. Barkley had also been easy to train, enforcing J.D.'s assumption that Barkley had been an AKC show dog. It was safer to keep him away from the populace until J.D. was sure he could be fully reintroduced into life with humans.

Barkley's mild anti-social behavior was acceptable to J.D. After all, if the animal was going to be a part of the armory community he needed to earn his keep, and house pet was not what J.D. had planned for him. J.D. was training Barkley to be a patrol dog. Barkley learned quickly and was an obedient canine, except when it came to attack mode. J.D. knew this was because the dog did not have an aggressive nature like German and Dutch shepherds or Belgian Malinois that were the vast majority of U.S. military working dogs. Except one day as the two were on foot patrol a few blocks from the armory, Barkley showed his true potential. He caught the scent of two half-mutes a moment before J.D. had realized their presence. Barkley went into full attack mode, trying to pull the leash from J.D.'s hand to go after the two predators. The sound of Barkley's furious barking along with a screech from J.D. sent the two stalkers fleeing. Barkley had proved himself as a useful animal.

It should have been a quick ride to his destination, but the city's decaying infrastructure caused a re-routing due to a massive flood on Chrystie Street a few hundred feet before the intersection of Grand. The body of water was immense and encompassed blocks east and west, as well as those ahead of him. J.D. knew Chinatown almost as well as he knew his own East Village. There were other ways to his objectives.

His first stop had been to the Lin Sister Herb Shop—not owned by one sister, but by Frank Lin and his sisters, Susan and Jane—on Bowery and Doyers Streets. He had broken into the store to acquire some herbs—specifically Yunnan Baiyoa—teas, ointments, Dit Da Jow, and, of great importance, acupuncture needles. He was happy to see that the rats, mice, and other vermin had not managed to find their way into the large cut glass apothecary dispensary jars and eaten the over 500 herbal remedies they sold.

Arriving on Mulberry Street, he pulled the Humvee in front of BLT Merchandise. BLT (letters which stand for the words "good fortune" in Cantonese) was a shop J.D. knew well. This had been the martial arts supply store from where he had purchased most of his martial arts gear, including his zai.

Over the years of patronage J.D. had befriended owner Jonathan Choy and his family, who helped run the shop. He also knew that most of what was in the shop display cases and mounted on the wall was for tourists. Most of what he had come for was on the shelves in the confines of the storage room. He had come for uniforms, footwear, equipment, and weapons.

The shop consisted of a small, narrow showroom, a small studio—where Choy taught children "black tiger" kung fu once a week—accessed at the back of the store along with a storage area. The store-front exterior consisted of two glass windows with an accompanying single commercial glass door separating them. The store entry was secured; its metal roll down gate was secured closed with a padlock on each side of its vertical runners. Nonetheless, J.D. had come prepared. He had brought bolt cutters.

He stepped out of the vehicle, taking with him the bolt cutters from in between the two front seats. "Stay," he told Barkley, in a firm tone and then closed the driver's door.

With two quick snips from the cutters, the heavy-duty security locks fell to the ground. J.D. took the looped length of chain and began to pull downward to get the vertical-lift-gate operator to retract the roll door. The noise was tremendous, unlike the gate of the Lin Sister's shop. He stopped his hurried action, paused, and momentarily waited, looking up and down the street. Barkley stared at him from the open passenger window. Nothing came running toward him. He saw no half-mutes bounding toward him, but J.D. knew this didn't mean there wasn't the possibility of them. "Anything can happen at any time, and probably will," was one of his philosophies. Caution was the word of the moment. He slowed his chain action, but the noise still reverberated down the street.

The glass door was also locked. However, J.D. had a solution for this, too. Again he used the bolt cutters, slamming the head of the tool into the glass nearest the lock mechanism. The glass shattered and fell away. He reached inside and unlocked the deadbolt. Entering, he walked past the display cases and to the back of the shop, and opened the unlocked door to the studio.

J.D. retracted a six-inch Cyalume ChemLight stick from the left leg pant pocket of his military pants, bent the plastic light stick, breaking the small thin-walled glass ampoule contained inside, and shook it, mixing its liquids. The chemiluminescence was immediate. He headed to the storage room. He didn't need the glow stick. It was more out of habit than necessity. After his blind rage of savagery against those who butchered Luci, he hadn't noticed that his eyesight had gained more night vision, only that in the days that followed they were painful. It wasn't until Doctor France's examination and testing that he realized he had better perception in the dark; however, his irises had also gotten marginally larger.

The last items J.D. brought out from the back were two small boxes. He placed them next to the retrieved goods on top of the glass display case closest to the entry door for a clearer examination. The boxes were marked, 'BRITISH GURKHA ARMY KUKURI KNIFE - Service No. 1, Kathmandu, Nepal.' He knew BLT sold many styles of martial arts weapons, but he had never seen any kukri in the shop. The two boxes were the only two that he had found, and he wondered if it had been a special order that had not been picked up. He opened one of them and removed the knife that was wrapped in high quality hand-made lokta paper.

The kukri blade was similar to the bolo machetes he had once carried. Both armaments were used by foreign country soldiers for warfare and by civilians as a woodcutting and general-purpose tool. However, the blade of the kukri, compared to a bolo, had a distinctive forward drop intended to act as a weight on the end of the blade and make the knife fall on the enemy faster and with more power. As for attacking, like his machetes, the kukri was most effective as a chopping/slashing weapon.

He removed the knife from its cotton wood scabbard that was covered in water buffalo leather. The weapon he held in his hand was genuine military issue, with a full tang, razor sharp high-grade ten-inch carbon steel blade with kaura notch, and a five-inch water buffalo horn handle with solid brass butt—identical to those used by the Gurkha of Singapore, India, Nepal and British Gurkha Regiments. The two kukri could be a replacement for his bolo machetes. However, he would need to combat test them before making a decision.

Abruptly, Barkley began a vocal tirade that was loud enough to reach the interior of the store. He took the two blades with him and dashed to the door.

J.D. knew better than to ignore a barking Barkley, and upon investigation he found that the canine was under attack by two very agitated half-mutes, who seemed to be particularly interested in getting into the vehicle to make Barkley their meal.

Barkley appeared to have the upper hand, almost literally. The dog had latched on to one of the creature's hands and was pulling ferociously as the creature was attempting to pull away. The predators were too consumed by their desire to get at Barkley that they did not see J.D. cross the shop's threshold or hear the noise of the broken glass under his feet as he made his way carefully to the street, unsheathing the kukri as he stepped onto the sidewalk.

It would have been quicker to dispatch these wretched once-humans with his sidearm, but pistols make noise and there had already been enough noise, and J.D. did not want to attract anymore of the creatures.

"Hey! Tweedle-dee and Tweedle-*dumb*. Come get some," he taunted, knowing that his acerbic words were not something they could comprehend. Nevertheless, his voice got their attention.

They charged, as they always did, blindly and furiously. A quick sidestep and a fierce slashing motion to the back of a neck, and the head of one lopped off and fell to the ground. The other turned quickly, reaching out inches from him. J.D. had no time to pivot, to make a proper defensive move, so he thrust the blades forward, and though the blades were not designed for stabbing, the blades still penetrated deeply into the creature's abdomen. The half-mute stopped, the look of rage leaving its eyes, replaced by astonishment, then blankness. It was dead.

J.D. retracted the weapons. A horrid cry broke the silence. J.D. quickly turned his head around. Abruptly a half-mute pounced on him from above, like it had fallen out of a void.

J.D.'s weapons tore from his hands as he and his enemy violently crashed to the ground, and then tumbled across the sidewalk toward the Humvee. Barkley barked furiously for a moment and then jumped out the open window.

Shrieking and tearing like two adversarial felines, it was a full on, a claws-out death match with both predators locked together, rolling around making horrible noises, as Barkley tried to come to J.D.'s rescue. J.D. tried desperately to grasp the grip of his pistol that was strapped to his right side, but the flailing claws of the half-mute ripped at him, preventing him from moving his arms too far away from protecting his face.

Suddenly J.D. was free. The half-mute had released him to turn on Barkley. The dog let out a squeal as it was knocked to the ground with his fur flying. J.D. let out a horrid screech and then drove the fingers of his right hand into the throat of the mutant as it turned back to him.

The half-mute paused shocked by the piercing of its larynx. Then it flailed, feverishly grasping at J.D.'s hand, which was still impaled in its throat. The creature gurgled, blood spilling from its mouth. Its cold eyes went dead and its body went limp. J.D. extracted his talons and threw the dead creature aside.

Barkley had not been down for long. He stood above the creature as he intently growled at the corpse. For a moment, J.D. hunched over shaking as he took in deep breaths. Then regaining his composure, he stood up and commanded Barkley to sit and be silent. J.D. picked up his weapons, and then began a thorough examination of the dog. The canine had not been seriously injured. Besides the missing fur the cuts he had received had barely penetrated the skin. It was most likely the yelp and tumble had been a glancing blow instead of a full-on talon swipe. J.D. rewarded Barkley's courage with his favorite tug toy. Barkley shook it vigorously in his mouth as J.D. kept guard.

As J.D. slid into the driver's seat, he looked at Barkley. Barkley looked at him, and then the dog whimpered. "That was too much work so early in the morning," J.D. told him, and then rubbed the animal behind the ears. He extracted a rag from underneath his seat and began to clean his blades. "We'll stay here for a few more minutes," he told the canine, "until you settle so I clean your wounds."

J.D. was still slightly shaking as he wiped his blades clean. He realized that it was more than nerves that was causing his trembling; his body needed nutrition. His post-viral transformation had caused a higher metabolism rate that demanded greater sustenance, especially after exerting himself in battle. He opened his backpack and took out a 24-ounce bottle of Gatorade carbohydrate energy drink and a plastic pouch of beef jerky.

He breathed deeply, trying to relax himself. He knew the kind of anxiety he had just experienced had previously brought on morphological change. His transmute genomes were already drifting in that direction and he feared that eventually he would change completely. This time though, there had been no headaches, no pain, and no burning in any of his extremities. He looked at his hands; still just talons and no other physical change. He put them to his face, slowly running them over his features, studying his facial appearance, as a blind person would often do to elicit an image of a person. Everything felt normal. He was relieved.

As he shared his meal with his companion, he came to the conclusion that it would have been wiser to have returned to his vehicle and waited to be sure the noise he had made opening the shop had not attracted any attention. There was no place in this world for bravado or stupidity. He had been foolish and had been in a hurry and not heeded his own words of, 'Anything can happen at any time, and probably will.' Then it happened again.

Barkley growled deeply. Something had alarmed him and J.D. was certain he knew what it was. A loud thud upon the roof, as if something had coming crashing down upon it. He instinctively grabbed his bladed weapons. Then a figure jumped from the roof onto the hood and peered in with a menacing look as it pressed a hand against the windshield. J.D. saw the half-mute's missing left finger. It was Four Fingers again. This time Four Fingers did something odd, he held up a necklace, dangling it so J.D. could get a clear look at it. Then Four Fingers pointed an index finger and let out a ghastly, angry cry as he looked at J.D. It leapt back up onto the roof and then was gone. This half-mute had certainly some weird obsession with him and it was eerie. J.D had no idea why the creature had held up a piece of jewelry. He pondered the encounter for a moment and then looked to the knives that he still held. With no desire to pick up another pair of bolo machetes, he would embrace the kukri. The blades suited him well. With a minor handle modification and practice he could become equally as proficient with the new weapons as he had been with his bolos.

Crimson-stained and wet from Luci's blood on that fateful night, he could not bear to retrieve his machetes. The weapon he mainly used to smite his enemies had been turned against him and used on his mate. Though using his bolos as a tool of revenge would have been sweet, the bitterness of how they had been used had traumatized him so deeply that the attempt to pick up the blades that Stone's men discarded induced uncontrollable trembling. For a moment, his mind wandered back to that night.

———————

Two of his men had died that night too, and his communications sergeant had disappeared. Sergeant Schumacher's intuition had been right. This was the third time he and his team had been attacked.

This could not be coincidence. Was it possible that Stone had infiltrated the armory with a spy? J.D. had once caught one man from Stone's horde hiding amongst the shadows of long unused buildings, watching the comings and goings of he and his men. That ended badly for the spy. That was also the night he found a small radio, but he had unwittingly stepped on it and broken it.

Even with their screening process in place it was not possible to do background searches, not in the post-apocalyptic, non-electronic communication, dystopian world. It was more than possible, J.D. thought, that there was someone on the inside.

His suspicion grew toward Sergeant Peter Shumacher, for he had miraculously escaped that night and returned to the armory unscathed. J.D.'s suspicions were further reinforced by a note Stone had written and attached to the severed head of Frasier Dunphy, who had been killed at the time of Luci's death. The note had been penned on white cloth in blood—the blood of the victim.

J.D. knew the message was for him. Though the note was unsigned, the signature was clear.

'Peter Peter pumpkin eater

Had a child but couldn't save it.

Peter learned to talk and tell.

In hopes of sending another to hell.' "

Stone was taunting him again.

His right hand trembled for a moment as a flashback of that horrid night filled his thoughts.

He had been caught off guard and shot with something. It should not have happened, but he had been distracted. Projectile vomiting can do that to you.

Beaten, weak and unable to break from the men who held him, Barlow and his men forced him to watch his woman's brutal murder. The grisly sight brought on overwhelming anguish that triggered his mutation. Like the comic character Dr. Bruce Banner changing into The Hulk, an acute metamorphosis began. Except unlike the transformation of the withdrawn and reserved physicist into the humongous, angry, green fictional superhero, J.D. only became uber-strong.

He heard himself roar with anger and anguish, and did not try to choke back the cry before he lost control of it. His sudden, violent outburst shook his enemies, seizing them with panic and fear. The rage had built so immensely from within that it exploded in a fury unlike it had ever done before.

Adrenalin-fed, virus-laden blood pumped into every muscle, every tendon, and every ligament, fueling his rage. He was not himself. He possessed more strength than any transmute and as much fury as a half-mute. He was savage and relentless in his attack against his tormentors, though it was an act that he could not recall.

When his gory, hateful rampage was over, the blood of his enemies was splattered across his clothes and face like a Hermann Nitsch abstract painting, while flesh from his enemies' throats and stomachs, skewered upon razored hands, adorned his talons like cubes of meat that make up a shish kabob. Then he collapsed, unconscious. The transformation had exhausted him and altered his physical being again —a change he wouldn't immediately realize.

# PART II

---

# THE DAMNED

"For each his revenge, will he forfeit his soul…"
— L.A. Starkey

# 1

## EXPOSITION

*JANUARY 23, DAY 290.*

Exposition.
Just filler.
A time waster.

The *really* boring part, J.D. thought to himself as he prepared to enter the conference room. It was the weekly staff meeting. J.D. hated these endless meetings listening to status reports, but as leader of the survivor group, he had to attend, though he believed his time would have been better spent hunting his enemies or scavenging for supplies.

*Paper work sucks*, he thought to himself, as he drew a breath, gripping the doorknob.

He opened the door and entered.

"Morning, gentlemen," he addressed James and Ryan, trying, but failing miserably, at a cheerful smile. He immediately noted that several personnel were missing and that there were two crude looking pedal devices sitting on the table. However, before he could address the matters, Ryan and James had stood at attention and saluted him, as they did every meeting. J.D. hated it.

"Ryan. James," he addressed them. "I asked you two not to salute me when we're in this room. Do I need to make that an order?"

"No, sir," they both replied simultaneously, and then sat after J.D. took his chair.

"Okay, am I early or are the other four late?" J.D. asked.

"They'll be here in a half hour after we discuss the promotion requests," Ryan said.

"Very well," J.D. acknowledged, and then turned his attention to the two mechanical devices sitting on the table. "So those are the pedal extensions, I assume?"

"Completed as requested, sir." James spoke up.

J.D. asked, "Has Peter seen them?"

"No, sir," James replied. "I thought you'd like to see them first."

J.D. picked one up one of them and examined it. "Panton did a fine job," he commented. "I think Chief Dunne will be pleased."

"It was actually a collaborative project of both Private Panton and Finlay Mackay," Ryan enlightened his commander.

"Well, let them both know they did a great job. So now, who's going to bore me first?" he asked, as he set the device down.

Ryan and James looked at one another.

"Never mind. I'll start," he announced. "The promotion requests. Make Wiese a master sergeant; bump up Dunne to... warrant officer two. Make Lott a SFC, Panton a corporal or specialist and McGann a staff sergeant," he told the two, with little concern.

James disagreed with his command decision. "With all due respect, sir, I don't recommend that."

"Which one and why not?"

"Dissension, sir," James informed him. "You're giving non-military personnel substantial promotions over trained military. Lott is currently a sergeant. If you don't do right by him we risk losing him. Don't forget he's here because he wants to be not because he has to be. Show him the courtesy and respect he deserves. That's why Ryan and I gave you the recommendation report for personnel promotions."

"Now I have issue with some of what you just said," J.D. rebutted. "I have always respected and appreciated the contributions Lott has given toward our survival—as I do all of you. But this isn't the military, and I never meant for our governing committee to be a military unit."

"Well, you're wrong," Ryan disagreed. "You started this military unit when James agreed to recognize you as leader and you began using rank to recognize our stations on the hierarchy of base leadership. You subsequently continued that trend with Lott, Wiese, Dunne, Panton, and every man and woman who has been sent out into the field to hunt down Stone or scavenge for supplies. And let's not forget that we operate our refuge as if it were still the 69th Regiment Armory and you even call us the 69th Infantry. With all due respect, *sir*. This is a real military unit and you are the only one that doesn't seem to realize that fact."

There was no arguing with Ryan's point of view, because he was right. Now J.D. had no choice but to own up to what he had started and recognize the governing body for what it truly was—the military.

"You're right, Ryan. You're both right. I started out—*we* started out to save people and give them a sense of community and safety, and in order to do that we had to put ourselves in an authoritative position to maintain order and discipline to achieve that goal. What we've created here is a military base and whether I like it or not, we are soldiers. Your words Ryan have made me realize that today. So, I will accept your recommendations and sign off on them, but I do have two issues with the promotion list."

"And what would that be, sir?" James asked.

"Neither of you are on it," J.D. replied. "So as the commander, I hereby promote you James to captain and you Ryan to first lieutenant. And I think I deserve to be brigadier general."

James and Ryan weren't sure if their commander was making a joke. J.D. of late had seemed to have lost his sense of humor.

"Just kidding—about your promotions." J.D. smiled, slyly, in jest.

---

Peter Dunne's supply report, read aloud by J.D., was the first of several reports that were concerning. Food stocks were getting low and sundry items like toilet paper were nearly depleted. This meant Dunne's scavenging team would have to journey farther north to search for supplies. Panton's facility repair report had also been disturbing. The armory's infrastructure was a mess, especially the plumbing. Although, Lott's vehicle repair report was satisfactory, he had also reported that fuel for the generator was near critical.

"Are you kidding me?" J.D. interrupted Paul Wiese, who was attempting to conclude his recruitment section of his personnel report. "*Peter* Dunphy?"

"Yes, sir. Peter and Frasier Dunphy. They're brothers."

"Yeah, I got that part. But *Peter*. Another Peter? *What?* Is this like the most common post-apocalyptic name? That's like—five now! All these damn Peters and you wonder why I'm always confused... I'm sorry, finish," he said, as he rubbed one hand to his face.

"They are both able bodied men and have passed Doctor France's physical exam," Paul continued. "They, too, await your approval for enlistment."

Refugees in January were no surprise to J.D. He knew that there would be people who would try and hold onto the past as long as possible, people who were desperately clinging to hope, praying and waiting for the world they once knew to be restored to some sort of normality. Except that way of life would never return, and those last desperate survivors who clung to the past were coming to the realization that the world of old was dead.

Strangely, most survivors didn't truly understand how lucky they were that the world ended so abruptly. If the pandemic had been prolonged, it would have caused worldwide civil unrest and famine. Dwindling resources such as food, medicine, and fuel would have set neighbor against neighbor and country against country in a battle of global survival. The quick zombification of the world didn't give much time for people to loot or kill thy neighbor or prey upon the weak. Although there had been a time when radiation from the Indian Point Power Station had drifted over the city, the window of exposure had been brief and only a few survivors that had come to the armory had signs of radiation sickness.

The City of New York was still a dangerous place. There were marauders, half-mutes, and transmutes. Diseases, such as cholera and dysentery, in post-apocalyptic Manhattan—at least in the armory—was not too much of a concern. Water was not an issue either. The city's vast underground network of delivery pipes were sloped at an angle from its upstate source which gives enough natural pressure to reach a fifth-floor apartment without the need of added artificial pressure. As long as there was pressure from the street you could flush the toilet and wash yourself. The downside was the dwindling fuel supply and the armory needed a lot, for the furnaces to generate heat and for the generators to provide electricity.

"It doesn't surprise me that we're still getting refugees, even this late in the season," J.D. commented. "Though I would have thought that most people would have fled the city for warmer climate or sought us out sooner. But I'm grateful. We could use the manpower. So, tag their files and I'll review them tonight. Ryan, you're next."

"I have one report of a petty theft that turned out to be just a lost item that was recovered. However, we have had two physical altercations this week, one resulting in substantial bodily injury. Doctor France treated the man and released him… Things are a little tense seeing that no one is allowed outside. Cabin fever."

"Understandable. Issue a memorandum to the effect that fighting no matter how incidental will not and cannot be tolerated. Anyone who is involved with physical violence will spend three days in lockup. And then figure out some outlet for their aggression. Add another movie night. Or if they want to kick the crap out of one another then start some amateur boxing night, and let them beat one another in a civilized manner. Understood?"

Ryan continued. "Suggestion, Colonel. Instead of adding a movie night or beat on each other night, how about a live music night?"

"Sure, Ryan, if you think that singing *Altar Boyz* and *Shrek* songs will calm the populous. Be my guest."

In the pre-apocalypse, Ryan had been an actor both of stage and screen, and J.D. was commenting on the two musicals he knew Ryan had preformed in.

"I was thinking more on the lines of a piano vocalist."

"Between training new recruits and civilians," J.D. spoke as he began to count with his fingers, "training with you, James, Peter, Katie, and constantly in staff meetings... I realize we've lost our arts and culture. And I respect that you desire to give them a sense of community and happiness through music. Except I don't have the time."

"With all due respect," Ryan replied, "I wasn't talking about you. Though I would need the use of your keyboard setup for the show."

Believing Ryan was asking him to preform again, J.D. was startled at the revelation that Ryan was referring to someone else. "Oh," J.D. remarked with surprise. "I wasn't aware of anyone else who could play piano."

"Her name is Christina Custode. Paul gave you her file to review several weeks ago. Did you not see it?" Ryan asked.

In fact, J.D. had not read her file. J.D. rarely read any file right away that had not been red tagged by Paul. Files with a red tag indicated a survivor with needed skills and was discussed in the weekly staff meeting, and then thoroughly reviewed later that day by J.D. for approval. However, those without red tags seemed to be read several weeks after Paul submitted them, and only skimmed over. J.D. never made a duty assignment for that was Paul Wiese's job, so he didn't feel the need to review the non-tagged files with any urgency.

J.D. did not acknowledge Ryan's question. The name Christina Custode struck a sour note with him. There had been an incident in J.D.'s past that had got him banned from performing at his favorite piano bar, and it had involved someone he had believed was part of another performer's party. That was of an up and coming piano playing songstress named Christina Custode. However, J.D. could not fathom how it could be the same songstress. She had been from Buffalo, NY.

"I'm sorry, did you say *Christina Custode?*" J.D. asked.

"I did," Ryan replied. "Why? Have you heard of her?"

"No, not possible. If it's the Christina Custode I'm thinking of—it can't be her. She's like from Buffalo. Is she?" J.D. asked, looking to Paul for an answer.

"I'm sorry, I don't have that information," Paul returned. "That isn't part of the information I collect, and it didn't come up in the interview. But if you'd like to find out, she's assigned to sanitary detachment, civilian bathroom detail."

Though J.D. believed the odds were against it being the same person, he still needed to know, but that would have to wait. There was another matter that needed more immediate attention, and that was of a staff member who was once again not present.

"Now," he said, in an annoyed tone. "I see Doctor France is absent once again. Anyone know where the quack is? This is the third meeting he's not attended."

James spoke up. "Unavailable, so he told me earlier."

J.D. addressed James as he aggressively tapped a talon on the conference table, "You know what? Cancel my subscription, cause I'm sick and tired of his issues. If he doesn't show up next meeting," J.D. informed his subordinate, "have him arrested and put in detention for a night. See how agreeable—No!" J.D. burst out in an angered tone, interrupting his sentence, as he slammed a fist to the table. His men were shocked by the outburst. "Strike that order," he counter-commanded. "It's about time I dealt with the pretentious son-of-a-bitch myself," he announced, clearly agitated. As quickly as J.D.'s anger arose it vanished. No one at the table thought too much of their commander's odd behavior. They all knew J.D. was under a lot of pressure as their leader and that the relationship he had with the doctor was for the most part adversarial.

"Peter," J.D. addressed. "I have read the report you submitted yesterday in regard to heating oil, and I concur. Work with John on securing the fuel we need for the vehicles, generator and the boiler, and make sure you do a full recon before taking the tanker out. No civilians on the team and no mention of the destination. I don't know if it was bad luck or if Stone has someone in our midst again feeding him information, but the skirmish last week nearly got two of us dead, and that is unacceptable. Understood?" John vocalized his acknowledgement as

Peter nodded his understanding. "On a personal note for Peter. I think I have an hour free after dinner if you have time to put down some more ink."

The small man shook his head yes. Peter was eager to continue his artistic endeavor upon his living canvas. In his twenty-plus years as a tattoo artist, he had done very few tattoos as large as the one he was inking upon J.D.'s chest. Performing his profession also gave him peace and tranquility, and helped ease his mind of thoughts of his stolen daughter.

"John. In regard to your request," J.D. said.

"Yes, sir," Sergeant First Class Lott answered.

"First, let me congratulate you on the fine job on acquiring the LAVs and buses. As for the request, I cannot authorize it at this time, since we do not have the fuel to spare. However, since you and Peter will be searching for said fuel, please use that opportunity to also recon for your steel plates. I'm sure you'll come across some street excavation site that never got finished. Notate it and once the fuel has been acquired, I'll authorize a salvage mission." John wanted the plating to use as armor for the buses stored at their secret storage facility. "If that is all, then we are dismissed." J.D. announced, glad to be done with one more painful meeting. It was time to seek out a songbird.

## 2

# PIANO GIRL

IT WASN'T GOING TO BE HER. IT COULDN'T BE, J.D. KEPT TELLING himself as he passed through the main hall and headed down the stairs to the basement where the public restrooms were located, first checking the women's before the men's. He couldn't see her face at first as he watched her diligently using a long-handled scrub brush on the inside of one of the tall urinals that lined the wall, until she turned slightly toward him. The shapely figured brunette with the unkempt hair and facial perspiration caught the man with the sunglasses hovering under the entry's archway out of the corner of her eye as soon as she had moved to the next urinal.

"If it's urgent I can stop," she informed him, as she squirted some liquid into the next porcelain trough, though she was almost certain he hadn't come to use the bathroom. In the time she had been on toilet duty she had never seen an officer use the civilian facilities.

J.D. remained silent.

She turned and looked at him, hoping direct eye contact would evoke a response. It did not. "Suit yourself," she said, and then started her cleaning again.

J.D. hadn't responded because he was dumbfounded. It just wasn't possible that the woman scrubbing the latrine could be the same person that he had met at Rockwood Music Hall on the evening that he knocked out who he believed may have been her boyfriend for making a very rude remark about his singing. Though J.D. could have forgiven the slightly inebriated male for his asinine comment, J.D. could not forgive him for the slap on the back that accompanied the statement. J.D. had knocked the jackass to the floor unconscious, and then was banned by management from ever performing there again. Nevertheless, there she was, a little older, a bit ruffled and dirtied, holding a toilet scrubber, but unmistakably the songstress from the piano bar.

Christina turned back to him. She had enough of the man's ogling from behind sunglasses. "Are you one of those sick dudes who gets off hanging out at the playground leering at underage children or just one of those creepy toilet fetish voyeurs?" she asked in an irritated tone without any sign of being intimidated. "Because if you don't back your ass up out of here, I'm going to scream like a banshee."

J.D. removed his sunglasses before he spoke. "Christina Custode? You are Christina Custode the singer from Buffalo, NY?"

"Niagara Falls," she quickly corrected.

"So it is you." He stepped closer to introduce himself. "My name is J.D. Nichols, I'm—"

Christina didn't need him to tell her who he was; she was fully aware of who was standing opposite her, even before she saw the tell-tale signs of his talons and his creepy black eyes.

"I know who you are," she told him, interrupting. "What is it I can do for you, Commander?"

"Do you remember doing a gig at the Rockwood Music Hall some years back, when the performer before you knocked out this drunk guy?"

"Is there a point to this conversation or have you just come to gloat?" she asked as she squirted cleansing solution into the last urinal that needed attention.

Christina's response told J.D. that she was fully aware that he had been the person who had knocked out her friend, but he had not sought her out to reminisce about the old days, so he got to the point.

"I have a proposition for you."

Christina laughed, and then said, "Well, I think we've reached the end of this conversation."

"Don't flatter yourself," J.D. came back. "This is strictly business."

"Ha," she scoffed as she scrubbed, "like I haven't heard that before," and then flushed the urinal.

J.D. was slightly irritated in her reply and it reflected in his terse response. "You must like being the latrine queen, cause you're doing a great job at making sure you're permanently assigned to shit duty. So, I'll leave you to it."

Christina bit her lip, immediately realizing she had been rash. Whatever his proposal was, it was at least worth hearing for she didn't enjoy her situation. She knew there were worse things than scrubbing toilets. She could be dead, or still suffering from the hardship of survival on the outside, or worse according to the stories she had heard from other armory survivors, a captive of the Stone survivor group. However, maybe what he had to offer was better than scrubbing shit in order to remain a part of the armory group, she told herself. She was just hoping it had nothing to do with prostituting herself.

"Wait," she called, stopping J.D. before he had made it to the archway. "I'll listen to your proposal."

"Very well. My XO seems to think we need some live entertainment to soothe the fraying nerves of our fellow survivors before the tension escalates and we end up with more than a few cuts and bruises. Since I am unable to fulfill that obligation as I have done in that past, I'd like to offer it to you in exchange for a temporary reprieve from this little slice of heaven."

J.D. wasn't about to reveal that he wasn't even considered for reprising his role as entertainer, even though he knew Ryan hadn't considered him for the reasons that J.D. had said during the staff meeting. It still didn't alleviate the slight he felt that Ryan had simply dismissed the idea of him performing again. At least he believed Ryan should have extended the courtesy of asking. He just hoped Ryan had chosen wisely for he hadn't actually seen or heard Christina play or sing. He had been thrown out of the bar before her set had begun.

"I'll play as many times a week as you want, but I want permanently off toilet duty and put on food prep detail, *and* I want you to teach me how to defend myself. Those are my terms," she announced with conviction in her position.

"*Unbelievable!* The queen of the scrub brush wants to negotiate. How about you pass the audition first before you start making demands." J.D. began to laugh as he turned, telling her to report to Sergeant Wiese when she finished her duty assignment.

"Hey, Commander," Christina called out as J.D. passed through the exit. He turned back. "For the record," she told him. "He was my boyfriend. And you were right, he was an asshole."

J.D. chuckled again. What had been a serious matter at the time seemed trivial and now laughable. However, it would be the last time J.D. would laugh.

# 3

## KNOW YOUR ENEMY

EVEN BEFORE THE PLAGUE, J.D. WAS A GIFTED COMBATANT AND FIERCE competitor. His strength and skills in martial arts was not derived from his mutant physiology, but enhanced by it. Skilled in weapons and hand-to-hand combat he was a masterful warrior, but he was not a trained military officer.

Stone had proven to be a cunning foe, one that was not reluctant to sacrifice his own men to gain what he desired, and what he craved was the armory. The armory had come under attack on several occasions. There had been a sniper, in an upper floor of a building across the street, who had killed one civilian late in November. J.D. and his men boarded up the entrances to the surrounding buildings as best they could, and set hand grenade booby traps. However, this did not deter his enemy. Two weeks later there was an explosion in an adjacent building. The remains of a man were found along with a mangled high-powered rifle equipped with a scope. The victim had tripped one of the booby traps set in a stairwell. Two nights later, apparently in retalia-tion, a group of Stone's men in Humvees simultaneously drove past the north and south gates and fired automatic weapons at the building and lobbed hand grenades into the compound. There were no deaths or injuries that evening, but it was evident that these harassment tactics were meant to intimidate. That attack was followed the next morning with a guerilla-style assault, while J.D. and his men were walking the Lexington Avenue perimeter inspecting the fence line for damage. This time Stone's men, led by Barlow, crashed an NYFD ambulance through the south perimeter gate in an attempt to gain access. Though the attack was quickly thwarted—J.D. having had the foresight to double the roof sentries after the previous night's drive-by attack—it left them shaken and with only one minor injury.

J.D.'s next encounter with Stone's group would have tragic consequences. It was a confrontation that brought a devastating personal loss. It was the loss of his beloved mate, Luci. It was a tragedy for which he blamed himself and a heartbreak he could not forgive. Plunged into despair and seized by hate, revenge was all he desired.

February had been bitterly cold and snowy, and strained the armory's heating system to the point the boilers were unable to warm the building above the low 60s. In order to raise the temperature in the main hall where the civilian population was located, parts of the armory were shut down. Heating ducts were covered and doors and windows sealed in order to direct as much heat to where it was needed. Even with some portable heaters that were found in storage, J.D. and his men could only maintain a 63-degree day temperature and a fluctuating 55 to 57-degree temperature after sundown.

March had been far from mild but the snow had melted. By the end of the month the fuel tanks for the boilers were nearly dry. As April began winter's chill slowly started to fade, but by mid-month heavy rains fell, flooding the streets and overloading the sewage system causing backups in the armory. April had brought the worst torrential storms J.D. could recall since Hurricane Sandy wreaked havoc in the fall of 2012.

J.D. and his team realized that the armory was becoming less sustainable and it was time to make plans to evacuate and head to Mechanicville. In order to relocate nearly sixty civilians that had now found refuge within the armory, an advance team would need to be sent ahead to prep the town for re-occupation. J.D. knew Mechanicville by now would have suffered some of the same infrastructure problems as New York was enduring.

The end of the snow had also brought the return of Stone's harassment tactics. The time had come for a new strategy in dealing with him and the threat he posed to the safety and well being of the armory. J.D. needed to take the fight to him.

Captain James Alexander was an indispensable part of J.D.'s team when it came to planning recons and re-supply missions, but James was not a tactician. Even if he had been, James was too busy developing the evacuation and relocation plans to give assistance. J.D. had no qualms about his lack of experience as a military strategist, but there was one thing he knew, and that was the art of war, not in a grand military fashion, but on a smaller combatant scale.

Not only had J.D. studied Bruce Lee's philosophies, embracing Lee's influences of Taoism, Jiddu Krishnamurti, and Buddhism, but he had also read all of Lee's books, incorporating them into his fighting and life styles. However, one influential book he had read had not been written by his idol, Lee, but penned by Sun Tzu—a great Chinese general during ancient China's Spring and Autumn Period— was an ancient book on military strategy. That was the book *Art of War*.

J.D. knew that Edward Stone was a psychotic killer and child molester with a narcissistic personality. He also knew that Stone was not a man without intelligence. Stone had proven to be a calculating, manipulative, and cunning enemy. His intelligence was not to be dismissed or underestimated. Yes, Edward Stone was a crazed killer, but he was also a formidable enemy, and had proven so on many occasions, both during the zombie apocalypse and in its aftermath.

The current tactics that J.D. had employed in defending themselves against the gang of murderous scavengers was not effective. J.D. knew that hiding away in the armory wasn't going to make Stone and his men go away. What was needed was an offensive tactic. He deferred to Sun Tzu.

There were certain passages that remained embedded in J.D.'s memory. Passages that he incorporated into his martial arts.

*Security against defeat implies defensive tactics; ability to defeat the enemy means taking the offensive.*

He knew how to do this.

*All warfare is based on deception.*

Martial Arts also utilized deception.

*Attack him where he is unprepared, appear where you are not expected.*

He knew the city better than his enemy.

*Let your plans be dark and impenetrable as night, and when you move, fall like a thunderbolt.*

The night was his domain, thunderbolts his fists.

*Hence the skillful fighter puts himself into a position, which makes defeat impossible, and does not miss the moment for defeating the enemy.*

He would give no quarter, as he had done in martial arts competitions.

*The quality of decision is like the well-timed swoop of a falcon which enables it to strike and destroy its victim.*

He was like a falcon—he was part transmute!

J.D. also knew that attitude and fighting skills were not enough to defeat the enemy. Sun Tzu also wrote that there are five besetting sins of a general, ruinous to the conduct of war.

(1) *recklessness, which leads to destruction;*

He was not reckless, so he believed.

(2) *cowardice, which leads to capture;*

He was not a coward. Mahatma Gandhi had taught him cowards could never be moral, and he had also proved his courage at the Javits Center.

(3) *a hasty temper, which can be provoked by insults;*

He had learned that power comes from self-restraint and that a quick temper will make a fool of you. Insults merely rolled off him like raindrops from a leaf.

(4) *a delicacy of honor which is sensitive to shame;*

The writings of Hsün Tzu had taught him, "The coming of honor or disgrace must be a reflection of one's inner power."

(5) *over solicitude for his men, which exposes him to worry and trouble.*

He no longer allowed himself to get close to his men.

However, above all there was one thing that Sun Tzu had emphasized, know your enemy. He knew exactly how to accomplish that goal.

# 4

## HAUNTER OF THE DARK

*MARCH 24, DAY 350.*

Where J.D. had once gone out mainly with his men, he now went out mostly alone, hunting for Stone's hideaway and the men who had killed Luci. Tonight his hunting had paid off, and he knew with relentless persistence he would find Stone, and where Stone was—that was where the prisoners were.

He had found his tactical advantage, and he used the enemy's need for light against them. He was trans-human and his enhancements were derived from the DNA of a spotted owl—and other genome resequencing the doctor refused to discuss. He was, therefore, a creature of the night, and the dark did not hinder him from prowling the city after sundown.

The enemy's use of light was useless unless he could see it, and wandering the city aimlessly would be pointless and futile, like looking for the proverbial needle in a haystack. Nonetheless there was one place, one vantage point, and one with a 360-degree view of the Manhattan skyline that would reveal where his enemy could be found

—and that was the observation deck of the 102-story landmark Art Deco skyscraper, the Empire State Building.

From his perch on the 86th floor he patiently watched the city below, first by searching for any light source. His tactical advantage he found was not simply limited to scanning the dark. He realized that his enhanced vision also could be utilized during the day. Though his eyesight was not as acute as a true transmute or that of an owl, it was superior to any human. With this, and his knowledge of the city, he could approximate where his enemy was skulking.

For two weeks he patiently watched and noted the areas in which he saw the telltale signs of moving vehicles or people. He observed in the southwest that, usually, after noontime until 8 or 9 p.m. there was a great deal of activity. At sunrise daily, he and Barkley made their way to the area where he had seen his enemy, and though his recons never revealed the enemy's hideout, it did reveal the enemy was scavenging.

With his intel, he was able to determine where his enemy was and where they were most likely to be next. They were currently in the West Village at Sheridan Square, the area in which West 4th Street, Barrow Street, and West Washington Place intersected. By the direction J.D. had calculated, they were heading toward 14th Street.

Patience and perseverance eventually paid off. He hit them three times, twice at night and once in the early afternoon. Weary from the hunt, he chose to return to his real home—his place on East 13th Street. This was not the first time he decided to rest at his pre-apocalypse residence instead of returning to the armory. His apartment was also a sanctuary away from his responsibilities and burdens as a commander. He knew that spending more than two nights away from his men was detrimental to their morale and their physical well-being. He still led some of the day missions and he still, when his other duties allowed, stood vigil on the roof watching for refugees or anyone who dared attack.

Tonight would be his only evening away for the week. There were duties that needed his attention back at base in the morning. Also, he wanted to tell his soldiers that there were three less threats they had to worry about.

He was at the corner of 13<sup>th</sup> Street and Second Avenue about to step off the curb to cross to the west side when he saw a faint set of headlights coming from the south. He knew it wasn't one of his patrols. There were strict orders that no patrol was to be out at night unless he was leading the team. He hadn't scheduled a patrol for another two days, so he knew it had to be another of Stone's. They must have found their men that he had ambushed earlier. The enemy was now hunting him.

It wasn't as if he had tried to hide the act; in fact, he had wanted Stone to know that he was the one who killed the three. Besides the talon markings left on his kills, he had left a note for Stone on one of his victims after the first surprise attack. It was a brief declaration he had written; it read: 'I will not retreat in the face of battle. I will give no quarter to the fallen. I will have no mercy for my enemies. I will never accept defeat. I will never quit.' He signed the edict 'Humpty Dumpty,' as a taunt.

J.D. was incensed and furious that Stone's men were violating his memories and intruding upon his piece of the night. This was his neighborhood, his home turf, and his little slice of what good in his life he had once had. It angered him. *How dare they violate it!* These trespassers, these undesirables, were a blight and not welcome. He could see the spotlight cutting across the darkness, relentlessly searching back and forth like a badminton birdie in flight. He knew this wasn't just any patrol; it was a search and destroy team and they were hunting for him. However the hunters were about to get a surprise. He had two fragmentation grenades that he hadn't needed when he caught the last patrol scavenging through a small liquor store, having been more interested in what they had found than watching their backs. He lay down on the sidewalk next to the curb, using a car to obscure his presence. As the military Humvee passed, he stood up and lobbed a grenade at them. It thudded on the hood of the truck next to the spotter, and then rolled off. There was no explosion.

The truck abruptly stopped. The light swept around to his position. They had found him.

"Don't take any of those wet boxes of ammunition," J.D. distinctly remembered telling his men as they looked over the cache of weapons and munitions they had discovered at the Javits Center. However, what he had ordered was either disregarded or they had brought back ones that they hadn't realized were water damaged.

---

The car shredded in front of him as 40mm rounds of a MK19-3 Grenade Machine Gun ripped through the vehicle's metal fabrication. The front windshield exploded. Fragments of glass and other debris burst into the air. Unfortunately for J.D., the enemy gunner didn't have to be a marksman to assure destruction of a target. The weapon was capable of major direct and indirect damage and it could penetrate through a vehicle and kill someone on the other side, if they were using it as cover. J.D. knew this, he had seen this, so he had been quick enough to get out of the way when the Humvee backed up and the gun turned in his direction. He had no place to go, but in a retreating direction. The spotlight swept through the dark in search of him. He had been lucky; it was night, and though the stars gave the streets some illumination, there was only a sliver of a moon this evening. Without the cover of darkness to make his escape, in all likelihood, he would have been gunned down.

J.D. had jumped out of the way as the bullets struck the first vehicle, and then had quickly rolled back along the curb past two parked cars. The gunner continued to fire, going from one car to the next, but J.D. had been quicker than the gunner and light operator. J.D. began his flight across the avenue by the time the spotlight had reached the third car. The noise of the machine gun had cancelled out the noise of his footfalls. As he dashed across the faded double lines that marked the center of the street he lobbed his last hand grenade like he was releasing a bowling ball. He hoped this one worked. It rolled toward the rear of the truck. He ducked in between two parked cars as the grenade reached its target. The back end of the Humvee reared up as the grenade exploded, just as the spotter caught him with the light.

J.D. didn't hesitate. He ran to the burning truck, and before the driver could get clear of the burning wreckage, he dug his talons into the man's throat and ripped it out. There was another in the Humvee, a man slumped in the passenger seat with his head against the window. The Humvee was a mass of flames and was about to be totally engulfed. J.D. looked at the unconscious man. It was too late; the driver's cabin was ablaze before he could get the door open. The spotter who had been sitting on the passenger side roof had been thrown off the vehicle when it exploded. The man had landed about ten feet away. The blast had stunned him, but he managed to right himself. He saw J.D. charging forward. He raised his pistol just in time and put three slugs into J.D.'s chest, not knowing J.D. was wearing body armor. The man stepped to the fallen J.D. to put one final shot into his adversary's head when he found himself on the receiving end of a leg sweep, which picked him up off his feet and knocked him to the ground. Before the man could recover, J.D. was atop of him about to tear out his larynx when J.D. saw the man's scar. It was the scar that Peter had described on one of the men who held him while Stone raped his daughter. J.D. punched the man in the face instead, rendering him unconscious.

It was not J.D.'s right to take this man's life. That right belonged to Peter Dunne. He would decide the fate of this man, and in the process maybe they would be able to extract the whereabouts of Stone's hideout.

He threw the unconscious man over his shoulder after securing his prisoner's hands and feet with nylon cable ties, and wrapped his mouth shut with camouflage tactical body tape. All trussed up like the proverbial *Christmas Carol* goose for dinner, a gift for Peter "Cratchit."

It was the first time Peter smiled since his arrival at the armory. In fact, Peter was borderline euphoric in his way of thanking J.D. as he peered down at the man.

"He's yours," J.D. told him, as he tossed the man to the ground before Peter. "Yours to do with as you see fit."

The man looked up; he recognized Peter. The prisoner's eyes bulged with fear as he thrashed and squirmed about in a vain effort to escape. J.D. slammed his foot down on the man's chest. The man convulsed slightly trying to catch his breath, but he got J.D.'s message.

"All I ask is before you kill him is try to extract as much information out of him as possible." J.D. requested. "But let's not do anything here. Let's make this party a threesome. I have an idea."

# 5

## LAGER LOUT

*April 6, Day 363.*

It was after midnight when J.D. wandered into McSorley's. This had not been his destination. He had just found himself there as he had every time he had killed one of his enemies or needed to think. Although on this particular night the comfort of one of his old haunts did not ease nor comfort his aching soul. This night his thoughts were of Luci, for it was this night that he had finally found those who had killed her. Tonight, he had not killed these men quickly or mercifully, but had methodically and slowly tortured them, hoping in some way their painful and prolonged deaths would give him some measure of satisfaction and peace of mind at finally killing those who took Luci from him. It didn't.

He sat at his usual table, the one where he always sat, the one in front of the kitchen next to the fireplace, the place next to where his and Max's picture hung. He sat with his feet propped up on the edge of the wooden table, a table filled with a dozen empty Jack Daniels bottles and many empty glasses once filled with ale, his chair tipped back precipitously on its two back legs, and his eyes focused on the singular glow stick on the table that dimly lit the backroom—the glow stick was for ambience. The black uniform he wore was soiled and sticky and his face speckled with his victims' blood that he hadn't realized had stained his pale, drawn face and makeup.

He was singing the Irish republican folk song *The Boys of the Old Brigade* as he played a bell accordion that he kept at the pub. It was a song he knew well, as he used to sing it on the ale house's anniversary; it was the only day the ale house had live music. However, upon reaching the first bridge of the song, he abruptly began to sing the refrain to the raucous Irish rock song *Rock 'n' Roll Paddy* by Shane MacGowan. His vocals were slurred and incoherent, and he was out of key. He was drunk; there was no doubt about it—*finally!*

He stopped his pathetic rendition and began to call out to Richie Welsh.

"Hey, Richie. Richie! Another round," he said trying to get the waiter's attention.

There was no response.

J.D. called out again, this time turning his head around 180 degrees to look toward the front room where the bar was located—having been seated with his back to the front room—while simultaneously outstretching his left arm, the one that he had barley been using to depress the instrument keys. His sudden head movement, arm gesture, and his inebriated state put him off balance. His chair tipped back, its legs slid out from underneath itself. J.D. tipped rearward, falling back toward the dirty floor. As the chair went crashing back he barely managed to rotate his head face forward. The back of his skull thudded hard and loud on the old wooden floor. His head spun. Everything turned a bright white and then dark.

"Are you all right?" he heard a voice in the darkness.

"I don't know," J.D. muttered as he looked up. Richie stood above him. "How the hell did I manage that?" he asked his old friend.

Richie helped him to his feet, as he said, "You haven't eaten and you've had a few rounds."

"Well, you know what Marry says about that?" he spoke, as he sat back in the chair.

"No. What?" he asked.

J.D. called out toward the kitchen to Marry.

"Marry! *Marry!*"

He heard her sweet Irish accented words arriving before her appearance in the doorway. "Yes, darlin'?"

"Tell Richie what you always say about eating?"

"And what's that? You should never eat on an empty stomach?"

"Aye! That's it."

"Yes, my dear. But I didn't mean you should drink until you're pissed," she sternly told him.

"I've only had a few."

"Apparently, a few too many," he heard her voice fade back into the kitchen.

"Well, that's not a lot," he told Richie.

"That's twelve rounds, J.D.—that makes twenty-four. And then there's all the whiskey."

"Yeah, well—it's my birthday!" he retorted. Except, Richie had vanished, and the whirly, swirly spinning and white shooting lights inside his head had now replaced the apparition.

J.D. looked up. He was on the floor, his accordion atop his chest. He raised his arm and depressed the illumination button on his watch. It was shortly after 0300 hours. His head throbbed as he stood up and set his instrument on a chair. He made his way out the door and to the street, dirty sawdust falling off the back of his head—with no thought about brushing it away. To his dismay, he was sober.

It was nearly 3:30 a.m. when he arrived in front of the Open Pantry on Second Avenue, near the corner of 12th Street. It had taken him nearly double the time it usually took. He chalked it up to having to stop four times to urinate.

He sat down on the bench that had been placed to the left of the door and directly under the large red stenciled window that read 'Open Pantry.' The bench he sat on was usually stored inside the shop when it was closed; there were two of them, but he had only dragged out one. He kept the coiling grill door rolled down and the green awning rolled up, as a precaution as not to draw attention to the fact that he frequented the shop. He had even gone so far as to replace the broken pane of glass on the door that he had shattered all those months ago when he had gained access, the day he had come with his old comrades and Max so he could have a Green & Black's chocolate bar. He had actually felt guilty for breaking into the storefront, but it had been worth it. The chocolate, as always, had been sweet, creamy, and delicious, and had satisfied his craving.

J.D., for the most part, always seemed to find himself sitting on the bench after one of his "search and destroy" missions, or the "hunt," as he thought of them. Sitting on this bench had always calmed his mind and soothed his aching soul, but tonight his mind raced with depressing thoughts of his past, thoughts of those who died in the plague and those he had lost since. Even thoughts of Joseph Joshua Daniel Young tormented him.

Joseph had died tragically at the hands of a half-mute. Though he never did like the ex-Marine turned civil engineer for the City's Department of Transportation, his untimely death still haunted him. He had been a member of his original group.

Tonight, though, was the first night in nearly a year that he thought about his parents, a painful memory, and like all his pain he tried to bury it deep within himself.

What was it about this particular night that triggered his recollection of the loss of his parents? It could have been the excessive drinking. It may have been spending his birthday alone. It may even have been the pending one-year anniversary of the end of civilization that was just days away. Except what it really was, was the cold, harsh reality that this night he realized the brutal, vindictive acts of murder he was committing in the name of vengeance had made him no better than his nemesis—a sick, twisted, sadistic murderer who had no regard or concern for human life and he was unmoved by the revelation. That indifference was the underlying cause for his brooding and anger. He had gone against everything moral and proper his parents had instilled in him, and he knew if they were still alive, he would be an extreme disappointment to them. That was the only regret he had about what he had become.

Anger. He felt more rage and anger than he had ever felt in 29 years. His anger was for the death of his family, for the loss of his love Marisol, and for the loss of his former companions, and those of his survivor group that had perished. Mostly, though, he was angry with himself. Angry for not being able to save Luci and angry for not being able to go with his friends and dog to England. Though above all, he suffered the greatest anger for not being able to keep the promise he made to Peter Dunne, to find and rescue his daughter Victoria and the others who were being held captive and abused. All of this fueled his hate for Stone and his followers. One way or another he was going to put an end to Stone.

## 6

# GOOD AND BAD CATS

*MAY 18, DAY 406.*

Caitlin quietly came into her father's sleeping quarters, and stood by the ajar door of the bathroom as her father tried unsuccessfully to camouflage his face. J.D. was trying for a look, something menacing to add to his fierceness—a facial painting that complemented his new haircut. However, after two attempts—two attempts Caitlin observed silently from the doorway—he threw the camouflage makeup into the sink in frustration.

"Dawd," a light, wistful call came from the other side of the door. "Dawd, what you do…? Why funny face?"

"Caitlin," he sternly reminded her, "have you forgotten your manners? What have I taught you about entering someone else's room?"

She apologized, "Sawee, dawd." She knew she had disappointed her father. She knocked on the bathroom door, "May come in, pease, dawd."

"Yes, Cat. Permission granted."

She pushed the door open and stood next to her father, who was hunched over in front of the mirror with both hands placed on the edge of the sink. Caitlin saw his frustration and concern.

"Dawd? You make funny face, purpose?"

"No, Cat. I was trying to make a mean face."

"Mean face?" she asked, giving him a perplexed look. "You want help?"

"You know how to make a mean face?"

"I think so. Like from movie?"

"*Movie?*"

"Yes," she announced, affirming. "Crow, dawd, like crow man."

"You mean Eric Draven, *The Crow?*"

"Of course, dawd."

"But, Cat, this is crow face."

"No, dawd. You do all wrong. No green. Not Grinch. Just black. Dawd already white—I come back. Dawd stay, no go. Okay?" she told him as she bolted out of the bathroom.

"Where are you going?" he asked as she ran out the door and into the hallway. All he heard was, "Dawd stay!"

---

The movie, *The Crow*, was one of J.D.'s favorite films, and was based on a comic book series created by James O'Barr. The series was originally written by O'Barr as a means of dealing with the death of his girlfriend at the hands of a drunk driver.

J.D. had watched the film with his daughter shortly after the death of Caitlin's mother. It was not something a normal parent would allow a small child to watch, but then again J.D. was far from a normal parent and Caitlin was far from being a normal child. Though he had reservations about her viewing the mature themed film—she was a child no matter how mature her physical appearance and emotional state had developed—he felt the message of the film would outweigh its violent content.

In the film a poetic guitarist, Eric Draven, is brought back from the dead by a crow a year after he and his fiancée were savagely tortured and murdered. Eric takes revenge for his death and the death of the woman he loves. When not on the hunt, Draven stays in the house he shared with his girlfriend, Shelly, spending most of his time there lost in memories of her. Her absence is torture for him, and he is in emotional anguish.

*The Crow*, he believed, paralleled his own life in many aspects and emotions he was experiencing. It also showed the brutal acts of revenge committed by the main character were justified, and he hoped his daughter would understand that he was much like Eric Draven in his commitment and desire to avenge the death of her mother. He had hoped to better explain his own actions through the movie, since it was extremely difficult for him to express himself and his emotional trauma directly to Caitlin. But as they viewed it together, all Caitlin wanted was silence from her father, not talk. She understood why he wanted her to see the film. Her words, 'Dawd crow man,' spoke volumes of her intellectual capacity.

After several minutes, Caitlin ran anxiously back into the bathroom, and then promptly exited. She knocked on the door. She had forgotten her manners again.

She presented her father with several makeup brushes and a black lip pencil.

"Cat. Where did you get these?"

"Katie," she told him.

"Katie? Did she give you these or did you take them?"

"No dawd," she said in a hurt tone. "Caitlin never take."

She frowned.

"I'm sorry, Cat. Sometimes dad forgets what a Good Cat you are… Why did Katie give these to you?"

"Katie teach Caitlin makeup," she proudly announced.

His voice reflected a tone of concern and anger when he asked her, "Katie puts makeup on you?"

"No mad, dawd. Only Katie makeup. Not Caitlin. I help Katie!"

"Okay. Dad sorry again… And what did Katie teach you?"

"Proper application to enhance natural beauty. Not look like made up."

He couldn't believe his ears. He had never heard his daughter speak such a well-constructed sentence, let alone one filled with words that were of at least an adolescent vocabulary."

"She did, did she?"

"Okay. Now Caitlin helps."

J.D. sat impatiently on the bathroom floor. He doubted that his daughter had the ability to do what she so boldly and confidently told him she could. His daughter held her small hand under her father's chin to steady him, her tiny claws poking his skin, scolding him to sit still. She drew lines vertically up and down his face from the center of the eyes. Then she painted his eyes with a larger brush, making sure to only take little dabs of black paint from her father's camo makeup case, gently applying and reapplying, filling in the eyelids like she was applying eye shadow. The final step was to paint his lips.

"No chap, Dawd," she told him. "Vitamin E," she declared. "Okay all done. Dawd look."

He stood and gazed into the mirror. He was amazed at the perfection in her craft. She had indeed done what she said she could do. The application was remarkable, a bit too remarkable. Caitlin must have spent a copious amount of time with Katie in order to be so perfect, even with her high intelligence.

"Thank you," he said, in a pleased tone, and then bent over toward her, "Give dad a kiss."

"No dawd, just hug. No smudge Caitlin's mean face."

"Okay, just hug," he spoke compliantly as his daughter squeezed him tightly around his torso, squatting to accommodate her.

"Dawd. Please read story before go."

"Cat. There's no time for a story now. Dad needs to go out into the dark. I'll read to you when I come back."

"Dawd," she pleaded. "No you won't. You be gone all night. You never read to me anymore. You never sing to me anymore."

He looked at her sad face that was almost in tears. She knew how to pull heavy upon his heartstrings. He picked her up in his arms and embraced her tightly, kissing her on her cheek, and then gently placing her on his bed.

"You're right, Cat. I'm sorry. How about you sleep here tonight? And I'll read you a little bit of your favorite."

"Good cats and bad cats," she excitedly replied.

"Yes, of course. But you have to promise to go to sleep and not be upset when I leave. Okay?"

"Yes, dawd. I pomise."

"Pinky swear?"

"Yes, dawd," she agreed, holding out the clawed little baby finger of her right hand. "Pinky swear."

J.D. went to his dresser and removed a book from the top drawer. He returned to her side and sat down on the edge of the bed. He opened the old and beaten book and began:

"*Good and Bad Cats*. Pictures and verses by Frederick White," he gently read aloud, as he watched her wonderment. " 'To Fuzzy Wuzzy. A perfectly good cat. Except when she is bad. Or (as is usually the case) utterly indifferent.' "

Caitlin settled back upon her pillow in anxious anticipation of the beginning verses.

> " '*A nicely mannered cat,*
> *At table,*
> *Behaves as well as she is able.*
> *And everybody says:*
> *"Why that*
> *Is really something*
> *Like a cat!"*
> *But when she gobbles bread and meat*
> *And uses hands for fork—*
> *Or feet—*
> *Then everybody says:*
> *"Oh, dear!*
> *Why do they have*

*That creature here?' "*

*Good and Bad Cats* had been a bedtime story his grandmother had read to him on a weekly basis as a child. *Good and Bad Cats* had been the fondest memory J.D. had of his grandmother, who, at the age of 82, had passed away in her sleep the August after his 27th birthday. J.D.'s mother had given him the book shortly after her death. Although, he had never read it, or opened its pages since her passing—since he had no children to read it to, until now—it was the most cherished physical possession in his life. Far more treasured than even his beloved Thai fighting sticks which he had received as a gift from his first love, Bonita.

J.D. didn't read just the first few pages, he read them all, showing her the accompanying black and white illustrations—the book having been published in 1911—of Fuzzy Wuzzy the cat.

When the last few words trickled from his lips, his daughter looked up at him and smiled, then asked, "Dawd? Why you go every dark? Why does Elty be dawd?"

In her broken words, he knew what she was asking. He had tried to be the best father he knew how after Luci's death. He often read to her and played piano and sang. Then when spring came he focused most of his attention on locating Stone. Caitlin briefly regained her father's attention back in mid-April, when the storms came, though at times the rain did not stop J.D. from venturing out on his quest. Now it was the third week of May and he had for the better part of the past three weeks nearly ignored her and placed her under the care of Ryan Duncan.

"Honey. Dad goes out every night to get the bad men, remember? To make all the bad men pay for taking mommy from us. And to find the missing children."

Caitlin knew her mother was dead. J.D. had explained death to her and had told her what had happened to her mother. So, when her father told her that the bad men had taken her away from them, she knew she was never coming back.

"You miss mawm?" she asked her father, with a longing voice and sad eyes.

He placed his hand gently to her face, cupping it lightly as if he were holding a butterfly in his palm. "Yes, Cat. I miss mom. I miss mom very much."

"You love mawm?"

He reassured her, "Of course. But why would you ask that?"

"Cause of fodo."

"*Photo?* I don't understand, Cat. What about photo?"

"Fodo on drezzer," she told him, and then pointed to her father's tall set of dresser drawers, the one in which he kept his grandmother's book.

He understood which photo she had questioned him about. It had been the group photo Ryan had taken moments before J.D. had taken his friends to Pier 17 at the South Street Seaport, the morning they had left for England.

"What about the photo?"

"Who is girl dawd hugging?"

"That was someone very special. Someone I miss very much."

"You love girl?

"Yes, I did. But I met Marisol before I met mom. You understand?"

Caitlin did not answer her father's query, instead she said, "Caitlin miss mawm, too," and then asked, "Mary Sol dead like mawm?"

"No, honey. Marisol went away with all the people in the photo. They went far away to a place called England."

"Monster, too?"

"*Monster?* I don't understand. What monster?"

"Short monster. By dawd's feet."

J.D. now understood her reference to his German shepherd. "No sweetie. That's not monster. That's my dog, Max."

"Dogd? But he doesn't look like Barky?"

"No, Cat, *Barkley*," he gently corrected his daughter with a smile. "Barkley is just one kind of dog. Before the plague there used to be all sorts. Max was my best friend, and he helped me rescue all the people in the photo from the zombies."

Caitlin had only known one canine, and that was Barkley, and she could not comprehend that there were other kinds of dogs. She gave him a confused look, and asked, "More dogds?"

"It's okay, sweetie. Max is gone, too. Max went to England." He paused momentarily and gazed upon the odd but beautiful face of his daughter. He looked into her brilliant blue eyes. She indeed was a reflection of her mother. "Okay, Cat. Time for sleep."

He kissed her forehead, then kissed her tiny lips, and whispered, "I love you." In response Caitlin grabbed him around his neck and held him tight for a moment, and whispered in his ear, "Please sing lullabee song to make me sleep."

As he tucked her in, he began to sing "Lullabye (Goodnight My Angel)" by Billy Joel. Before he finished the second verse, she had fallen asleep.

It was time for J.D. to be a bad cat again. It was time to hunt.

# 7

## WAY OF THE LITTLE DRAGON

*MAY 27, DAY 414.*

There had been no more training of survivors. Furthermore, the instructing J.D. did with his troops had been relocated to a large storage room in the basement. It was there Katie O'Hanlon was headed to test her defensive skills with her master. It had been five months since she had begun her training, and she was confident that she would pass. As she neared the entry, she saw Jonas McGann exit the room with Liz Hudson waiting in the hallway for him. The two kissed as they greeted one another. Katie had become friendly with Liz, so she heard firsthand the harrowing story of Liz and Jonas' survival. It wasn't any surprise to Katie that the two had become lovers having shared such a traumatic experienced together. As Liz and Jonas moved from the entryway, Jonas nodded his head in passing to her and gave Katie a knowing smile. It was odd. Jonas had never once smiled at her before. As Katie moved to the threshold she almost ran into Christina as she exited.

"Careful," Christina warned. However, she was not telling Katie to watch where she was going. "He's in an unforgiving mood today," Christina finished as she exited.

J.D. was practicing with Peter Dunne as she entered. A full-on match was taking place with Peter wielding his staff as J.D. bare handedly defended himself against the short man's powerful advance. She stood in the doorway and watched J.D. as his lean body glistened with the perspiration that covered his chest and back. A small golden cross around his neck bounced lightly as he countered the staff's jabs and swings with hand strikes. The large tattoo of the angry dragon that adorned his chest rippled across his torso as if it were in flight as he moved and flexed his body. She had seen him with his shirt off only a few times, but that was before the new body art that covered his chest had been completed. The tattoos that adorned his physique were one of many things that attracted her to him. Katie even thought the grayish stripe of mutated skin that ran the length of his spine was erotic.

She had desired him for a long time, though she had hated him at first, the day he had hunted her down, tied and gagged her, forcing her from her sanctuary. Nevertheless, she discovered he had a gentle side to oppose the brutality, and that was shown with his love for his daughter. She had dropped subtle hints, which went unanswered, and only fueled her want for him more. She had fantasies about her commander, sexual fantasies that she did not share with anyone. She wanted to feel his hard, muscular body atop her. To feel his sweat dripping from his chest down onto her breasts as his he drove his hardness deep inside her wanting loins as they had hours of intense, passionate sex. She had not felt a man's touch, let alone the pleasure of an orgasm that wasn't self-induced even long before the plague, and now, seeing his glossy, glistening body and new artwork, the want and desire to have J.D. was even more intensified.

She knew that he was aware that she was watching, but he did not stop the fight. She had arrived three minutes early and he would make her wait to the exact time he had given orders for her to appear. Katie stared intently at him, partly out of the excitement and pleasure she got from seeing him partially undressed but also out of amazement at the fluidity and intensity of his movements, as he jumped and leaped over the staff as Peter swept it toward his legs. However, it appeared to her that J.D. was continuously on the defensive and that Peter had the upper hand using the weapon. Then J.D. let out a cry and instantly the staff was snatched from Peter's grip and used against him. With a quick and forceful sweep across the man's legs, Peter was knocked off his feet and the end of the staff pressed against his chest. The bout was over. For a moment Peter didn't move, he was clearly dazed. J.D. reached out and helped the man up. After they bowed to one another, J.D. handed Peter back his staff and said, "Outstanding, Peter. You've come such a long way. I look forward to our next practice."

As Peter departed, he gave Katie a wicked smile, like he knew something that she didn't.

"Come," J.D. finally said, as he motioned her over to him. She stood silently before him. "I know you are extremely competent in hand-to-hand and have excelled in knife skills," he said as he circled her. "You've trained hard with me and have proven your ability and desire to learn. Ryan and James have informed me that you have shown great leaderships skills and could make a good team leader... So, you come before me today to test your skills. Are you planning on using those zai?" he asked, seeing them tucked into the belt of her karate uniform.

Over the past ten years J.D. Nichols had trained in many different martial arts styles and with a variety of weapons. His weapons familiarity was extensive, though the practical use of most of the armaments he knew was limited. The nunchaku was the first weapon he learned many years after seeing Bruce Lee use them in his films. Although, J.D. became extremely adept in their use, he had barely practiced them in the years since his instruction by an Okinawan Kobudō master.

He was also familiar with basic elements of the bo, also known as a staff, and had recommended it to Peter Dunne, due to its reach and striking power. With the zai his skills were self-taught and short lived. Like many of the weapons he had explored, it was not a perfect match for him. However, the weapons he excelled in, and had continued to practice throughout his life, were his bastóns—Filipino fighting sticks

—and a pair of Bolo machetes. These felt right to him, the ones he was lethal with. The ones he had become one with.

Katie knew her master was not skilled in the use of the weapons she had chosen. He had told her so when he gave her the instructional book to them. This she believed would be to her advantage. Katie knew it was impossible for her to best J.D., but she didn't have to. All she needed to do was prove she was competent in the weapon she had chosen in order to pass the test. She had no doubt that she would excel for she believed that with zai in hands she would be lethal against anyone other than her master.

"Yes," she confirmed.

"You choose a weapon in which I have limited knowledge, one that I was not able to give you proper instruction in. Learning from a book is a poor substitute for practical instruction. I for one know. I commend you on your initiative and dedication in learning it... However, I don't believe you're ready—and before you say anything, I am well aware of the hours you spend practicing every day. All the sparring you've done with James, Ryan, and Peter. Nonetheless it takes hundreds of hours of practice and sparring to achieve a level of proficiency with any weapon."

She gave him a look of disappointment. She was sure that he was going to send her away. He saw the look on her face, but did not acknowledge it. He continued.

"However, if you think you are skilled enough to meet the challenge of being tested on the use of your pointy batons, so be it. But don't think I will go easy on you. On the battlefield our enemy will give no quarter, and none should be expected. To pass you must prove yourself. Is that understood?"

"Yes, *sifu*," she replied.

"Take a moment and stretch, then we shall begin."

He turned away from her and went to a table in the far corner of the practice room. He paused momentarily to quench the needs of his dehydrated body by consuming an entire 32-fluid ounce bottle of Gatorade in several seconds. He took a bite of a chocolate bar, and then wiped the perspiration off his face with a small terry cloth hand towel.

For a moment, he stood at the table sucking on the half-chewed chocolate in his mouth. Chocolate was a difficult commodity to come by lately and he wanted to enjoy its texture and taste. When the sweet had melted off his tongue, he picked up his martial arts uniform shirt and accompanying belt and put them on. Katie was disappointed he got dressed, but she knew his body would only distract her—and this was not a time to be distracted.

"Anytime you're ready," she told him, anxiously waiting to prove herself.

He picked up his bastóns and turned back to her. "Just giving you the opportunity to warm up, but you chose not to."

"In combat, there will be no warm up," Katie told him, and then bowed and took her fighting stance.

"Very well," J.D. replied. "I hope your ability exceeds your ambition."

"You doubt my ability, master?"

"Only if one accepts his weaknesses can one achieve strength. But perhaps today will be different. Perhaps today the student will teach the master."

She was prideful in her boast. "Then let the lesson begin."

Katie was headstrong like he had once been. He saw a lot of himself in her, but he knew what was inside himself was dark, dangerous, and unpredictable. That was something he needed to beat out of her before her ego elevated, and he was about to give her the trashing of her life, like he once experienced as a teenager in an Eskrima match in the Philippines.

J.D. said, " 'Pride goeth before the fall,' " he warned, as he approached her.

J.D. bowed to Katie, and then took his fighting stance, displaying his Eskrima sticks.

"*Sifu*, sticks?" she asked, believing he was going to test her using his bare hands.

"Since you are using your little pig stickers, I thought it only fair if I used my bastóns. After all they're just sticks," J.D. told her, giving a sly smirk.

However, these were not merely sticks. They were true Eskrima fighting sticks made from a dense hardwood called Kamagong—also known as Ironwood—that was only found in the Philippines. This was the most precious gift he had ever received, for it had come from the woman who had taught him the meaning of respect and humility, and taken his virginity.

She had caught his knowing grin, and it concerned her. Perhaps this is what everyone earlier had been smiling about.

J.D. saw the sudden trepidation in her face. "Very well, I do want you to feel that your test is fair, based on your current ability, so I will use only one."

J.D. stuck one of his bastóns in the belt of his uniform top, and then waved her on, indicating to begin, but before she had made a second step toward him, he took the offensive and came at her hard and fast. He was merciless in his attack. She tried to ward off his advance by using an inside sweep block, and then followed by a downward block to counter yet another offensive move, as she had learned from the book he had given her. Except, he had lightning fast reflexes acquired from years of training and his transmute DNA. With every counter strike or defensive move she made, he was able to out maneuver her and land forceful blows. First, he struck her in her arms and torso, concentrating on her right side, pummeling her hard enough in the chest that she bent over trying to catch her breath.

"Need a rest?" J.D. asked, but not in a taunting tone, as he spun around her left side and came up behind her. "Good. Because there is no rest on the battlefield," he said, as he struck her hard against the back of her leg under her buttocks. The painful sting made her rise quickly. He then took his bastón and slammed it onto the back of her knees in one precise and painful sweeping motion, knocking her off her feet and sending her crashing backward onto the floor.

She quickly stood up. Her stubbornness and his taunting innuendo would not allow her to give in. She assumed a left-foot-forward stance with the zai, meaning both weapons pointing toward her, gripping the right hand sai, a single weapon, by the blade. As J.D. attacked, she attempted to execute a horizontal strike with the left-hand sai. She had assumed that when the sai blade contacted the bastón, it would cause him to lose his grip. However, J.D. knew the move she was attempting; after all, it had been his technical book she had studied.

Indeed, Katie had thought wrong, he had not loosened his grip. As she reached forward with the right-hand sai, attempting to hook the inside prong around his knee and pull backward until he fell to the floor, J.D. came down with a quick and forceful snap with his unarmed hand and slapped it across her arm just above the wrist. She immediately dropped the sai. She anticipated he was about to execute another counter that would come to her head, but he had feigned the move and instead struck her repeatedly upon her thighs with a complement of swift stick strikes. Her leg gave out and she fell down, landing on her sore buttocks.

J.D. gave her a glare of disappointment. "Now you are thinking," he scolded her. "What did I teach you? Reflex!" He imparted words from Master Lee's philosophy, " 'Empty your mind. Be formless, shapeless like water.' "

He had spent many hours teaching her Jeet Kune Do and Okinawan Shorin-Ryu Karate-Do, and she had been an apt pupil. Nonetheless in his mind the zai had made her stupid; she was relying too much on the weapon and not on the principles he had taught her. "If my stick were fangs," J.D. told her, "your legs and arms would have torn from your body."

Katie rose again. She hobbled, and tried to go on the offensive. The pain in her leg was intense, but she was not going to give in. She wanted to be a team leader and the only way was to pass this challenge. However, her offense quickly turned to defense. She was able to block most of his leg strikes, but once again she found herself on the floor; this time her other thigh had taken a beating. There were no words from her master after this round, but she could see the disappointment in his eyes over her performance. He signaled her to rise, and instructed, "Hold your fangs and make them arms. Hold your arms and make them fangs."

Twice more she had found herself sitting on the mats having been struck down by her teacher's relentless brutality. Every time she had fallen, he had stopped, stood in silence, and allowed her to get up. This infuriated her even more than his earlier taunting, for she had been so sure that it was her that was going to be doing some of the knocking down, not entirely the other way around.

J.D. could see the pain and agony she suffered and was silently proud of her in her fortitude. She had sustained his attacks for nearly ten minutes, far longer than he had been able to the first time he had fought against an opponent more skilled than himself. He knew that her body would not be able to take much more punishment; she could barely stand. He tucked his weapon in his belt with the other. He would finish her lesson in bare hand combat.

J.D. had trained in many different forms of martial arts, but he was most adept in three: Jeet Kune Do; Okinawan Shorin-Ryu Karate-Do in which he held a shodan, one who holds a beginners black belt; and the Filipino martial art of Pekiti-Tirsia Kali—Eskrima style from the southern Mindanao regions of the Philippines—in which he had achieved the rank of Instructor Guru. However, he felt his greatest achievement had been earning the rank of Associate Instructor Level 1 in Jeet Kune Do/Jun Fan Gung Fu. Regrettably, he had suffered a neck injury while responding to a medical emergency call and was forced to reschedule his upcoming Associate Instructor Level 2 test, and then the end of the world happened. Though he knew he would have passed his test it still bothered him that he would never be given the opportunity to prove himself before *his* master.

As Katie stepped forward, attempting to deliver a series of offensive straight punch moves with the point of the sai held outward, J.D. countered with a block. She then countered with a strike using her right non-weapon hand, and followed with a quick jab again using her weapon hand. J.D. sidestepped to the left. Taking control of her arm, he said, "Little Dragon seeks the path," an alteration of a line from the Bruce Lee film, *The Way of the Dragon*, and then delivered two quick blows to the upper arm and neck, the first with his forearm followed by a quick closed hand strike to the nerve cluster in her exposed neck. The move was called Palamoot. It is one of the most dangerous moves he had learned while studying Pekiti-Tirsia. The close range of the move normally does not generate enough force to do permanent damage, only enough to stun one's opponent, unless it is executed using a weapon.

She faltered. She had been forced to release the last sai and had suffered a dizzying blow. J.D. had been easy on her. He had barely struck her neck, though it had felt to her like someone had hit her with a 10-pound hammer. The blow she suffered was delivered with the intent to disorient, not cause unconsciousness. Bewildered, she fought desperately to maintain her balance.

The move had been precisely carried out and completely effective. However, he did not stop there. "Big Dragon snaps his tail," he voiced, and then followed with a quick snap strike with his foot aimed at her inner thigh that connected with the femoral nerve. She dropped immediately to the floor. The inside low-leg karate kick he had executed was known as Gedan Mawashi Geri and he, too, had experienced the intense pain it could cause. The test was over.

He extended his arm to help her from the floor. She stood up and then abruptly collapsed, unconscious. J.D. carried her to her room and laid her down upon her bed.

Katie awoke to the blurry sight of fluorescent lighting that highlighted a dull white painted ceiling and walls, which had become dirtied from time. For a moment, she was disoriented. As she looked around, she realized she was lying on her mattress in her narrow room. She didn't remember making it to her room. She must have been carried, she reasoned. It must have been J.D., who had brought her and turned on the lights. An intense pain seared through her lower extremities and across her right breast. She realized that she must have passed out from the pain.

J.D. entered her room unannounced through the open doorway with two cases in his hands. In the right was a long, thin, leather carrying case; in his other was a small black pouch. He was also fully dressed in his military uniform, and she wondered exactly how long she had been unconscious.

J.D. set the larger down under the side of the bed before sitting next to her, and then informed her, "I need you to remove your karategi."

"*Why?*"

"I need to examine you?"

"Come to play doctor?" she asked, painfully. "Don't think I'm up for that."

J.D. ignored her comment. He had not had a sense of humor in a very long time. "I've come to rub some Dit Da Jow liniment on you. It will help with the pain and swelling... Do you have underwear on?

"Yes, *why?*"

"I'm a paramedic, not a gynecologist," he said frankly with a bit of snark. "I only need to see the impact areas, then apply the liniment... Are you able to get undressed?"

"I don't think so. I'm—"

"That's okay. I understand. I've been where you are now," he told her, and then untied the belt that held her uniform top closed.

"You really are a paramedic? I thought it just another cock-and-bull story I hear whispered... like you drink the blood of rats and pigeons."

J.D. did not answer her paramedic question; instead, he began to tell her a story as he cautiously and gently disrobed her.

"That first real Eskrima fight I was in, I was beaten so bad that I was carried from the ring unconscious and back to my hovel. The only medical care I was given was a bottle of Fighter's Friend, and told to rub it on where it hurt. The only problem was there were places I couldn't reach—like everywhere. I was so badly beaten that I lay in bed for over a day unable to move... I would have probably remained immobile for longer if it wasn't for the fact that I had to urinate so badly—and I wasn't going to piss myself."

"So how did you manage to get to the bathroom?" she asked, as he pulled off her pants.

"*Bathroom!*" J.D. scoffed. "I didn't get to any bathroom. I crawled out of my hut, managed to roll myself sideways and urinated. Thank the Creator above I was slightly uphill and it was nighttime."

Katie chuckled. The pain of which made her wince.

"You find that amusing. Well, keep it to yourself. I've never told anyone that."

She was as undressed as he needed to her be. He had not

completely disrobed her. He left the shirt of her tournament style karategi open, having removed the uniform belt, exposing her grey sports bra. She was also wearing white underwear with a violet, flowered pattern, which he pretended not to notice. His self-conscious behavior had not gone unnoticed. J.D. pulled out the knife that was strapped to his leg from its sheath and brought it toward her.

"What's that for?" she asked cautiously.

"I need to cut off your top, so I can see the rest of the impact sights."

"No, you won't—" she declared.

"I need to—"

"—why do doctors always want to cut off your clothes?"

"—in order to put the ointment on. This is strictly professional," J.D. tried to explain.

"I'm not worried about you seeing my breasts. I just don't want you to cut my clothes off. You think I can go to the store and just pick up another? Pull it off."

"It's tight, it should be cut off. I don't want to cause any undue discomfort."

"That's sweet and very… professional of you. But I think I can handle a little undue discomfort."

He understood the clothing objection. The paramedics had cut away one of his favorite rock shirts on that fateful night he had found himself in the back of the ambulance heading to a trauma center after being shot in the chest. The recollection of this brought on thoughts, not of the tragic night, for his body would forever carry reminders of that night but of his friend David DiMinni. The shirt had been from the band The Dominion. The Dominion had been a band with blues, progressive rock, Indian and Middle Eastern influences, dubbed "Moroccan roll," and had been fronted by David, or DD Dominion as he had been known in his rock star days before becoming a conEdison employee. J.D. had not known David then, nor had they ever met, until the fall of the world.

He obliged her.

After removing the uniform top he moved closer to her, leaned in, and gently took her arms and placed them around his neck. "Hold on," he softly spoke, and then carefully pulled her upper body up enough to reach down to the hem of her sports bar to pull it up. When he had guided it up as far as her neck, exposing her breasts, he placed his left hand behind her back as support to remove the garment from around her neck. He could smell her musk. He fought the urge to sniff her, but he could not help be aroused. After placing the grey top down, he took his free hand and placed it upon the soft warmth of her back and smoothly moved lower. He picked up her top and laid it across her breasts, hoping to avoid any further stimulation. Katie took his gesture as modesty and gentleman like-demeanor, which made him even more desirable to her. She could have flirted with him, but with his uneasiness at her naked chest she felt it was best for the moment to not say anything.

He ran his hands gently over her legs, first the right—which had suffered the most damage—and then the left, moving slowly up her thighs over the purple and blue spectrum of colors that her contusions had now become, searching her injuries for any hematomas.

Katie's body was lean, strong and muscular. Her well-developed definition had become more toned than her dancer's physique had once been. She had trained hard to increase her agility, stamina and muscular strength. Her body was trim and rock-hard but had not lost its femininity. She reminded him of the comic book character Elektra, a Greek ninja assassin who wields the zai as her trademark weapon.

As he moved across Katie's ribs, she grimaced more than she had when he had run his hands along her lower extremities. Her ribs and right breast were extremely tender. There was the possibility that he had hit her hard enough—though he had not used full force—to have fractured a couple of ribs. As a paramedic, he would have instructed his patient to go to the hospital for x-rays. Though the armory hospital was equipped was an x-ray machine, it would only confirm or deny the existence of the hairline fractures.

Before he sent her to see Doctor France for x-rays, and not to unduly alarm her at the slight possibility he had done more injury than he intended, he asked her to breathe deeply and then to cough moderately. After which he requested she should cough as hard as possible. There was no sharp pain associated with these actions. He was satisfied that he had not fractured her ribs.

He took the bottle of liniment out of its small pouch and opened it. The aroma quickly filled the air of the small room.

Katie commented, "It's very…"

"Aromatic?" he responded.

"No, pungent… So what is it, again?"

"Dit Da Jow. That's Cantonese. Its literal translation is 'fall hit wine.' It's a bruise liniment to stop pain, reduce swelling and inflammation—and unblock blood stagnation and blood stasis. It'll help increase your blood flow and tissue healing response."

"You do sound like a doctor—"

"Paramedic," he reminded her.

"—and is dit dow ja standard issue in a medical kit?"

He corrected her, "Dit *Da Jow*. No, part of my personal kit." He began to apply the liquid. "Of all the weapons I offered to teach you, you decided on one I barely knew."

"I tried, but none felt right to me. The zai feels like an extension, part of me."

J.D. knew exactly how she felt. He had been taught that the ideal weapon must come together perfectly with the fighter, and maximize the warrior's impact, lethal range, and control. Nonetheless she relied on the three-pronged weapon as a mainline of defense, and this needed to be corrected.

"When my attacks merely sting the enemy and I know my hands and feet are useless because they cannot inflict pain, then I must use a 'substitute weapon'. My bastóns, my kukri… They are my substitute weapon."

J.D. took her wrist and held up her hand, telling her, "Let these be your fangs first."

She glared up at him, "I'm sorry I failed you."

"Have you now? Is my approval that important?" he asked.

"I wanted to show you I was worthy of a promotion. I want the responsibility of team leader."

"Did you try your best? Did you give all that your heart, soul and body could give?"

"Yes. And more," she told him, in a pained tone.

"Then where is the failure in that? If you try and do not succeed, that is not failure. The failure is in not trying at all. Besides, no one here has ever beaten me."

"But—I thought—but you promoted the others. And you said I would have to beat you to earn a team leader position."

"*Did I?* Are you certain? Or did I say, 'you have to prove yourself'?"

She thought about it for a moment, and then realized that proving herself was what he had told her. "You sound like my father," Katie told him. "He always would say, 'You only fail in life if you do not try to succeed.' "

"Your father was a wise man," he told her. "You did well. Better than I expected, but not half as well as you could have if you hadn't relied on the pig stickers." J.D. changed the subject to dancing. "Do you still dance?"

She thought it an odd question; they were in the midst of a conversation about failure and out of nowhere he asked about dancing.

She replied warily. "On occasion. *Why?*"

"Your muscularity and strength are outstanding—"

"Are you making a pass at me?"

"—however, your balance and focus are off. You may want to practice pirouette in retire—à la seconde—or even better fouetté rond de jambe en tournant. It will help improve these deficiencies."

"Is that what you do?" she jokingly replied.

"Not anymore."

She didn't believe him. "You're a dancer?"

"No. But I did take ballet lessons."

She laughed out loud, "*You?!*" and then once again grimaced from pain.

"You seem to find great humor in that, too, don't you? Well, that's another secret you're going to keep," he sternly warned her. J.D.

replaced the cap on the liniment bottle. He had completed applying the herbal remedy to the front portion of her body.

"I'm sorry. I just find it funny, you doing ballet."

"So did the kids at elementary school. I was the only one in my school taking dance, and the only boy in my ballet class. It was fun learning dance with all the girls, but it wasn't fun getting my ass kicked on a daily basis. I really hated my parents for that... As a child, my mother always wanted to be a ballerina, but her family was too poor to afford lessons. So, she never could pursue her dream. I guess me taking lessons was her way of living out her lost dreams."

"And this lasted how long?"

"The lessons? I put an end to that early. I kind of persuaded my mom that if she stopped forcing me to take ballet, I wouldn't fight her on the piano lessons. Of course, I didn't tell her I wanted to learn piano."

"You're quite a Renaissance man. Sensitive and sexy."

"Katie, just stop. I've gotten all your subtle and not-so-subtle hints. I can't give you what you are looking for."

He had finally broached what she had wanted him to acknowledge for so long. She had been beginning to think that he had never noticed her or her hints of desire for him. Except his response was not what she had hoped for.

"How do you know what I am looking for?" she asked.

"There's a reason I don't get close to anyone. And—"

She cut him short. "So, you're saying you're not attracted to me?"

He was, and the transmute side of him desired her deeply. Though Katie had suffered a substantial beating from J.D., and, for the most part, had overcome the pain, he wasn't sure she would be able endure the frenzied and often rigorous and painful acts of transmute coitus. There was also no room in his heart for anything but a sex partner, for his heart ached with love lost, and his loss consumed him, so he declined.

"What I was about to say," he spoke, with slight irritation having been interrupted, "is that everyone I've loved or cared about has died or left—my friends, my dog, Marisol, then Luci—men under my command, who trusted me with their lives—dead! There's nothing left inside me. Do you understand?"

She wasn't going to make his rejection of her easy on him. "Don't get all mushy on me. I'm not looking for a ring, I'm just looking for a lay." She forced herself to rise and put her arms around his neck and gave him a deep, erotic tongue kiss.

J.D. didn't immediately spurn her advance. The taste of her tongue inside his mouth aroused him. He put his mouth to her neck, sniffed and then pressed himself closer, nuzzling his mouth under her ear and repeatedly kissed her. Katie breathlessly moaned. She could feel herself getting moist. J.D. could sense her arousal and it stirred him. He dug his talons into her back. She winced, more out of pain than pleasure. He knew under her present condition he could cause her severe bodily damage. He pushed her away and told her, "No. This can't be. I'll break you."

He took her hand and placed the bottle of liniment in it. "I think it best you finish the other areas. I need to attend to armory matters."

As he departed, he paused at the doorway and drew a long breath. Raising his left arm, he placed his hand on the doorframe and spoke, but did not turn to her as he did.

"Consider yourself on temporary medical leave. Report to Major Alexander at 0900 tomorrow for your new assignment. Understood?"

"Yes, sir," she replied, in a reserved tone, regretting making her feelings known to him.

"Good day, *Sergeant*," he spoke as he walked into the hall.

A smile came to O'Hanlon's face. She had gotten half of what she desired. She had been promoted.

---

J.D. returned to his makeshift dojo and to his martial arts, hoping that the intense workout that he was intending would take his mind off of Katie O'Hanlon, but it did not. Her scent, her tongue and the feel of her soft flesh was something he could not shake.

As the day waned and darkness fell on the city, his desire for her only intensified. He wanted her, but he feared in her weakened condition she could not endure his intense thirst for carnal pleasures, and was unsure that he could temper his aggressive passion to ensure he would not do her harm. His workout had not been a diversion or a release of his desire for her, so he set out on a hunting expedition, hoping the tracking down and eliminating more of Stone's men would lessen his lust for her.

---

The thoughts of J.D.'s muscular form, the tattoos that adorned him, and the sensation of her tongue upon his made her moist and wanting. Katie knew that he was not normal in many aspects of his physiology because of his mutation, but the brief exchange of bodily contact proved to her that he was still a man that had sexual needs, and she wanted him inside fulfilling her needs as well as his.

It had been a long time since Katie had had a man sexually gratify her. She had a boyfriend before she moved to New York and he was attentive to her needs, though he had been as inexperienced in love-making as she at that time. She had been dating an older guy for nearly a month before the plague, and she had every intention of consummating the relationship on their eighth date, but the end of civilization put an end to her getting laid. She masturbated twice hoping that the self-pleasure would relieve her sexual frustration, but her orgasms just aroused her libido even more.

---

It had not been a productive night. He had not come across any enemy patrols nor was he any closer to finding Stone's newest basecamp. After showering and dressing into a simple black cotton Kung Fu uniform and matching pair of Kung Fu shoes, he walked the floor of the armory hall. It was after 1:00 a.m., and most civilians were sleeping, though a few remained awake in whispered conversation or reading by candlelight. He stopped briefly to check on his two sentries before heading to the upper floors where the private rooms were located. Katie was still heavy in his thoughts. He decided to visit her under the guise of seeing how she was feeling. If she still wanted him, he would oblige her. He needed to get laid, too.

---

A light rapping came to her door. She knew that the only person that would come calling this late would be J.D., and she had prepared in hopes he would change his mind. She turned on the small lamp that sat on the nightstand and replied, "Come in."

As he closed the door behind him he said, "I know it's late but I wanted to see how you were doing."

He moved across the room and sat on the bed next to her. For a moment, they looked at one another both knowing the real reason why he had come to her room. Katie broke the silence.

"What are you waiting for?" she asked. "Take me," she told him and pulled back her bed covers to exposure her naked body.

J.D. did not refuse the invitation. All he said was, "Let me know if I get too rough."

She gasped with equal parts discomfort and pleasure the first time he penetrated her. She was not sure if he was well endowed because of his mutation or that he was normal and that the only man she ever previously had sex with was under endowed.

He took her forcefully three times, digging his talons into her and thrusting his manhood deep into her with uninhibited vigor. She returned the pain in kind by biting him hard on his neck, shoulders and chest, and it heightened his pleasure. After his third rapid orgasm his ferocity seemed to diminish and was replaced by less wild but still impassioned intercourse. He allowed her to repeatedly quench her needs for a while, and then they began an exploration of one another's bodies. They continued well after dawn satisfying one another.

When their sexual tryst was over, she had felt pleasure in ways that she had never experienced. She was even more exhausted and in discomfort than she had been from her martial arts beating, but she was sexually gratified.

When it was time for J.D. to leave, there were no thank-yous or sentiment between them. He rose and dressed in front of her, as she lay naked upon the bed watching him. He sat back down and then scooped her up in his arms and gave her a passionate kiss, and then gently laid her back down and departed.

J.D. felt more relaxed and calmer of mind than he had in a long time. Katie O'Hanlon was just what he had needed, but he knew a repeat of their time together would be unlikely. He had other plans for her.

# 8

# COMMANDER! MY COMMANDER!

PAUL WIESE STOOD UP FROM HIS CHAIR AND RAPPED LIGHTLY ON THE commander's door. Paul was now a warrant officer. Once having been distrusted by J.D., he went from civilian to valued soldier—being put in charge of all base personnel recruitment and oversight along with being J.D.'s personal assistant—all because of one pivotal moment that earned his unquestionable trust.

---

J.D. had not always trusted Paul as much as he did now. J.D. was leery about him when he first came to the armory begging for sanctuary. He had been a member of Stone's gang—but not just any member. He was part of Stone's crew that had captured Ryan and tied him to a tree at Astor Place. Ryan had been sick then, ill with shingles, but Stone's gang believed he had been infected with the mutant plague and were intent on killing him. J.D. and his former comrades saved Ryan, and let Stone's men leave unharmed, but with a stern warning to stay out of their territory.

When Paul showed up at the armory the night before the old team members were to depart to England, J.D. thought it highly suspicious.

However, circumstances and fates change and with Paul helping Ryan rescue J.D. at the pier, and with Ryan and Doctor France as Paul's champions, J.D. granted Paul's request for asylum.

Asylum had not been the only reason Paul had come to the armory seeking shelter. It was his conscience and morality that brought him to J.D.'s doorstep. Having been with Stone—for a brief period, though J.D. doubted the validity to Paul's claim—he knew the brutality Stone inflicted on those who did not obey and worship him. Worse was that he knew the rumors of what Edward Stone was doing to his young captives were true.

An early dawn raid had been planned and though J.D. suspected a trap, he and Ryan had no choice but to go. They took Paul with them. J.D. warned the man if it were a ruse, he'd make sure he was the first to get a bullet. When they arrived at where Paul said he and the others had made their base, Stone's men had gone. They rushed back to the armory; J.D. believing the location had been used as a ruse to lure them away to give Stone an easy opportunity at seizing their fortress. An attack never came, and J.D. realized, after some convincing from Ryan, that Paul had been sincere. However, a good intention, no matter how noble, doesn't automatically award you with trust. J.D. was still unsure of where Paul's loyalties lie. He was further unconvinced at the tale Paul spun of his escape from Stone's grip. It was just too unbelievable.

This all changed in mid-November. Doctor France was liberal with wanting anyone who showed up at the gates to be given sanctuary. In his eyes everyone should be given aid and comfort, even those who appeared dubious. J.D. had never known France to be generous or compassionate, which struck J.D. as suspicious, but he could not determine Frances' endgame and let him have his way within reason.

There had been a screening process in place, but more often than not, and almost always when J.D. was away from the armory, the screening process was bypassed. The refugees were rushed into the armory's medical facility for immediate care, whether they were in distress or not, before they could be thoroughly checked for weapons or contraband.

Disregarding the screening process was dangerous and J.D. knew eventually Doctor Frances' blatant disregard for the safety of the armory would come back to bite them all in the ass.

A group of refugees arrived at the gate one early afternoon. J.D. had been gone for a day; no one knew where and no one questioned why. James and Ryan were in a meeting with John and Peter Dunne. Jonas was on sentry duty on the roof and Peter Schumacher, Sr. was in the communications room. When word of new arrivals was passed by radio from Jonas to Schumacher and then relayed over intercom to James and Ryan, Richard France immediately went to the main armory doors to wait for James and/or Ryan. If it had been up to France, he would have immediately gone to the perimeter gate, opened it, and allowed the refugees entry. However, Doctor France was no longer allowed to have the keys to the compound gates. Only J.D., Ryan, and James had the authority and the ability to open the gates, and this completely annoyed the doctor. To him it was an impediment on his ability to efficiently and rapidly respond to the medical needs of any refugee who sought help.

Ryan responded to the call and under guard brought the five refugees into the compound. One survivor appeared to be very ill, and before Ryan and his men had an opportunity to search the man, Doctor France tried to whisk him away. Ryan ordered France to desist and begrudgingly France acquiesced, though he protested greatly at what he described as heavy-handedness in the treatment of the ill. Upon inspection they discovered a large hunting knife concealed under the man's shirt, the man claiming it was for self-protection. Ryan confiscated the weapon.

The following day the man seemed to make a miraculous recovery, France taking the credit for his superior medical treatment. The thin, wiry individual with the dirty blonde-hair was released and allowed to join the general population in the drill hall.

It was not unusual for Paul to be in the drill hall most days for he had been given the task of doing initial interviews with new arrivals to see what kind of useful skills they might have, and then reporting his findings to Ryan. J.D. had allowed Paul the luxury of his own room, since he did aid Ryan in his rescue. However, there had been one stipulation to the amenity. Since Paul was civilian—a status Paul wished to change but J.D. had refused—and was being allowed a luxury that was reserved for base personnel, Paul would have to keep the upper floors, including the hospital, clean, if he wished to keep his private quarters —bathrooms too.

Nonetheless interviewing was not what brought Paul down to the civilian population that evening; it was the children. There had been a few children amongst the refugees and Paul had decided just because the world had ended that it was no reason for education to end. Three evenings a week, after completing his daily duty assignments, and out of his love for teaching, he held a reading and spelling class for the children.

As he walked through the drill hall, he caught a glimpse of a man looking at him. At first, he thought nothing of it as he passed the nervous man and went with books in hand to his destination. However, as he conducted his reading class, he noticed the man was still watching him, and then he realized he couldn't recall interviewing him. When Paul looked toward the man, the man would suddenly avert his eyes from Paul's direction. It happened three times and Paul had an uneasy feeling that the man was studying him, but for what reason Paul did not know. When reading and spelling time were over Paul decided he was going to get a proper look at the fellow who was placing so much focus on him.

As Paul stood and said farewell to his class, J.D. came into the drill hall with Ryan and began speaking with the new intakes. The man was waiting to speak with J.D., as were the other new refugees, all eager to meet the base commander. However, the body language the skinny man was portraying suggested something entirely different. It wasn't an excited anticipation he was exuding; it was anxiety.

As Paul drew nearer, he suddenly realized this man was no ordinary refugee; it was one of Stone's men. There was a glint in the man's right hand, an object. J.D. moved onto the next refugee, greeting and welcoming them to their safe haven, promising he and his men would do everything they could to keep them safe and comfortable. The man moved slightly toward J.D. and Ryan as Paul quickly approached.

Something slid from the man's sleeve into his hand. It was some sort of pointed weapon. The man turned his head slightly, and seeing Paul in a hurried approach gave him a wicked smile.

Paul was still too far away to do anything but yell, so he screamed as loud as he could, "*Weapon! Weapon!* He's got a weapon!"

J.D. looked toward Paul and saw him pointing in his direction. Abruptly someone pushed Ryan to the ground from behind. J.D. saw a blade coming toward him and quickly sidestepped. The blade barely missed. As J.D. moved his foot, it became entangled with Ryan's and he lost his balance. The man raised his knife again and as he did Paul forcefully tackled him.

There were screams from the civilians when they finally realized what was happening. Paul and the man tumbled to the floor and rolled away from J.D. and Ryan. Paul let out a howl of pain. The man had stabbed him in the left shoulder at the upper pectoralis major near the shoulder joint. It was a surgical scalpel the man was wielding. Paul sat on top of the man's chest struggling to hold the knife at bay.

Ryan had painfully scrambled on all fours across the floor before J.D. could recover, which had been surprising since Ryan was still in a sling and his recent wound had now been re-injured in his fall. The assailant rolled over in an attempt to free himself of Paul. A pistol suddenly pressed against the man's temple.

Still on his knees, Ryan ordered, "Drop it, drop it now!" The attacker looked at him. He could see the nervousness, the fright in Ryan's eyes. Ryan felt the gun trembling on the man's temple. Paul rolled clear. "I said drop it!" Ryan demanded again.

"Sure," the man said, but then moved to swing the weapon. The pistol went off. The scalpel dropped.

Ryan rose and then looked at the brain and blood spatter coating the floor. A deep red pool began to spread out from the large hole in the man's head. Ryan excused himself. J.D. understood. He too had needed to vomit the first time he had killed someone.

"I was wrong about you, Wiese." J.D. told Paul. "No more mops. Report to Lieutenant Alexander in the morning. I'm putting you on special assignment. Consider your request for enlistment granted,

Private Wiese. Dismissed," he said, and then saluted his newest recruit, giving him a smile. "Now stop bleeding all over my floor. Go see Doctor France." Paul returned the salutation and the smile.

J.D. picked up the scalpel that had fallen from the dead man's hand. James had come running with a few men at hearing the sounds of the shot. "I think we need a body bag," he told James. "And I think I'm going to have a talk with Dick," he said, showing James the weapon.

Several hours later the light tower was lowered, and the beacon that illuminated the night sky extinguished permanently. There would be a moratorium on further refugees allowed into the armory, until a more secure process could be implemented. The moratorium only lasted for a few days, when Michael Panton's group arrived.

---

"Come," came a voice from the other side.

Paul opened the old wooden door with its frosted glass window, stepped through the archway, and shut the door behind him. He did not salute his commander; it was not required. "Sergeant O'Hanlon wishes to see you, sir."

"Does she now? Send her in."

Paul stepped back into the smaller outer office and addressed the sergeant, having left the commander's door open. "The commander will see you."

Katie saluted Paul. "Thank you, Sergeant."

Paul returned the salutation.

Katie saluted her commander as she approached J.D.'s desk. He did not return the salute.

"At ease, soldier," he replied instead. "What's on your mind?"

"I've come to request not to be promoted and reassigned, sir," she answered him respectfully, but with a reflection of anxiousness in her tone.

Katie placed the leather case that her teacher had left under her bed on the lip of his desk. J.D. glanced at it and then looked up at her.

"Request denied. Is there anything else, Sergeant?"

"No, sir."

"Don't you have to be somewhere in a few minutes, Sergeant?"

"Yes, sir."

"Then I suggest you pick up your weapons and dismiss yourself. You have a tactical meeting, and I highly suggest you don't make Major Alexander wait."

She began to move toward the door, then stopped, turned back to her commanding officer, and addressed him.

"Permission to speak freely, sir."

"Permission granted."

"Please forgive me, *sifu*." She humbled herself before him by getting down on one knee with a bowed head. "I know by allowing you into my bed we crossed the line of commander and subordinate. I've dishonored you and shamed myself. But please do not punish me by sending me away. I beg you."

Her begging forgiveness reminded him of the old Hong Kong kung fu flicks of the 1970s, he so loved to watch.

"At ease, soldier. And Katie, get up off the floor." She did as he instructed. "Is this what you think it is a punishment? Katie, we are not the military of old. What we did last night is no one's business but our own."

"Then why are you sending me to Mechanicville?"

"It's a command decision, and frankly I do not have to explain myself. However, since you are an exceptional warrior and kind to my daughter, I will tell you... I promoted you because you are ready for the next level in command responsibility. And that step is to be second in charge of the civilian relocation. I did not make that decision lightly.

This is an extremely dangerous and vital mission. There are very few in this armory I trust implicitly. You and Major Alexander will be commanding a very large column of supply and combat vehicles, and most of our civilian population. Your fighting skills are exemplary. That's why I'm placing you on the Alpha Team."

Katie's expression went from disappointment to appreciation at the compliment and trust he had in her.

J.D. added, "You're the first protégé I've ever had that's shown exceptional promise. I know if anything should happen to me you'll be there to continue the tradition of martial arts. And you are ready; you just don't know it yet. Do you understand?"

"Yes, sir. And thank you, sir."

"Oh, don't thank me, Sergeant. This isn't a holiday. You're going to have a lot of work and a lot of responsibility. I need that town fully operational by the end of June. Do you understand?"

"Yes, sir."

"Good. Then report to Major Alexander, you are dismissed."

She turned to leave.

"*Sergeant!*" J.D. called to her.

"*Sir?*"

He asked, "Aren't you forgetting something?"

"Begging the commander's pardon, sir!" She saluted him, having forgotten.

"Sergeant O'Hanlon. I was referring to the zai. Those are a gift. They were the ones I used to train with. They're yours now. Put them to better use than I did."

She smiled and picked up the case.

# 9

## IN A MIRROR, DARKLY

THE DOCTOR HAD WARNED J.D. IF HE DID NOT GET SLEEP HIS condition would worsen. However, he had not heeded the doctor's warning and had begun a dangerous downward spiral in his mental behavior.

He sat on the padded examination table with his shirt off. The doctor had concluded a first round of questions, followed by the administering of an EKG, drawing a blood sample, listening to his heart, and taking his blood pressure. J.D. had been poked, prodded, and interrogated and the doctor had still not come up with a conclusion. He was physically sound, as far as the doctor could see from his preliminary exam.

"So, besides your headaches, what other symptoms are you aware of?" France asked. "Are you still having hypersexuality issues?"

"Not at the moment. And I keep telling you, it's severe migraines."

"And have there been any of the accompanying physical changes after the onset of the headaches?"

"No."

"And is this what brought you to the conclusion that these are migraines?"

"I'm a paramedic, remember? I know a migraine when I feel one."

"No, I have not forgotten, especially since you have made that quite clear since the day we met. However, that does not qualify you as a doctor. And since I am, I will be the one who determines the diagnosis." The doctor took a note pad and pen from his table. "You do not have any symptoms of a migraine. There is no nausea or vomiting. No increase in your sensitivity to light. You have no sensitivity to noise or smells. Your headache does not get worse with routine physical activity. And you have no history of migraines in the past. The only symptom of your headache is the severe throbbing. This is not a migraine... Have you been taking the medication I previously gave you?"

"Yes."

"Do you have difficulty doing tasks?"

"No."

"Short attention span?"

"*What?*"

The doctor looked at him disapprovingly. "You are quite amusing, Mr. Nichols. Now answer the question. Short attention span?"

J.D. replied with irritation, "No!"

"Irritability would be a yes," Doctor France noted dryly.

The doctor's questioning became tiresome to J.D. "How much longer with the questions? I'm busy. I just need something for the headaches."

"I am not at liberty to be dispensing medication just because you think your problems stem from migraines that are not migraines."

"What problems? It's just a fucking headache...! You know I could just go out and get something on my own."

The doctor countered with a stern tone, ignoring J.D.'s threat of finding his own medication. "That would be your decreased need for sleep, mood swings, depression, decreased self-control, irritability, rage, and your risk-taking behaviors, Mr. Nichols! Do you think that no one has noticed? You snipe at your men. You prowl the streets at night. When you come back, *if* you come back, you are dirtied and bloodied; you proceed to pace the halls or stand vigil on the roof, not even having the courtesy or decency to wash. Your behavior is concerning.

You exhibit symptoms of a chemical imbalance. More precisely hypo-
mania, however—"

"*Bipolar?!* You're saying I'm bipolar?! Listen, you quack! You're
not even a real doctor, just some bureaucrat with some fancy degree
who can't tell a headache from a hemorrhoid!"

"*I* have a degree in biochemistry. What do you have? The great J.D.
Nichols: warrior, hero, paramedic. The great savior of mankind! Well,
let me tell you something, Mr. Nichols. Any first year EMT student
could conclude your headaches are not migraines."

J.D. stood up and pointed his finger at the doctor, but before J.D.
could speak France laid into him. The doctor had grown livid over his
belittling comments. France burst forth in an angered tone. "I have put
up with your insults," he said, as he touched the index finger of his left
hand onto that of his right, and then proceeded to touch the next digit
as if counting out—accenting his finger animation with forward hand
thrusts—"your threats, and your indignations ever since we met. Yes, I
helped destroy the world. Yes, that is unforgivable." He directed his
finger now at J.D., punctuating the resentment he felt toward his
tormentor. "But do not—do… you do not have the right to question my
ability as a physician. If it was not for me volunteering to stay behind,
there would be no one here to give aid and comfort to the sick and
injured, no one to extract bullets and shrapnel from the men who fight
for you on this holy crusade you are obsessed with. For this, I have
earned the right to respect in regard to my ability as a care provider.
So, shut up and sit back down until I give you leave, or I will have you
declared medically unfit for duty and remanded to my care pending
review. Do I make myself clear, *Colonel?*" France ended, condescend-
ingly using J.D.'s military title.

It had been J.D. who had given the doctor the power to declare a
person physically or mentally unfit for duty. In an effort to bring order
back from the chaos and to protect the innocent from harm, he, Ryan,
James, and, begrudgingly, Doctor France, had constructed and insti-
tuted a series of governing laws that all in the armory must follow
explicitly. One such article gave Doctor France the authority to evaluate the mental and physical health of any soldier and judge them fit or

unfit for duty, and if deemed unfit would be relieved from his or her duties until the doctor deemed otherwise. This was for the protection of the common good, and this included J.D.

Doctor France had put his commander on warning, and J.D. knew he was over the proverbial barrel.

"Volunteered my ass!" J.D. scoffed, knowing full well the doctor stayed behind knowing he would probably have been executed for his hand in ending the world if he had gone to England. "Well, at least you finally grew some balls, Dick," J.D. congratulated him. He resentfully sat back down.

"Now, shall we continue?"

"By all means. Carry on, doctor."

"Unfortunately, the body doesn't have a built-in dipstick for me to check the chemicals which relay messages from nerve to nerve, and without the availability of a PET Scan, I am forced to evaluate your neurotransmitter levels by looking for indicators in thought, behavior, mood, perception, and/or speech that are considered related to levels of certain neurotransmitters. You have many of the outward signs of bipolar disorder but you are not bipolar. I will run your blood and check your dopamine, serotonin, norepinephrine, and gamma aminobu-tyric acid levels. However, I think that will be moot. We are both aware of what is really the underlying cause of your symptoms. And there is nothing that can be done about it. I can adjust your current medication to help counter some of the symptoms; nevertheless, I also highly suggest you get some sleep, and I do not mean for one or two hours. You need to be getting a minimum of six hours daily before you take your meds. You may be part transmute, but even transmutes need sleep."

"I can sleep when I'm dead," he informed the doctor.

"Well, if you do not get sleep you may soon be dead, or worse, you may get someone killed by a lack of clear judgment. So, I am ordering you to go to your room and get some sleep."

"And what about my headaches?" J.D. asked.

"Clearly you were not listening. It is your brain chemistry. Your lack of adequate sleep and your constant worrying has exacerbated your condition. However, I am sure I can find something to help alleviate the discomfort."

J.D. did not have a choice. He knew the doctor was serious, and he knew if he disobeyed France's order the doctor would inform his subordinates. There had always been a standing rule with regard to his behavior. It had been established at the GCC with his original team, and the order J.D. had given to protect his friends and dog was that if it was felt that he was a danger to others he could be expelled or, worse, terminated. His decree had carried over. He went directly to his room with his added regiments of medications. He slept for four hours.

———

J.D. had a great reason to be concerned about his condition. The original antigen that he had injected himself with had not eliminated the virus from his body. What had prevented J.D.'s complete mutation into a transmute was the antigen in unison with his own immune system that had forced the virus into dormancy.

However, dormancy was only a temporary state, and the virus with its accompanying mutations had re-emerged on several occasions. The doctor noted that the re-emergence of the virus was triggered by severe stress. J.D. had changed the day he had been attacked at Pier 17 and again the night he lost Luci.

He was sure it was only a matter of time before his transmute side took over. This would put everyone on the base in danger, for his transformation would not be like Luci's but more aggressive and dangerous like the males of the species.

What J.D. did not know and the doctor had no intention of revealing, was that there was something more sinister happening to him.

# PART III

## THE DARKNESS

"Passion and shame torment him, and rage is mingled with his grief."

— Virgil

# 1

## TATTOOS & SCARS

JOHN DAVID NICHOLS HAD BEEN THROUGH MANY YOUTHFUL TRIALS and tribulations, and even a near death experience from which he had emerged a better person. He had also mellowed over the years, becoming more empathetic, and though at times his faults would seep through his strong but gentle exterior, he had overcome most of his shortcomings through the discipline of his martial arts and meditation. He had even found his life's calling as a paramedic for Saint Vincent's Hospital, a career that brought him much satisfaction.

However, he was no longer the man he once was either before the plague or since the loss of his love Marisol De La Garza and his original survivor group. He was lonely and missed their companionship and that of his dog Max. Ryan was a friend of sorts, but his relationship with Ryan was different from those who had left him. He and Ryan's relationship was one of more commander and subordinate, not like the one he had with David. He did have Barkley as a canine companion, but he certainly wasn't Max.

What had changed him for the worse was the horrific loss of the mother of his child. He was a tortured soul, a man who had become disillusioned, reclusive and distant, filled with a hate and revenge that consumed his total being, with a madness-fueled fixation in his resolve in finding the missing and to punish the man who was the cause of so much suffering to so many.

The Trixoxen virus that had mutated J.D. to a trans-human had been beneficial to a certain extent. The transformation had left him with the ability to turn his head completely backward, useful in surprising the enemy, with minimal change in the elongation of his neck. His fingernails had fallen off. The nail beds had been replaced with flesh, but his fingertips had spontaneously sprouted talons. These were not proportionally long compared to an owl's, but they were just as sharp and as deadly, and were sheathed in keratin—making them a lethal weapon that could rip flesh. Though at times his talons proved to be challenging when attempting something that required significant manual dexterity, he adapted—at first clipping them with dog nail clippers, but less as time went on.

Although his visual acuity had been hyper extended, the only outward change in his eyes had been their color. They had become midnight black. There had been other changes, too. The strength, agility and stamina the doctor had told him about were there—he had developed more fast twitch fiber in the muscles of his arms and legs—but the high metabolism that was associated with it demanded more food for energy, far more than he had consumed even when he was heavily training in his martial arts disciplines.

His higher tolerance to pain and rapid cellular regeneration that gave him the ability to heal quickly from injuries was also advantageous, especially since he had been shot through the leg and found that after four days it had healed with only a scar remaining. There seemed to be no damage to his leg, no loss of function whatsoever. There had been one final major transformation to his outer metamorphosis and that was a four-inch wide long patch of transmute skin that ran from the base of his skull down the spine to his coccyx. Of course, there was also the complete loss of body hair, except for his scalp. It was great that he never had to shave—*anywhere*.

However, there was one other change that Doctor France neglected to inform him or was unaware of—hypersexuality. His sexual compulsivity to copulate hadn't been an issue, for he enjoyed the immensely heightened gratification, the longer duration climaxes, and the ability to have multiple successive orgasms without a waiting period that his mutation provided. The problem was his nearly constant erection and his increased need to fuck, since Luci's death. He feared he would not be able to maintain control much longer, so he sought the doctor's help.

After running a few tests, Doctor France reported that his persistent genital arousal disorder, or his "raging hard on," as the doctor had referred to his heightened state in an unsuccessful attempt at witticism, was not due to lack of sexual release or increased testosterone levels. There was a high probability it was a physiological change in the frontal and temporal lobes, which was the area of the brain for regulating libido. This was also the area of the brain that Doctor France had told him long ago was where most of the neurological and physiological changes occurred during mutation into a transmute. Certain parts of the brain associated with reasoning, planning, speech, emotions, problem solving, and memory, had been impeded, while other parts of the brain had heightened sensitivity important to cognitive inhibition and memory for negative emotional information—heightened aggression, less fear, and a memory for anything bad that may have happened to them. This, the doctor had told him, was the root cause of his unremitting headaches.

Suffering a neurological disorder was something J.D. never considered could happen, or at least he denied it could happen. It didn't seem possible since all the acute changes had happened early on. France reminded him that further transformation was possible considering the virus had not been eradicated from his system, but rather had become dormant with periodic bursts of further mutation, referring to his skin change.

J.D. now understood that his outbursts and violent nature was a result of a transformation in brain function that caused his heightened aggression, decrease in fear, and a sensitive memory for traumatic experiences. Even though the doctor told him an X-ray would be required to verify any brain abnormalities, he declined. J.D. was certain the doctor's preliminary diagnosis was correct, which was the first time J.D. ever took anything the doctor told him at face value. The doctor gave him some medication and told him to follow his prescribed regiment with the additional pills.

Though J.D. had become more demanding and less tolerant of mistakes, he refused to put anyone's life at risk above his own. Lead by the front was something he remembered once hearing, and it was this creed he adapted, taking point and commanding every mission. Not all of his men liked him; they thought him at times callous and overbearing, but every one of them respected him and followed his orders to the letter for they knew that everything he did was for them and for the children. When things got rough between his men and his demands, Ryan was the buffer, the one who could smooth things over, explain his behavior. Ryan was second in command, the one that stayed by his side through everything.

Sleep was something J.D. rarely had the luxury of. Even when there was time he was still unable to reach a deep and restful slumber. An hour or two, three at best, was his usual, but this to him was fine. To sleep too heavily was to allow the memories of the past to invade his mind, to remind him of a time that was no longer and of friends who were no longer a part of his life. These memories reminded him of who he once was, and today, of all days, was a day he did not wish to remember those days of past. Today was a day that there was no charity or forgiveness in his heart. Today was the day he would question one of Stone's inner circle—the red-haired stuttering man.

---

Peter Jonathan Dunne, the dwarf. A man who had more hate and desire for revenge in him than J.D. Peter, by sheer will and determination, had found his way to the armory a week after James' arrival, and over a month after the encounter with his and his daughter's kidnappers. Doctor France was amazed after hearing this man's tale of survival. The wounds and trauma that he had suffered to his face alone should have killed him, but not to have succumbed to a massive mouth infection astonished France, especially after what Peter had relayed about his fight to survive and ward off infection. He had lain in the pit for what he believed was several days, until the swelling of his face had gone down enough that he could pry his eyelids apart, enough to get slivers of vision back. After discovering he had not broken any bones having been tossed into the pit, he struggled for a day to crawl out and make it to the closest bodega. He hid in the back of the store in a bathroom drinking Gatorade and vitamin waters for nourishment and rinsing his mouth out with salt water every few hours, taking in and expelling liquids through a straw. He had also made a jaw sling to hold his jaw back in proper position, once the swelling had gone down enough that he could push his dislocated jaw back into proper alignment. He spent four weeks hiding and recuperating, fearing that they would discover he was gone and would come looking for him to finish the job.

The scars ran deep on this little person. He had been forced to kill his own son and wife in order to survive. Then when he thought the world was once again becoming safe, he and his daughter were dragged from their apartment. He awoke with hands bound behind his back in a basement with others who had been kidnapped, but his daughter was no longer with him.

He asked the others if they had seen her, but they warned him not to ask, for it would cost him his life. When they came for him, he pleaded with them to tell him where his daughter was. The man responded with, "The little bitch is entertaining the boss. Do you want to see? Do you want to see what a good little fuck your daughter is?" The supervisor gestured to his two men. One with a scar on his face wacked Peter to the back of his head with a long club. In a daze Peter fell to his knees, and then the two men dragged him from the basement and took him to a room where his daughter was being held. His daughter, Victoria, was naked and strapped across a small table. Her face was bruised and bloodied. Her eyes pleaded to her father for help as she struggled, but he could not save her. They held him tightly, two each holding an end of a broom handle firmly against his throat, while the supervising man stood next to them.

There was a man standing in the room, his back was to him. He was wearing no shirt, and held a knife in his right hand. One of Peter's restrainers spoke.

"Boss, this little freak wants to see his daughter. I thought you might like some added entertainment," the tall man with a balding crown atop of his head stated.

The man turned around. He was of average height with blonde hair and blue eyes.

"That's what makes you my perfect right arm, Barlow. We think alike."

"I doubt that, Stone, no one thinks quite like you."

"Would you look at this fuckin' smurf!" Stone exclaimed, smiling, as he gave the captive a once over. He walked over to him, spinning the knife in his hand. "Do you have a name, smidget?" Stone spoke calm and softly, as he prodded his captive with the tip of the knife. "Well, speak up smidge."

Peter gasped for air trying to speak. The man with the knife smacked the closest of the two who were pressing the pole too tightly, a man with a distinct scar on his face.

"Ease up, assholes," he addressed the two men. "The midge is trying to speak… So, what is it midge? What's the name?"

"Peter," he muttered, trying to catch his breath.

"Peter? Well, *Peter*. Did you help make this juicy piece? She don't look like no midge, though she certainly is fun sized." Peter's restrainers laughed. "It must be true what they say about midgets then? Is it?"

"I don't know," Peter responded. "I'm not a midget."

"Not a midge? Then what are you, an Oompa Loompa, a Hobbit?"

"I'm a dwarf."

"A dwarf? A dwarf you say?" The man held out his hands, gesturing like he was weighing objects. "Dwarf, midge, munchkin, who gives a shit! You're a freak, a midge. And I want to know if it's true what they say about midges."

The man cut his shirt open and pulled it back. A large smile came to the blonde-haired man's face.

"Holy shit, look at this," he told his cohorts. "He's got tattoos all over him. Tattoos on a midget! That's fucking hilarious. He's a sideshow freak."

The others started to laugh.

Stone took his knife and cut the dwarf's belt off. "Time for the unveiling!"

"For God's sake," Peter pleaded, "not in front of my daughter. She's only—"

"*God?!*" Stone asked. "There's no God here. Only me, the King of New York! Hail to the king!"

"Hail to the king," one of Peter's restrainers stuttered to get out.

"She's only eleven. Please," Peter begged.

"*Eleven!* Damn, a little old for me. Well when you get served lemons, you just have to make lemonade," he taunted, as he ripped open the man's pants and pulled them down exposing his genitals.

"I guess the stories aren't true," the blonde-haired leader spoke with disappointment. "What an anti-climax. Oh well," he said as he moved toward Peter's daughter. "She's got a lot of spunk, this one," he cruelly tormented. "Usually they break so easily." He stepped behind the girl and slapped her ass, and then raised her head so she could see her father, clearly.

"Smile for daddy, baby. It's gonna be a moment worth remembering."

He unzipped his pants and pulled them apart, exposing his erect penis.

"Oh, I hope this hurts, you little tease," he whispered sadistically to the half-conscious girl.

Peter struggled and began to loudly protest. He tried to break free but the three guards were too much for him.

"Shut him up. Shut him up, God damnit!" Stone shouted, his calm demeanor falling away. He looked down at his penis and became irate. "You fucking little prick," he shouted, great anger in his tone. "Look what you've done. Look what you've done," he ranted as he stepped around from behind the girl exposing his flaccid state.

He zipped up his pants and went to the man. He grabbed the back of his hair while the others held him tightly.

"You little piece of shit. How dare you come in here and make demands and ruin my fun," he angrily spoke with enraged eyes, as he pulled Peter's head back, making sure he was looking up.

Stone raised his ring-adorned right hand into the air, making a fist, and began to repeatedly hammer away at the little man's face, pulverizing it into a bloodied, disfigured mess. He continued to beat his captive even after he passed out. The dwarf's face was bloodied, his lips split apart, his face began to balloon and his eyes became swollen shut.

"Jesus, that feels so good," he spoke, pleased with the damage and suffering he had inflicted. "I feel the wood comin' back."

He went back to the table where he had placed the knife and picked it up along with a pair of pliers. He returned to the unconscious Peter and opened his mouth, grabbed the man's tongue with the pliers and outstretched it. "This will teach you to interrupt me," he said sadistically, then cut out his tongue. Blood poured from Peter's mouth.

"Oh, God, that feels so good," he announced, relishing the deed. "Take the little freak back to the basement as an example to the others. Then tomorrow throw him in the meat pit... Damn, my dick is hard."

The others left the room, dragging the mutilated and nearly dead Peter with them. The blue-eyed man waved Peter's tongue in front of the sobbing girl's face.

"Oh, shush, shush," he spoke to her, as he stroked her dirty, matted golden hair, and then wiped the tongue across her face to clean away the tears.

"We'll save this," he told her. "Maybe you'd like daddy to lick your pussy later."

———

Peter rose early, too, and was already prepping for the upcoming interrogation of the stuttering man. Not only was he going over the instruments he would be using for the questioning, but was rehearsing for his and J.D.'s show for their Theatre of the Absurd.

# 2

# BORSTAL BREAKOUT

THEY HAD BEEN HAILED AS HEROES, THE SAVIORS OF THE UNITED Kingdom, of Great Britain and Northern Ireland. The data they had brought from Doctor France helped significantly in developing a vaccine against the secondary plague; thousands of lives had been saved. Within six months after their arrival, the massive cleanup of the remaining half-mutes throughout the United Kingdom had been completed. Ireland was now reopened and people moved home. Industry and trade began again. Farmers returned to their fields, store keepers to their shops, and factory workers to the plants. The country had returned to a certain normalcy, as much as could be after three-quarters of their country's population had perished.

Kermit had been promoted to Chief Warrant Officer and given the duty of overseeing the specialized teams that had been put together to eradicate the non-human threat, which included eliminating trans-mutes, a job which was offensive to him, knowing that transmutes posed no threat—having witnessed this back in New York with regard to Luci. To him it felt like he was conducting genocide. As distasteful as the murderous acts were, he had to follow orders. He wasn't in New York anymore—these were the rules of a sovereign nation that he swore to defend, so there was no choice but to do what he was instructed to do.

Sam had been promoted to Staff Sergeant and assigned to Logistics Management and it was now he who was second in charge of logistical planning of operations deployments, sustainment, recovery, and support procedures. David and Julie were given honorary ranks of Technical Sergeants in the United States Air Force and were contracted as Engineering Technicians. Marisol got her wish; she got to go to school. Though Marisol wasn't able to go to an English University, since they had remained closed for the first six months after their arrival, The United States Air Force, as a thank you, allowed her to train in computer science technology alongside other soldiers without enlisting.

Their bonds of friendship remained close. They were all assigned housing in the same building, and spent as much of their off time together as possible. Once a week Kermit would invite them over to his apartment and cook for them, and even prepared something special for Max and Otter. But even after all the good things that came from their leaving New York, none of them were truly happy, and none of them wanted to believe that J.D. was dead. Every week as they sat around enjoying each other's company they talked about home.

Home, however, was far away and a place they knew they would never see again, but their time in England was drawing to a close. The British government had now re-established its sovereignty over The United Kingdom and as a year had passed those non-citizens who so valiantly had defended the nation were no longer needed or wanted.

Since the safety of the UK had been secured there was no longer a need for armed foreign troops on its sovereign soil, and therefore the British military felt that RAF Croughton, was no longer needed and should be closed. The United States Air Force base was owned by the British government and was on lease to the United States; under international law, like diplomatic missions, RAF Croughton benefited from an extraterritorial status, which didn't allow the host country to enter the representing country's base without permission. However, since the government of the United States no longer existed, international law would no longer be recognized or honored by the UK. They declared that the US Air Force base's lease was now forfeit and in lieu of back payment all its properties and contents belonged to the British military, and all its occupants were to disarm. If any U.S. military personnel wished to continue its service to the well being and protection of the United Kingdom then they would be welcome to enlist in Her Majesty's Armed Forces, or otherwise retire.

The orders of the British government were final; there were no diplomatic channels to go through to work out an amicable settlement nor was there any way to appeal its decision. The United States Armed Forces was to be disassembled and its aircraft, vehicles, weapons, and supplies confiscated. Eighty-seven men and women, not including a few children, were being forced out of the only refuge they had left. The British government had slapped them in the face by offering them refugee status or inscription into their military without the courtesy of equal rank or pay.

When notice arrived by government courier, not even showing respect enough to send a military commander to deliver the news, an emergency meeting of the Joint Chiefs of Staff was convened. This staff meeting consisted of the four highest-ranking officers of what was left of the U.S. Forces. It consisted of Major Russ Ramsey, Air Force; Colonel Jake Westfield, Army; Lieutenant Colonel Jacob O'Reilly, Marine Corps; and Captain William Baker, Navy. The meeting was called to see if there was anything that could be done to dissuade the British government in their decision. Having failed to get the Brits to rescind their orders, all subsequent meetings were conducted in secret in the late hours of night. They had come to the only decision that could be made, and that was to protect the citizens of the United States in the best way they could, and that would be to guarantee their God given rights and the rights their forefathers had fought so hard for in the Revolutionary War. They would leave, taking with them as many supplies as possible.

The British government had given RAF Croughton seven days to pack up their personal items, prepare for inspection, and depart, all under the watchful eyes of the occupying British Forces. Of those seven days, the Joint Chiefs had used two in a fruitless effort to convince the Brits to change their minds, but they weren't even given an acknowledgement by the British Home Office. Once they realized that drastic measures had to be taken to assure the safety and well being of personnel and civilians, it took them another two days to work out the plans for their escape.

This plan could only be accomplished successfully if they could sequester, without incident, the 27 British Airmen who were jointly running the base and not having Her Majesty's Armed Forces made aware of their plans. Secrecy was of the utmost importance, so it was decided that at 0300 hours on the sixth day, seven men would be summoned, armed, and given instruction to subdue the 27 British subjects and place them in holding. Once this was accomplished all troops would be called to duty and fueling operations would commence, followed by loading of weapons, medical supplies, food supplies, and finally passengers onto five Boeing C-17 Globemaster IIIs, because they were the United States Air Force's air transportation workhorse—having broken 22 records for oversized payloads—and two Lockheed C-5 Galaxy aircraft. Only seven airlift transportation planes were to be used, because there were only seven pilots remaining who were certified and trained on the large airlift aircraft.

Of the 27 Royal Air Force members, most were enlisted pilots who were billeted in the same sleeping barracks, while five administrative officers were living in an officers' quarters on the opposite side of the base. The plan called for the five officers to be subdued first, then the rest.

The plan had been scrutinized down to every detail possible in the short time they had to come up with it. However, three items of importance were the last to be decided, the first being should they destroy all remaining U.S. military property on the base or let it fall into British hands. Also, where on the United States east coast should they land to refuel and what would their final destination be? They had discussed many options but, in the end, they chose the closest air force base to Cheyenne Mountain Air Force Station—Andrews AFB—as their final destination. Though they had not heard from any military base in the

U.S. since the fall of the Western half of the country, a British military satellite had detected a heat signature at Cheyenne Mountain. It was possible, since the mountain complex was a fortress, a military force may have survived.

When discussing their refuel destination there was clearly only one logical place in Major Ramsey's mind, and it was McGuire AFB in Wrightstown, New Jersey. Though Stewart ANGB in Newburgh, New York was almost the same distance from New York City as McGuire, the location was quickly eliminated from consideration. Stewart ANGB had been the base they used when they had come to pick up Doctor France's data nearly a year ago. They had already salvaged most of everything worth taking. McGuire was the only choice in Ramsey's opinion, for it was also larger and better equipped, and was more likely to have fuel. It was also five minutes away from Fort Dix, another place that might still contain large amounts of resources— including vehicles—which meant they didn't have to take ground transport with them. They did decide on taking one U.S. Army AH-64 Apache attack helicopter and one USAF HH-60 Pave Hawk with them just to be on the safe side.

In the end the Joint Chiefs decided it was better to leave what they couldn't take intact as not to piss off the Brits. It was their hope that the Royal Air Force would not stop the transport planes from leaving the UK once in the air, unless they had a reason; blowing things up might just be that reason.

As planned, in the early hours of the morning on the sixth day, far before the dawn broke the horizon, their plan was put into action. It was Kermit who led the subduing strike team in a decisive military engagement, swiftly taking the sleeping British airmen by surprise and without incident. It had helped that Her Majesty's enlisted personnel were all billeted in one building, and the two British officers who resided in a nearby building were easily subdued by another, smaller team. Major Ramsey also headed a team that subdued those RAF personnel on night duty.

Once word came that the base was secure the exodus quickly commenced. When all cargo was loaded, military personnel aboard, and civilians safely seated, the large planes taxied into position. The operation had taken less than three hours. With darkness waning they departed.

Everything that led up to the loud rumble of the departing winged giants taking flight—leaving only the smell of fuel exhaust clinging in the chilly, damp English morning air behind—had been an MRX, a Mission Rehearsal Exercise. The real mission was to leave British airspace alive.

The planes had been in the air less than two minutes when an edict had come from RAF High Wycombe, which were the Command HQ and the Combined Air Operations Centre for the British.

There had been no politeness in the Royal Air Force's request for the United States to return to base, and though Major Ramsey wanted to tell the Brits to go fuck themselves, he restrained that verbalization and went with diplomacy. When discretion failed and a squadron of RAF Harrier GR9 fighter aircraft—mostly armed with AIM-9 Sidewinder missiles—intercepted them, Major Ramsey informed British Command HQ that if it were their desire and intent to deliberately target non-combatants and shoot down unarmed aircraft, then it was a moral decision they would have to make. The United States was not going to surrender under any condition, and they were going home.

Seeing that the Americans were not going to be intimidated and not finding a justifiable reason to murder civilians, especially children, British civility returned and common sense prevailed. The Brits had gotten what they wanted—the Americans gone and their airbase returned. As the jet fighters departed, High Wycombe gave warning. If any United States aircraft attempted to enter into British air space ever again, they would be considered hostile and immediately fired upon.

The sun had risen, the sky was clear, and the promise of a new life lay beyond the horizon. It was a good day for America.

# 3

# FURY OF THE DRAGON

*AUGUST 19, DAY 499.*

The hooded man lay stomach down, strapped over the length of a long table. He was naked. His feet touched the floor, his genitals dangled below the edge of the table. His hands were strapped behind his back, and his torso bound to the table. He was cold, hungry, frightened, and disoriented from the drug he had been injected with—just the way J.D. wanted him. The room was dark for added sensory deprivation, which accented the uncertainty of the captive's situation.

Captured prisoners had previously been taken to the 9th Precinct for interrogation, far away from where the team made their home. This started the night J.D. had captured the man with the scar across his face. It was J.D. who had come up with the idea of using the 9th Precinct for conducting interrogations. This was for the sole purpose of keeping the vile business of information extraction from civilians and anyone with a moral conscience—for Chief Warrant Officer Dunne was very inventive in his methods of obtaining intelligence on the enemy.

J.D. knew the precinct well; his father had been a police officer with the 9<sup>th</sup> for 22 years, before retiring to Arizona. J.D. had often come to visit his father and most of the senior officers knew him. Even though the police station had been renovated after his father had retired, the layout still remained nearly the same, and J.D. knew where the most isolated part of the building was that could mute the noises of Peter's extraction techniques from the outside world.

There were only a few who had first known what went on at the police station. James and Ryan were indifferent toward their commander's tactics and ethics in regard to information acquisition and punishment. They knew in order to survive, extremes were necessary when it came to Stone and his men, and they were glad J.D. had championed the cause, because they both knew neither had it in them to do what J.D. could do.

Paul, though, who had been imprisoned and forced to do hideous tasks against his moral character under Stone's control, was in total agreement with his commander's ways. Admittedly, he was unsure if he could actually torture and kill. Even so, Paul was all for eliminating Stone and his men in any manner necessary.

The police precinct had been abandoned in late July, when the final civilian population was relocated to Mechanicsville. With no longer a reason to hide what was being done—J.D. had told his remaining staff that he was not above doing whatever it took to find the children—there was no reason to continue using it. There had never been a guest in the new interrogation facility that was setup in the basement, for it had become more increasingly difficult to capture Stone's men alive. However, this morning, a warm early August day, a very special visitor was being held, one that Peter and J.D. were both acquainted with—the stuttering man. This man was not only the stutterer who had stood by Barlow's side at the gate that fateful day when Stone made his appearance; he was also the other man who had held the broom handle against Peter's throat.

J.D. never conducted the "interviews" himself. That special pleasure was reserved for Peter, for to torture a bound prisoner was not J.D.'s style; there was no sport in it. Only the chase was fair and challenging. The hunt gave him the exhilaration and the thrill his transmute side desired. Nonetheless that was not to say that he did not participate in the event. J.D. was the warm up act, the ringmaster, the carnival barker, and he was very adept in terrorizing a prisoner using psychological techniques.

Each prisoner was different, and each prisoner was handled accordingly. Those that were of a strong will and defiant in nature were approached more matter-of-factly, for to menace a person with threats and a crazed personality would appear comical and be ineffective. However, for those who were scared and weak of spirit, crazy worked well, and today was one of those days for J.D.'s maniacal sense of humor.

J.D. slowly pulled the door open, allowing the full effect of the squeaking hinges to resonate into the dark room. He stepped through the archway, closing the door behind him. As he casually strolled up to the table's edge, he played a haunting melody on his bell accordion. J.D. stopped playing, squatted and began a light and rhythmical tapping of his talons on the tabletop.

The prisoner could not see J.D.'s approach or that he had squatted in the blackness of the room at the opposite end of the table with his chin on the table's edge, for his head was covered. The prisoner called out in a frightened tone, "Who—who—who's there? What do—do—do... do you want?"

J.D. was only six inches from the man's face, and could hear the fear in the man's erratic breathing and his alarmed squirming, trying to wriggle free from his bindings. He removed the pillowcase that had been placed over the man's head and afterward remained silent for a moment, just two feet away from the man's face.

A beam of flashlight illumination abruptly played across J.D.'s face. "Boo!" J.D. said, looking straight into the man's eyes, his head propped up under his chin by a small pillow.

The man screamed out in horror at the ghastly sight of the creature before him, and as he did, he urinated. He fought desperately to free himself, but could not get free of his bindings.

What had given the stuttering man such a fright was J.D.'s appearance. Besides the black eyes staring at him, he was greeted with a most unusual guise. J.D. had not only painted his face with camouflage make-up in an unconventional manner, but had also shaved the sides of his head, shaping his hair into a Mohawk in order to give himself a fiercer and more menacing look. His overall facial appearance was a cross between Wez from the film *The Road Warrior* and the character Eric Draven from the film *The Crow*. His manifestation and demeanor were that of a depraved madman, and he was.

"Are we seated comfortably?" he greeted the naked man with a large grin.

The man stuttered out a response. "Wha—Wha-wha—"

J.D. grabbed the man's face and squeezed his checks together, causing the man's lips to purse.

"Wah, wah, wah! Stone got your tongue, too, Stutters?"

"You, you, f-f—f—freak."

"Quite the little speech impediment you have there. Let me introduce you to someone else who has a spee—spee-speech impediment," he told the man, taunting him.

"Drum roll, please," J.D. requested, and then began a rhythmic strumming of the tabletop. The room suddenly lighted with the warm illumination of the overhead light.

"Tah-dah!" J.D. proclaimed, and then stood aside as he hand gestured to Peter dressed in full green surgery garb, his face masked as not to reveal his identity.

"Holy shit!" J.D. exclaimed with great astonishment and glee. "Look. It's Doogie Howser!" J.D. ran up to Peter. "Mr. Howser, Mr. Howser. I'm your biggest fan. Can I have your autograph? Wow, I'm so excited that I got a semi." J.D. turned back to his captive, who had a look of confusion on his face. "Aren't you excited, too?" He then turned back to Peter. "Wait a minute. You're not Doogie Howser. Doogie Howser is dead! He died in that *Harold and Kumar* movie. So, who are you?"

Peter responded with a shrug and a hand gesture that indicated he didn't know. He then began hand motions that appeared to be the game charades.

"*Charades?!* Oh, I love charades," J.D. announced.

Peter stood with hands on hips.

"Person!" J.D. shouted. "I know, I know—Hearts, stars, clovers, blue moons, gold and rainbows, and red balloons!" he said in a fake Irish accent. "Oh, Stutters, it's your lucky day. He's the Lucky Charms leprechaun!"

Peter gave him the "fuck you" finger, and then made a few more charade gestures.

"Ooh! Ooh! Ooh! I know, I know!" J.D. exclaimed. "You're Buddy the Elf."

Peter gave him a double "fuck you."

"Man," J.D. spoke with disappointment, "I really suck at charades... Your turn, Stutters," he told their prisoner. The man shook his head no. "Ah, don't be like that, Stutters." J.D. leapt up on to the table and sat by the man's face. He leaned sideways and placed his elbow in the middle of the captive's back, and then placed the palm of his hand under his chin as he reclined. J.D. took his index finger and ran his talon on the canal opening of the man's ear in a teasing but painful manner. "*Please?!*"

The man grimaced. "Wha-what d-d—do you want?"

"A lot of tha-tha-things, actually. A cup of vanilla hazelnut coffee. A Black & Green's toffee chocolate bar. A really good blowjob. Stone's location!"

"I—I-I can't do—do that."

"*Damn!*" J.D. exclaimed disappointed. "I was really looking forward to that blowjob... Well, I guess I'll just have to settle for Stone's location then."

The man again shook his head no again. "He'll k-k-k-kill me."

J.D. stood up and withdrew one of his Eskrima sticks and cracked the man across the top of his skull. "Don't be a dipstick, Stutters," he said angrily. Stutters cried out in agony and began to weep. J.D. drew a breath and sympathetically apologized. "Oh, I'm so sorry, Stutters. Sometimes I forget my own strength. Can you forgive me?" he asked, as he gently rubbed the man's injury.

"It h-h-hurts."

J.D. kissed the man's head and whispered in his ear, "One man's pain is another man's pleasure, and right now I got a chubby. Now, I'm going to ask you one more time, and if you tell me, I promise I won't kill you." The man sobbed, but would not answer the question. "You see that man there, Stutters. Do ya?" He turned to Peter. "Show him who you are, Peter. Show the man what he had a hand in. Show him your pretty face!"

The man averted his eyes as Peter revealed his scarred features.

J.D. leapt off the table. "You see that fucked up face? Take a good look. Look at the man, Stutters!" J.D. shouted in an enraged tone as he shook his captive's head by his red colored hair. "Look at him good," J.D. demanded. "Don't you remember? It wasn't *that* long ago... Maybe a visual? Would a prop jar your memory?" J.D. called to Peter, "Props my good man, props. Bring in the props!"

Peter left the room and as quickly as he had exited he returned, pushing a four-wheeled food service cart draped in a white sheet into the corner of the room. Atop the pushcart was a wooden pole. Peter picked up the staff and began to twirl it, jabbed it in the air, and then smacked its ends on the floor. He jumped, spun, landed, and then repeated the movements as he moved forward. Though to the man it appeared to be some demented dance, it was actually staff fighting moves from Shaolin Kung Fu that J.D. had taught him.

"Wha-wha—what kind of f-f-freak show is—is this?"

J.D. squatted down next to him and pulled his head up again by his hair so he could get a good look at the little man before him. J.D. stroked the man's injury and told him, "The kind that's going to make you squeal... like a pig."

Peter stopped his martial arts movements in front of the table, and as a taunting jester he made the "tah-da" stance.

"A short man with a pole held across his throat by you and a scar-faced man. Does that ring a bell?" J.D. asked

The man sobbed, "I-I-d-d-don't know. He's just some mige-mige-mi—" The color withdrew from his face, replaced by a pale look of fear. He now realized who the dancing man was.

Stutters began to tremble, he pleaded with J.D. trying to bargain what he knew of Stone in return for a reprieve. It was too late.

"That's my warrant officer," J.D. told him. "He's very good at his job. You know what that job is?" he asked with a wicked smirk. "That is to extract information. And he's very good at extracting things... He's going to hurt you, Stutters. He's going to hurt you so much that you're going to beg him to kill you. But the more you scream and cry for mercy the more he's gonna hurt you. That's what he does. You think about that poor innocent child that Stone raped and tortured in front of his eyes. You think about his daughter as Peter ass-rapes you with that pole," he told him, as he pointed to the staff gripped firmly in Peter's hand. "You think about *that!*"

He kissed the man on top of his head and whispered to him, "There's no love like love lost. No pain like a broken heart. No greater anguish than losing a child... and I'll be in the corner watching Peter prove that."

J.D. pulled out a condom from his top shirt pocket, and slapped it down on the table in front of the man's face. He turned to Peter and told him, "Don't forget the condom. No glove, no love." He picked up his accordion and began to play once again.

The man squirmed frantically as Peter gave a twisted, evil grin. The man called out to J.D., who sat in the corner. "You can't do-do—do this. You prom-promised you wo-wouldn't k-k-kill me... if-if I told you!"

"And I won't," J.D. grinned as began to play his accordion again, "but he will."

---

Stutters let out a howl of extreme pain and agony as Peter drove the pole into his rectum.

"Matthew Downey," a voice came from the corner of the room. "That's barely a few inches," J.D. declared. "You're screaming like a little bitch. Is that how you squealed bending over in prison? Yes, we know your name. We know you were at Rikers with Stone and Barlow. We know much about you, Stutters," he taunted.

The man cried out, pleading, his speech impediment missing as he begged, "Please. I'll tell you whatever you want to know."

"Give him some more, Peter," J.D. told his chief, and then addressed Downey. "No, Stutters. It's not a time for talk. It's a time for payback."

The anal probing continued for several more minutes.

"I think we're ready now," J.D. said, seeing their captive was nearly unconscious.

Peter extracted the feces and blood-smeared pole from the man's anus. He placed it in the corner of the room and then went to his cart and rolled it toward the prisoner. Retrieving a hand held digital recorder, Peter turned it on, and then placed it on the table next to Stutters. He turned back and picked up a 14-inch bolt cutter. Peter snapped its jaws in front of the restrained man, and gave him a pleased grin.

With tear-filled eyes and anguished voice, Stutters begged for mercy, except there was no forgiveness in Peter's heart.

Stutters could not tell them where Stone was hiding, for he did not know. He could only tell them where they had set up operations—and this was not in the same location where the captives were held. Nevertheless, the information was useless. Stone's men never stayed at the same location for long, especially since they knew they were being hunted.

However, what Stutters did reveal, before Peter cut out his tongue, were two very important things. The first, to Peter's relief, that some of the children, including his daughter, were alive and with Stone. The second piece of information, and equally as important, was that Richard Barlow knew where Stone could be found, and Stutters knew when and where Barlow could be found alone.

"Loose lips sink ships," J.D. spoke as he continued to play his bell accordion.

'Italian Wine Merchants' were the last words Matthew Downey would ever speak. Then his tongue was gone. Stutters was left alive and taken to the same pit where Peter had been thrown into. Peter's revenge, at least for this man, had been extracted.

Richard Barlow had a passion for vintage wines, red mostly, and one region in particular—Langhe, Italy. Having been born into an extremely wealthy family, he had wanted for nothing. But with all his family provided him, it could not take away the boredom. The endless parties, the women, the young boys, the expensive designer clothes, flashy jewelry, the imported European cars—nothing seemed to satisfy him or give him the rush of life he desperately thought he needed and deserved—so he found it in murder. He had been a thrill killer.

He, like Stone, had been awaiting sentencing, and he, like Stone, had been one of the few survivors at Rikers Island after the living dead had expired. His alliance with Stone had been beneficial and the new world order in the aftermath of the plague provided a much more favorable world for him, rich with possibilities and ripe with countless survivors to abuse and exploit. He could go unabated in whatever he chose to do. That was until he discovered that a people's champion and savior, a military commander, still remained alive, and began to interfere with his personal agenda.

Though most of his vices were no longer important to him, there still remained one obsession, Giacomo Conterno Barolo Monfortino Riserva. This rare, special reserve wine had always been, and continued to be, his favorite, and was one thing he refused to do without.

Barlow relished the way it flowed from the glass with stunning depth and purity, caressed his palate with a rich tapestry of dark plums, cherries, smoke and licorice, the layers of aromas and flavors emerging with a sensual enveloping personality within the glass. This was one addiction he needed to quench, and it was this one habit that led to his capture.

Stutters had told them of his persistent need for this wine and his endless effort to locate it throughout the metropolis. Like worshippers are drawn to church on Sunday, he was drawn to his cathedral of the sacrament every seventh day at noon.

He had found a wine shop that had an extensive array of vintage wines, and many bottles of his holy Conterno Barolo, and that was Italian Wine Merchants. Stutters knew this because Barlow would always bring two bottles home in a brown paper bag imprinted with the shop's name.

J.D. had recognized the store's name immediately. It was co-owned by famed Italian chef Mario Batali. He knew the shop's location. It was near his old neighborhood, in the Union Square area.

---

J.D. sat atop the armory's roof with a pleased look upon his face. To say it was a smile would be an exaggeration, however, it was one of satisfaction. Stutters had been punished and he now knew how to get to Barlow. He sat in his usual spot that gave him the best vantage point to see both entry gates. Barkley nestled at his feet, the moon glowing brightly, the stars shinning, and the critters of the night scampering about pleased him. He had forgotten how serene the night could be when he was doing nothing but keeping guard from his perch. However, the serenity of the moment was about to be broken.

Barkley whimpered and raised his head from off his outstretched front legs. A moment later the canine stood up and growled. Barkley was alarmed and agitated. Then J.D. could smell it. It was a half-mute. How could this be? J.D. thought. Half-mutes don't prowl the night. Then he saw it approach the gate. It was Four Fingers and he was carrying something. The creature tossed the object over the fence and then fled. J.D. went to investigate.

J.D. was aghast over the discovery. Four Fingers had tossed in a severed head, but it wasn't just any head. It was the detached skull of Ann-Marie, and there was something partially dangling from her mouth. J.D.'s horror turned to grave concern. If Ann-Marie had been killed by half-mutes then what of Michael Adam? J.D. bolted with Barkley to Hearst Tower.

Ann-Marie's body was ravaged to the bone. The half-mutes had made a feast of her leaving only discarded intestines and gnawed bones. To J.D.'s relief none of the remains belonged to James' son.

Nonetheless that didn't mean the child was safe and alive. He headed to the upper floors to where Ann-Marie had made their "nest," hoping the child was safe and sound, and he and Barkley weren't headed into an ambush.

Michael Adam Alexander was right where he could always be found, unharmed and very happy to see J.D. The young lad had grown at the same rate that Caitlin had. However, Michael Adam's features leaned more toward the male transmute side. Even with him looking slightly more like a transmute, it didn't diminish his capacity for learning. He had comprehended some basic human language skills almost as quickly as his daughter.

J.D. knew he could not leave the child to himself. He was not mature enough to hunt or defend himself. He knew the child had to come back to the armory with him. J.D. just hoped that the boy could understand that his mother was dead and he needed to come with him for his own safety. Michael Adam left with J.D. without resistance. He had heard the shrieks of his mother and the unknown cries of something else. The boy knew something bad had happened for he knew his mother would not have abandoned him for so long.

# 4

## DARK PLACES

*August 24, Day 504.*

Today was a most extraordinary day. This was the greatest capture they could have achieved, aside from Stone himself. This was Stone's right-hand man, a man privy to all of Stone's dark secrets and plans, and as his second he would surely know where the hideout was to be found. So today J.D. decided to talk with the one called Richard Barlow alone, before Peter joined in the conversation.

J.D. had waited for Barlow alone in the darkness of Italian Wine Merchants. Like clockwork the man had arrived on time as Stutters had confessed he would. Barlow never got to reach for the wine he desired. J.D. had been waiting for him. Knocked out, tied up, and stuffed into a body bag, J.D. arrived with his bundle at the armory and took him directly to the basement and locked him into a darkened room.

They had kept him in isolation for three days: no food, no clothes, and no bathroom. All he was allowed were two buckets. One empty to use as a toilet and the other filled with water to use as he saw fit.

Richard Barlow sat naked in a chair facing the door, which stood in front of the desk in the cold, low lit room that smelled of piss and shit.

J.D. entered dressed in his usual attire, black uniform and boots, gloves that covered his claws, sunglasses that shaded his eyes, his kukri strapped to his chest, a sidearm on his right hip, a knife strapped to his right thigh, and his Eskrima sticks in his right hand. He had forgone the makeup and had tucked his Mohawk style hair up into his cap. He had also taken off his BDU shirt and wore only an olive drab A-shirt.

J.D. didn't speak as he entered the room. He just stood in front of the door as he closed it behind him and stared at the man.

After a moment the man spoke out, "What the fuck you looking at, huh? You want me to stand up? You want a good look at me?"

The man stood up and exposed his fit and trim physique. He was muscular, though not as well defined and as large as J.D. However, J.D. knew the naked man would have made a formidable opponent if it had not been for his own enhanced strength and agility of his mutation.

Barlow grabbed his genitals and yelled, "Here! Here, get a good look… You like that, bitch?"

J.D. did not utter a sound. Instead, he pulled out a pair of boxer shorts from his left pant pocket and threw it at the man. Again J.D. said nothing, but twirled one of his sticks in his right hand, as the man dressed.

"*What?*" Barlow spoke with irritation. "What the fuck now? Am I supposed to be scared? You with that stick in your hand. Is that supposed to intimidate me? My daddy used to beat me with a bigger one than that, until I took it from him and beat him senseless. So, go ahead tough guy, c'mon over here. Show me what you got!"

J.D. spoke in a measured tone of voice. "Your name is Barlow, Richard Barlow. Is that correct?"

"*What?* You going to be the good cop? You wanna be my friend, get to know me, get me to tell you about the children? Fuck you, I'm not talking."

"Strange, for someone who isn't talking you've just said a lot."

"Fuck you, asshole. Go ahead and give it your best shot. But you get nothing from me."

J.D. stopped twirling his stick and moved away from the doorway.

He placed his weapons down on the desk's top and pulled out an opposite chair and sat.

"You have it all wrong, Richard," he began to explain. "I'm not here to get you to talk. No. I'm just here as a courtesy before the inquisitor arrives. So please, have a seat. Go ahead... I know you and Stone were in Rikers together. I know you're a convicted murderer and I know that Stone is a real sick son-of-a-bitch, convicted of numerous murders and a long list of other offenses. I know this because there have been several others of your psychotic group I've had the displeasure to speak with. Stutters was the last. Or as you called him, Matthew Downey. He, too, was defiant like you, for half a minute. But in the end, when the inquisitor came, he was cryin' for his mama, giving up everything, begging for the pain to stop. Have you ever had needles stuck in your eyes? It really hurts, I hear."

"Fuck you!"

J.D. remained calm and focused.

"*Fuck me?!* Are you sure? From what I hear you like to fuck little boys!"

"Balls deep night and day," Barlow boasted, taunting J.D.

The mere mention of the act sickened and enraged J.D. J.D. lost his composure, snatched up one of his sticks, and without rising from his chair slapped it across the man's face. Though Barlow was stunned, bleeding from his mouth and in obvious pain, he didn't cry out. Instead he licked the blood from his split lip, and then spit it at J.D. Barlow had gotten to him, and J.D. knew he had been bested.

"How original," J.D. said, keeping his voice calm, unruffled, as he took off his sunglasses to wipe the spit from his face.

The man saw J.D.'s eyes.

"Seen them before, freak!"

J.D. took off his gloves and placed them on the desk next to his dirtied sunglasses.

"*Freak?!* You wanna see a true freak?" he asked Barlow, and then rotated his neck around.

J.D.'s parlor trick came in useful when he wanted to shock and disorient an enemy or use his ability for a tactical advantage. However,

Barlow was neither horrified nor impressed. Unmoved he replied, "Save the circus act for the boons and retards. You see, I know much about you, and I know Stone has planned something very special for *Caitlin*."

J.D. felt the anger welling up inside him again. He wanted to snap the man's neck for the threat against his daughter, but he knew he couldn't. The information he knew about Stone and the whereabouts of any remaining survivors superseded his desire to kill the man. No, he wouldn't kill him, just yet, but he was going to put a very big hurt on him. He pulled out a Pneu-Dart tranquilizer gun and shot Barlow. The dart logged in Barlow's pectoral muscle.

Barlow looked at the dart and laughed, then said, "Seriously?"

"Wait for it," J.D. said.

Barlow's smirk fell from his face. He felt oddly woozy. Then his voice rose in panic, as he felt the loss of use of his extremities. "What the fuck did you just do to me?"

"That was totally cool watching that smug grin fall right off your face," J.D. told him, almost ecstatic with the results. He then held up the pistol and smiled. "Got this off one of your men. Was it what you used on me that night at the fire?" Barlow didn't answer. "Makes no difference," he told him. He reached across the table and pulled the dart from Barlow's chest, and told the slumping man, "Just a small amount of paralytic. Enough to make you cooperative, but not enough to render you completely speechless," he assured.

After securing Barlow to his chair so he wouldn't slip from it, and then placing both of Barlow's hands palm down on the table, J.D. sat next to him on the tabletop. He pulled out his knife from the sheath strapped to his leg and pressed its point into Barlow's breast.

"You're a smart man," J.D. began, "so I'm sure you know that interrogation doesn't mean sticking a gun in someone's face and threatening them if they don't talk. Interrogation is a process, sometimes a long, extremely painful procedure. Do you know in ancient China they used to torture men to death by slowly slicing into the flesh with precise cuts, starting with parts on the body that would inflict the least amount of pain to the greatest? The flesh is cut from the body in very small pieces," J.D. enlightened him, as he slowly rotated the knifepoint into the man's chest. "Slices so precise that neither vein, nor artery, nor nerve would be severed until the end. It's true. It was called Líng Chí, the Death of a Thousand Cuts. They could keep men alive for days, screaming in all that pain." He ran the 420 modified stainless-steel military knife down Barlow's chest, cutting him enough for the blood to flow, but not deep enough to do severe damage. Though Barlow could feel the pain from the blade slowly slicing across his flesh, he remained silent and defiant.

"In Vietnam," J.D. continued, "during the war, the Viet Cong used thin pieces of bamboo on captives, driving them under the nails, or into the under part of the eye socket. Or my favorite—piercing them into the testicles. The Asians had such unique ways of maximizing pain while prolonging death... However, as I recall, it was the Spanish Inquisition that is credited for the most brutal and torturous forms of punishment in the recorded history of modern man. The Inquisitors would do things to people you couldn't even imagine. Not even coming out of your sick, twisted little mind. They had all sorts of mutilation devices, even one which resembled a nutcracker and was used to crush *testicles*. The Spanish Tickler," J.D. said, and then held out his right hand and curled his fingers as he explained. "Four sharp metal talons about the size of four fingers of a man's hand resembling a cat's paw served to rip a person's flesh to shreds and to strip it off the bones."

As intimidation J.D. clawed himself along his left forearm, ripping four thin lines down his flesh. He held up his bleeding arm and let the blood drip into Barlow's lap.

"But my favorite is The Pear," J.D. continued. "It was a device that expanded after being inserted orally, anally, or vaginally. Talk about ripping ya a new one. 'Confessions' were freely given then... Last but not least, there was one very simple, effective technique. That was vivisection. They would use a sharpened instrument to cut you open from groin to sternum while you lay strapped to a wooden table. The accused—men, women, children, it didn't matter—would be screaming in such horrific agony while the Inquisitor's men reached into the body cavity and pulled out the intestines first," J.D. animatedly gestured as he expounded, "always saving the vital organs for last, all to extract confessions from the accused. And they did this all in the name of God."

Barlow seemed to be unfazed by his captor's ranting. His eyes remained hard and cold.

J.D. continued, "Oh, but that was in a much more civilized time. These days, well, there seems to be a total disregard for human life. It's all about raping and murdering. Sodomizing children, killing trans-mutes, and beating dwarves."

J.D. now paced the small room, as he explained to Barlow what was going to happen.

"I have a series of questions for you," J.D. began. A knock came at the door, interrupting. "Oh, how timely. Come!"

A short man wearing a black hooded mask entered pushing a food service cart.

"Oh, must be lunch time," J.D. said, and then asked Barlow. "You hungry? You look hungry. I know I feel a little peckish."

J.D. moved to the cart and pulled off the white linen covering from the first tier.

"*What?* Surgical instruments and tools? No lunch?" he asked the masked man.

The short man shook his head no.

"That's a shame, Peter. Where are your manners? Every condemned man is supposed to have his last meal."

He turned back to Barlow. "You know, the world has really gone to shit. It's just so hard to find good help these days with all those pesky half-mutes and you and Stone murdering survivors... Oh, but how rude of me. Here I am admonishing Peter for his poor manners and it seems I've forgotten mine. Richard, meet Peter. Peter, say hello."

Peter raised his hand and circled it left to right gesturing his greeting.

"Peter doesn't talk much, you see. He's got this speech impediment."

"Another fucking midget," Barlow declared, his speech slurred from the effects of the narcotic. "It's like the circus. Two freaks for the price of one."

There was now a hardness and ferocity in J.D.'s voice. "Better than a Coney Island Circus Sideshow attraction." J.D. grabbed his adversary by the throat and then spoke into his ear, "If it is curiosity that you seek, then behold the vicious freak," he said as he gestured to Peter. "He'll make you laugh until you cry, then you'll die, then you'll die."

He released Barlow and then told him, "And this is not just another midget as you so impolitely put it; he's a dwarf with whom you are well acquainted. Peter, let Richard see your pretty face!"

Peter stepped over to the chair and took off his mask to reveal his scarred features.

"Well, fuck me!" Barlow exclaimed, still slurring his words "If it isn't the midget with no tongue. Don't worry, Stone put it to good use," he taunted. "That little bitch daughter of yours never came so good."

J.D. slammed down one of his sticks atop Barlow's head; this time the man cried out.

"I would explain it to you," he told Barlow with immense disdain, "but I don't have the time or the crayons."

Peter went to his cart to retrieve a digital recorder and microphone with accompanying stand from under the covering of the bottom tier. He came back to the desk and set it up, pointing the microphone toward Barlow.

"This is Peter Dunne. I affectionately refer to him as my inquisitor," he let Barlow know. "Remember when I asked you if you ever had needles stuck into your eyes? Well, you're going to be begging for that simple pleasure. See, Peter used to make his living as a tattoo artist. He did some outstanding work on me recently. It seems he also has a unique gift for extracting information. He makes Doctor Mengele look like Mother Theresa.

There are only four simple questions you're going to answer." J.D. continued, moving the recorder atop the desk closer Barlow. "The first is, what is the location of Stone's hideout? Second: In what part of this location will he be holding his captives? Thirdly: Will there be anyone else besides Stone at the location? And finally... Who's the spy that has infiltrated our ranks? See, just four simple questions… Oh, and since you brought it up, you may want to tell Peter about his daughter."

J.D. pointed to the corner of the room. "I'm going to be right over there, Richard, sitting, and asking you those questions over and over until I'm satisfied it's the truth… You may ask why I'll be conducting this interview from the corner of the room… Go ahead," he told Barlow, baiting him. Barlow refused to answer. "No? That's okay, I'll tell you anyway. There's going to be a lot of body fluids splattering everywhere and I don't want my bell accordion to get soiled." Barlow gave J.D. a confused look. "Oh, did I forget to mention that? During the interludes, those moments where Peter will be encouraging you to answer honestly, I'll be providing the entertainment."

J.D. moved to the pushcart and retrieved his instrument from the bottom shelf, and began to play "Send in the Clowns." He moved to Barlow and began to sing to him, and then moved to sit in the corner; as he did he smiled at Peter and gestured for him to proceed. Peter returned the smile with an extremely pleased look on his broken face as he held the hammer and nails in his hand.

"Question one: What is the location of Stone's hideout?" J.D. asked.

Barlow refused to answer. Peter gave a crooked smile, and then drove a nail through their captive's right hand, securing it firmly to the desk. Barlow flinched, but refused to cry out.

J.D. continued the questioning as he played. However, before he could finish his song, a knock came on the door. It was Major Duncan. He had come to deliver an urgent message from Chief Wiese. J.D. stepped out of the room as Peter held two large fish hooks up in front of Barlow. Ryan had come to report that the trap had been sprung, but Wiese had not captured any of Stone's men. They were friendlies. In fact, they were more; they were true friends.

A cry of pain resonated from behind the closed door, but Ryan did not react to it.

"*What?* Where are they now?" J.D. asked, concerned.

"Being brought in, sir," Ryan responded.

"Take care of it," J.D. told him. "I can't be disturbed right now."

"Yes, sir," he replied, understanding the delicate nature of the current situation.

J.D. re-entered the room and returned to playing, and again he did not speak. Then after a few moments of watching Peter implement a few more of his warm-up techniques, J.D. started the questioning again. However, Barlow still refused to answer. For the second round, Peter's tool of choice was a scalpel. Seeing it, J.D. began to play what sounded like "Like a Virgin," a song recorded by American singer Madonna. However, when J.D. began to sing it was actually "Like a Surgeon," a parody song recorded by "Weird Al" Yankovic. Peter was amused at J.D.'s choice of music. He gave a little shuffle in time to J.D.'s music as he moved from his surgical cart back to Barlow.

Peter executed his craft with methodical precision. It was gruesome the things the man was capable of, but it was also cathartic for him. Peter relished every painful twitch his victim made, savored every agonizing scream. The more pain he caused the better he felt. J.D. once knew the feeling all too well, releasing the anger and hate inside him, but that seemed to him so long ago. Now even the thrill of the hunt had evaded him, and he was desensitized to the tormented cries of Peter's interrogates, and watching neither brought pleasure nor repulsion, just indifference. Nonetheless, J.D. knew that torture was a necessity when captives refused to cooperate. Richard Barlow was a very obstinate subject.

J.D. continuously repeated the questions, but Barlow was strong-willed and refused to yield any information. J.D. walked up to the man, raised his chin and looked into his enemy's face.

"I guess you need some private time with my inquisitor. So, I'll leave him to it. Perhaps you'll be more talkative when I return." He turned to Peter. "Try the nails in the testicles. I think that may loosen his tongue."

Barlow's eyes finally lit with fear.

———————

J.D. went upstairs to the main hall, where the detainees were being held. There before him were Kermit, David, Sam, Marisol, and two uniformed men he didn't recognize. Except this reunion of old friends was not a joyous occasion, as one would have expected with friends that had bonded as closely together as they had. This meeting, for J.D., was filled with apathy, so it appeared. Though J.D. seemed to be unemotional in seeing his old comrades, he was puzzled at their return and angrier than elated to see them, although he refused to show either feeling.

The group, along with his dog Max, and another canine called Otter were supposed to be in England. So how and why had they returned, especially now, at the most critical point in their struggle against Stone's forces? J.D. needed to know.

"Got yourselves caught, did we?" J.D. immediately noticed there were three absences. "So where's Julie, Otter and Max?" he asked.

"Julie and Otter couldn't make it, and Max—"

"Ask Piss Pants," Marisol cut David's sentence short with a bitter tone, pointing an angry finger. "*¡Pendajo!*" she cursed, directing her pejorative at Chief Wiese.

No one had called Paul Piss Pants is a very long time.

"Chief," he said sharply, furiously. "Chief Wiese front and center!"

J.D.'s harsh demanding demeanor was out of character for the man they had left behind, and it surprised them all.

Paul responded to his superior, quickly standing before him at attention and saluting. "Sir. Yes, sir."

"What the hell is going on?" J.D. demanded to know.

"*Sir?*"

"Where the hell is my dog?"

Paul asked, "You mean that German shepherd, sir?"

"No, Wiese, I mean the poodle. Of course, I mean the shepherd," J.D. snapped. "How many dogs do you think there are, Mr. Wiese?"

"Just one, sir."

"*Well?*"

"No, sir. We did not kill the animal, sir. As per your orders we do not kill animals or transmutes without your direct authorization. The dog, sir, is still outside."

"You left *my* dog outside? You wanna be busted to private, Wiese?"

"No, sir."

"Then what are you standing here for? Go get him. *Now*, Chief!"

He turned his attentions back to Kermit and company, his anger quickly shifted back to a tone of considered indifference. "I take it you're in charge, Kermit, with all that new brass on your collar. My apologies, for my lackluster enthusiasm in seeing all of you, but you've come at a bad time, and you've clusterfucked my trap for Stone. I also see you've brought some company. So I can probably assume this isn't a family reunion. Looking for the doctor, perhaps?"

As Kermit began to respond, Max ran into the hall to his master's legs and vigorously rubbed up against them. Chief Warrant Officer Wiese had chased behind.

Slightly breathy Wiese announced, "Your dog, sir."

"Yes, Chief. I can see that." J.D. knelt down and returned the affection his dog had shown with his own vigorous rubbing and vocal praise. "*Gute hund*, Max. *Gute hund*." Max gave his master a generous portion of licks.

He turned back to Paul. "Take a body bag down to Chief Dunne. And relieve Corporal Panton, so he can piss and get chow." He stood up and turned to Ryan. "Major Duncan, give them back their gear, so Chief Brown can call whomever to let them know his team is okay."

Addressing the two unfamiliar soldiers, he told them from behind sunglasses, "As for you two men. My name is Colonel Nichols. I do not know you but if you are under Brown's command, then as warfighters I expect you to conduct yourselves accordingly. My men have orders to shoot anyone who threatens the well being of this base. And I wouldn't want either of you to get in the way of a bullet because one of you gets all Gung Ho."

The higher-ranking man responded with, "We don't get 'Gung Ho', Colonel. We're Navy Seals."

"Excellent. I'm glad we understand one another. Gentlemen, and madam, consider yourselves guests. Get something to eat and then we'll have a debriefing in the war room." Addressing Kermit, he put his attentions back to business. "Chief Brown. Please call your base and let them know you have made contact."

---

In the short time J.D. had been gone, Peter had continued his body modifications of Barlow. Besides both of Barlow's hands having been nailed palm down to the table earlier, his head was now propped up with a device that resembled a medieval Heretics Fork. In addition to the eight fingernails and two nipples with fish hooks still embedded in them that Peter had removed during J.D.'s questioning, he had added several pieces of filleted flesh, a thumb, and three molar teeth to the contents of the stainless-steel tapered bowl on the table. However, removing body parts wasn't the only thing Peter had focused on. To maximize pain, Peter had stuck several acupuncture needles inside each lower eyelid and was in the process of probing Barlow's molar cavities with a dental pick, focusing on his exposed nerve endings. The exploratory was so overwhelming excruciating for Barlow that he could not hold back his anguished screams, and had become severely disoriented and delirious.

"So. Has he answered any of the questions, yet?" J.D. asked, returning to the interrogation room with Max alongside him.

Peter shook his head no.

"*None?*" J.D. asked, as he knelt down next to Barlow. "Defiant until the end, are we? Or is it that you know if you answer we're going to kill you? Well, I hate to disappoint you. But you don't deserve to die quickly. We're going to let you rot and fester. A nice slow death of dehydration and infection. Out where Stone can see you."

Richard Barlow looked at his nemesis with glassy eyes and began to laugh. It was the hysterical laughter of a still insolent but delirious man. Then when he spoke, J.D. was shocked at the words he uttered.

A rambling of disjointed phrases filled J.D.'s and Peter's ears. The colonel stood up and looked at his chief. They both could not believe what the man had revealed. J.D. now knew who the traitor amongst them was.

"Finish it," he told his chief. Without hesitation Peter dug his knife into the man's mouth, cutting out his tongue. Barlow's screams were momentary, and then he passed out. The Heretic's Fork penetrated deep into his flesh. The blood poured from the wounds.

After placing Barlow in the body bag, J.D. scooped the man up and threw him over his shoulder. Escorted by Chief Warrant Officer 2 Wiese and Chief Warrant Officer 3 Dunne, J.D. left the bloodied inter-rogation room with Max and headed upstairs. Next stop was the perimeter fence.

As the group made their way up the staircase of the basement, Major Duncan and three subordinates were escorting Kermit and his team up to the second floor. All of them saw the colonel carrying the bundle across his shoulder and they stopped. Except what the real distraction had been was Chief Dunne, who was in the rear of the procession.

The little man with the disfigured features strutted up the stairs with a distinctly pleased look upon his face, grinning widely. His white butcher's smock was covered in blood and he was wearing protective goggles atop his head. He stopped, briefly, to wipe his forehead and face clean of the blood splatter, and then hurried on to catch up with his commander.

Having seen Ryan near the upper floor, Paul quickly hurried to report to him. He pulled Ryan aside and whispered something in his ear. There was something wrong, Kermit and his group knew from the way Ryan and Paul had quickly departed with one of their soldiers, leaving only two as escort.

---

J.D. and Peter joined Ryan and the others for a debriefing, but this was still not to be a happy and joyous reunion. He had come to give them an edict, and that was to tell them they were not welcome.

Sergeant Schumacher had been waiting by the doorway to the conference room as instructed by Major Duncan. He was instructed to remain at the door with the guard until he was summoned. When they entered, Max followed behind his master, followed by Chief Dunne. They were both now dressed in proper military uniforms—though the little man's clothing was still too big even after it had been altered. J.D. removed his military cap to reveal his Mohawk hairstyle as he entered, which garnered a few odd looks from his former teammates. Max headed toward Marisol, but J.D. was quick to correct him using the Dutch verbal commands he had been trained to follow. Max quickly went to his side and sat down next to his master at the conference table.

"Attention!" Ryan announced, and raised his hand to salute. Everyone stood, even Marisol and David. J.D. still hated being saluted, but he had accepted it. He returned the salute.

The two Navy Seals were purposely missing from the debriefing. J.D., did not want them privy to the action he was going to take after he debriefed Kermit and his team, but mainly he didn't trust the two Seals and did not know what their agenda was. For all he knew they could have come to assert their military authority and lay claim to the armory or had come for him. For all concerned, J.D. had them escorted to the Garyowen, a bar on an upper floor, to enjoy the amenities of the club, but instructed two sentries be placed outside the doors. For the safety of everyone in the armory he told the two navy warriors that their weapons would be returned upon their departure from the facility.

"Please, be seated... Pardon our lack of amenities," J.D. addressed the gathering. "But we're prepping for final pull out of the city. We've only stayed this long in hopes of locating some missing women and children, but we were unsuccessful."

"How many people have you saved?" Kermit asked.

"One hundred and seven, provided the rest of us get out safely. We're at a critical point. The trap you fell into was set for Stone. I was hoping he'd come to rescue his right-hand man. However, there's nothing left to rescue now."

"Torture and murder, J.D?" Kermit remarked. "That's not like you."

If it had been anyone else that had made the comment, J.D. would have grown angry against the inflammatory words and gone off on a tirade, but he kept his composure and presented Kermit with the brutal truth.

"Well, Chief. You see that man sitting there?" J.D. pointed to Peter. "Barlow had his hand in nearly beating my chief warrant officer to death. They cut out his tongue and threw him in a pit to die. This after being forced to watch his 11-year-old child being raped and sodomized by Stone. Barlow and his partner Stone have kidnapped at least 23 women and children we know of. So, if I have offended your morals or some military code of conduct, then so be it. We do whatever it takes, by whatever measures and methods to find out where the kidnapped survivors are located. If it means torturing a few sick fuckers in the process then that is my burden of command. And for the record—we didn't kill that sick fuck. He got the same treatment as he gave my chief. Now, Kermit, I suggest you make arrangements to return to wherever you came from. Go back to England. It's better for all of you. That's—"

Caitlin burst into the room and ran to Ryan for protection. Chief Wiese was fast on her heels.

"Chief, what is the meaning of this interruption?"

Paul snapped to attention.

"Sorry, sir. But she's fast... and she kicked me, sir, *really* hard."

J.D. addressed Caitlin, the hardness of his previous tone melting away in the presence of his daughter.

"Caitlin. Is this true? Did you assault Chief Wiese?"

She clung to Ryan's legs as she looked at her father with a sad face.

"Yes, dawd."

Kermit and company were stunned. However, it wasn't Caitlin's odd physical features that prompted baffled looks from them; it was that she had called J.D., "dawd."

"And why did you do this?"

"Cause Cheep Weez won't let me see monster."

"*Monster?* What monster?"

"The monster over there," she told him, pointing to Max.

"Caitlin. He's not a monster. I told you, he's a dog. His name is

Max. Don't you remember the photo? And the chief is right. You can't see the dog right now."

She looked up at Ryan. "Elty. Tell dawd to let me see monster."

"Honey," Ryan spoke softly to her, "I can't tell Dad to let you see the dog. Your dad is the boss. Okay? Now you need to go with Chief Wiese."

She protested. "Not fair. I want to see monster."

"*Caitlin,*" J.D. scolded, in a firm, but not too harsh tone. "Is that the proper way to act in front of guests?"

"No, sir," she answered her father, sorrowfully.

"Okay. Then tell everyone you're sorry."

"I'm sawee," Caitlin spoke remorsefully.

"Now apologize to the chief for kicking him, and promise you won't ever do it again."

"I sawee, Cheep Weez. I won't again. I promise."

"Dismissed, Private Nichols," he told her.

She saluted her father as she and Paul left the room.

J.D. stood up and announced, "Meeting adjourned. Major Duncan will make arrangements for your safe return to your pickup point. Good day."

"*That's it?*" David question. "After all this time, we get a fuck-you-very-much? We don't even get to tell you why we came back?"

"Mister DiMinni. The reason for your return does not concern me. If you've come to rescue me then you're wasting your time. Give Her Majesty my regards, and tell Master Sergeant McDaniels thanks for such great marksmanship," J.D. remarked about the man who had shot him on the pier.

Marisol cried out, almost bursting in tears as she spoke, distraught over J.D.'s callous and austere demeanor. "How can you be this way? These are your friends. Don't you care anymore? How can you treat us this way, after all we've meant to each other?"

J.D. snapped, "I'm not that man anymore. There's nothing here for any of you except death and disappointment."

"I don't believe you. You're lying," she told him.

Coldly he responded, "Lying? You want to see the real me? You want to see who I've become? Then I'll show you. Major," he addressed Ryan, "Send in Sergeant Schumacher, and have the prisoner sent for."

Ryan exited, and then re-entered with Sergeant Schumacher.

"Sir, reporting as requested."

"At ease, Sergeant."

J.D. moved to the other end of the room and sat on top of the table at the end where his old friend, Sergeant Drukker, was seated.

"Sergeant," he addressed Peter Schumacher, Sr. "Up until an hour ago I thought your incompetent buffoonery was a deliberate act, one to distract me. But I was wrong. Though your heart is in the right place you truly are an incompetent soldier. And for this I am sorry. You will be missed."

Peter Schumacher was confused. *"Sir?"*

"Sergeant Schumacher. I hereby grant you an honorable discharge from the 69th Infantry Regiment. Consider yourself a civilian henceforth. Have a good life, Peter."

"I'm confused, sir."

"Undoubtedly. You're a dentist."

None of J.D.'s old team understood why he had remarked that he was not the same person as they had once known. Though they had seen a harder side of him earlier, he still maintained his unique sarcastic sense of humor.

"Yes, sir. A damn good one, too, sir."

"Yes. You've proven that. But let me put this to you bluntly. As a warfighter you suck. You're just not soldier material, and it's not for a lack of trying. I understand why you volunteered for service, but I should have kicked you back to civilian long ago, so I'm doing it now. So, when you leave in the morning you leave as a dentist. Is that understood?"

"Yes, sir. I'm sorry I was a disappointment to you, sir, but I'm—"

Sergeant Schumacher stopped short in his sentence when he saw his son brought into the room with his arms tied behind his back.

Ryan whispered in J.D.'s ear, and then showed him a small walkie-talkie.

"*Sir?*" the sergeant asked. "What is going on? Why have you arrested my son?"

J.D explained. "For months command has suspected a spy. That spy, we thought, was you."

The sergeant was still confused. "What, Colonel? I don't understand. What does this have to do with Peter?"

J.D. clarified. "Since January, Stone and his men have caused this armory to suffer unacceptable losses on mission, too many times for it to be random. Nine of our men and women are dead. I knew we had a leak, but I wasn't sure whom. I thought it was you. That's why I told you who we were holding captive in the basement. You were the only non-command personnel who knew. Not even the sentries were told who they were guarding. I truly hoped Stone would come for him. That's why I set a trap outside the armory. But he didn't... I guess loyalty means nothing to him."

"Are you saying, sir, that you truly think I'm a spy."

"Not anymore. Today I found out who the spy is. It's your son."

"*My son!* That's impossible. Why—why would my son do this? Where is your proof?"

J.D. pulled out the interrogation room audio recorder from his pant leg. He played it for him. In a raspy, pained and hysterical tone Barlow repeated, "Old King Cole, Old King Cole. Merry Old Soul, Merry Old Soul—Hail to the king. The king is coming. The king is coming. Hail to the king, old soul."

"Colonel, I don't understand. What do the rants of that man have to do with my son?"

"That was Barlow's voice. 'Hail to the King!' That's exactly what your son said the day he returned to you. Remember? 'To a great man. Hail to the king!' He's the spy. He's the betrayer!" J.D. pointed an angry finger at the young lad.

"It can't be. It just can't be. You're mistaken. Barlow, Barlow lied. It's not true!" Sergeant Schumacher declared, but what his son had toasted that day echoed in his mind.

"It is true." J.D. said plainly to the elder. "What reason would Barlow have to point the finger in the wrong direction? He wouldn't even give up Stone, not even to save his own life. I truly thought it was you."

J.D. now turned to the younger Schumacher.

"Everything pointed to your father. You set him up perfectly. That was until Barlow started his outburst, then it struck me." J.D. turned from them both and walked back to the table. He unsheathed one of his Gurkha kukri blades that hung over his chair back. He stepped back to the young Schumacher and looked directly at him.

"What I don't understand," J.D. spoke, as he glared into the young man's eyes. "What I don't understand is why. Why turn on your own father?" He stepped back from the boy. "Little Peter suddenly appearing on our doorstep. The only child to ever escape Stone's house of horrors. Four months of enduring such torture, but never could tell us from where he escaped. Psychogenic amnesia, isn't that what the doc said? Brought on by extreme emotional, physical, and psychological trauma. What shit!

Such a happy reunion that day. Remember that day, Peter?" he addressed the boy. "What was it you said that day at the celebration party?" J.D. asked rhetorically, as he held out his hand to Major Duncan. Ryan placed the walkie-talkie in J.D.'s hand.

"You remember. When you raised your glass in toast. 'Thank you all for giving me back my life.' With your glass raised high, you said, 'To a great man. Hail to the king!' Giving your father a big and loving smile. What an odd thing to say I thought. 'Hail to the king.' You weren't saluting your father; you were giving us all warning, weren't you? All this time, Stone's little spy."

"*No*, no, Colonel. This can't be true," Peter Senior pleaded. "There's got to be a different explanation. *Peter*—Peter, tell, tell me he's wrong."

The boy said nothing as his dad begged for a reason that could satisfy a father's aching heart.

His father kept pleading, "Peter, please tell him he's wrong."

J.D. recited, " 'Peter, Peter pumpkin eater. Had a child but couldn't save it. Peter learned to talk and tell. In hopes of sending another to hell.' Stone's little poem is clear now. *Two* Peters. Father and son."

"It's your fault, father," the adolescent child coldly responded. "You let go. You let go of my hand. You let go of my hand." His voice grew angrier and colder the more he spoke. "You were supposed to protect me! I waited for you to come. I waited for you to save me from those men. The things they did to me! You don't have any idea. You were supposed to *protect* me!"

"Forgive me. Please, please forgive me. One minute you were there and the next you were gone. They took you so fast... I couldn't find you. So, I sought out the place of the light. The place we were headed to. I thought someone could help. I couldn't save you by myself. I sought out the light. Please forgive me. Please!?"

"They did things to me," the young man began to cry. "They did things to me and I hate you for it. I hate all of you for it. But Edward saved me, protected me from the others; showed me that it was all of your faults. He promised if I helped him, he would punish all of you. Wait 'til he comes. He'll kill you all! Then I'll be happy. Happy to see you all die!"

Tears began to flow from Sergeant Schumacher's eyes. His son had betrayed him.

J.D. held up the object that was in his hand revealing it to everyone in the room. It was a walkie-talkie. He turned back to the boy.

"It was you. That night we went to the fire," J.D. said. "Your father told me he had an uneasy feeling... You came to see your father off. It wasn't what you said; it was how you said it—like you knew it would be the last time you'd see him. I've been so blind. All these clues and I looked in the wrong direction."

J.D. handed the walkie-talkie to Peter Senior. "Not one of ours," he told him. He continued to address senior, confronting him on his cowardice. "That was the night I thought you were the leak. You just disappeared that night. Then later turned up here, not a scratch on you, telling everyone I was dead. You ran. I thought you set me up. But you were right, you were just afraid."

He drew close to Peter Junior, placed the blade against his jugular, and spoke softly in the youth's ear; his voice never rising above a fierce, frigid whisper. "Good people died because of you—" And then revealed a secret that only he and Doctor France knew, "My unborn child and woman died because of you. For this, I'm going to gut you alive and hang you on the perimeter fence next to Barlow so your entrails hang around your feet."

He stepped back, away from his prisoner. "Peter Schumacher Junior. In accordance with the articles of the 69th Infantry Regiment and as the commanding officer, I have it within my power to find you guilty of aiding and abetting the enemy and 13 acts of conspiracy to commit murder. I therefore sentence you to death, to be carried out immediately."

J.D. turned back to his friends. There was a cold hate in his eyes.

"You will all bear witness," he told them, pointing the Gurkha to everyone sitting at the table. "You will all see how I deal with traitors."

"J.D., are you serious?" Sergeant Drukker asked with surprise. You're not really going to gut him, are you? Chief," he addressed Kermit. "That's not right. He should be taken out and shot."

J.D. turned back to Drukker and gave him an intense glare of contempt.

Kermit did not agree either with the method that he believed the boy's death sentence was to be carried out, though he did whole-heartedly agree with J.D.'s guilty verdict and death sentence. What J.D. was about to do was not a sanctioned military method of execution—but then again, J.D. did not have to conform to any of the old ways of the military. J.D. Nichols was the commander of these men and they appeared to be loyal to him. Although, Kermit disagreed, he was not going to interfere with his authority.

"Stand down, son" he told Drukker, putting a hand to his arm. "It's not our place."

However, before J.D. could turn back to the boy to enact his revenge, three shots rang out. Young Peter slumped to the floor, his hands still tied behind him. Schumacher Senior fell to his knees in anguish. His pistol dropped from his hand, he muttered over his sorrowful tears, "He was my son. The shame is mine. My responsibility to punish."

A guard rushed in. J.D. returned to his chair and picked up his other weapons and his hat from off the table. He looked at Chief Dunne and ordered, "Take out the trash and secure it to the south gate. I want Stone to see his failure." J.D. walked to the door without any further acknowledgment to his guests. As he approached the exit, Paul and two other soldiers ran into the room. J.D. spoke softly to Paul. "Escort the sergeant back to his room. He's honorably discharged. Inform Sergeant Hanson there'll be one civilian on the convoy."

J.D. bent over and picked up the hand-held radio that had been dropped. The last word he spoke was, *kommen*, as he left the room. Max immediately followed him.

There was a moment of silence as the body of Peter's young son was removed under the direction of Chief Warrant Officer Dunne. When the task had been completed, and all had departed, a burst of outrage erupted.

"Now, son." Kermit addressed Ryan. "You want tell us what the hell is going on around here?!"

"It's simple, Chief Brown. We're at war."

"Frankly, I don't give a shit about your internal issues or how you deal with them," David told Ryan. "But as for the people who helped save your ass, you know, us, you should do us the courtesy of at least explaining how our friend went from being an occasional insensitive jerk to an outright callous asshole, *and* how he ended upon adopting a transmute daughter."

Ryan didn't like his remark about J.D.'s character and let him know so. "I'd be very careful what you say around here, DiMinni," Ryan warned. "Our commander has a fearless devotion to duty and a great steadfast allegiance to this city. And no one has ever disagreed with his command decisions! He's earned the respect and praise of the people. We are all loyal to the colonel. He's personally saved my ass more times than you have. As for that child, that little girl is the commander's flesh and blood *and* my godchild."

"*What?*" Marisol gasped in shock and disbelief.

"It's true," Ryan revealed. "She's the colonel's daughter."

"Well, now I think you do owe us an explanation, *Major*," Kermit told Ryan.

"Don't think me ungrateful for what you all did for me, and don't take what I'm about to say the wrong way, but you shouldn't have come back. Everything changed after you left. J.D. has changed. Hell, I've changed. I used to be an actor. Now look at me, second in charge in the middle of a war with a madman."

"So, what happened?" Sam said, interrupting. "How did J.D. end up with a transmute for a daughter?"

"You saw Paul Wiese, the one J.D called Piss Pants? You see he's a warrant officer now."

Ryan tried to condense the events of what had happened since they left, but even the highlights were lengthy.

"This female transmute sat in the truck and kept holding him all the way back to the armory," Ryan told them. "And when we got here she followed us in. Well, the doctor freaked when he saw her, and Luci's reaction was unsettling. I ended up attending to J.D.'s wounds because Luci wouldn't let France anywhere near him."

Kermit was impatient with Ryan's long explanation, which still hadn't answered any of their questions. "Son, can we speed this up, and get to the crux of things?" Kermit asked, interrupting, having nearly run out of patience.

"Sure. So, J.D. is out for hours. When he wakes, he can barely remember what happened. Doesn't remember you left, doesn't remember getting shot, doesn't seem to remember anything. When I told him, Luci was outside his door waiting and she was pregnant. He looked at me, got out of bed, pushed me out the door, and then locked it. In his room for three days, won't come out, won't eat, and refuses to see anyone. Then someone drives up to the gate. Next thing I know there's J.D. coming out of his room, all dressed in his blacks, machetes strapped on and machine gun in hand. He orders me to follow him. That was the first time I ever heard him actually give an order. So, I did. We went to the gate. That's how Lieutenant Alexander joined our ranks; he accepted J.D. as his commander. The weird thing he really was a Lieutenant and actually had been a member of this armory."

"What about the baby? How can that girl be J.D.'s? She's too old," Marisol wanted to know.

"Yeah," David added. "And where was Luci all that time?"

"I'm sorry, Marisol, the child *is* his. He named her Caitlin Marcela. Caitlin, he told me because it was a good Irish name. But he never did say why Marcela."

Marisol knew, and she was surprised. Marcela had been her mother's name.

"As for Caitlin's age, she's almost a year old. However, the doctor says she aged faster because of her transmute DNA. He puts her physical age around four or five and maturity around seven. She's extremely bright, and very precocious, as you saw... As for Luci, she sat outside his room for three days, never made an attempt to get in. Just sat patiently waiting for J.D. to open the door and let her in. He did eventually, the day Lieutenant Alexander came.

After Caitlin was born, he made sure everyone in the armory knew Luci was the mother of his child, and that they were both to be treated with dignity and respect or else get out. There were 15 or 16 of us back then. Everyone accepted it without question, as would any new refugee or they were turned away."

Kermit asked, "So what's all this about women and children?"

"It was Paul who first told us about them. He said he had heard and seen things when he was a part of Stone's group, about women and children held captive and abused. Then later, a few days after Lieutenant Alexander arrived, Peter the dwarf came. He told us about Stone, too. Well, sort of. As you heard, Stone cut out his tongue, so he had to write his story down."

"So who is this Stone? I thought Piss Pants was part of that Renquist gang."

"Richard Barlow called himself Renquist. Barlow was Edward Stone's enforcer. Edward Stone is one sick piece of shit... Anyway, J.D. starts leaving the little one in my care and goes out on patrols with a few of our men looking for Stone's prisoners, doesn't have any luck. One night there's this fire on the west side. J.D. goes out to investigate, takes Luci, Sergeant Schumacher, and the Dunphy brothers with him. After an hour or so Peter Senior comes back, says that they were ambushed and everyone is dead. We were getting ready to leave when I heard this angry scream just resonate in the night air. I knew it was the colonel. We looked for him but all we found was the smoldering bonfire, that and the burnt corpses of the Dunphy brothers, and a lot of Stone's men torn apart. The next night the colonel shows up. He's all crusted in blood. But there's no Luci. He never spoke a word. He went up to his room and shut the door. He didn't come out for a day. I went to check on him. I heard him weeping. That was the last time I ever heard him cry. That was the day he changed."

"He cried over her?" Marisol asked.

Ryan responded to Marisol quickly. He knew by her tone she was hurt.

"*No mi hijita. Usted no entiende. Él clamó para que usted también.* He cried after you left, too. He cried for all of you. Those three days when he locked himself away, he was sobbing. I didn't know what he was crying about at first, but then one day I found Caitlin in his room looking at a photo. It was all of you. It was the one I took before you left that night. He had made a shrine of it. That's when I knew he was crying for losing all of you."

There was a silence for a moment. They were perplexed by this man they had once called friend, a man who had helped to save them and who had later, by election, become their leader. Why was it that a person who had once been so caring and loving toward them was now so cold and distant? David broke the silence.

"I thought you said you didn't speak Spanish?"

"If you are referring to that day at Astor Place," Ryan replied, "when I asked J.D. why he was speaking Spanish to me. I never said I didn't know Spanish."

David responded, "Oh."

"Yes, that's all very nice, but what in the hell is going on?" Kermit asked. "And why the attitude and indifference? Even if he had something against the rest of us at least I would have expected he'd be happy to see Marisol. He acts like he doesn't care. Was he in love with Luci? Is that it?"

"Oh, no, no. You really don't understand. I don't think he was ever *in love* with Luci. I think he did love her, but she was the mother of his child. It was more of an act of responsibility and loyalty. As for his behavior, he distances himself from everyone. He's afraid he won't be able to protect you."

"He doesn't think we can protect ourselves?" Sam asked.

"He stopped getting emotionally involved with people after Luci died. He has no friends. No attachment, no pain. Everyone here is either civilian or one of his subordinates. It's not that he doesn't care, it's because he does. You were the closest thing he had to family, and now he fears for you. He feels responsible for everyone. Every time someone died under his command, whether it was a soldier or civilian, it took something away from him. He's taken on the burden of saving all of humanity and it's rotted his spirit.

Now gentlemen, and Marisol, I must end this. I have a meeting with the colonel. We are doing final departure in the morning and I have to finalize our plans with him. Please make arrangements with your base for a pick-up point. I'll be back shortly with an escort for you."

Ryan moved for the door, but was interrupted by Kermit.

"Hold on there, son. Why is it everyone is trying to get rid of us? Aren't you a bit curious to why we came back?"

"Kermit, we don't have time to be curious. There's too much going on right now. Its best if you all go back to England like Colonel Nichols asked. It's better that way, better for all of us."

"We didn't come back just for the sake of wanting to, we came back because we had to," Kermit informed Ryan. "England doesn't exist for us anymore more. We were forced to leave. We had to come back, everyone."

"What do you mean by *everyone?*"

"I mean every last U.S. citizen—civilians and armed forces alike. We left England and are now at McGuire Air Force Base… 94 of us."

"Is this something the colonel should be concerned about? What was the specific nature of your mission?'

"*Mission?* There's no mission. The Chiefs of Staff gave us permission to look for you as a courtesy. They knew the rescue team that extracted us last year shot J.D. and left him to the half-mutes. So, they gave me permission to come back to the armory to see if you were still here and if by some miracle J.D. was still alive."

"Is that the only reason you've come, or was it the doctor?"

"Why would you even ask that, after everything? Why would you suspect an ulterior motive?" Kermit asked disappointedly.

"Your arrival the day before withdrawal is suspicious. And in these times, everything is suspect to me; especially when you come with two Navy Seals. Are they aware that J.D. isn't a real colonel?"

"You know us. How could you think like that?" Marisol pleaded.

"Listen. There's no secret agenda here, Ryan," Kermit enlightened his host. "When we left J.D. was a sergeant, remember? And the doctor was dead. And that's the way we left it; no one except us knows differently."

"Yes, but he introduced himself as colonel. They'll be suspicious. Now, I really must leave you. If there's anything you need just let the guard at the door know and he'll arrange it."

"Wait a minute, wait a minute! Let me finish," Kermit requested, nearly demanding. There's more I need to let you know."

Ryan gave him five more minutes.

# 5

# A LONG JOURNEY INTO DAY

"COME," J.D. SPOKE, AS THE KNOCK CAME TO HIS OFFICE DOOR. IT was Ryan.

Ryan had earned a Major's rank and had not only earned the trust, respect, and admiration of the troops and his commander, but was also the only one that J.D. wholeheartedly trusted with his daughter. Not even Paul, though he had earned J.D.'s trust in watching over her when needed, had gained the entitlement of care provider. This honor was exclusively given to Ryan.

"Is everything ready?" J.D. asked.

"Yes, sir."

"You sure? You know how she loves her music and her movies— and her books. She'll be quite unhappy if you forgot to pack every- thing. You know how she can be."

"Everything is packed, including the Blu-ray player."

"Good. And are you all set?"

"Begging the commander's pardon, but I'm not going. My place is here, until the very end."

J.D. was angry with him. Ryan had never challenged a command decision before.

"*Begging the commander's pardon?* No! No, you may not beg my pardon! That wasn't a request, Major, it's an order. You will be on that convoy. Do you understand? An order!"

"No sir, I will not. I will not go. I will stay."

"How dare you. I could shoot you for this."

"You could, sir. But you won't. And I still wouldn't be going."

"Damn it, Ryan. Cut the crap. You've never disobeyed me, why now?"

"Because my job isn't done here. I told you I wanted to stay and help as many survivors as possible. I told you this the night we made contact with England. That time has not yet come."

"Goddamnit, Ryan. If the children are alive then Chief Dunne and I can handle it. You know I need you to lead that convoy. And you know you're the only one I trust with implicity with my daughter and Michael Adam. So Goddamnit! As a friend, I'm asking. Please do this."

"That's the first time you've ever called me friend. I appreciate that, J.D. You know Caitlin means the world to me, and I would never do anything that would put her in harm's way. That's why I have no reservations about staying. Chief Wiese can lead the convoy as well as I. Paul is more than capable of watching over Caitlin and Michael Adam. I wouldn't say that if I truly didn't believe it. Paul cares deeply about her. You forget he was expecting his first child before the plague. You've never given him the same trust as you've given me. The trust he deserves. You should. He would protect her with his life, as would I."

"Damn you to hell, Ryan Duncan. If our friendship means anything, you'll take care of your godchild. Damn you, damn you for... Just get the hell out before I change my mind and shoot you out of principle."

"No, sir."

"*What?* Going to disobey another order?"

"No, sir. There's the matter of our friends. I know why they came back, and it concerns me."

In a way J.D. was actually disappointed when Ryan explained the situation to him. He had hoped that the sole reason for their return was out of concern and interest in finding out what had happened to him, though he was still angry about it all. Even though he had hoped his friends were well and happy, and would never return for their own sake, he had hoped the reason for their abrupt appearance had been motivated by friendship and loyalty. However, that was not the case, at least not in whole.

At least the integrity of his command, what little there was left of it, for the moment would remain intact. After tomorrow it wouldn't matter what the returning military wanted. They could have the city and what was left of it, which was little, at least below 86th Street. Over many months J.D. and his men had hit as many hospitals, pharmacies, grocery stores, food shops, clothing stores, and anywhere else they could scavenge supplies. Almost all of what they had acquired had been shipped out of the city and up to Mechanicville on two separate occasions. This third and final transport was solely for the purpose of evacuating the armory's remaining military personnel. However, there was no place for men with deceit in their hearts and blood on their hands in Mechanicville, as the doctor would soon find out.

It was now late August. If necessary, J.D. had hoped to stay until October, but things had not gone as planned. Rodents had ravaged their food stores, and they could not waste vehicle fuel or divert manpower from protecting the armory to travel the distance needed to find a possible replacement source. There was just enough fuel to get them to their destination. Also, there was little remaining diesel to power the generators to last until October, even with conservation efforts. Ammunition was the only supply that was abundant.

Of the twelve men remaining at base only Ryan Duncan and Peter Dunne knew where the survivors had been sent. This was a necessity in assuring the secrecy of the town. That decision had proven to be a wise choice.

Only the senior and second in command of each relocation team mission had been told their destination. There had also been a contingency plan put into place to make sure each convoy wasn't followed out of the city as an extra measure of security to protect the convoy and their destination. Further security measures had also been taken in keeping the town a secret after arrival. Only one brief transmission four times a month was allowed from the town to the armory, unless there was an emergency. The transmission dates were only known to James Alexander in Mechanicville and Ryan and J.D. at the armory, along with the dates and times pre-set before the first convoy departed. As a further precaution a codename for the town had been pre-established. Gladly, an emergency call had never come.

This first convoy leadership had been given to third in command of the 69th Infantry Regiment, Major James Alexander. Second mission team leader duty was assigned to Sergeant Katie O'Hanlon. The B-Team, the team that would protect the rear of the convoy was Jonas McGann and Liz Hudson. All together there were 12 soldiers, 34 civilians—mainly men—four cats, one dog, six Humvees, nine LMTV cargo trucks, one MTV LWB truck, three Strykers, and two NYPD Police buses all loaded with supplies that had been stored at a secret storage site.

A month later and several weeks ahead of schedule, O'Hanlon and Custode returned to the city with a small team to collect the remaining, civilians—mostly women and children—transport vehicles, and nearly all the outstanding supplies, leaving enough food, fuel, weapons and ammunition for a team of twelve to survive until October, or so they thought.

---

J.D. had made his goodbyes to his daughter, a teary farewell that nearly brought him to his own tears. Though he kept in control of his emotions, it had not been easy for him.

"Dawd? Where we go?" Caitlin asked in a concerned tone.

"You, young lady, are going to a special place where you can be outside and run around and play in the grass. A place where you don't have to worry about bad men trying to hurt you."

"Dawd, what is gwass?"

Caitlin had rarely been on the outside of the armory. It had been too dangerous for anyone to be outside with the constant threat of attack, so she did not know what grass was, for she had never seen any.

"Grass is... Well, it's green. And... It's... You know, Cat, I don't know how to tell you so you'll understand. You'll just have to wait and see. But I promise you will love grass. And Katie is there."

Caitlin had not overlooked her father's reference to only her going to a special place, and knew that his mentioning of Katie was to distract her.

"Dawd? How come you say Caitlin go. You go, too. Dawd go to special place, too. Okay? Elty and Cheep Weez and Mickel go, too."

He smiled at her tentatively, trying to cover his uncertainty about Ryan.

"Yes, Caitlin. Elty go, too. But he may not be in the truck with you. Chief Wiese may watch you and Michael. Okay?"

"Why no Elty watch me? Not fair."

"Ryan has many responsibilities. He's going to be in charge of everyone."

Caitlin grew anxious at her father's evasive responses. "Not dawd? Dawd is boss. Dawd has to go!"

He gently put his hands on her upper arms.

"Caitlin. You need to be a good cat, okay?" He tried to relieve her anxiety with reassurance. "Everything will be fine. Dawd is going to look one more time for the children. You remember our talk about the children. Right?"

"Yes, dawd," she answered, understanding its importance to her father.

"Then you know how important it is to find them. So be a good cat for me. Go with Chief Wiese when he comes to get you. Okay?"

"Okay," she agreed, reluctantly conceding.

He offered her a consolation prize to help ease the pain of their pending separation.

"I'll tell you what. When it's time to leave, I'll make sure Marisol and Max ride in the truck with you and Barkley. How about that?"

She was ecstatic at the prospect. She shouted, *"Monster!"* with great enthusiasm and joy.

He pulled his daughter in and held her tight for a moment, not wanting to let her go, but knowing he had to. There were matters that needed his attention. He kissed her good night.

---

After having met with Chief Wiese and Major Duncan to go over final preparations, and after enjoying brief playtime with Max, J.D. retired to his room. It was nearly 1800 hours when he lay down upon his bed. He knew that sleep, if it came, would be brief, which was perfectly fine this night, for later he would have to bid farewell to his men and make sure that they departed on schedule.

J.D.'s furry companion lay at the edge of the bed, content to be in his master's presence once again. Lying silently, J.D. stared up at the dirty off-white ceiling thinking and reflecting. His mind wandered from his upcoming farewell to his men to Stone, and then to his dog, and finally to Marisol.

Marisol had kept Max's obedience reinforcement up, and even made sure he always had on his doggie pack filled with everything J.D. had taught her to put in it. She was a good woman, a loving and attentive woman, and though strong headed and foul-mouthed at times, he had loved her for who she was and how she made him feel. But that was long ago, a time before hate and revenge devoured his soul and left him empty.

What lay in the darkness of his mind when he shut his eyes had now become reality. He felt he had lost his humanity, fallen too far into the pit to find it again. His hate for himself and his enemy devoured him.

Now his friends had returned and he should have felt happy. This was not the case. There was no place in his life for them now. There was no place in his life for anyone, not even his daughter. He had become something unspeakable—a raging monster—and there was no way of going back. He needed to remain behind so that Caitlin would not be stigmatized with the sins of the father.

Ryan had been only partially correct. J.D. did indeed still care about his friends, and he was concerned about how well he could protect them, but there was more to it, a more selfish reason. He cared what they thought about him and he was afraid that the memories they held of him and what they had shared together would be wiped away if they saw him transform into his true self—the predatorial trans-human. David once had quoted Andre Gide, 'It is better to be hated for what you are than to be loved for what you are not.' At the time he had agreed, but now all he wanted was to be loved and remembered for whom he had been. So he had given them just a glimpse of what he was capable of, let the demons loose enough to reinforce his cold exterior, enough to show them they were no longer welcome and he was not the person they had known.

He was stirred from his tossing and turning by a knock on the door.

"One moment," he spoke, as he sat up in his bed and picked up his shirt. "Come," he said as he began to button it. He stopped; it was Marisol.

Max sat up as Marisol entered.

"Why are you here?" he asked, but she didn't respond. She approached him; there was anger in her eyes. He knew he was about to get slapped.

She raised her hand, but he was quick. He grabbed onto her wrist, "Not this time," he warned her, having remembered a time long ago when she had slapped him in anger. Nevertheless, she too was quick and it was not his face she was interested in. She kneed him hard in the groin and began to swear at him in Spanish.

"¡Cabron! ¿Cómo se atreve usted a tratar nos de esta manera! ¡Usted Pendajo!"

J.D. had not heard what she had been screaming at him. He had been caught off-guard. It was apparent to him she had continued with her self-defense studies, for he knew he hadn't taught her that move. He was in pain, severe testicular agony, pain which radiated up into his guts.

From his pain grew anger, anger at her but even more with himself for letting her get the better of him.

"*Almeja*," he gasped. He had called her a name that no man should ever call a woman, especially a Columbian girl with a quick temper.

"*¡Vete al carajo!*" she yelled, and then punched him square in the solar plexus.

The punch had not affected him, but it had further roused his anger. It burst forth. "You want it rough, is that what you want?" he yelled, and then grabbed her by the throat and lifted her into the air, his talons digging into the soft flesh of her neck. "I'll give it to you like you've never had it."

She held onto his arm to stop him from choking her. He turned around and tossed her on the bed like a crumpled piece of notebook paper into a wastebasket. Max fled to the corner of the room and cowered. It was the first time that his fearless canine retreated without an order.

He immobilized her before she could rise, sitting on top her pelvis, pinning her to the bed. He removed his shirt and tossed it to the floor. She hadn't seen the cross around his neck when she had kicked him, but there it was—the platinum polished cross pendant with its round shaped diamond accent. She had received it from her grandmother as a Quinceanera gift, and in turn she had given it to him as a token of her love. Though J.D. had been hesitant in accepting it, partly because he thought it "sappy," he took the gift and promised to leave it around his neck from that moment on. But this was not the man who had pledged his love to her. That man, the one of gentleness and understanding, the one that made her "first time" special was gone.

J.D. was fierce. His cold, frightful eyes scared her as he tore at her vest, fumbling chaotically to release it. She repeatedly struck at him, first slapping, and then punching his face, drawing blood, trying to get free. He ripped open her BDU shirt, and then tore away her army issued green A-shirt to expose her full, ripe brown breasts. He grabbed her hands and forced them to her side.

J.D. sniffed her neck, and then released her hands and grabbed onto her head. He began to lick the small trickles of blood that ran from the small puncture wounds he had inflicted upon her. He had often drawn blood in his mating rituals with Luci. The sweet taste of Marisol's blood sexually excited him.

She could feel his manhood rising up as it pressed against her body. She wanted him, she had longed for him and burned for him to be inside her again—but not this way! He was vicious and brutal, and he was hurting her. She still loved him, with heart and soul, but without the tenderness it was too much to bear. His rage and aggression deeply frightened her, enough that she feared for her own life.

He appeared blind in his blood tasting, and he did not notice when she slipped her knife out of its quick release military holster that was strapped to her hip. She closed her eyes as she raised it above his back; she ached inside at the thought of hurting the only man she had ever given herself to. She plunged it into his back with all her strength.

The blade struck him to the left of his mid-thoracic vertebra, barely penetrating his thick transmute skin. He felt the sensation of something strike him, but that area of his back was highly desensitized. She struck him again; this time the knife went deeper, striking him along the delineation of where his transmute flesh met his human. He reared up and spun his head around. The knife was lodged in his back. There had not been too much pain where she had stuck him, but it still hurt. He pulled the embedded knife from his flesh and placed it against Marisol's throat, pressing the razor-sharp military blade just above her larynx.

"You're pathetic and weak," he told her, then grabbed her hands and put the knife into them, squeezing them tight around the textured grip. "Try it now!" He held onto her hands and forced the tip into his chest, just below the tattoo of a dragon in flight, the one Peter had given him to cover up a youthful injury. A trickle of blood began to run.

"*¡Te odio!*" she screamed at him. "*¡Te odio!*"

"Do it." Do it or I'll kill you!" he warned.

"I'll hate you forever," she now screamed at him in English. "*Forever!* Do you hear me?!"

He told her again, "Pathetic and weak," and then added. "How did I ever love you?" He grabbed the knife from her and raised it up. His arm came crashing down. The knife plunged into the mattress next to her head. "Get out. Get out before I change my mind," he warned, and then released her.

She ran from the room crying, clutching her torn shirt closed as she did, and nearly ran into Kermit as he approached the doorway. She bolted passed him, not saying a word.

Kermit burst in and angrily shouted, "What the hell is going on? Did you just—?"

"*Never,*" he told Kermit.

Kermit saw the knife protruding from the mattress. "Then what—?"

"Just a lesson in reality. She'll understand eventually. What is it that you want, *Chief?*" he asked as he buttoned his shirt.

"I know you, son; you're planning something. So, you want to tell me?"

"Just a strategic withdrawal, that's all," he said as he extracted the knife from the bed, and then handed it to his old comrade.

"Cut the crap and tell me what I need to know. I'm worried about you."

"Don't be, Chief. There's—"

Kermit cut him off. "That's exactly what I mean. You're addressing me as a soldier. You rarely used my rank, and here you are using it every sentence."

"Chief Brown. Strange," he commented, and then sat at his desk to put on his boots. "You used to be a master sergeant. Didn't know they made cooks warrant officers."

"I'm not a cook anymore. I'm a Tactical Commander."

"Ah well, their loss."

"Now I know something's wrong. You used to make fun of my cooking. Whatever you got planned I hope it's not something reckless that will endanger others."

J.D. was hurt and angered at the notion that Kermit could think ill of him in such a way. He slammed his fist on his desk in protest.

"*No,* no I was never reckless! Never with anyone's life but my own! You know that. Don't you dare! Don't you dare accuse me—I have always put the good of the group first. My life always before the lives of my soldiers. If anything, you put the lives of your team in danger," he angrily chastised Kermit. "You came looking for me. You got captured. What if those hadn't been my men? What if they had been Stone's? You and the others should have gotten on that chopper when my men took you back. It was your responsibility to keep your people safe."

"I know why you stayed," Kermit told him. "I knew how hard it was for you. And you were right. You made the right choice. It was hard on us all not having you around. We missed your smart-ass and your obsession to outdo David with all those damn movie quotes. But mostly we just missed you. Son, you're family. And our family was torn apart. It affected us all, but it nearly tore the heart out of Marisol. Whatever it is you got planned, whatever you're scheming, all I ask is you don't break that little girl's heart again. You'll never know how hard it was for her to survive without you. I just thank God we were there for her; I shudder to think what would have happened if we weren't."

"Well, I shudder to think what Stone would have done to all of you, especially Marisol. You foolishly came looking for me, when the odds were I was dead. And don't give me some cock 'n' bull story that Marisol needed closure."

"It wasn't just for Marisol. It was for all of us. Though I can see I'm just wasting my breath on you."

Kermit moved to exit; as he did J.D. called to him.

"Kermit. None of you should be here. You're continued presence will jeopardize the mission objective. You're to go with my men. You can live that life I wanted for all of us."

"That's the other reason we came looking for you. Some of the civilians wanted to make a fresh start away from the military. Command granted their request. I'd like to have those civilians relocate with you, but I'd need your assistance. The military is pulling out and heading to Colorado Springs the day after tomorrow. That doesn't give those staying behind a lot of time, and they can't be left unprotected. They just don't have the training. Will you help?"

"What makes you think I would welcome them with open arms when you just told me they're untrained. I need warfighters or people with special skills who can help our community prosper and thrive."

"That's a bit harsh, isn't it?" Kermit asked of his callous comment.

J.D. did not want to turn any survivor away, but the harsh reality was that taking in more unskilled people would not be for the betterment of the survival group. The uneducated that had been part of the armory had been tasked with doing menial labor, such as laundry and facility cleaning. Upon arrival in Mechanicville they were put to task in helping to construct security barricades and fencing, along with cleaning out buildings and homes, sorting the useless from the items that could be used in their survival. J.D. truly did not need any more unskilled laborers.

"Is it?" J.D. snapped. "Perhaps in England you had unlimited resources to feed the masses, but here—here we'll barely have enough to get through the winter. Taking on more mouths to feed, more people to protect, will jeopardize our community's survival. That's just the unforgiving truth."

"How about I clarify? These civilians may not be able to protect themselves very well, but they weren't required too. Many civilians learned farming. There are also two doctors, a gynecologist and a surgeon, an electrical engineer, a carpenter and a plumber. And how about Master Sergeant McDaniels? He and a few others want to make a new start, too. Are they suitable for your community now?"

"It's also a matter of transportation. I'll give you an answer later, after mission briefing. Now if you will excuse yourself, I have other affairs to attend to."

As Kermit neared the door, J.D. asked, "Why Colorado Springs? What's the significance?"

"A heat signature," Kermit replied. A heat signature on a satellite photo. They think there may be someone still at Cheyenne Mountain." As Kermit stepped out the door, he spoke, "Sometimes if you chase the dragon too long, you become the dragon."

J.D. went to the corner of the bedroom and picked up a dusty guitar case and a large bottle of Jack Daniels that stood next to it. He knew it was just a matter of time before David would pay him a visit. He went to the roof with Max.

J.D. knew it was unsafe for any of his men to stay at the armory. After many exhausting months of searching he had given up hope of finding any of Stone's captives. By now, he believed, they were dead.

It was time to leave. Except to leave and let Stone have what he had desired for so long was unacceptable. Edward Stone and his band of killers and rapists would have to earn the prize; they would have to survive him.

J.D. dismissed Michael Panton from roof sentry duty. With walkie-talkie in hand, he stood at the edge of the building and taunted his nemesis.

"Stone. Stone. Are you listening? I know you're out there. I have a final riddle.

'This thing all things devours:
Birds, beasts, trees, flowers,
Gnaws iron, bites steel,
Grinds hard stones to meal,
Slays king, destroys town,
And beats the highest mountain down. '

What am I?" There was a long silence. J.D. was uncertain that anyone, especially Stone, was listening. "Give up, Stone? The answer is time... It's time, Stone. It's time to put an end to this conflict. Your little Peter Pumpkin Spy is dead. We hung him on the perimeter fence, as we did Barlow. But here's some good news for you. My men are leaving in the morning. They're leaving me all alone, Stone. Just me and this big armory. You can have it, Stone. That is if you and your half-wits have enough balls to take it from me... I'll be waiting. I'll even leave the front door open for you."

J.D. pitched the walkie-talkie across the street toward the Baruch College building and then retreated to the center of the roof and sat down on the large covered trunk. He thought about what he had purposely done to Marisol, but he knew it was necessary. He needed for her to hate him. For her to hate him enough that there would be no reason for her to try and stay behind. After a moment, the scuffle of footsteps came from behind him. He knew it was David; he recognized the sound of his footfall. Even Max knew who was approaching, barely raising his head in recognition.

J.D. asked, "No gun this time, David?" as he neared.

"You left the lights on," David commented as he neared. "I thought you liked to do your thinking the dark?"

"I still do, but just not here. Besides, tonight's a special occasion. I wanted the tower lights on."

"Where's the beer?" David asked, referring to the last time he and J.D. had spent time on the roof sharing camaraderie and friendship, as he joined his old comrade.

"Drinking has no appeal anymore, since my metabolism won't let me get piss-assed, but what kind of host would I be if I didn't offer you something." He handed David the bottle of Jack Daniels. I have something else for you," he said, handing him a guitar case that had been sitting to his left.

David unlatched the case and opened its lid. He removed the soft cloth that lay on top and revealed a new guitar. He was astounded.

"*Holy shit!* Where the hell did you get this?"

J.D. responded, but didn't answer his question. "It's a Yamaha Wes Borland Signature Semi-Hollow Electric Guitar. It has a Takumi-Kezuri constructed body carved from one block of Alder with a three-piece Maple neck, and Rosewood fingerboard with 24 frets. The bridge is a Finger Clamp Quick Change Tremolo System and the pickups are YASH-designed Custom33 Split-field Humbuckers. So the brochure says."

"Where the hell did you get it?" he asked again.

"Picked it up on one of my visits to the Guitar Center on 14th Street. Saw it in a glass showcase and it reminded me of you, so I took it."

"This is—I mean. WOW… How can I thank you?"

"I'm sure I'll think of something," J.D. replied, waiting for a moment before he put his plan into motion. It was a favor and the guitar was just a prelude.

David began to tune the guitar. "Seriously, J.D. This means a lot to me. I was really disappointed not being able to take any of my guitars with me. Took me six months to get one when I got to England, then that was just a cheap piece of crap."

"Funny you should mention your guitars."

"Yeah, I see my room is completely empty. So go ahead and give it to me."

J.D. trusted David implicitly. Theirs was a mutual bond of friendship that had been forged in survival and he trusted him with his life. He had no reservations in revealing the location of David's personal affects.

"All your personal belongings were shipped out. They're in Mechanicville."

"*What?* Mechanicville? *Our Mechanicville?*"

"Yes. I couldn't bear to throw out anyone's stuff. Therefore, when the first convoy left, I made sure they took your personal effects up. Even some of what you didn't get from your Gramercy apartment."

"I don't even know what to say. I mean, we weren't supposed to come back."

"I know. I did it for me. Just wanted something to remember you by. My own personal DD Dominion museum... So what happened to Julie?"

"I did exactly what you told me to do. 'Make babies, grow old, tell our grandkids stories about what we did to survive.' At least we started."

"*You* had a kid?"

"Yeah, The other day in fact, in mid-air. Right after we took off. Named her after you. Of course, we had to make a slight adjustment since she is a girl. Named her Janna Davida Pei Chen DiMinni."

"Why would you want to go and name your kid after me?" J.D. asked, with a tone of disappointment, shaking his head with disbelief.

"What's wrong with that? You saved my life—twice! Saved Julie's, too. We're grateful. You're one of the good guys. Our friend. Hell, family."

"No... I'm not one of the good guys. I've tortured and murdered people, all to get to Stone. None of this would have happened if it weren't for me. To do what I do, David, takes conviction. But more often than not, it is the resolve to do what is ugly and necessary. You say I'm one of the good guys, a friend, family, and I say you're wrong. There's nothing left of that J.D. Nichols, not even what was a paramedic."

"And I say you're full of shit. You've convinced yourself that everything you've done has taken away your humanity, and France is right there backing you up on what a monster you've become." J.D. gave David a look of surprise. "Yeah," David continued, "I had a chat with Doctor Evil—and he's still a douche. From what I've heard most of those people you helped save wouldn't have survived much less followed you, if you hadn't the conviction to do what was ugly and necessary. Maybe you're trying to convince yourself that killing doesn't bother you, so you could do what needs to be done."

"I'm not pretending," J.D. responded. "I'm telling you it doesn't. I've had this anger inside me for a very long time, far longer than I realized, even before we met. Meditation, martial arts, it barely quelled the repressed darkness... When Stone's men slaughtered Luci in front of me, I let that demon out, the true me, my trans-human me."

For a moment neither spoke; it was an awkward silence, a silence that David decided to break. "So what happened?" he asked.

J.D. stood up and walked to the edge of the building and looked down onto the brightly lit compound, peering down at the corpses of Private Schumacher and Richard Barlow that had been indignantly stripped, bound and left hanging on the perimeter gates. He stood in silence for a moment, and then turned back to David.

"January 9. Luci, Caitlin and I were here, on the roof, just... being in the darkness, watching the stars. A light began to glow from the west. Dimly at first, but then the sky lit with a great dance of light. You could smell it, too—thick, pungent. Like burning diesel.

Then came the screeches. Loud, pained—echoing—filling the night air. Caitlin began to cry, telling us we needed to go help.

I took a few men with me. Luci insisted on coming. I wanted her to stay with Caitlin. I always made her stay, no matter how much the night called. But this night she insisted. She wanted... She wanted to feel useful, to be a soldier again. All because I made the doctor repair her DNA, giving her back some of her lost humanity."

He paused for a moment, gathering his thoughts, trying not to choke on his words.

"There were five of us. It wasn't too difficult to locate the fire. It was a raging beacon. When we drove up, I couldn't believe what I was seeing. None of us could believe it. It was worse for Luci and me.

There were transmutes. Three, maybe more." J.D.'s tone grew sad and pained. "The smell, God the smell—I thought they had all gone, sought warmer climate." His lament grew more anguished, the sound of his ache trembled in his words as he recounted the event. "But there they were, tied up, on top of that structure, that big pile of debris... It was ablaze, like a giant wicker man. They burned—they burned them alive—the child... I puked. I ran to the curb and puked. Then I got shot. Shot with some kind of tranq dart.

When I awoke, I could barely see—my face had been pummeled, my ribs shattered. Four men held me, pulling my arms taught with rope, holding me up. Then I saw them, Stutters, Barlow and eight or nine others. Some of them had Luci. She was trying to get free, trying to get to me. But she couldn't. Several others had one of the Dunphy twins. I couldn't tell which one. They picked him up and tossed him onto the pyre. I heard him scream when he began to burn. I looked around for the rest of the team, but I didn't see them.

Then they turned on Luci. I struggled. I couldn't get enough strength. They were all laughing. Laughing this sick drunken laugh. Then Barlow said something to me. Something about being a freak. About my eyes, my hands. Then he struck me with a pipe. Smashed me in the face. I remember the blood running down my cheek, the taste of it on my lips.

They held my head up. Those sons-a-bitches, they... They—they had my machetes. They butchered her. Butchered her and made me watch! Then something inside me—something wanted out. It was the darkness, the rage.

For a moment I shook violently. They dropped me. They dropped me and laughed. Laughter sick and perverse. Then I exploded. I remember letting out this scream... Then blackness. I must have passed out, because when I awoke, I was lying next to Luci, soaked in blood. My clothes, my hands—all stained red, thick with flesh and entrails. But it wasn't hers. It was theirs.

I had killed them, five of them. I had ripped out their throats, ripped out their guts. And I did it with my hands." J.D. held up his claws and looked at them almost with admiration. "I don't remember doing it. I just remember looking at the corpses, feeling nothing. No regret, no satisfaction, just numb... and a driving need to hunt the ones who got away, Barlow and Stutters. And I have—most of them— hunted them down. And tomorrow. Tomorrow it ends."

David was horrified by the story J.D. relayed, but he refused to believe that the man who just moments ago had given him a guitar as a gift had become the self-proclaimed monster.

"That kid you were going to gut," David asked, "you really would have done it right there?"

"It wasn't his entrails falling out around his feet I wanted to see, it was him choking on his own blood and spittle after I cut out his betraying tongue... All the time it was little Peter," J.D. continued, "not his father. I should have known, should have seen," he told David with a tone of regret and anger in his voice toward himself. He paused briefly, reflecting, then continued. "The little bastard. He was the cause of a lot of good people dying... Just showed up on Christmas morning. Came right up to the gates and started calling out for his father. Everyone thought it a Christmas miracle, the only child to escape from Stone. It was no miracle, just a bullshit fairy tale.

Except today, today everything fell into place, everything was clear. I understood I was looking at the wrong person. For all the murders he had a hand in—for Luci, for the Dunphys, and all the others—he earned a death that should have been slow and agonizing. But his father saw it differently. Didn't he?"

"Ryan told us you never found the children, never found Stone."

"The children. I don't believe they're alive. As for Stone, I don't have to look for him anymore. He'll be coming to me. So that brings me to you, to all of you. You should have gotten on that chopper. There's no place here for any of you."

"Sorry that the people who truly love you came back to see if you were still alive," David told him.

"And the argument Kermit had with those two Navy Seals?"

David took another swig from the bottle. "So you heard? Well, it was about you from what I gathered over the helicopter noise. Kermit was saying something about being a warrior and a guardian of freedom, and protecting the American way of life. All the Navy guys could do was point a finger, ordering him to get us on the chopper. Then Collins pulled a gun. Then I heard Kermit say something about being loyal to his first team and resigning from the military. Then he walked away. Collins kept yelling at him, telling Kermit he would be shot for desertion even after we all got back in the Humvee."

"If he cut off ties with the military, how you going to get Julie back?"

"Yeah. I was kinda shittin' myself on that one, but Kermit told me that's why Drukker went back. To oversee all the civilians that didn't want to continue on, and she'd be safe. Julie was already pissed at my leaving. Don't want to even think what she'd do if I abandoned her."

"Your failure to do what I requested has complicated the situation. For this, I'll need a favor."

David quickly returned, "Oh, hell, no. The last time I did you a favor I got a punch in the face from Marisol—and she refused to talk to me for two months. If it involves her, I'm not going down that route again."

"It does and you will."

David shook his head with disbelief. He knew J.D. was going to ask him the same thing he had asked the last time they had a talk on the roof, and that was to make sure he watched out for Marisol when J.D.

could not. This also told him that J.D. had no intention of going to Mechanicville, like he had not gone to England. However, England had been a place he could not have gone and David had understood, but not this time.

"No. You ask too much of me. Forget whatever you're planning. Take Marisol and Max, and let's all go to Mechanicville like we had planned."

"Even if I had found the children. Even if I believed that those who I helped eventually wouldn't turn on me for what I've done in the name of survival, there is one thing that will never allow me to find a place, and that is that one day the sickness inside of me will take over. I won't put my daughter's life or anyone else's in jeopardy because of it."

"So, I'm right. You are full of shit. You still care. It's that you're afraid. You're afraid of failing and afraid of falling off that pedestal that so many have placed you on. Afraid that someone else you care about will die under your watch. You alienate yourself under the guise of being a monster, telling yourself that it is in everyone's best interest because you're afraid of being hurt. That's so deceitful, selfish and disrespectful. You're a coward."

David's comment had cut him deep. For it was the truth. He had once told Joseph Young, a member of his original team, to take responsibility for actions that caused the death of Joseph's younger brother at the outbreak of the plague and to atone for the cowardice. Although, David had never been privy to that conversation, the statement was still painful. Nevertheless, J.D. blocked out the voice that told him David was right that he should follow what he moralized and take responsibility. However, his obsession with punishing Stone had consumed him, blinding him.

"Whatever your scheming. Whatever this plan is of yours, it's going to get you killed," David warned him. "And how do you think Marisol is going to react to that?"

"What I'm planning is to finish what I started, what Stone started. He will answer for what he's done."

"With his life? Will that help? Give you closure?"

"For every life he took, for every family he destroyed, I will see to it he suffers a hundred-fold—in the most unnatural way possible!"

"In this delusional game you're playing is there a chance you'll win?"

J.D. remained silent.

"*Well...?* You don't even care, do you? As long as you get your revenge."

"All I need is for you to watch over Marisol," he told David. "Take her, get in the Stryker and go to Mechanicville with my men. Will you do this for me?"

"Damn you to hell. I'll keep her safe, but not for you, for her. She's my friend, my family. And you never hurt family."

"Then we're done here." J.D. looked at his wristwatch. "I have an assembly to go to and your presence is required. "*Kommen,*" he called to Max, and they departed.

## 6

# GOOD NIGHT NEW YORK

J.D. REFLECTED ON THOSE RESTLESS NIGHTS WHEN HE HAD GONE OUT alone, often wandering the once familiar streets of his neighborhood and its boundaries. His mind was never at ease, and in those streets he felt shadows, ghosts of his past. On one such night his journeys took him past Union Square, west on 14th Street, and past 5th Avenue to the place where he had purchased his electronic keyboard. As he entered the store he was greeted by a large banner, which hung from the ceiling that read, 'The World of Yamaha Artist Week, April 7th – 13th.'

This would be a place where he would come often to clear his mind and play the Yamaha grand piano that was on display. The shop was also where he would find the guitar for David, and all the accordions he would acquire. He thought about the first time he sat at the store's piano and began to play probably the world's most known piano tune, "Chopsticks." He played it the way the piece should be played in 3/4 (waltz) meter, not as most people played it with the stresses as in 6/8 time. The piano was out of tune, but not too badly.

He paused for a moment to think, and then chose to play the instrumental "Le Depart" by the Style Council. However, it quickly turned into another one of their songs, "The Paris Match." When he was midway through the verse sung in French, he stopped again. It still hadn't felt right to him. When all else failed, J.D. defaulted to what he considered to be one of the greatest contemporary piano songs ever written: "Life on Mars" by David Bowie.

---

He stood in silence in the back of the hall waiting for the arrival of Ryan. As he recollected back to that first night's visit to the Guitar Center, a slight smile, as fleeting as it was, came to his face. Even though the post-apocalypse world had a lot of suck to it, there were still moments that had become memorable for the better. However tomorrow it would all be put right. He was about to address his warriors for the last time.

"Attention in the hall. Commander on the floor," Ryan declared.

The troops snapped to attention.

"You may be seated, please," Colonel Nichols told them. "First, I would like you to welcome Chief Warrant Officer Brown, David DiMinni, and Marisol De La Garza, who will be joining us on the trip to our new home. I fought along side these men and woman during and after the time of the living dead and the rise of the half-mutes. They have been in England for the past year, until the British decided to throw them out. I won't go into the details of how they got there or how they returned; however, let me assure you that the folks that sit here with you are as good and as honorable as any amongst you. I will also tell you I trust them with my life, and they have earned the right for a place at our safe haven.

Your mission tonight is vital and simple. You go to your new home and join the other team members and your families. Our struggle here is over. The children are lost to us. There is nothing left to do, but live our lives in a safe place with those who love us.

I know it has been hard on you all, being separated from family and friends, not knowing their location, not having any contact with them. You have all shown great fortitude and courage in this. I assure you this was done to protect them. But tonight that ends.

Men. It has been a privilege and an honor serving with all of you.

You have all done me proud. God bless you and God bless the 69<sup>th</sup> Infantry Regiment… Major, you have the floor." J.D. stood at attention and saluted his troops one last time. "Carry on," he spoke, as he snapped off the salute to everyone in the hall.

They rose and returned the commander's respect.

J.D. went to his office and had Kermit sent for. The meeting was brief. He agreed to let his civilians join the new community, with one stipulation.

"Can you still contact your base?" he asked Kermit.

Kermit was curious to J.D.'s odd question. "Yes. Why?"

"You remember what I told you my daddy always said? Well, I need one," he said, and then explained his stipulation.

---

It wasn't long before Doctor France came to his office demanding to know why his research equipment or personal affects had not been moved to the staging area.

"It's simple…" J.D. explained. "You're not going."

Outraged the doctor yelled, "What do you mean I am not going?! Of course, I am going. I did not work this hard at making sure you kept me alive just to be left behind."

"You're only alive because you served a purpose. After tonight that purpose will no longer exist," J.D. enlightened him.

"If it was not for me you would still be that pathetic, broken man who was hiding in his room, instead of the hunter/killer you have become."

"And what is that supposed to mean?" J.D. asked, curious about the doctor's odd comment.

"Where do you think your courage and your ferocity comes from? From channeling your inner Bruce Lee?" the doctor sarcastically asked. "From your evolving transmute side? No! It came from *me!* I gave you what you needed to keep this facility safe, the driving desire to punish those who would take it from us."

J.D. demanded clarification "Speak plainly," he snapped.

"You wanted to save the world but your martial arts honor and religious philosophies were getting in the way of doing what was necessary—to kill our enemies without restraint or remorse. I freed you from your moral compass and reticence by activating that repressed part of your transmute brain."

"You did *what?*"

"Yes, Mr. Nichols, I unleashed the monster you feared you were becoming. The truth is your headaches are simply a combination of post-traumatic stress, fatigue and insomnia, not a symptom of further mutation."

J.D. was stunned at the admission. The doctor had convinced him his health was deteriorating from further mutation. He screamed, "Then what the fuck was all that medication for?"

The doctor replied, "A pharmaceutical cocktail for stimulating the frontal and temporal lobes to keep you alert and drive your aggression and rage."

"You sick fucking bastard! You convinced me I was on the verge of no longer being human."

"No. Mr. Nichols, you convinced yourself of that! I was merely capitalizing on what you wanted to believe. It gave you justification for the atrocities you needed to commit to keep us all alive."

J.D.'s rage exploded. He lifted his desk and overturned it.

"That's right, let it out," the doctor told him, "but not on me on that sick son-of-a-bitch who preys upon the weak. The one who rapes, tortures and murders innocent children. Children like your own daughter."

The shouting between the doctor and J.D. had not gone unnoticed by others in the armory. Ryan, Kermit, Paul and David rushed into the office, weapons drawn, just as France said, "Be the killer I made you; don't give Stone the chance to find our new home."

"Arrest him," J.D. ordered his men.

Without hesitation Ryan and Paul seized Richard France.

"No, *no*," the doctor protested loudly, struggling to get free. "You should be thanking me. I have given you the will and means to defeat our enemy, and this is how you repay me?"

" 'I am in no mood to be deceived any longer by the crafty devil and false character whose greatest pleasure is to take advantage of everyone,' " J.D. warned him.

"Camille Claudel?" David whispered, recognizing the quote from his days at university.

J.D. reached into a leg pocket and retrieved five bottles of pills and held them up, announcing, "My sanity was purposely turned to madness and put to use. I am not a monster by my own hand but one created by a man who had his own agenda," he informed everyone, dropping the vials onto the floor, and then stomped on them.

"*Fool!*" France shouted, his countenance expressing the utmost extent of condescension. "Reject what I have made you and risk defeat."

"You may be my creator," J.D. replied sharply, "but you are not my master. Put him in basement lockup," he instructed. "I'll deal with him later."

The doctor warned, "Our enemy is merciless; we cannot afford pity. Kill or be killed," he warned, as Ryan and Paul forcefully escorted him from the office.

"Thank you, gentlemen, that will be all," J.D. informed David and Kermit as he put his attention to righting the overturned desk and picking up the scattered papers.

"*That will be all?*" Kermit asked. "I think there is much to talk about."

"I am extraordinarily busy, gentlemen," he replied pointedly ignoring him and David, as he sat and began to sort through the disheveled paperwork.

"This changes the plan," Kermit informed him.

"No, it does not."

Kermit asked, "Why not?"

"Can the revelation of knowing I am not a monster make up for the monstrous things I have done?"

"Don't be such a pussy," David admonished him. "You have hurt others, gone to extremes; so what? You need to own that shit. If it weren't for you, I'd bet most of your survivor group would never have

The Romero Strain349

made it. Like myself. And if they can't accept what you've done to protect them, and be grateful for it then fuck 'em! You don't need them, because they're not the kind that'll have your back."

"You can't forget or forgive what's been done," J.D. told David.

"You've taken so many lives in this battle, now you are so filled with regret and guilt, that you avoid believing that your life has meaning even to others," Kermit expressed.

"*My life?*" J.D. asked. He sprang up from his chair, angrily. "It is my duty to stop Stone before more people suffer—even if it means I must sacrifice my life," he educated Kermit.

"Your life is not for you alone," Kermit voiced. "If you self-sacrifice it to protect the weak or those you love, those people left behind will always have a sadness having lost you. They'll never be happy. When you learn to live between the fear of your own death and the will to die for what you believe in, only then will you be able to defeat your enemy."

With those final words, David and Kermit departed.

J.D. sat with his face in his hands contemplating Kermit's ideology. His mind was too clouded from the doctor's drugs to think clearly. He felt his head begin to throb, but at least this time he knew it was just a headache.

---

David and Kermit walked out of J.D.'s office in search of Ryan, who they believed had a more rational and objective mind, in hopes of convincing him to go against his commander and alter the plan.

"No," Ryan firmly told them. "I will not alter the plan. I will not go against J.D.'s orders."

"This is insane," Kermit responded in a heightened and agitated tone. "The only thing that man is doing is digging his own grave. His mind is clouded from the drugs he's been taking for God knows how long; he's unable to think rationally. The plan is going to fail and he'll die needlessly."

"The plan stands. Even if I thought it unsound, there's nothing I can do. I simply don't have the manpower to engage in an all-out battle with Stone's forces."

"Then give David and me enough weapons and ammunition and we'll back him up."

"No. Our enemy is watching. If they don't see that J.D. is the only one here, we lose our only chance at luring Stone himself out of hiding. If we don't accomplish that, then there's a possibility he and his men can find us again."

David was not satisfied with Ryan's answer. He knew he needed to resort to blackmail if he and Kermit were to elicit a change of mind. "Damn it, Ryan. We saved your life," David reminded him. "Have you forgotten? You owe us," he insisted.

"Your attempt at extortion is futile. I will not betray J.D.'s trust, and I advise both of you to do the same. Let this matter go."

"Are you threatening us, son?" Kermit asked, giving him a look of disdain.

"You both made promises to him. Did you not? You, David, gave him your word to see Marisol to safety, and you Kermit, need I remind you of your deal? Will you break your words?"

Ryan was well aware of J.D.'s fail-safe for the armory if it fell into Stone's possession, and he wanted Kermit to know he knew it without revealing it to David, who was certainly more attached to J.D.

There was nothing more to say, Kermit and David knew it, but it didn't mean they liked it. Their old survivor group creed was much like the military belief, to never leave a man behind. Although it had been necessary when they departed for England for J.D.'s own safety, this time it wasn't needed, and it gnawed at them.

Ryan, too, knew that he could not go against his commander's request. If Stone had any suspicion there was anyone remaining in the armory then the plan could go afoul. "Damn it," he muttered, and then kicked his desk in aggravation.

# 7

# DEAD RECKONING

*THE STRATEGY HADN'T GONE AS PLANNED.*

He crawled out of the armory on his belly with crippled, bloodied legs, two bloody smears upon the armory floor, marking his way like snails leaving behind their slime trails. He painfully made his way to the archway of the main entrance, through the opened heavy oak doors, and across the main landing of the portico. Arriving at the next set of steps he pulled himself forward twice, before his body weight and gravity took over. J.D. slid down the steps to the bottom landing near the sidewalk of Lexington Avenue. He lay stomach down, but face up and perpendicular across the landing. His head tilted slightly to one side hanging over the first step. One arm was bent at a right angle toward his head, the other slightly tucked under his lower abdomen. With backward head and blurred vision, he stared up through black-colored eyes to the sculptured winged eagle that formed the keystone of the entry arch.

As he lay bleeding, he thought it should have been magnificent flying off the balcony doing a forward flip, majestically making a perfect landing like a gymnast dismounting from a set of uneven bars, and then ripping out the throats of two of his enemies with his bare hands, blood spraying into the air, like he was in a Shaw Brothers

Studio film from the late 70s—but it was not. Without the full effect of the drugs he felt the fear of his own death, no longer having the sensation of invincibility, and it frightened him. Perhaps the doctor had been correct, he had been given the will and means to defeat his enemy through chemical stimulation and now without it he had failed. Or perhaps it was the simple fact the Stone's men were numerous, far too many for him to dodge all the barrages of bullets from his enemies' weapons. He knew he was in serious condition, but he refused to die just yet. It never occurred to him that the doubt and fear he was experiencing was mostly psychological, and not the loss of chemical courage. For the drugs were still in his system.

It hadn't been one bullet that had penetrated his leg, like what had happened at Pier 17. He had been shot multiple times, most of the slugs lodged in his upper legs. Three shots had struck him in his left leg. Another impacted his right leg. The gunshot wounds weren't immediately life threatening—providing he could remove the projectiles.

Stone had been extremely careful and calculating in his seizure of the armory, waiting a full day to make a play for it. When dawn broke the day after J.D.'s men had left him, Stone's men came. There were more of them than he thought Stone had. There had been more than a dozen men that had come into the armory looking for him, and he had dispatched ten of them. The rest J.D. believed had fled, since none of his enemy had followed to finish him off.

There were footfalls approaching, but J.D. could not turn his head to see who it was. He was teetering on the brink of unconsciousness. He knew the odds were it was the enemy. If Edward Stone were smart, as he knew he was, he would have held a reserve to be called up as reinforcements.

J.D.'s head abruptly turned. He felt a sole of a shoe pressing on his face. His head rocked to-and-fro. He looked up. It was Stone. A young girl with blonde hair with her hands bound behind her back and a dog collar and leash around her neck stood next to him, firmly restrained by two of Stone's men.

Stone came around and stood above him, his back to the armory. He looked around to be sure they were alone. "My, my. Look at the state you're in," Stone casually spoke as he looked down to J.D.'s mutated eyes. "It's true. The plague changed you. I heard all sorts of things about you. Does that surprise you? No, I guess it wouldn't. Little Peter was so sweet and willing to please—and oh so obedient," he told him, a smile of satisfaction on his face. "And such a wealth of information." Stone looked around again as a precaution, and then with a pleased smile Edward Coleman Stone squatted next to J.D., and then taunted, "So, Colonel. Here we are. And there is my armory. It still stands, every brick, every stone. And there you are, a broken, defeated freak." Stone's smile grew wider. "The strong live. The weak die. That is just how it is. That is a simple fact. And you are one of the weak. Weak because your life is just to protect weak people, so you don't understand your own happiness or how to enjoy life."

J.D. did not respond, but just gave Stone a blank stare.

Stone gestured to his men to bring the girl forward.

Edward Stone's voice was calm, but held great disdain for his enemy. "You see what I brought you? I brought one of my children. I heard this one is very special to you, the one that belongs to that little smidget whose tongue I cut out. I thought about slitting the little bitch's throat and watching the life drain from her as I fucked her off to eternity," he said coldly, "but I thought the better of it. You see I wanted you to witness her death. Watch her die in front of your eyes, knowing that you failed to save her, to save any of the children."

J.D. gave Stone a look of acknowledgement.

"Yes, Colonel, some are still alive—the special ones." Stone grabbed the leash and pulled the girl to him. "But this used up piece of cunt," he told J.D., "I'm going to do to her what you did to the only friend I ever had. I'm going to butcher her and tie her to the fence," he conveyed. "I want you to understand the depths of my pain and anguish over the loss of Richard."

Stone put a knife to Victoria's throat. He shivered with anticipation. "Tell me you're sorry," Stone demanded. "Tell me you're sorry for killing Richard, and maybe, just maybe, if I truly believe you, I'll spare her life."

J.D.'s lips began to move, but no sound came from them.

"*That's it*?! Come on, Colonel! I want to hear you apologize!" he shouted, his calm demeanor turning to rage. He pressed the knife firmly against Victoria's throat as a warning.

J.D. looked at him, and then in a raspy tone said, "Do it."

From the building directly across the street from the armory's entrance a shot echoed. Before the sound had diminished the man who stood closest to Stone dropped to the ground; his skull blown apart. By the time Stone and the other man realized what had happened, J.D. had all ready grabbed Stone's closest leg, piercing it deeply with his talons, and had yanked him. Stone let out a howl of extreme pain, just as the second man collapsed from a bullet through the throat. Edward Stone dropped the knife and Victoria ran into the armory.

Stone grabbed at the knife that had fallen less than a foot away from him. He grimaced under the extreme pain of the talons piercing his leg but was determined to reach the weapon. J.D. could feel he was losing his grip around Stone's leg. He closed his eyes and let his humanity go. A fierce intensity rose in his face. He let out a screech nearly as loud as the one at the bonfire. What Edward Stone saw in J.D.'s face as he rose scared the hell out of him. He grabbed the knife, but it was too late. J.D. knocked it from Stone's grip, and then grabbed him by his shirt and pants and lifted him high into the air. Stone flailed attempting to get free. J.D. turned and threw the man into the compound. Stone crashed onto the pavement, becoming unconscious. J.D. let out another shriek, but before he had finished he, too, collapsed and then tumbled down the stairs.

The plan had not gone exactly as J.D. and Peter had strategized, although the outcome had the desired results. Stone had been captured alive.

J.D. was aware that torturing Stone to get the location of any surviving hostages—if there truly any—would be futile. Stone was not the type of person who would give up their whereabouts, even if it meant his own life. Nonetheless, J.D. was pretty certain that if any of his captives were still alive, Stone was the sort of person that would want to keep them close. Obviously J.D. was in no condition to search for them at the moment.

J.D. was more concerned about the welfare of Peter's daughter and the securing of their unconscious enemy so he lied to Peter regarding his injuries, telling him that they were merely flesh wounds and nothing he should be concerned about. Peter did not have to look far for Victoria. She had been inside the second set of double doors watching the commotion after hearing the screech. Victoria, too, had heard stories during her imprisonment about the mutant leader of the armory, who screeched like an owl and was hunting down her captors and brutally slaughtering them. Her curiosity with the screeching man overshadowed her instinct for flight. She watched as the wounded man lifted her tormentor in the air and tossed him like a beanbag, knocking him senseless. She didn't immediately come out of hiding when she saw her father, in part because she was shocked to see him alive after Stone repeatedly told her that he was dead and in a pit rotting, and partly because she was unsure if Stone was truly incapacitated. When Victoria saw her father securing Stone, she timidly and cautiously stepped down the stairs toward him. She began to sob in his arms as he held her, not for what she had endured but for what Stone had done to her father.

After retrieving a chair and J.D.'s backpack, Peter held his daughter's hand as J.D. gave her a cursory exam. Victoria was remarkably physically sound, considering the physical abuse she had endured—though he could not render a diagnosis on her mental welfare. With no apparent broken bones or lacerations—though recent bruising and scarring were evident—Peter, aided by his daughter, put his attention to Edward Stone. After dragging Stone from the armory across the compound and to the fencing, Peter retrieved a ladder and long rope from the armory, tied the double-braid nylon cord around Stone's chest and under his arms, stood atop the ladder and looped the free end over the top parallel pole of the chain link fencing, and then pulled it back to where J.D. was seated. It took both them to hoist Stone into place, though J.D. barely felt like he had helped. Sitting in his chair with bleeding legs, struggling to pull back on the rope, he had been the anchor as Peter prepped Stone for a crucifixion.

After lifting the now naked Stone onto the fencing, but unable to raise him so that his feet were off the street, Peter lashed the child molester meticulously to the perimeter fence with heavy cable ties and rope, directly across from and facing the armory entry—Peter Schumacher, Jr. and Richard Barlow had been hung on opposite entry gates, bodies facing toward the street, as a warning. Peter then began a few body modifications.

When the deed had been done, and Peter satisfied with his work, he stood with his daughter by his side, and stared at his mutilated enemy, enjoying the moment. Except, Peter's minute of triumph, of satisfaction, was disrupted by his daughter's abrupt outbreak of sobbing again. In her father's arms she let loose the months of pain and suffering she endured, the perverse sexual cruelty and sadistic torture that Stone took great pleasure in dispensing.

Then through broken cries, as she held her father tight, Victoria revealed the fate of the other captives. A fate that both he and J.D. believed had been cruel death. Through mutterings, both out of exaltation of being with her father again and emotional distress over her long ordeal, she told him that, only a few blocks away, there was a van.

With pistol in one hand, his daughter holding the other, Victoria led Peter to where the vehicle was parked. Seeing the waiting windowless, full-body cargo van perhaps 15 feet from the intersection, Peter made his move. Bold and angry, Peter approached the two men standing outside the vehicle in full view with pistols drawn. Before Stone's men had a chance to raise their weapons, he shot both of them twice in the chest. The driver's door burst open, Billy Miller moved to exit, but Peter was upon him before he could. Peter Dunne unleashed his fury in a hail of gunfire. Blood spattered on the interior of the van's cab, sending a crimson coating onto the windshield and driver's door. The scraggly blond-haired man slid out of the vehicle, but Peter's anger had not been quenched. He finished off the ammunition magazine into Miller's head.

At first, in his blind fury, he had been deaf to the screams and cries of the children who were locked behind the cab's heavy metal mesh partition. As his rage subsided the cries of the children became clear. They were locked in the cargo area. Peter climbed into the vehicle and removed the keys from the ignition. He attempted to unlock the dividing wall, but there was no key on the ring that would unlock it. He quickly exited and went to the back door. The only windows on the van, with exception of those found on the front of the vehicle, were on the rear swing out doors. However, the windows were barred with the same mesh as the partition and the doors were also secured with a heavy padlock. The side cargo door had also been secured.

Victoria had waited, crouched and hidden in a doorway near the intersection. When the gunfire had stopped, she waited a moment before she emerged from her hiding place to see if her father was safe. Peering around the corner she saw Peter moving to the back of the van. As she approached, she called out to him, "Poppa. Poppa. I'm sorry, he has them. He always has them. He's the only one," she cried.

Peter understood. Stone had the keys with him. They must be in his clothing that had been stripped from him. They hurried back to the armory.

Out of twenty-three children—boys, girls, and young women—only eleven had survived. Peter's daughter told them the others had been killed for disobeying him or being used up; this was what Stone had told her.

# 8

# OPERATION SPOILED BRAT

J.D. SAT IN A CHAIR ON THE STREET FACING THE COMPOUND FENCE. HE cut open his left pant leg with his survival knife and then jabbed a syringe into his upper left leg in several different places. He grimaced in pain. He poured isopropyl alcohol over his wounds, and as he did, he let out a howl of pain from the overwhelming burn of the astringent. The local anesthetic hadn't taken effect. His self-operation was about to begin, anyway.

Though J.D. had the ability to heal quickly, his cellular regeneration would not happen unless the bullets were extracted. He would have normally slit the three wounds open with a scalpel, and then taken a pair of Kelly forceps and removed the slugs. Except today, he was without surgical instruments. Instead, he took his knife to make the incisions, and then used the talons of his index finger and thumb of his right hand to dig deeply into the bleeding hole and pull out the first bullet.

Only two slugs had to be removed from his left leg. One gunshot wound had exited out the back of his leg. After applying the brown rusty-red colored topical antiseptic solution Betadine as an antibacterial, he gauzed and wrapped his leg, securing the bandaging with camouflage cohesive wrap. He then removed the bullet from his right leg, another painful procedure.

Richard Stone began to wake. J.D. looked up at the bloodied, naked man. Stone mumbled, but words failed him. Two fleshy, bloody globs fell from his mouth.

"Now that was truly disgusting," J.D. commented. "By the way... those were your balls."

Stone tried to look down to his groin, but his head had been secured to the fence by razor wire. The fine, near surgical sharp metal strips sliced into the thin flesh of his forehead. Terror and panic seized him. His eyes lit with fear. He was bound to the fence; arms extended and feet together. He wanted to know if he had been castrated. Were his precious testicles truly laying in a lumpy mess upon the street?

As Stone struggled with the realization of his situation, J.D. continued. "I know Stone, you're dazed, confused. Wait til the pain sets in— another five/ten minutes, perhaps—when the morphine wears off."

Stone tried to speak, but his tongue and mouth failed him.

"You must have a lot of questions. Like why the lack of speech? Let me explain... No, there's way too much. Let me sum up... You were about to slit Victoria's throat. You thought I couldn't stop you... but as I once told you, you're pretty stupid if you think there's no one watching my back... He's a short guy, a lot of tattoos, you cut out his tongue, made him watch while you sodomized his daughter," J.D. reminded Stone. "He had my back. You see not only did you scar him physically, but you also scarred his soul. You took that from him what he cherished most, all that he had left in the world—and destroyed it. I promised him that he would have his revenge."

J.D. pulled out a bottle of Bushmills Malt 16-Year-Old Irish whiskey. It had been in the backpack that Peter had retrieved from the armory. David had given the liquor to J.D. as a belated birthday gift, just before departing for Mechanicville.

"It's a shame," J.D. told Stone, "Such a fine whiskey as this, and I can't even get a buzz from it. An unfortunate side effect of my mutation. Well at least I can still enjoy the flavor."

J.D. suddenly slumped into momentary unconsciousness.

"Seems I'm a rude host," J.D. said, as he awoke, and then tore open a bag of beef jerky that David had also gifted to him. "Another side effect," he said, as he spoke with his mouth full. "Higher metabolism demands constant nourishment. So where was I? Yes. Victoria. Your balls... Strange about Victoria," he spoke, wiping his mouth. "You'd think after all she's been through, she'd be so traumatized she'd be a shell—quite the opposite. You see Victoria was the one who requested your privates be removed, though she wanted your cock cut off and shoved up your ass. That was until I explained that cutting off your cock would cause you to bleed out too quickly. I couldn't have that. Balls in your mouth was her alternative. She's got some issues. But don't we all?"

J.D. grimaced in pain.

"Strange about pain and me, it makes things so much clearer. I thought it didn't matter if I lived or died, as long as I took you out, except it does."

J.D. looked at his watch. Time was running out. "Shit. Gotta speed this up." J.D. continued. "Not enough room in the Humvee for me and all the children."

Stone's eyes lit up with hate; he squirmed trying to get free.

J.D. took another swallow of whiskey.

"Oh, did I forget? Yes, we found them. They're gone. Far away."

There were two other reasons why Peter took the children and fled, and Stone was about to find out.

"Time's running out, Stone, for both of us. So, I should finish."

Stone kept squirming, trying to speak, but only making gurgling noises.

"Having difficulty speaking?" J.D. picked up a fleshy lump that had been resting between his legs and beheld a tongue. He held it up momentarily, skewed upon one of his talons, long enough for Stone to comprehend, and then J.D. casually discarded the discolored mass to the pavement like a used tissue.

"Just fuckin' with ya. It's Barlow's," J.D. said with a grin. "You've been injected with a mega dose of Procaine. Peter wanted your tongue but I said I have a better use for it. As for your missing eyelids... Well,

I wanted to make sure the last thing you would see in this life is the last thing you'll never have—the armory."

Stone struggled again. Anger welled up in his lidless eyes, hot with the heat of hatred.

"There is no good way to kill you," J.D. spoke again. "No torture that would be long enough to equal the pain and suffering you have inflicted on so many. All the lives you have destroyed. However, I swore I would find you and make you suffer, even if it meant my own life. Can you feel the drugs wearing off, the pain welling up in what's left of your nutsack? By the way, you see that crown of razor wire upon your head? That was my idea. Hail to the king!"

J.D. looked at his watch again, and then gulped down the last of the caramel colored liquid. He lobbed the empty bottle at his adversary. It struck Stone squarely in the chest. Stone winced. "C'mon, bitch, start screaming. We're running out of time."

The pain began to return to J.D.'s legs. He pulled out a vial of morphine and a hypodermic syringe from his backpack, prepped it, and then injected himself in the thigh of his less wounded leg. He paused, looked up into the clear late summer sky, and waited to feel its effects.

When the morphine began to alleviate the pain, J.D. rose from his seat and hobbled to Stone, and looked him in the face. "I wanted to make sure you never hurt another child again. I wanted to make sure you got a royal ass-fucking. So, I made an arrangement in case I failed."

---

"I'll grant you anything you ask for—as long as it's something I'm willing to give." Kermit had told J.D.

What J.D. had asked for, though, was not in Kermit's power to grant. It was something only his superiors could carry out.

"And if they agree, how will they know you got out?"

"They won't."

Kermit shook his head in disagreement. "I don't like it. There's no margin for error."

"If I'm not out by then, then I'm already dead. And it won't matter, will it? But I will not allow that murderous pedophile to have free reign over this city or any other. If I fail then that's what will happen. The children are lost, gone. At least let the grieving families have the consolation of knowing that sick fuck got it in the end."

Kermit could not argue with J.D.'s statement. No one, even with the smallest of moral conscience, would want to allow such evil to continue.

---

"However, that's not even the best part," J.D. told Stone. "I lived. And there's still time! Now how's that mouth of yours?" J.D. grabbed Stone's face with his hand and gave it a hard squeeze, digging his talons into the man's cheeks. Stone let out a whine of pain. "Not quite there yet," J.D. commented.

Stone began to whimper and cry. He realized that he was not going to be able get free.

"Oh, no, no, no. Don't cry," J.D. told him, and then damped away Stone's blood accented tears with his shirtsleeve. "It'll be over soon, when our guests arrive. Well, not too soon I hope for you." J.D. looked at his watch again. "Plan B," he announced, and then hobbled back toward his chair. As he did he asked, "Ever come across any of those day mutants? You know the ones who always seem to be attracted by loud noises?"

J.D. retrieved four stun grenades from his backpack, and then turned back to the restrained man. Stone saw the grenades. His face lit with fear and panic.

"Eyes closed, cover your ears," J.D. said to him. "Oops, sorry. I forgot," he sardonically apologized.

One at a time J.D. tossed the grenades toward his foe. One at a time they released a bright flash, but more importantly a loud invitation.

J.D. moved onto the first landing of the armory entry, just under the portico. He didn't have to wait long for a response to his invite. From the ajar south gate came Four Fingers and his mutants. They moved cautiously into the compound. They saw the panic-stricken man strapped to the fence. The group wanted to move quickly to the free meal, but Four Fingers was hesitant, he held his followers back. With suspicion he looked to his foe, who stood at the armory's entry, and then pointed an index finger at him.

J.D. goaded him. "Yeah, here's one for you, too," he told Four Fingers, as he flipped him the bird. "You want a piece of me? You want a piece of J.D. Nichols?!" he shouted at Four Fingers. "Well, here I am! What are you waiting for?" J.D. let out a piercing screech. However, this time Four Finger's and his half-mutes didn't seem to be too intimidated.

Four Fingers returned a shrill, angry cry, and then waved to his followers. They beset upon Stone, ripping the flesh from his bones so fast that the man never screamed out.

"That was a total disappointment," J.D. said as he watched them quickly butcher the restrained quarry.

When the group was finished with shredding Stone, Four Fingers called to them like he was giving an order, motioning to the exit. The mutant minions began to depart.

"Hey, Four Fingers, that's it?" J.D. taunted, hoping to provoke the half-mute leader. "C'mon. All these months of stalking me, trying to kill me every chance you could find. Now here I am all alone and you pussy out?" However, Four Fingers ignored him, as he fell in behind the last of his group.

Nonetheless, J.D. refused to let it go. The creature had brutally murdered Ann-Marie as an act of revenge for something that had to do with a heart-shaped pendant, the pendant that Four Fingers had displayed to J.D. after the Chinatown attack. The same one that he had discovered stuffed into the mouth of Ann-Marie's severed skull.

J.D. threw the pendant at Four Fingers. It hit the leader in the back of the head. Four Fingers looked down to the jewelry and then picked it up. He let out a piercing cry, and then turned back to J.D.

J.D. could see the hate and anger in his eyes. He had definitely gotten Four Fingers' attention.

"That's it," J.D. said, as the half-mute leader moved toward him.

"I'm the man. J.D. Nichols. The one who did whatever it was to piss you off." J.D. was anxious, adrenalin pumping as he slowly backed up the last set of stairs as Four Fingers made his way up toward the portico. "That's right. C'mon," J.D. shouted, trying to bait him so he would follow him into the armory.

As Four Fingers crossed under the portico and to the first step of the second set of stairs he stopped. He paused momentarily to probe the dim lit entry to where his foe had disappeared. Four Fingers cried out, and then turned and fled.

J.D. emerged from the armory, kukris in hand. The mutant did not fall for J.D.'s trap. The creature was much more intelligent than he had anticipated. The adrenalin and morphine began to wear off, and the burning pain came again to J.D.'s wounds. J.D. took a step and his legs faltered. He tried to stand but he couldn't. He needed more morphine. He grabbed his pant leg for more, but the pocket was empty. He looked out to the compound to where he had been seated. His backpack was still by the chair. The morphine was in the backpack. He looked at his watch. His countdown timer read, 33 – 32 – 31 – 30....

"Buddha's balls," he muttered. He was out of time.

## 9

# THE FUTURE IS UNWRITTEN

"THE LIFE OF J.D. NICHOLS IS AN EXTRAORDINARY ONE," DAVID SPOKE aloud to the crowd, from behind a lectern at center stage. "One of dedication, loyalty, love, humor, and above all—friendship. Except try as I may I cannot find the words to honor him, to do justice to his life. Luckily, I had help. Today, on this our first anniversary, let us not only honor those who gave their lives in our service but also honor those men and women amongst us that made it possible for us to be here today. The following are the names of those men and women who did not die in the line of service, but are alive today, because of John David Nichols' extraordinary courage, uncommon valor, steadfast devotion to duty, unrelenting perseverance, and unselfish acts of bravery...

Colonel James Alexander, Lieutenant Colonel Ryan Duncan, Chief Warrant Officer Five Kermit Brown, Chief Warrant Officer Four Peter Dunne, Chief Warrant Officer Two Paul Wiese, Sergeant Major John Lott, Master Sergeant Katie O'Hanlon, Staff Sergeant Liz Hudson, Staff Sergeant Jonas McGann, Sergeant Stephen Drukker, Sergeant Taylor Hanson, Sergeant Michael Panton, Corporal Christina Custode, Corporal Oneil Andrews, Private Brian Mann, Private Tupper Thomas, Private Peter C. Brown, Private Jamie Conlan, Private Brian Dye, Private Keith Crawford, Private Jason O'Rourke, Julie Chen, Marisol

De La Garza, Barkley, Maxamillian Nichols, canine extraordinaire—and myself, Sergeant First Class David DiMinni.

Citizens of Mechanicville. It gives me great honor to present to you a man I call friend, General John David Nichols."

A roar of applause from an enthusiastic crowd filled the Mechanicville High School auditorium in honor of their leader. As J.D. stepped in front of the lectern, the audience as well as those on stage rose to their feet applauding, showing their love and admiration to the man who had given them comfort, protection and leadership in a time of chaos.

At that moment, J.D. realized his family was not just those who were close to him, but the community, for they all shared a common bond. They all had survived and they had done it together. He was overwhelmed with joy, and grateful that Kermit had broken their deal and also disobeyed his order and had come back to the armory to rescue him.

"Thank you, David and thank you citizens of Mechanicville. I am truly overwhelmed and moved by that tribute."

J.D. became uncomfortable with the adulation. "Please. Please. I beg of you. Please do not applaud me. It is I who should applaud you, for your generosity, your understanding, your friendship, your loyalty, and for your love. Thank you. Thank you all."

J.D. gestured to the crowd and applauded them.

He paused as he looked down to the speech he had prepared and then set it aside. He looked to his wife Marisol and daughter Caitlin and Michael Adam, along with Max and Barkley, in the front row and he smiled.

"I had this speech—I worked on it for a week—even my daughter helped with it. Except now as I look at it, here before all of you, it seems—It's not... It's not what I need to say."

When the audience finally returned to their seats J.D. spoke again.

"It is a great honor and privilege to be able to stand before you today for this dedication ceremony and even a greater pleasure having been chosen by you the citizens to be the one to unveil our new town sign."

J.D. stepped away from the lectern and to a nearby covered, heavy-duty easel and pulled the cloth away to reveal the town's new signage. The audience cheered, for they all had a vote in renaming the town.

Returning to his lectern, J.D. announced, "This day we celebrate the re-settlement of Mechanicville. Through the hard work and dedication of all of you, we have taken momentous steps forward in building a sustainable future. Over these past months, I have learned that the past can truly be the past, and the future is indeed unwritten. Therefore, let us write a new chapter in our life story. With the changing of our town name from Mechanicville to Bethlehem, I feel it is time for another change, to demilitarize our town, taking us from a state of full military strength and authority to a state of vigilant guardedness."

The audience was uncertain, voices arose.

J.D. addressed their anxieties. "I know you have concerns. There are still marauders out there and half-mutes, and with the strong show of military force you feel secure. However, a police state is not a state of freedom and growth; it is a state of fear and stagnation. Look at all we have accomplished so far. We have electrical power, fresh produce, a fire department, a town newspaper and this school. Imagine what we could accomplish moving forward, setting our fears aside, coming together as a community to make our lives better.

Therefore, in order to accomplish this goal without compromising our safety and well being, we will be begin the demilitarization process by forming a police department that will regulate and control the affairs of our community, maintain order, enforce the law, and handle any civil crime.

Our military will still stand on guard to defend our borders and protect our power station and crops. But by taking away the burden of internal security and civil discipline, and giving those responsibilities to a civilian force, we can not only begin to restore civil liberties, but we will be able to reassign our military personnel, giving them the task of expanding our town borders by opening up areas that have been restricted, and rescind the current curfew, thus giving us more civil liberties and enough free housing for everyone.

Let us as a community, as a family, move forward and begin writing that new chapter. I thank you, the people of Bethlehem."

The town's people's concerns had been placated. They stood once again and applauded their leader.

J.D. motioned for them to sit. "Now, I've bored you long enough. Let's get this celebration started with some music." J.D. moved to where he had been seated and picked up his accordion and joined David, Christina, and several other musicians.

"This was written and arranged by our own songbird Corporal Christina Custode," he announced as they began to play. Christina had passed the audition.

J.D. looked around to his fellow musicians and to the citizens of Bethlehem, and he saw their joy and contentment, and he was pleased. Although he drew comfort and pleasure at seeing their happiness, he was also aware that contentment could lead to complacency and complacency in their post-apocalyptic world could mean their destruction. They would always need to be vigilant and on guard if they were going to survive and prosper.

# EPILOGUE

## WHAT LIES BEYOND THE DOOR

FROM OUTSIDE THE DOOR TO THE ROOM WHERE HE WAS IMPRISONED, Richard France heard the jingle of keys in the padlock. He hurried to it, believing it was his release, but his hopes were quashed when he heard the voice of J.D. Nichols.

"Everyone is gone, Dick. You and I are all that remains of this place," J.D. told the doctor. "I'm not letting you free; that you will have to earn. What I am doing is releasing the lock. It will remain on the door. If you are resourceful, then you should be able to clear the lock from the latch."

"You are insane!" the doctor shouted at him from the other side, and then ordered. "Let me out now! You need me."

"Dick," J.D. calmly replied. "I'd be careful as to the shouting. I'm expecting company. Edward Stone and company. If I lose, I'm sure he'd love to meet you."

"You bastard!" France cried.

"I'm leaving now. You'll know when it's time to make your escape. I'd wish you luck but I'd be lying."

France grabbed the doorknob and jiggled it violently.

"You son-of-a-bitch!" he shouted, but did not know if J.D. had heard his curse.

The sounds of gunfire had ceased. France had hoped that J.D. had done what he had promised: to kill Stone. Then came some loud noises that sounded like grenades. He waited long after the explosions ended, just to make sure. Now there had been no sounds for a very long time.

He jiggled the doorknob and rattled the door trying to get the padlock to unhook from its latch and fall free. For several hours he kept up the attempt, but could not escape. When he was near exhaustion and about to resign, he heard what sounded like voices outside his door. He strained to listen. It appeared to be several people in low conversation, though the few words that he heard uttered were indistinguishable.

France began a rapid succession of fist pounds on the door. He was not sure if those outside his door were friend or foe, but he knew if he remained imprisoned he would perish.

A voice arose. It was just one soft word with a reflection of puzzlement. "Who?"

"*Who?*" France replied. "Doctor Richard France. That is who?" I am locked in. Please let me out."

"*Who?*" the voice repeated.

"Who?" France said with irritation. "Just open the door—Take the lock off the door!"

France began rattling the doorknob. "The lock. The lock above the doorknob! How hard can it be?"

"Lock," the voice whispered with puzzlement.

France heard the padlock drawn from the latch and then drop to the floor. He pulled at the knob and the door swung in.

"Thank God you came—" he began to thank his saviors. France's face lighted with fear. "No. No! How is that possible!" he shrieked in terror, as he retreated.

The mutant with a missing finger looked at him with cold and menacing eyes, pointed, and then spoke his intention in a voice that sounded like a bad imitation of Golem. "Eat. *Hungry*."

"No, wait! I'm not the one you want," France told the ravenous pack. "You want the colonel. You want J.D.!"

The group moved in.

"*Jaydee?*" the four-fingered creature inquisitively half questioned, like he was familiar with the name.

"Yes, J.D.," France repeated.

Four Fingers held up a necklace, and angrily said, "*Jaydee!*"

## THE END

# ABOUT THE AUTHOR

**TS Alan** is an American author of horror, supernatural fiction, and suspense, but also frequently incorporates elements of fantasy, science fiction, mystery, and satire. Alan has published four novels, and eight short stories.

As influences on his writing, Alan lists Clive Barker, Dean Koontz, Stephen King, Edgar Allen Poe, and O. Henry, among others.

Alan is also the co-founder of the entertainment website Zombie Education Alliance (zombieeducationalliance.com).

His writing credits also include two short stories published in *Devolution Z* magazine, a short published in an anthology called *What Went Wrong? (Legendary Stories)*, and shorts published in anthologies called *Whispers of the Apoc* and *Silence of the Apoc*, and others.

For more information visit TS Alan at: www.tsalan.com